D0254992

Praise for _Jewish N...

"_Jewish Noir II_ is a fun, eclectic, globetr...
by its embrace of classic Jewish themes: love of langu..., ...
for justice, and the irresistible charm of a good story."
—Jesse Kellerman, author of _The Golem of_
Hollywood and the Clay Edison series

"Jews and crime: two cultural storylines that are
never far from each other. And this entertaining
anthology showcases them on the highest level."
—Andrew Gross, _NYT_ bestselling author of _Button Man_

Praise for _Jewish Noir_

"A fine anthology, true to both the noir frame and the Jewish theme."
—_Booklist_

"Every reader will have his or her favorites, but this anthology
is heartrending and spine-chilling in its entirety."
—_Library Journal_

"Powerfully describes a woman's struggle to
reconcile survival with morality."
—_Publishers Weekly_, on S.J. Rozan's "The Flowers of Shanghai"

"A very desirable book for the lover of noir in all its fascinating varieties."
—_Jewish Book Council_

"There are rarities and delights throughout Wishnia's collection."
—_Jewish Journal_

"[Noir] can be an alluring match for gray winter days."
—_The Forward_

"An excellent anthology."
—_Mystery Scene_

JEWISH NOIR II

Edited by Kenneth Wishnia
and Chantelle Aimée Osman

ISBN: 978-1-62963-822-5
Library of Congress Control Number: 2020934734

Cover by John Yates / www.stealworks.com
Interior design by briandesign

10 9 8 7 6 5 4 3 2 1

PM Press
PO Box 23912
Oakland, CA 94623
www.pmpress.org
Printed in the USA

CONTENTS

A SHANDEH FAR DI GOYIM
(YOU SHAME US IN FRONT OF THE WORLD)

THE GOD OF MERCY

THE GOD OF VENGEANCE

AMERICAN SPLENDOR

Foreword

Lawrence Block

Fifteen years ago, I got to spend the night at Terrace Hill, the Iowa governor's mansion in Des Moines. I was on a book tour in aid of *The Burglar on the Prowl*, and in my experience book tours don't come with a lot of perks. Sometimes a bookstore presents you with a logo-laden coffee mug or T-shirt, but that's about it. You are, after all, not a rock star. You are a mere writer. You don't get to insist there be no brown M&Ms in your dressing room. You don't get any M&Ms, brown or otherwise. You don't get a dressing room. What you may get, if you're lucky, is a coffee mug or a T-shirt sporting the store's logo, for which you thank all concerned profusely. (After you've done this a time or two, you learn to leave the stuff in your hotel room.)

But when I embarked on that particular book tour, Tom Vilsack was governor of Iowa, and his wife Christie was a dedicated reader and a great booster of literacy. When she learned I'd be visiting four Iowa libraries, including one in Des Moines, she extended an invitation. I turned up in time for iced tea and conversation on the porch with her and her husband, then drove off to another library event up the road in Ames. I returned to Terrace Hill and slept the dreamless sleep of the pampered, and in the morning I got dressed and went down to the kitchen, where the wife of the governor prepared my breakfast—my breakfast and hers, that is to say. It was ham and eggs, and the eggs were perfectly acceptable, but the ham was absolutely superb. I said as much, and Christie told me it came from a particular farm in southeast Iowa, and that she'd never had better.

I was blogging every night during the tour—I can't remember what made me think this was worth doing—and I blogged about that breakfast, with particular reference to that slice of ham. (Well, I think it may have been two slices.) It was, I noted, the best ham I'd eaten since I'd been a boy on Starin Avenue in Buffalo, New York. My mother always bought hams from a Buffalo butcher named Nate Gordon, and for all I know he got them from a farm in southeastern Iowa, because they were just wonderful.

My parents were Jewish, but we belonged to a Reform temple, and I grew up a couple of generations removed from the laws of Kashruth. We observed the holidays, I attended Hebrew school to prepare for my bar mitzvah—but we ate ham and bacon and shellfish without a second thought.

But something occurred to me as I was sharing all this in my blog. My mother never served anything with the work *pork* attached to it. No roast pork, no pulled pork, no pork chops.

I wish I'd had a chance to ask her about this. She died in 2001, two weeks and two days after the towers came down, and there have been many things I'd have liked to ask her since then, but this would certainly have made the list. Why ham and bacon but no pork chops or pork sausage or—

It had to be the word, and it could only be an unconscious choice. We were Reform Jews: we'd no more separate milk and meat or have separate dishes for Pesach than we'd grow *peyes* and strap on *tfilin* or do any of that Orthodox *mishegas*, but we were Jews, and everyone knows Jews won't eat pork, and—

So I shared this revelation in the blog and got an immediate response from a woman who reported the same damn thing from her own childhood. Ham, sure. Bacon, why not? Fried shrimp, oysters Rockefeller—but nothing that called itself pork.

She didn't know why either.

א

Over the years, I've written introductions for quite a few volumes of short stories. In each instance, I can only suppose someone thought it would be to the book's advantage to have a few words of mine start things off. If nothing else, the task at least requires me to put aside some other and more important piece of writing, something that's probably giving me trouble and that I'm yearning for an excuse to abandon. And more often than not I begin by advising the reader to skip the foreword and get on to the happier business of reading the stories.

And what is one to say in an introduction or foreword? That the stories are excellent? Well, perhaps they are and perhaps they are not, and you don't need me to tell you one way or the other. In the present instance, you and I could both take the merit of the stories for granted, and I could go on at some length about the two words of the title, *Jewish* and *Noir.*

I already tackled the second word in my foreword to *At Home in the Dark,* my cross-genre anthology of dark stories. Maybe I can write a little about Jewishness.

Here's every Jewish holiday in three sentences: "They tried to kill us. We survived. Let's eat!"

While the third sentence is the generally the chief reason for getting together, one and two would seem to define Jewishness—and make combining it with noir almost inevitable. Because ever since Haman got sore at Mordecai, no end of people have put the subjugation and extermination of Jews at the top of their wish lists.

Perhaps the worst result of the Holocaust, a well-bred Englishman was heard to say, was that it made anti-Semitism an untenable position. For a while, anyway.

Shall we move on to the second precept?

"We survived."

And that, it seems to me, is at least as remarkable as the fact that, again and again, they've tried to kill us. There's a line spoken by George Arliss in *The House of Rothschild*—for an upright Episcopalian, the fellow played a lot of Jews. "We are evidently eternal," he said, and so are we.

You know, I think that's more remarkable than the persecution. For over two thousand years of Diaspora, the Jewish people have continued to exist. Hated and persecuted and scapegoated everywhere, expelled from one country after another, we have gone on living and have gone on being Jews.

What keeps us going? What explains that Jewishness has somehow survived the destruction of the Temple and the dispersion of all of its people?

I could go on—but why? I'd much rather change the subject. I don't have a firm enough grip on the hem of History's garment to dazzle you with my erudition, so let me shift gears altogether and amuse you with wordplay.

Playing on words has precious little to do with noirness—*noirishkeit*? Never mind. Nor can we claim it as the particular property of the Jews. But it's certainly more fun than thinking about the Holocaust, and one thing that has struck me over the years is how much it's a matter of pure luck.

A late friend of mine, the science fiction writer Randall P. Garrett, was a high-church Anglican who took the whole business seriously, though not without humor. He met regularly with his spiritual advisor, an Episcopalian canon, and their long conversations were occasionally marked by jokes Randy told, and told well. Some of these were, if not precisely off-color, a few degrees removed from lily-white, and Randy thought to ask the man if it was inappropriate to tell such jokes in that particular setting.

"Oh, not at all," the clergyman replied. "They're fine jokes. Besides, I can always use them as fodder for one of my sermons."

"It's a wise canon," said Randy, "that knows its own fodder."

Now the brilliance of such a piece of spontaneity is not something I need to point out to you. One can do no more than ponder it, and nod in admiration. But one thing that strikes me is Randy's great good fortune in having the opportunity.

His spiritual advisor could as easily have been a bishop or an archdeacon. Or a dean, a provost, or a prebendary. If he's anything other than a canon, there's nowhere to go with it. "It's a wise prebendary that knows its own fodder?" No, I don't think so.

And, of course, the canon has to say *fodder*. If he calls those off-white jokes anything else. . .

Well, you get the idea. The canon gave my friend a gift, floating one belt-high right over the middle of the plate, and Randy did the rest.

I received a similar gift some years ago on a visit to Ashland, Oregon, where my friend Hal Dresner had just about finished overseeing the building of a house. It might have been described as a château, and was the sort of thing God might have done if he'd had the money.

It was topped by a newly completed tile roof, to which Hal pointed. "Can you believe," he said, "that there's thirty-two thousand pounds of ceramic tile on that roof?"

I said, "Sixteen tons, and what do you get?"

Now that's not up there with Randy's canon fodder inspiration, but it shares the element of fortuity. If the number Hal mentions is anything other than thirty-two, I don't get to quote the Merle Travis song. Look at our exchange if he'd rounded it off:

Hal: "Can you believe that there's thirty thousand pounds of tile on that roof?"

Me: "No kidding? Sure is a lot of tile."

Wonderful.

❦

And here's another example, and it's bound up in Jewishness, as you'll see, and whether or not it touches on noir is up to you to decide.

It was in July 1964, and I had just accepted an editorial position in Racine, Wisconsin, at Whitman Publishing, a division of Western Printing and Lithography. I was at the time an avid coin collector, and after I'd sold a couple of articles to the *Whitman Numismatic Journal*, I was invited to come edit the thing. It was the first job I'd had since leaving college for the life of a freelance writer, and it would be the last, but it served me well for the twenty months I spent there.

I went to Racine and settled into the job, while my then wife stayed in Buffalo long enough to see to the packing and moving. Before she was to join me, a colleague invited me over for dinner. He was Neil Shafer, and he sat at the desk next to mine in Whitman's numismatic division. Neil was—and still is—an expert in the field of Philippine coinage and paper currency. He was also no longer the only Jew in the employ of Western Printing and seemed grateful for my presence.

So I went to the Shafer home for dinner. He had married fairly recently, and his wife, Edith, was enthusiastically keeping a kosher home. It's perhaps worth noting that she had not grown up in one herself. I believe her parents were Reform Jews in Milwaukee, who found her new commitment to the dietary laws puzzling; as for Neil, while he certainly identified as Jewish, he was not at all observant.

I don't remember what we had for dinner. It goes without saying that it was not baked ham from a farm in southeast Iowa.

I don't recall what the three of us talked about either. But I do remember that we had coffee after the meal, and that Neil asked about the cake that reposed in the kitchen. Edith reminded him that the cake had been made with milk and butter, and they'd had meat during the meal, so that she couldn't serve him a piece of that cake until a specific amount of time had passed. (An hour? Two hours? Hey, I'm the last person to ask. I grew up on cheeseburgers, you'll remember. And Nate Gordon's ham.)

Neil did not welcome this news, and he made his views known. And Edith stated her position, backed by the authority of rabbis all the way back to Hillel. And the conversation, peppered with no end of darlings and sweeties and honeys, did nothing to change anyone's view of the matter.

And during a pause for breath, I uttered these words: "Neil, there's something you have to realize. You can't have your cake and Edith too."

I know. And it didn't hurt a bit that Neil was irredeemably addicted to wordplay and quite the master of it.

But consider the fortuity, will you? Had her name been anything other than Edith. Had the designated dessert been pastry or pudding or, really, anything but what it was.

"Neil, you can't have your Banana Cream Pie and Florence too."

Yeah. Right.

❧

No, I won't apologize. Why should I? Didn't I tell you to skip this foreword?

Now it's time for the stories. *Jewish Noir II*, a rich collection of wonderful tales wonderfully told. They're what we're here for, and they're here for you. All you have to do is turn the page.

So what are you waiting for?

Introduction

Out of the depths I call You, O Lord. O Lord, listen to my cry.
—Psalm 130:1–2

Oy, vey iz mir. Where do I begin? Things were bad enough when the first volume of *Jewish Noir* came out a few years ago, but they've taken a much darker turn since then.

We've all seen the headlines: with the rise of far-right nationalist parties, anti-Semitic hate crimes and incidents are up in Europe, led by Germany (a 20 percent increase) and France (a 74 percent increase), but they're up 90 percent in New York City, home to half of the US Jewish population. FBI statistics show that the 684 incidents of anti-Semitic hate crimes recorded in 2016 were greater than all other "religiously motivated crimes of bias and bigotry combined" (Weisman). White supremacist propaganda that "the Jews own and control everything in America" has become more acceptable on formerly "moderate" websites (Perlstein). Conspiracy theories blaming "the Jews" for the 9/11 attacks still circulate among alt-right and far-left fringe groups (Kestenbaum). And of course, the white supremacists and neo-Nazis staging a torchlight parade in Charlottesville, Virginia, in August 2017, chanting, "Jews will not replace us," were labeled "some very fine people" by the sitting president of the United States, who went on to declare that the majority of American Jews are either idiots or disloyal—that is, they're lousy Jews—because, well, they aren't the other group of American Jews, namely the politically conservative ones.*

I hesitate to say more about such words and actions, since we all know that anything I set down here will be outdated in about five minutes

---

* The president's exact words as reported on August 21, 2019: "Any Jewish people that vote for a Democrat, I think it shows either a total lack of knowledge or great disloyalty" (Hirschfeld Davis).

1

by some fresh outrage. But words have power, and when the president of the United States speaks, people listen—and act. For example, on October 18, 2018, the sitting president tweeted "deliberately deceptive videos" of a crowd of people receiving cash handouts in an unidentified Spanish-speaking country and related it to the caravan of Central American migrants heading for the US border with the caption, "Can you believe this, and what Democrats are allowing to be done to our Country?" (Alterman), retweeting a post by Representative Matt Gaetz (R-FL) that questioned whether progressive billionaire George Soros was behind it (Soros apparently standing in for the "international Jewish bankers" of earlier anti-Semitic tracts).

Nine days later, on October 27, 2018, a hate-filled moron referenced *that exact tweet* ("HIAS likes to bring invaders in that kill our people. I can't sit by and watch my people get slaughtered. Screw your optics, I'm going in"), then murdered eleven people at the Tree of Life Congregation in Pittsburgh simply because they were Jews. In these volatile times, reflexively retweeting such an obviously anti-Semitic accusation is pretty much unforgivable.

And if that weren't enough, the *New York Times* reported that "Israel's Ashkenazi chief rabbi refused to refer to the Tree of Life as a synagogue because it is Conservative, a non-Orthodox branch of Judaism not recognized by the religious authorities in Israel" (Landler). In other words, the victims of this particular mass murder were Jewish enough to be targeted by an anti-Semitic sociopath, but they're not Jewish enough for a chief rabbi in Israel? And some wonder why relations between Israel and progressive American Jews are fraying.

The Tree of Life synagogue shooter also mentioned his belief that "Jews are the children of Satan" (Roose), an idea that comes from no less an authoritative source than the New Testament itself: the Gospel of John depicts Jesus telling "the Jews" that "You are from your father the devil, and you choose to do your father's desires" (John 8:44). This verse associating the Jews with Satan has stoked anti-Jewish hatred for the past two thousand years (Levine & Brettler). Thanks, Jesus.

Not content with such broad condemnation from the Savior Himself, David Duke, former grand wizard of the KKK, tweeted the comparatively trivial accusation that "Jews dominate porn—why are 'Christians' ok with that?" An idea that nevertheless found its way into the four-thousand-word diatribe posted by a nineteen-year-old man before he opened fire at a synagogue near San Diego in June 2019, killing one person and wounding three more, blaming Jews for "causing many to fall into sin with their role in peddling pornography" (Kuznia).

We might have once been able to kid ourselves into believing that such views only existed on the fringes of society, but recent events have shown that at least 40 percent of the population supports such "extremist" racist ideology in one form or another.

It all starts with ignorance.

The ancient Greek historian Thucydides (ca. 460–400 BCE) testifies that certain forms of propaganda have always worked: "Most people will not take trouble in finding out the truth, but are much more inclined to accept the first story they hear" (quoted in MacMillan). Closer to our era, visionary Jewish science fiction author Isaac Asimov wrote in 1980: "There is a cult of ignorance in the United States, and there always has been. The strain of anti-intellectualism has been a constant thread winding its way through our political and cultural life, nurtured by the false notion that democracy means that 'my ignorance is just as good as your knowledge.'" (quoted in Rosenblum).

Jewish tradition celebrates a love of learning. The rabbis of the late-biblical and post-biblical era were all teachers. *Rabbi* means *teacher*. We are teachers in a society that often shows contempt for higher education, which is a nice way of saying that Jews are generally educated enough to know bullshit when we hear it.

But anti-Semitic propaganda, fairly unique among the many channels of hate flowing through our society, requires believing multiple, highly contradictory stereotypes: Jews are clever enough to manipulate world financial markets and media, and engineer the election of an African American president who couldn't possibly have won without our behind-the-scenes scheming, but we're too stupid to vote reliably for the Republican Party. Put another way, "Jews are both all-powerful puppet masters and sniveling weaklings, rapacious capitalists and left-wing anarchists. The Holocaust never happened, but man, was it cool" (Weisman).

Right. The Holocaust. On July 9, 2019, we were treated to a news report about a high school principal in Boca Raton, Florida, who said it was his duty to stay "politically neutral" on the subject, because "Not everyone believes the Holocaust happened." He continued: "I can't say the Holocaust is a factual, historical event because I am not in a position to do so as a school district employee" (Mervosh). At least he was

3

removed from his position. But what are we to do when a sitting president can get away with saying, during a public speech to the Republican Jewish Coalition's annual leadership meeting in Las Vegas, that the "Democrats are advancing by far the most extreme, anti-Semitic agenda in history" (Orr & Isenstadt)? I'm sorry, but when you hear the phrase "by far the most extreme, anti-Semitic agenda in history," a name should come to mind. And that name is not Nancy Pelosi.

And so Holocaust denial continues to stalk the earth like the zombie idea that it is, when the reality is that "Every American Jew has people they lost" in the Holocaust, according to Rachel Silverman, a genealogist who specializes in Jewish family history. "It's just the matter of the degree of separation" (Murphy).*

And it doesn't look like things are going to get better anytime soon. Welcome to the world of *Jewish Noir*.

Kenneth Wishnia
The Depths, aka New York
December 2019
Kislev 5780

Postscript

Oh . . . dear . . . God . . .

We have seen some *very* dark stuff arise out of the swamp of racist hatred recently, and let's just say that the vast majority of Jews have never been in a position to say, "Oh, they're just coming for the Gypsies. We don't have a thing to worry about." Because if they're coming for one group of undesirables, they're coming for us next. If someone hates Blacks and Latinos, believe me, we're next on the list. (One exception: racist Jews like former senior White House advisor Stephen Miller. Fuck that guy. Now *he* is what is known as *a shandeh far di goyim*.)

Our lives have been repeatedly derailed by pandemic madness, and now we find ourselves engulfed by a poisonous cloud of lies intended

---

* One final example: In November 2019, federal authorities arrested a man for allegedly planning to bomb a synagogue in Pueblo, Colorado. He used numerous Facebook accounts to post messages promoting racist violence, including one saying, "I wish the Holocaust really did happen," because the Jews "need to die" (Turkewitz).

to stifle our voices, restrict our rights, and justify violence against us. A current conspiracy theory asserts that the Jews created the COVID-19 virus to kill off the world's non-Jewish population. Because we're immune? Because we need the living space? (Okay, sure, we could use the real estate, but that still seems like an awful lot of bodies to bury . . .)

On a lighter note, cabbage sure takes a beating in these pages, and there is also a *Star Trek* reference, continuing our proud tradition of including at least one *Star Trek* reference in each volume of *Jewish Noir*. (Thank you, Rabbi Schneider!) After all, Captain Kirk and First Officer Spock were Jewish—or at least played by Jewish actors, and one scholar of the TV series notes that the "common values in the *Star Trek* universe and Jewish belief [are] the idea of a more liberal, inclusive people, where 'other' and 'difference' is an embraced strength as opposed to a divisive weakness" (Nagourney).

Progressive Jews have a long tradition of siding with the oppressed, and fortunately they outnumber reactionary Jews by at least 3 to 1 (in the US, that is).

And so the struggle continues.

K.W.
Deep inside the Raging Hellscape
March 2021/Adar-Nisan 5781
Revised (again!) January 2022/Shevat 5782

Works Cited

Alterman, Eric. "Chronicle of Deaths Foretold." *The Nation*, November 8, 2018, 10–11.
Hassan, Adeel. "Hate-Crime Violence Hits 16-Year High, FBI Reports." *New York Times*, November 12, 2019.
Hirschfeld Davis, Julie. "Trump Accuses Jewish Democrats of 'Disloyalty.'" *New York Times*, August 21, 2019, A1, A20.
Kestenbaum, Sam. "9/11 Conspiracies Blaming 'the Jews' Still Rage." *The Forward*, September 16, 2016, 10–11.
Kuznia, Rob. "Some Extremist Groups See Porn as a Conspiracy." *New York Times*, June 9, 2019.
Landler, Mark. "Support for the President in Pittsburgh, but It's Coming from Israel." *New York Times*, November 2, 2018.
Levine, Amy-Jill, and Marc Zvi Brettler. *The Jewish Annotated New Testament*. Oxford: Oxford University Press, 2011, 156, 176.
MacMillan, Margaret. "Gathering Storm." *New York Times Book Review*, May 13, 2018, 11.
Mervosh, Sarah. "Principal Who Tried to Stay 'Politically Neutral' on Holocaust Is Removed." *New York Times*, July 9, 2019, A18.

Murphy, Heather. "Ancestry Digitizes Millions of Holocaust Records and Offers Access at No Cost." *New York Times*, August 3, 2019, B3.

Nagourney, Adam. "Jewish Roots of 'Star Trek' Are Explored by Exhibition." *New York Times*, January 5, 2022, C1, C6.

Orr, Gabby, and Alex Isenstadt. "Trump to Jewish Republicans: Democrats Pushing 'Extreme, Anti-Semitic Agenda.'" *Politico*, April 6, 2019. https://www.politico.com/story/2019/04/06/trump-jewish-republicans-democrats-anti-semitic-1260169.

Perlstein, Rick. "Guns, Extremism, and Threats of Escalation." *Washington Spectator*, May 1, 2017, 1.

Roose, Kevin. "Social Site Let Suspect's Hate Spill Unbridled." *New York Times*, October 29, 2018, A1, A14.

Rosenblum, Mort. "A Wolff at the Door." *Washington Spectator*, February 1, 2018, 2.

Turkewitz, Julie. "Colorado Man Is Arrested in Plot to Bomb Synagogue. *New York Times*, November 5, 2019, A20.

Weisman, Jonathan. "A Robocall with Devil Horns." *New York Times*, November 19, 2017.

Introduction

So, I have to say—in the interest of full disclosure—I'm not Jewish. So, when Ken did me the honor of inviting me to be his coeditor on this anthology, I admit, I hesitated—but I'm certainly glad I said yes. The stories, some true, some fantastical, some horrifying, all opened my eyes in so many different ways, not only to Judaism, but also to the human condition. Was I really the right person for the job? I still don't know the answer.

What I *do* know is that this anthology is important. And the stories in this book apply to everyone.

This is the second volume in the Jewish Noir series, but this isn't anything like what you've seen before, and the world the first volume was published in certainly isn't the world we live in today.

On the day I originally wrote this, five people had been stabbed in a rabbi's home in an act of "domestic terrorism." The next day, two people were killed in a church shooting. Then came a global pandemic. Then the hate got worse. Shortly after revising this introduction for the second time, a rabbi and two others were taken hostage at a synagogue in Colleyville, Texas. Rabbi Charlie Cytron-Walker credits the active-shooter and security courses he's taken with his and his congregants' survival. The days following saw many people share stories of metal detectors, armed guards, and other precautions at their places of worship. Which, sadly, was nothing new and not enough. Antisemitic incidents are being reported at record levels and hate crimes are rampant.

None of us are safe, and all of us are relevant.

I was fortunate—honored, actually—to coedit this volume. And in doing so, I've learned a lot. About culture, about people, about humanity. About Yiddish. One of the first things I learned, being relatively new to this, was that there are three central tenets of Judaism. First, that there is one God, incorporeal and eternal. Second, that people are to act with justice and mercy. And last, but perhaps most importantly, that all people deserve to be treated with dignity and respect.

You'll see these tenets appear in various ways throughout the stories, which we've organized into six overarching themes:

Legacies, which teach us the importance of what has come before, what we have lost, and why we need to remember, like a family heirloom in Elizabeth Zelvin's "The Cost of Something Priceless" or family memories of the Triangle Shirtwaist Factory fire in "Taking Names" from Steven Wishnia.

Scattered and Dispersed, showing us an international viewpoint; Xu Xi takes us to Hong Kong, and Joy Mahabir to Trinidad.

A Shandeh Far Di Goyim (**You Shame Us in Front of the World**), stories of embarrassment and dishonor: a young boy's bar mitzvah is memorable in Jill Block's "Wishboned," and an elderly woman uses compassion as a weapon in Lizzie Skurnick's "To Catch a *Ganef.*"

The God of Mercy, illustrating the kindness of man—a sister would do anything for her brother in Eileen Rendahl's "Brother's Keeper"—and **The God of Vengeance**, our other, darker, face, like Kenneth Wishnia's story dramatizing events depicted in the book of Judges 4–5.

Lastly, **American Splendor**, tales that could only happen here in America, like Rita Lakin's "The Nazi in the Basement," where wartime events witnessed by a young girl in the Bronx can never be forgotten.

Unfortunately, a lot of what we have in this book—the central tenet, if you will—is fear. Right now, we are scared. All of us. That's why we have so many stories in this book about people—sometimes quite literally—being torn apart by the stresses of modern society. Of having multiple identities. Of external forces that make us choose something that we don't want or believe in. We don't have control.

This book isn't a solution for that. But, I hope you take away something from reading it, no matter your location, creed, belief, or religion. It seems so simple. So obvious, so old. Yet right now it's so rare. How could we have forgotten? The solution is to be kind, merciful, and understanding of ways and lives that are not yours—most of all, to treat everyone with dignity and respect.

You are relevant, and that is a responsibility. Share it every day.

Chantelle Aimée Osman
December 2019/January 2022/February 2022

LEGACIES

Taking Names

Steven Wishnia

A white-haired firefighter in full dress uniform tolled a silver bell. Elementary school children and distant descendants laid roses on the sidewalk as the names of the dead were intoned, the bell tolling again after each one.

Tina Frank, seventeen years old.

Rosie Freedman, eighteen.

On this March day in 1911, this building that now housed New York University's biology department had rained a screaming bloody mess of bodies, as dozens of Triangle Shirtwaist factory workers plunged nine stories to their deaths rather than get burned up like a pile of cotton scraps.

Molly Gerstein, my great-aunt, age seventeen.

Sarah Kupla, sixteen.

Women carried Gibson-girl blouses over their heads on stick frames, each with a sash across the front bearing the name of a victim. The ladder on a parked fire truck extended to the sixth floor. Fire ladders couldn't go any higher in 1911.

Kate Leone, fourteen years old.

Jennie Levin, age nineteen.

Charlie Purpelberg, laminated city press card hanging from his neck by a beaded chain, scribbled descriptions and quotes in a thin notebook. A black baseball cap with an orange OnTheClock.org logo, his gig for the day, covered his bald pate.

"The Triangle Shirtwaist factories of today are in Bangladesh. They are in meatpacking plants in North Carolina. And they are on nonunion construction sites here in New York City," a speaker, Andrea Vivino, a midlevel Laborers official wearing the union's orange T-shirt, declaimed. Charlie had met her a few times, knew her as warm and outgoing, she'd helped him out on a story when the top brass were closemouthed.

He spaced out for a moment, remembering the murky family story of his great-aunt Reyzl, who had either been fired or quit Triangle the week before the fire. Was it talking union, or sexual harassment, or some secret scandal the greenhorn girl got tangled into? No one knew the details, and she'd died in the flu epidemic of 1918. He clicked back to alertness.

"Eighteen construction workers were killed on the job last year," Vivino continued. "Four have died so far this year. All but one were on nonunion jobs. And when that happens, it's not an accident. It's because they cut corners on safety."

❧

Charlie was halfway through his bagel the next morning, alternating bites with sips of coffee while checking his email and posting his article on social media, when the text bell pinged. *Construction worker killed in accident. Bushwick. Lafayette Ave bet. Broadway and Bushwick.*

He got there an hour later. The block ran north from Broadway and the J-train el. Mostly three-story buildings of flat clapboards or yellow-ish-beige stone with round alcoves curving out of the front. A few modern ones, six stories high. They looked prefab, like they had just patched on IKEA panels of brick and balcony. And this one, ten incomplete stories and two not built yet, green sheetrock insulation on the lower floors, naked steel skeleton on the upper ones.

Police had yellow-taped off the scene, almost two-thirds of the block. An hour or so before someone had been walking the edge of the eighth floor, bolting together the framing, with others below laying rebar on the floor for concrete, when he slips, the kind of sudden malapropism you wouldn't make if you were mindful, but who's always mindful? Maybe he drops a bolt and grabs for it. Grabs at empty air. No harness. Off balance. Empty air, two and a half seconds, one hundred feet, hit the ground double nickels on the dime. The cruel laws of gravity.

A small crowd milled in the space just in from the corner; a couple TV cameras, print reporters with smartphones and notebooks, neighborhood people, and two or three cops watching over them. Charlie spotted Frankie Medina and Lavon Stackhouse, two organizers from the Trades

Community Project, a campaign to reach nonunion construction workers loosely backed by various Laborers and Ironworkers locals. They made an odd-looking pair, Medina short, bushy-haired, and wiry, Stackhouse big, shaven-headed, and burly.

Medina was raging. "The fuck? Guy didn't have a harness, wasn't tied off, no nets, no nothing. Union job, you'd be tied off so tight or they'd close the job down in three seconds."

"This contractor tells the guys to buy their own," rang in Stackhouse. "They're supposed to pay 350 bucks for it, and they make like 15 or 20 an hour. Yeah, right."

"None of the guys want to talk," Medina told Charlie. "They're all scared shitless of ICE." He bowed his head to his phone and tapped the glass. "I might be able to get you somebody."

"You know anything about the contractor?"

"ESS, Emerald Structural Solutions. *Long* history there," said Stackhouse. "I'll send you the list. Two fatal accidents on their jobs, one in a collapse, one in a fall. I said they pay their guys like fifteen, twenty bucks—that's *when* they pay them. We get a lot of stories that they pay late, they don't pay overtime. Somebody complains, they tell them they're gonna call ICE."

Medina's phone pinged. "Let's take a walk," he told Charlie. "Guy will talk to you, but he doesn't want to be seen with you or us."

Medina led him across Broadway, under the train, and around one of the sharp-angle corners. Introduced him to a short Mexican, maybe in his thirties, in a gray hoodie and orange Under Armour T-shirt. "*Este es Charlie, un periodista,*" Medina told him. "*No se necesita saber su nombre.*"

"*¿Qué pasó?*" Charlie asked in thickly accented Spanish.

"*Ramón se cayó.*" The guy went off too fast for Charlie to catch more than a few words and phrases: "*octavo piso,*" "*Ramón,*" "*peligroso.*" "Damn, I need to learn a lot more Spanish," he thought.

"He said he didn't see it, he was on the sixth floor," Medina translated. "Ramón was on the eighth floor when he fell."

"*Tuvo . . . como se dice* 'harness'?"

Medina translated it.

"No," the man said. "*Una vez, el jefe* tell me, 'Look like you are wearing rope.' I say, '*No está seguro.*' He say, '*Hielo.* You know what *hielo* is *en inglés?*'"

"ICE," Charlie answered. "*¿Conoce el hombre matado?*"

"*No muy bien. El era hondureño, del Bronx.*"

"All we know is that the guy was named Ramón," Medina repeated. "He didn't know him very well. He was Honduran, lived in the Bronx."

"*¿Cuánto se paga aquí?*"

"*Para mí, diecisiete dolares la hora. Pero me debe por dos semanas. Mil cuatrociento dolares.*"

They owed him $1,400, two weeks' pay.

"*El viernes, le pregunté, '¿Cuándo me lo pagará?' Y el me dijó, 'Hielo.* You make fucking *problemas*, it get *muy frío.*'"

❧

The street was blocked off; he wasn't going to get any closer to the site. He could get basic details and the dead man's name, if it was available, from DCPI, the police press office. The medical examiner's office probably wouldn't have anything for a couple days.

He got close enough to shoot a picture of the construction billboard. The building was part of the mayor's OneCity Housing program. He wrote down the names of the developer and the contractors.

This was going to be a research gig from here on out. The neighborhood was gentrified enough to have a coffeehouse with Wi-Fi, suburban molded-plastic chairs around blocky wood tables. He spread out his laptop, phone, notebook, and pad, and sketched out what he needed to find out. What the project was. Who were the developer and contractors. Department of Buildings records of violations, unpaid fines. Names of the two previous fatalities.

The developer, UrbanEquity, had a one-page website with a Queens Plaza address and phone number. He reached its voicemail, and got: "The mailbox is full. Goodbye." He sent an email.

ESS had no website but a phone number posted on several business-listing sites. The number listed was out of service.

A two-sentence response from the City Hall press office. "This is a tragic accident and we will fully and thoroughly investigate its causes. We are partnering with the most qualified and cost-effective developers to create an unprecedented amount of affordable housing for tens of thousands of New Yorkers."

The Department of Buildings: "The matter is under investigation. We have issued a stop-work order. We cannot comment further at this time."

Two hours and two cups of coffee later, he'd put together a lead.

The contractor on a Brooklyn building where a construction worker plunged to his death early this morning has a "long history" of safety violations, according to a union official at the scene.

The man fell from the eighth floor while working on the building's frame, according to police and witnesses. Police said they were withholding the name of the victim pending further identification and notification of relatives. A coworker said he was a Honduran immigrant named Ramón.

The 120-unit building, on Lafayette Avenue in Bushwick, is slated to contain 30 affordable apartments as part of the mayor's OneCity Housing program. The city Department of Buildings said it has issued a stop-work order.

Lavon Stackhouse, a Laborers Union organizer working with the Trades Community Project, said that Emerald Structural Solutions, the framing contractor, had a "long history" of safety violations, including two fatal accidents. Department of Buildings records show it was cited for violations after the first of those accidents, in 2016, and issued a stop-work order in the other, in 2018. The records do not indicate whether it paid the roughly $6,000 in fines levied.

The coworker, speaking in Spanish through an interpreter and asking not to be named, said the contractor had not provided harnesses, basic safety equipment to prevent falls. He also said that he was owed two weeks' pay and that when he asked for it, a supervisor threatened to call immigration authorities.

He finished a draft of the story, reread it, entered corrections. Checked his email one more time before filing.

There was a message from the Ansell Weiss Associates PR firm, with a statement from UrbanEquity: "Our thoughts and prayers are with those impacted by this tragic accident. Safety is our first and foremost consideration in our relationships with our contractors. We are proud to partner with the City of New York to create affordable housing."

He cut-and-pasted it into the story.

Two questions. The spokesperson from Ansell Weiss was Jake Waxman, a former intern from the *Eye*, the alternative weekly that had employed Charlie before it threw in the sponge in 2013, a victim of the Great Recession and the decimation of print media. Charlie remembered him as an overbearing young-radical type, what was he doing there?

And why was this obscure developer using Ansell Weiss, the same

PR firm as Joshua Roth's JSR Associates, one of the city's largest and most politically connected developers?

That would have to wait for the follow-up.

He attached the file to email and hit "Send."

※

There were two possible angles for the follow-up, he thought.

First, JSR Associates and the contractors it used. Joshua Roth was loudly and aggressively anti-union, not wanting to concede that large-scale development was the building trades' turf. "Unions are like bedbugs. You find one, you have to fumigate the whole house," he'd told a real-estate trade weekly in 2017.

And the Lafayette Avenue project was part of OneCity Housing, the mayor's affordable-housing program. In exchange for 25 percent of apartments defined as "low-income," they got to build it twelve stories tall, twice the size the block was zoned for. The formula used to set rents defined "low income" as roughly the median income in the city, which was well above the median in this neighborhood. So, an "affordable" two-bedroom apartment would go for around $1,250 a month, cheap by market standards, not cheap if you were a single mom taking home $620 a week. The other 75 percent of the apartments would be luxury.

The deeper story: The mayor had been discreetly but steadfastly against using union labor in the program. Why? Informed speculation number one, cost-benefit. It's cheaper. Two, he's clueless, the kind of upper-class liberal that gets outraged about workers making $8.50 an hour instead of $15, but can't conceive that somebody who works with their hands would deserve $30 and benefits. Three, a pay-to-play pragmatism. He'd made the deals for what could be done with who he needed to do it, with "don't make the perfect the enemy of the good" the incessant rejoinder to critics.

Maybe. The bottom line: They are being built by contractors with a history of wage theft and fatal accidents.

Where does the trail go? Into a cloud of shell companies, swirling around some unknown nucleus?

He felt big-story buzz. OnTheClock didn't run long-form pieces. He queried his editor at the Lens, a website attempting to carry on the tradition of the *Eye*, but paying about a quarter as much.

He had a start, a listing of accidents and wage-theft allegations at ESS from Medina and Stackhouse, material that could be cross-checked with available public records. They said they'd get him more on the web of contractors and subcontractors, more allegations of wage theft, injuries and deaths, unsafe conditions.

UrbanEquity looked like a JSR operation. Buildings Department records online listed overlapping principal officers and property-management companies at the same addresses. For a company with a one-page website and a phone they didn't seem to answer, but using the same high-powered PR firm, that made it pretty obvious.

And campaign-finance records, once you pored over pages and pages in a 1980s-computer all-caps font, revealed a network of contributions from JSR. Like most large landlords, they had separate limited-liability corporations for different properties, insulating the enterprise as a whole—and also, through a loophole in state law, enabling them to give the maximum corporate contribution from every single one, a bit under $5,000 each. Checking out the LLCs through the city housing agency's online records was also tedious, but it yielded the same pattern of principal officers and property-management companies at the same addresses.

They'd used that loophole to funnel millions of dollars to the mayor, the governor, and dozens of elected officials. The names of the recipients were like a litany of the last decade's scandals. State Senator Frank Fiorini of Queens, an outspoken foe of same-sex marriage who'd diverted $900,000 in campaign funds to buy a house for his boyfriend by the beach in Breezy Point. City Councilmember Dontae Lamar of Brooklyn, whose kickbacks from city contractors included getting two of his girlfriends on their payrolls. Assemblymember Ariel Bender Bernstein of Manhattan, the city's first trans elected official, embezzling $65,000 from an LGBT community center they were on the board of. And former state Senator Diego Suarez of the Bronx, now doing twenty-four to twenty-seven months in federal prison for purloining $2 million in Medicaid payments and spending it on, among other things, $28,000 worth of lap dances in one night at Sin City Cabaret.

The most obvious: Councilmember Lupe Morales, who switched her stance to vote for a spot rezoning that let JSR do a twenty-three-story luxury building in her Washington Heights district, after she'd received $39,600 from eight connected LLCs while running unopposed for reelection.

The mayor's re-election campaign had gotten at least $295,000. That didn't include his personal PAC, which was set up to take dark money.

Corruption is the most truly diverse aspect of New York City's politics, Charlie thought. Black, white, yellow, brown, male, female, gay, straight, from Albanian to Zimbabwean, they've all got their fucking hands in the pot.

❧

The spokesperson for the Laborers, a skinny young guy who looked like he'd lifted more textbooks than cinderblocks, had emailed him the complaint they'd filed with the Brooklyn DA's office, a listing of various wage-theft and unsafe-job allegations against several contractors. Secondhand, but enough of it could be cross-checked to be usable.

In one of the wage-theft cases, from 2018, Emerald had gotten off with a warning. But two other contractors now on the Lafayette Avenue job, Cross-Boro Concrete and TGI, had signed a consent decree agreeing to pay their workers on the books.

His cell phone bleeped. "Y'all not gonna believe this," Lavon Stackhouse's voice boomed out. "TGI. They signed a court order to pay workers on the books, so they set up a phony check-cashing place."

He met Stackhouse and Medina by the Gates Avenue stop on the J later that afternoon. They walked over to a street on the south side of Broadway, the Bed-Stuy side. Stackhouse pointed out a vacant lot behind a corrugated-metal fence, scrawny ailanthus trees growing in the gaps, a security guard at the gate.

"They've got a trailer back there. That's where it is," Stackhouse told him.

Charlie wandered over toward the gate. "Private property," the guard growled when he was still about twenty feet away. The two larger ones behind him moved up to block the gate. They smelled of Mob like stale garlic on bad pizza.

"Okay, so how do we show this if we can't get in?" he asked when he got back.

"Talk to the guys," Medina said. The Friday-afternoon parade of men in cement-crusted jeans and work boots was beginning to flow down the block. Medina discreetly accosted individuals. Some ignored him or sped up. Some said they couldn't talk. A few stopped and described the scenario. They lined up, handed in their checks, and got cash. Then the checks would be torn up.

One guy showed his check. It was handwritten, with the deductions scribbled on the memo line.

Charlie asked him, "Did they give you a W-2 form?"

"*¿Doble dos? ¿Qué es?*"

"Did you get a tax refund?"

"I don't have tax papers. I get cash."

He took a cell phone picture of the check, with the man's finger covering his name.

By looking legit, the company could steal a guaranteed amount. It was a decent amount too. Take $160 in deductions out of a $600 paycheck, and you've clawed back a quarter of your labor costs.

"How do we prove they're ripping up the checks?" Charlie asked. "I'm not asking anybody's status, but guys who are scared shit of ICE generally don't wanna put their name on the record, you know?"

"Find someone who's really pissed off, and I've got an idea," Medina said.

They didn't have to wait long. A guy with a Virgin of Guadalupe T-shirt under his gray hoodie came by—the man he'd talked to from the Lafayette Avenue job. He asked what was going on. Medina told him.

"*¡Hijo de la chingada!*" he cursed.

"*¿Tiene un smartphone?*" Medina asked.

"*Sí.*"

"While you're waiting on line, call somebody," Medina told him. "Shoot video while you're talking. And then text it to me."

"It doesn't have to be perfect," Charlie added. Medina translated.

"And whatever you do, don't get caught," Stackhouse finished, and Medina translated.

The video that arrived several minutes later was blurry, with the camera angles sometimes spinning like a drunk with a zoom lens. But it showed what needed to be showed. Cash dispensed from a gray metal box being stuffed into envelopes, and checks being shredded.

❧

He had the story. City hires politically connected developer whose shell company hires contractors who've found a novel way to steal workers' pay. Backed up with records and video, albeit blurry video, and correlated with campaign contributions. Heavy on innuendo, but proving the association was easier than proving their motivation. That's the way money works in politics. As the anonymous woman whose online personal ad featured a closeup of disembodied pussy said, "All donations are for my time only and do not include acts that may happen between consenting adults."

JSR Associates statement: "Safety is our first and foremost consideration in our relationships with our contractors. We are a merit shop and we are proud that we are providing the newest Americans opportunities for gainful employment at competitive wages."

City Hall statement: "We are partnering with the most qualified and cost-effective developers to create an unprecedented amount of affordable housing for tens of thousands of New Yorkers. No contributor to any of our campaigns has ever received any consideration that they would not have received as an ordinary constituent."

The encyclopedia of quotations in Charlie's brain spewed up an echo. The mayor would not be flattered to know that he'd plagiarized Richard Nixon's Checkers speech, except for the gender-neutral language.

❧

The story went up Thursday morning. Charlie went through the morning rites of coffee, bagel, email, and social media. Within minutes his inboxes were popping.

Jake Waxman had posted a message on behalf of JSR Associates: "This self-styled journalist is spouting the classic anti-Semitic trope that Jews are evil, money-grubbing landlords. We are proud that our merit-shop contractors are providing the newest Americans opportunities for gainful employment at competitive wages that have been denied them by corrupt special interests whose leadership is pale, male, and stale."

That line's gotta be a new definition of chutzpah, Charlie thought. But not for long. Nasty comments flooded his Twitter account, @charlie-purple. *Fake news. Scandalmongering hack. Self-hating Jew. Takes halal meat up the ass. Shilling for racist unions. Look how much Roth contributes to charity, only bitter losers want to carp and tear it down.*

His phone rang. Sarah, his editor. "I just got a call from the City Hall press office, complaining that your story was 'misrepresenting our success in creating and preserving an unprecedented amount of affordable housing in the city.'"

"Well, what do you want me to do?"

"Nothing. It's a good piece. We'll say we stand by the story. If there's anything factual we need to correct, I'll let you know."

"Thanks. I'll be here. By the way, you see that Jake Waxman is calling us anti-Semites?"

"Yeah. Haters gonna hate. Ignore it."

"I'm getting a shitload of vile bile on Twitter."

"Welcome to the club. Trolls gonna troll, and who knows how many of them are bots. And be thankful you were not created a woman. It'd be a lot worse."

"I can imagine. I already got a couple ISIS-dick-up-your-ass messages. What's the story with him, anyway? You remember what he was like at the *Eye*."

"Yeah. He likes the proximity to power, and making six figures at the age of twenty-five doesn't hurt either. And you know the Upton Sinclair quote, 'It is difficult to get a man to understand something when his salary depends upon his not understanding it.'"

Charlie checked his email again. The notifications were coming in every few seconds. But the tide of bile was turning. The comments on @charliepurple were waxing in the direction of "agent of the Jew-controlled far-left media" and "commie-fag Jew."

His phone started to beep and vibrate. "Go back where you came from, faggot." Where? My mother's womb in Rego Park? Speaking of my mother, the next caller wanted to inform me of her proclivities for the penises of terrorists and camels. Another call. Hissing noises, then a hangup. Oh shit, I've been doxxed. Another one. More hissing noises—this time, he recognized it as a stretched-out sibilant syllable, "gasssssss," and then a disguised-voice growl, "You're going to be vaping with Zyklon B very soon."

He riffled through the settings on his phone, trying to find a way to silence it except for calls or messages from his contacts. No dice. Not unless he could find a call-screening app.

He decided to put his phone on silent and change his voicemail message: "If you have a legitimate reason for calling, please leave a message after the beep. If you are calling to harass or threaten me, press 1 for *gey kakn oyfn yam*. Press 2 for *chinga tu madre*. Press 3 for *kiss mi batty, rassclaat*. Press 4 for *idi na khui*."

But he'd still have to go through the messages to get the legit ones. The phone showed three voicemails from area codes he'd never seen—321,

740, 458—and one from an actual contact. Elena Mavraki, a former coworker at the *Eye*. They'd been good friends, maybe might have been more if they hadn't both been attached. He'd sort of lost contact with her, except for bits and pieces on social media.

He called her back.

"So I hear the cyberlice are crawling all over you," she said. "Anyway, I like your voicemail message. You know you're a New Yorker when you think you're multilingual because you can curse in five languages."

"Yeah, it's like it's got a life of its own. I mean, it's a local story, I can't believe people in Oregon and Florida are even reading it."

"I got doxxed once, but it's too long a story for now. Listen, you need a break. Why don't you come out to Queens tonight instead of sitting home waiting for harassing phone calls? My friend's klezmer band is playing in Jackson Heights at Los Subterráneos. It's a really cool coffeehouse."

"Okay. Wanna have dinner first?"

They met on Roosevelt Avenue and 74th Street and had Nepalese food, chili paneer—spelled "chilly" on the menu—and momos, the Himalayan version of ravioli, wontons, pierogi, or kreplach.

"So you wanna hear about how I got doxxed?"

"Yeah."

"Do you remember the story I did about my family?"

"Yeah."

It had been her big career break, a cover story in the *Eye* about her parents' odyssey. They were Romaniote Jews from Greece who'd escaped in 1940 just after the Italian fascists invaded, to Cyprus and then London and then Astoria, Queens.

"The *Eye* archive site republished it a couple years ago, and somebody in the neo-Nazi world noticed it and posted it on one of their sites, and it went viral from there. Then somebody decided to look me up on the web, where your basic personal information isn't hard to find. Used to be they'd have to have a Queens phonebook and all they'd see is 'E Mavraki' with no address. So I got calls like, 'Hi, Elena, you live at 33–03 28th Street, and I'm gonna fuck you up your fat ass, bitch.'"

"I remember that. It was a great story. Were you scared?"

"At first, but then I was more really annoyed. It was like getting nasty personalized robocalls. And I thought about it, and it's not likely that some keyboard warrior's going to drive all the way here from Ohio or Texas."

"Except for the schmuck who shot up the pizza place in DC because he believed Hillary Clinton was running a pedophile ring out of tunnels in the basement."

"Oy, the *mishegas* these people believe."

"It's bizarre, you work your ass off on a piece and you feel lucky if a few hundred people do more than skim it, and then you've got a whole army of cretins obsessed with hating you. It's like Frankenstein's monster coming to life."

"You're right it's got a life of its own. I've come to realize that there's a scarily large number of people who are possessed by being pissed off. I don't have to tell you what about, you know the gestalt. And they spend their whole lives online, looking for something to be more pissed off about. When something gets on their radar, they go off on it, and the more they do, it spreads like a chain reaction. It turns into a psychotic feeding frenzy."

"I don't understand why they went off on this story. I mean it's a totally local piece, a lot of arcane going-through-documents details. Why?"

"Once the Jew hashtag got pinned on you, that's all they needed. I got that, and because my parents escaped, that brought out the 'they should have gassed you too' angle. Plus I'm a woman, which means that when you accomplish something and they know you wouldn't fuck them in a million years, they want to put you in your place. And because JSR is calling you an anti-Semite, that spread it around, and they like that you're getting it from both sides."

"Well, at least someone's reading our stuff." They both laughed.

The conversation lulled for a moment, and Charlie got distracted by the way she looked. Pleasantly *zaftig*, he thought, warm brown eyes, a gloriously hooked nose, and full lips, the dark curls of a few years ago now an unruly mass of old-lady gray. The way she lit up when she laughed. Very intriguing. Some women are beautiful because of their age, not in spite of it, he thought.

"Are you still in Astoria?" he asked.

"Yes, I'm on 28th Street. Same place."

She said I instead of we, he noticed. "Are you still married?"

"Wow, we really haven't talked in a while," she said. "He moved out December before last. How about you?"

"No, I split up with my girlfriend a couple years ago."

"Very intriguing," she replied, camping it up with a bit of affectation, and a smile he read as having depths well beyond flirtation.

They walked down Roosevelt Avenue, threading through the streams of people speaking Spanish, Bengali, and Chinese, women with strollers and shopping bags, around taco carts and produce stands, past bodegas blazing white lights, bachata basslines booming out of barroom doors, all under the oceanic rumble of the 7 train. Los Subterráneos was under a sporting goods store featuring jerseys from Barcelona in Spain and Barcelona from Guayaquil, down a flight of stairs from the sidewalk.

It was a softly lit room, brighter than a bar, with red walls and a black floor, tea-light candles on the tables, selling beer, wine, and empanadas as well as coffee and tea. About fifteen to twenty people were there, a table of Jews on the elderly side, a few Latinos, a middle-aged woman by herself with a laptop and a chai latte, a Chinese couple that looked like students, another couple deeper into their twenties, the woman with dreadlocks.

They could tell the band was having a good night from the moment they walked in. It was a four-piece, two women up front on clarinet and violin, men on upright bass and congas. The bass player had dyed black hair and the pale, withered face of an old rocker weathered by liquor and drugs. Elena pointed to the clarinet player, whispered, "That's Alyssa."

Alyssa introduced the next song. "We're gonna do one by Belf's Rumanian Orchestra," she said. "Recorded in Warsaw in 1913. It's called '*Oy, 'sa Falshe Velt.*' It's a Lying World."

"Painfully appropriate," Charlie whispered.

The bassist vamped it in, then pulsed an eight-note riff with a Terkisher rhythm, the percussionist punctuating it on a poyk, a marching bass drum with a small cymbal on top. The clarinet and violin sprightly and mournful, like there was joy but also eternal sadness at the evil of the world. The Jews' blues.

The band sped up for the next two songs, "Odessa Bulgar" racing like a Yiddish hoedown, and a version of "Mousourlou" that Alyssa torched like Naftule Brandwein doing Dick Dale. At the end of the set Elena complemented her and introduced Charlie. A boy of around seven poked around the percussion instruments, under the eye of the bassist. "Rafi, can you show Aaron a rhythm?" he called to the drummer.

Elena suggested they go upstairs to vape some weed. The streams of people flowed a little thinner, tired working men and women coming home, two men in open shirts with their heads cuddling each other's shoulders, curvy taxi dancers in short, low-cut dresses having a smoke outside a nightclub. She passed him her vape pen, slipped her hand into his. "Forward of me?" she smiled. "We're not working together, and I'm not married anymore. We can do this."

They came back in with their arms around each other, the sound system playing Prince Royce's bachata version of "Stand by Me." The band opened the second set with a klezmerized reggae tune, Augustus Pablo's "King David's Melody," the conga reverberating in the space matching their mood. The next song stretched out on the Middle Eastern side of klezmer, the clarinet and violin doing long hypnotic trills over an undulating midtempo groove. Elena and Charlie oozed closer together, touching each other, then slipped into an embrace and a kiss, tentative at first, then wallowingly deep. The band segued into a *zhok*, a slow jam with a heartbeat bassline and scratched guiro percussion, the clarinet and violin trading long, mournful phrases that sounded like a last-call singalong in a long-gone Bessarabian tavern. Elena and Charlie kept at it, reveling in the sensations and their new connection, oblivious to anyone offended by the old ones acting like that. When you're our age you'll be grateful if your *eyver iz nit in der keyver, keynehore.*

The man coming down the stairs barely registered on their optic synapses. A pudgy putz in camouflage, with a few pubescent squiggles of wannabe beard. The more important detail not seen yet: The AR-15 rifle behind his back, modified to full automatic, with a 100-round drum magazine attached.

It took less than two minutes for him to empty it.

Leaving behind carnage. Fragments. Shards of life. Shreds of life. A shattered cup of chai latte.

❧

The suspect headed for the Brooklyn–Queens Expressway. *Get me off these shitty little city streets*, he raged, *fucking red lights on every block, where a man can't drive free like in real America, only a cuck mangina could stand to sit stuck waiting for all these assholes to move. And waiting for the fucking pedestrians to cross, a bitch with a stroller and two kids. Fucking sluts invade us and breed like rats.* He contemplated ramming into all four of them. *They will not replace us now! No, now's the time to get out of this pit.*

Parking enforcement agent Syed Choudhury heard the bulletin on the police radio and remembered a van with Pennsylvania plates he'd ticketed around the corner from the scene. Aside from that it was blatantly blocking a driveway, he'd noticed the stickers, "Pork-Eating Crusader" in English and Arabic, and "Lead Is My Precious Metal," with a picture of a bullet.

He called in the plate number. It was a white Ford Transit Connect registered in Ulysses, Pennsylvania, a small town three hundred miles west of the city.

Police spotted it on the Triborough Bridge. The suspect noticed one on his tail, one on his side, and swerved off at the exit for the Bronx. He ducked off the Bruckner at the first exit, going down the off-ramp past a stew of pallets and cranes jumbled under the expressway. Shithole city, he thought.

His brain screaming to get away, away from the traffic, he made the first turn off the service road, a hard right onto East 136th. A side street of plumbing supply shops and neat brick houses. The next block was emptier, his headlights catching ailanthus trees, chain-link fences, and a yellow metal grate. The street narrowed to go under a railroad bridge, the air smelling like stale beer. He sped toward the corner, thinking about turning. Cop cars blocked both sides. He jammed through the stop sign. Giant gas tanks ahead. Left or right. And then two cop SUVs blocked the intersection, and blinding white lights exploded on from both ends.

"Come out and put your fucking hands on the car!" a cop with a bullhorn barked.

To his left were chain-link and corrugated-metal fences topped with razor wire. He could see rifle barrels poking out between the cop cars.

"Do anything stupid and you're fuckin' dead," the voice barked. He opened the door. "Slow, motherfucker!" it snapped. "Keep your hands out! Show your face!"

He slowly turned counterclockwise and submissively placed his hands on the roof of the van. A phalanx of backlit shadows in black body armor advanced on him. Legions of android soldiers. Monster turtles with Kevlar underbellies. "Stay still!" the voice barked.

One grabbed his left arm, another his right, and slammed them into handcuffs. His eyes adjusted to the light. He was in the South Bronx. And every single one of the dozen-odd cops was black, brown, or beige.

Police officials said the suspect surrendered without incident. That wasn't 100 percent true. In custody at the 40th Precinct, he had to be given a pair of ill-fitting sweatpants, because, as Officer Katie Ortiz put it in a 138th Street bar after the four-to-twelve shift got off, his own pants were "like a blowout diaper from my two-year-old."

"I feel bad for whoever's in the evidence room," said Joe Pierotti.

"He went from racial holy war to rectal holy war," quipped Jameel Morgan. "How the mighty have fallen!" They clinked beer bottles, slapped palms, knocked fists.

Police officials said there were indications the suspect had targeted Queens, particularly Jackson Heights, but could not yet determine how or why he selected Los Subterráneos. They believed a manifesto found online had been posted by him about twenty minutes before the shooting began.

It said New York City was a "cesspit of fecalized races" and continued,

"We preserve our strength and a future for white children by preserving our purity. The pestilent races mix their genetic filth. It must be cleansed with blood."

In other words, he wanted to exterminate pretty much everyone on the 7 train.

And he said that according to the *Protocols of the Elders of Zion*, this was the result of a Jewish plot to undermine Western civilization by infesting the Nordic nations with immigrants from inferior countries.

We do not need to dwell on that or even mention his name. It should be erased from the Book of Life. He doesn't deserve the publicity.

Let us remember the eighteen lives he erased. Eighteen is supposed to be the number of life.

Evelyn Weinberg, 83, retired teacher, grandmother of four.

Morris Schwartz, 79, retired, grandfather of two.

Shelley Sokolow, 71, retired.

Estella Vega, 19, barista, student at LaGuardia Community College.

Anthony Quesada, 23, bartender, father of one.

Juan Carlos Olmedo, 38, coffeehouse owner, father of two.

Emanuel Chao, 21, student at Queens College.

Allison Li, 20, student at Queens College.

Roxanne McNair, 25, poet, teacher's aide.

Giovanni Pérez, 27, IT worker at Elmhurst Hospital.

Shaila Rahman, 42, treasurer for nonprofit organization, mother of two.

Charles Purpelberg, 63, journalist.
Elena Mavraki, 64, journalist.
Alyssa Rosen, 56, clarinetist.
Rachel Edelstein, 47, violinist, mother of one.
Rafael García, 52, drummer.
Mick Greenberg, 62, bassist.
Aaron Greenberg, 7, his grandson.

❧

May their memory be a blessing.

That seems so minuscule next to the magnitude of their loss.

It's normally the nicest realistic thing you could say about someone who died.

Sanctuary

Doug Allyn

In the first furious days after Pearl Harbor, everybody wanted into the fight. Quakers were enlisting, and even nuns wanted guns. Jake Abrams was as ready as the rest, but with one difference. Jake actually knew about fighting. Firsthand.

He'd won his first Boy's Club bout at ten and still sparred six-rounders in Columbus Bottoms clubs to pay his tuition at Ohio State. Jake knew the taste of his own blood and the soul-searing pain of a liver shot. He didn't hate the pugs he faced in the ring, just wanted to beat them. Fighting Hitler or the Japanese wouldn't be much different.

When his college roommates, Izzy Kaminski and Moise Shefler, marched down to the army recruiting office to enlist, Jake went with them but at the last minute didn't sign up. Mo and Izzy were legacies, the sons of wealthy men. Jake's father was a pawnbroker in the Bottoms, who'd taken on a second mortgage to scrape up money for med school. Jake owed the old man the courtesy of a phone call first, at least.

A mere formality. Isaac Abrams hated the Nazis like cholera. Jake expected his father's blessing. A "go with God," maybe even an "attaboy."

Instead, he got silence, an ominous hum on the line.

"Listen to me carefully, Yakov," Isaac Abrams said. "The newspapers, the radio people, are all saying this fight will be over in a year. They are wrong. I have a letter from your Uncle Chaim, in Germany. He says these Nazis are practical men who study war like Hasids study Talmud. In public, they revile Jews, but their armies need food, so they leave Chaim to work his farm. They mean to win the world, so they plan for a long fight. You will be more useful to America as a doctor. Finish your schooling first, then enlist. There's no hurry, son. This war will wait for you."

His father and uncle were right. By Christmas, the Nazis had rolled through Europe, looking every inch the supermen they claimed to be. Invincible. Which didn't make Jake's situation any easier to swallow. Overseas, the Allies were getting shellacked. France collapsed, then Norway, while Jake sat through lectures, ashamed of the studies that shielded him from the draft. And then it got worse.

Izzy Kaminski vanished in Sicily, vaporized into a red mist by a German 88. A sergeant with one arm brought Izzy's mother his medals and a map of Messina that marked his grave. Moise Shefler was next, cut down by a Nazi sniper while Jake sat snug in his dorm, cramming for finals. He skipped his graduation ceremony to stand in line at the enlistment office.

For a blue-collar kid who'd been training half of his life, Officer's Candidate School at Fort Leonard Wood was a walk in the park. Jake emerged as Captain Yakov Isaac Abrams, MD, and promptly shipped out for the European Theater. The troop transport was crammed with young warriors, eager to fight, and impatient with Jake's first aid lectures.

"Stop the bleeding, close the wound, call for a medic," was the mantra he repeated over and over again to teenaged troops who were so keyed up he doubted they heard a word. Five weeks after their ship docked in Liverpool, Jake jumped into the largest amphibious invasion in human history.

Normandy.

Jake's unit waded ashore at Omaha Beach on D-Day plus three, brushing past brutally torn bodies floating in the surf like driftwood.

On the beach, work details were clearing away the corpses so the newsreel cameras could record the marvelous victory while glossing over its terrible cost.

Jake paused beside one corpse, a kid he recognized from the ship. A shrapnel shard had ripped him open from the groin to the knee. He'd closed the gash with safety pins from his sewing kit. Apparently, he'd recalled Jake's lecture, though it hadn't saved him. Jake murmured an *El Malei Rakhamim* for the dead, then moved on.

His first field hospital was a huge canvas tent without partitions, where emergency surgery was going on beside wounded men on stretchers waiting their turn. The tent roof was marked with an enormous red cross, a major mistake because the Luftwaffe soon began targeting the tents. Wounded soldiers are more trouble than dead ones.

After quitting the tents, Jake's unit continued their bloody work in burned-out basements, church naves, cow barns, any building with a roof. The Nazis still strafed them, but the medical units were harder to identify now. Bombed out buildings were everywhere.

Surgery in the barns was a nightmare. Repairing the godawful wounds of war as the ground shook and the lights winked out during shellfire was all but impossible.

Jake changed units nearly as often as he changed shirts. Though he was attached to a specific command, docs were often left behind when an outfit leapfrogged ahead, then reassigned to whichever unit replaced them on the line.

The constant relocations made anything more than casual acquaintances nearly impossible. Jake would sometimes step into a basement surgery and not recognize a single soul in the place.

He finally made one friend, though. Artie Weiss, a cocky, sawed-off runt from Brooklyn. They were called into the commander's hooch on their first day with Patton's Third Army. A battle-weary sergeant told them to take off their Mogen David stars, and mail them home, then issued them new dog tags, with their religion listed as Christian.

"Our right to wear these stars is one of the things we're supposed to be fighting for," Artie said furiously.

"You're absolutely right, sir," the sergeant sighed. "But in some actions, the towns and grounds can change hands a dozen times. If you're captured, and the Germans learn you're Jewish, you'll be executed on the spot. Or worse."

"What's worse than being executed?" Jake asked.

"The camps, from what we're hearing. Please, guys, mail your stars home. They're not worth your life."

"Actually, they are," Artie said. But he pocketed his and traded in his old dog tags for the counterfeits.

Outside, he and Jake exchanged names and thumbnail histories. "What are you going to do about your star?" Artie asked.

"What the man said, mail it home. I'm not religious, I only wear the David to please my mom. You?"

"I'm keeping mine. If the Nazis grab us, I'll say it's yours," he added with a sly smile. "Somebody said you're from Ohio? Do you know anything about Michigan?"

"Not much. I did a semester at U of M med school. Combat trauma. Why?"

"I've been reading up on a town on the north shore of Lake Michigan," Artie said. "It's called Valhalla. I'm moving there once this shit's over."

"Why there?"

"Valhalla is the Viking heaven, my friend, and this place sounds like it. A quaint little resort town, sandy beaches, trout streams, virgin forests, power boats and sailing. Hell, it's sanctuary, *boychik*. I did the math. Geographically, it's about as far from this craziness as we can get. You should come with me. We'll open a general practice together. Wear our Mogen Davids on our fucking hats if we want to."

Valhalla. Sanctuary. Right. Jake knew it was just a pipe dream. He heard them every day. Most GIs clung to a cherished hometown fantasy that starred their high school sweethearts and a little house with a white picket fence. They'd babble on about them as Jake was severing their shattered limbs, or bandaging their blinded eyes. If a daydream helped them bear their pain, fine. But in truth, even if they survived their wounds, the nightly artillery barrages and occasional strafing by mad dog Messerschmitts, their reveries were unlikely to come true. Artie's was no different. Except for his friend's maddening attention to detail, Valhalla was just another impossible dream.

Still, a good many of their off-duty hours were spent poring over maps, discussing the fine art of fly fishing, or what they'd name their sailboats, harmless fantasies that helped to counter the horror of the torn bodies and shattered dreams they faced every day, or worse, walked past without stopping, knowing the wounded man would die with or without aid. They had no time for the dying, nor much comfort to offer. Simple necessity meant saving their efforts for those with some hope of survival.

Which sometimes included Germans. Division policy dictated that enemy wounded would be seen last, but Jake and Artie patched up a good number of Wehrmacht soldiers and officers who would have blown their heads off had their situations been reversed. Artie, of course, proudly wore his Mogen David while he worked, making certain every Nazi he treated saw it. Two SS officers, a colonel and his aide, actually complained about being treated by a Jew.

No problem. Jake had them pulled from the line and sent back to the POW compound. The colonel bled out in the night. His aide, a lieutenant, in agony from a ruptured spleen, made so much noise a medic issued him six syrettes of morphine. He promptly injected all six, overdosed, and put himself down like a dog.

No great loss. No more complaints either.

Madness? Of course. But in war, irony and insanity are never in short supply. Artie and Jake would often joke about performing circumcisions as their Wehrmacht patients faded out under the anesthetic, but in truth they treated the Germans with the same care they gave their own, obligated by their oaths and their honor.

Until Buchenwald.

Mid-April 1945, Jake and Artie were attached to the Sixth Armored Division of Patton's Third Army when the unit encountered its first death camp.

They were among the first through the gates, called there because the battle-hardened GIs didn't know what else to do. There were no guards on the gates or the gun towers. Corpses were stacked outside the barracks like cordwood, and the inmates who were still breathing were scarcely more than skeletons. It was a miracle they were alive at all, and many wouldn't survive the day, let alone the week. The very air bore a stench of death and corruption that seemed to ooze through their skin into their souls.

Artie spoke enough Yiddish to get directions to the camp's medical facility, but what they found there was worse than the stacked corpses. Most of the "patients" were dead or dying, and they hadn't been there for treatment anyway. They'd been guinea pigs for experiments that would've sickened De Sade.

The only semifunctional human they encountered was a half-mad male nurse, a Pole, who said the Nazis had fled a few days before, but the last orders they'd received from Berlin were to execute the inmates, then obliterate the camp with explosives. The collapse of the Thousand-Year Reich wasn't slowing Hitler's Final Solution, it was speeding it up. In his final act of insanity, he meant to murder the Jews, to the last man, woman, and child.

All of them.

They stumbled out of the infirmary, stunned by the sheer horror of this place. Dropping to his knees, Artie spewed in the dirt, coughing up everything he'd eaten in a week. Jake rested a hand on his friend's shoulder, the only comfort he could offer. And then he stiffened.

"What is it?" Artie demanded, glancing up, spitting to clear his mouth.

"My uncle," Jake said. "His farm is maybe thirty, forty miles north of here."

"Your uncle's German?"

"A German Jew, a farmer. He got a letter to us early in the war. The Nazis needed his crops, so they let him be, but this country's falling apart. They'll kill him now, kill his whole family. I have to get them out."

He flagged down a passing Jeep, rigged for battle. It had Thompson submachine guns in its scabbards, and an M1919 Browning .30 cal mounted on a tripod in the back. A freckle faced troop with a bandaged forehead was at the wheel.

"I'm going with you," Artie said, as the Jeep pulled up.

"No," Jake said, scrambling in. "This is personal, and this hellhole needs all the medical help it can get. I'll be back in a few hours. Let's go, driver."

"Yes, sir. Where to?"

"A country village called Posenstedt. Maybe thirty miles north."

"Sir, the ground north of us is still in enemy hands. We can't—"

"It's a backwater, Sergeant! There won't be any troops there and we aren't going to the village anyway. I've got family a few miles this side of it. If that's a problem for you, get the hell out. I'll drive myself."

The hard-eyed vet hesitated, but only for a moment.

"Hell, I'd rather be anyplace else on the planet than this shithole," he growled, slamming the gearshift into first, gunning it out. "What's in Posenstedt?"

"My family," Jake said.

"Good enough for me," the sergeant nodded, working a wad of chaw around in his cheek. "I'm Sergeant Puchinski, sir. Pooch to my friends."

"Pooch," Jake nodded. "I'm Jake."

"No sir, you ain't," Pooch grinned. "You're Captain Jake, sir. If we land in the crapper over this, I'm just a lowly grunt following your orders. Sir."

They blew through the camp's north gate without being challenged. It would be hours before any sort of order was restored. With luck, they'd be back before that.

Rolling through the countryside on the narrow dirt road, it was hard to believe they were in the middle of a war. This was farm country, open fields neatly kept, planted mostly with corn, the shoots poking out of the earth. The only reminders of the carnage all around them was the railroad embankment that ran parallel to the road. It had been blasted into ruin by Allied bombers earlier in the war, its tracks hopelessly twisted now, rusty rails reaching skyward as though begging for mercy.

The few farmhouses they passed appeared to be abandoned, none of them showing any smoke from a chimney. No sign of life.

Then, as they rounded a curve, they nearly ran down a platoon of German soldiers, a half dozen Wehrmacht regulars marching along the roadside in single file. They looked spent, exhausted, but they were still armed to the teeth, staring dumbfounded at the American Jeep, casually driving through their midst.

"Wave to them," Pooch said, smiling around his tobacco chaw. Jake waved. One of the Germans actually waved back, though he was instantly cursed by another. Still, miraculously, none of them raised a weapon.

"*Mach weiter!*" Pooch yelled as they blew past. "*Der krieg ist vorbei.* Don't look back, Captain."

"You speak German?" Jake said, surprised.

"Milwaukee Polack, born and bred," Pooch grinned. "The whole town speaks German."

"What did you tell them?"

"Keep going. The war's over. And seeing two Yanks out for a Sunday drive? They're thinking maybe it is."

But it wasn't.

The next farmhouse they came to had been burned to the ground. A single chimney, standing amid a few blackened, skeletal timbers was all that remained.

His uncle's farm, Jake was sure of it. A crude, yellow Star of David had been painted on the front gate. Pooch pulled into the yard, then slowly circled the ruins of the house.

"No bodies, no graves," he noted somberly.

"Not here," Jake agreed.

"We should go back, Captain."

"Not yet. If they're alive, they'll likely be held in the village."

"Unless they're back in that camp," Pooch said, spitting over the side of the Jeep. "Look, Captain, we've been dumb lucky so far. A few

Kraut soldiers is one thing. Going into a town is something else. We could have trouble."

"Good," Jake said, jerking the tommy gun out of its scabbard. "After seeing that camp? I'm up for some trouble. How about you?"

"Yeah," Pooch nodded grimly, "I guess I am. Lock and load, Captain. This could get interesting." Pooch pulled his own weapon, racked it, then handed it to Jake. "Hang on to this, sir. We're gonna make an entrance."

They roared out of the farmyard at full speed, bouncing onto the road, headed north to—they had no idea what. They found out soon enough. A few miles further on, they crested a hill to find a small farm village laid out before them, seemingly untouched by the war. Posenstedt.

"Sweet Jesus, it looks like a picture postcard," Pooch said.

"Too small to bother bombing," Jake nodded. The village consisted of a few dozen houses with manicured yards on both sides of the dirt road, elaborately trimmed with Bavarian gingerbread. A white clapboard church with a single spire stood at one end, a brown brick railroad station at the other, closed now, with boards nailed over its doors and windows.

Pooch never slowed. He roared down the dirt road to the center of the village, skidding the Jeep to a halt in a cloud of dust.

"Here we go," he said grimly, taking his Thompson from Jake, climbing out of the Jeep. Switching the weapon to full auto, he fired a burst in the air.

"*Herren!*" he roared at the top of his lungs. "*Raus! Raus mit uns!*"

Nothing. Not a sound, not a soul. No response at all.

"*Raus!*" Pooch yelled again, and this time Jake joined in, both men shouting "*Raus! Raus! Raus mit uns!*" Firing their guns in the air.

This time it worked. The church door inched open and an elderly clergyman edged out. He wore a long black robe, white collar, some kind of cap over his wispy gray hair. He stumbled down the steps and fell to his knees in the street, hands in the air. Clearly terrified.

Jake was past caring. Stalking up to the priest, he pressed the muzzle of the Thompson against the old man's forehead.

"Captain?" Pooch cautioned.

Jake ignored him. "Chaim Abramson," he said slowly and distinctly. And it was enough. The old man nodded, swallowing. And mumbled something.

"What did he say?" Jake demanded.

"*Der eisenbahnhof,*" Pooch echoed. "The train station."

"The station's closed. The tracks were blown to hell a long time ago. The farm was only torched recently. What does he mean?"

"I don't know, but that's what he said," Pooch said grimly, looking away, clearly embarrassed at seeing the old priest on his knees in the dirt.

"Okay then, let's go," Jake said. Seizing the old man's robe, he hauled him to his feet, then gestured with his weapon, pointing toward the railroad station. Pooch opened his mouth to argue but read the rage in Jakes eyes and shrugged. Taking the old man by the elbow, he steadied him, and spoke quietly to him, explaining. The priest nodded and led them down the street to the closed station, but he didn't stop there. Instead, he marched a dozen yards beyond it, pointing down the empty track.

Jake walked past him, following his rough directions, but saw only the railroad grade, torn up in the distance, and the embankment on the far side.

"What the hell, Pooch? If he's claiming they took the damn train, he's lying. These tracks we passed were bombed out early in the war and my uncle's farm was burned within the past few weeks. So what's—" He broke off, reading the sickness in the sergeant's lined face.

"Look down, Captain."

"What . . . ?" Jake glanced down at his combat boots, and then again as he saw that the ground wasn't just gravel. There was brass mixed in with it. Empty cartridges. Jake knelt and picked one up. Common as dirt in this war. 7.92 mm brass from a German MG 42 machine gun. And as he straightened, he realized the embankment across the tracks was pockmarked with bullet holes. And stained black with blood. It took a moment for the scene to register. What must have happened here. And how it was done.

"They lined them up against the embankment?" he asked.

"Captain—"

"Ask him!" Jake shouted.

Pooch did as ordered, and the old man explained, pointing down the tracks. Pooch nodded, swallowing.

"Well?"

"He, um, he said they dug their graves first."

"Who dug their graves?"

"Your . . . your family, sir, your uncle, two boys, one girl. His wife, your aunt, I guess? They were killed last month. And there were others too. POWs. Polish laborers. Maybe a dozen. All executed here by the SS."

Jake said nothing, just nodded slowly, absorbing the scene, imagining what it must have been like.

"Where are they buried?" he asked at last.

"Where they fell," Pooch said. "The villagers shoveled some of the embankment down to cover the bodies. Afterward."

But Jake wasn't listening. He'd wheeled, and headed back up the road into the village at a trot, firing his weapon into the air, then firing another burst that raked across the front of the church, slugs slamming into the old clapboard facade.

"Out! Out! *Raus mit uns!*" he roared. And this time a dozen or so townsfolk obeyed the madman shouting in the street.

They streamed out of the church, instinctively clustering together on the steps. One woman knelt, raising her hands in supplication, and then a few more followed suit, and then the rest dropped to their knees as well, cowering before the madman who was still stalking the road, ranting at the houses, though all the villagers were already kneeling in front of the church.

Terrified.

Jake could see it in their peasant faces. And that's what they were. Peasants. Farm families. Old men, old women, a few girls. No boys at all. The only men of military age were missing limbs, or otherwise injured, likely invalided out of the Wehrmacht. They'd seen death many times, and recognized it now in Jake's madness, knowing how quickly this could end. Expecting to die.

And Jake realized they were all expecting to be killed. Not just the soldiers. All of them.

And then he realized why.

These villagers knew what had been done at the train station, and shared the collective guilt of it. And now their hour of reckoning had come. Vengeance, in the guise of a crazed American Jew, herding them into the street to wreak God knew what on them. Ready to kill them all.

And for a single mad moment, it almost happened. Jake was only a heartbeat away from emptying his submachine gun into the crowd.

"Captain?" Pooch said softly. "You don't want to do this."

"The hell I don't!" And it was true. Jake *did* want to do it! He needed to do *something* to balance the books for Buchenwald, for Kristallnacht, and all atrocities in between and the hatred at the root of them.

But even in a red rage, only a word away from committing mass murder, he couldn't quite pull the trigger. No matter what crimes had been done here by the Nazis and their adherents all over the damned world, he simply could not hate these people the way they hated his. Righteous rage for their crimes burned in him like a fire, but it hadn't quite consumed his soul. He would not sacrifice what little remained of his humanity on their bloody fucking altar.

Lowering his weapon was one of the hardest things he'd ever done. But he did it. Then he stalked back to the Jeep, climbed in, and folded his arms to wait for his driver.

The villagers stayed on their knees, their eyes locked on Jake like radar, terrified he might change his mind. But even when he didn't, none of them breathed any easier. They'd been reprieved from retribution, but only for this day. The Russian beasts would be on them soon, and there would be no mercy from them.

So the dazed crowd remained in the street until the two Americans and their Jeep disappeared in the dusty distance before they finally, reluctantly, rose to return to the church, avoiding each other's eyes as they did so.

The drive back to Buchenwald was less than thirty miles. They should have covered it in a few hours. It took five days.

Ten miles out of Posenstedt, they were spotted by a lone German fighter, a Focke Wulf 190. The Allies had air superiority now, so the Jerry pilot was probably fleeing for his life, but he risked a few moments to make a single strafing run at the lone American Jeep he caught in the open.

One pass, one burst of 7.92 machine gun fire. At the last minute, Pooch spun the Jeep into a broadside power slide that avoided most of the rounds, but a half dozen slugs stitched the hood, destroying the Jeep's four-banger engine, and a ricochet punched through Puchinski's shoulder, blowing him out of the vehicle as it skidded off the road into a drainage ditch and flipped over. Jake was catapulted a full forty yards before crashing down in the muck, unconscious.

When he woke, it took him most of an hour to crawl back onto the road. Pooch was on the ground, leaning against the upended vehicle, pale as a ghost, his right hand clamped over the savage wound in his shoulder, stanching the flow of blood.

Jake salvaged the Jeep's first aid kit to patch him up, but it was clear they weren't going anywhere. They were at least twenty miles from

American lines and the Jeep was a total wreck, including the radio. Pooch was too weak from blood loss to cover any distance on foot, and Jake couldn't leave him.

They had weapons and water. All they could do now was wait to be rescued, or executed, by one side or the other.

Four days later, they were spotted by a Ranger scout in a Jeep, who gave them a lift back to Buchenwald.

At the camp, Jake and Pooch shook hands like the strangers they were again, and parted without a word. Jake reported to the medical facility, expecting to get thoroughly chewed out for going AWOL.

Instead, his boss waved off Jake's explanation and told him to take a seat.

"I have hard news, Captain. I know you and Captain Weiss were close. While you were—gone, Captain Weiss went into Stratsfurth, a village south of the camp, to vaccinate the children and treat serious injuries. On the way back, his Jeep hit a mine. Artie and his driver were both killed. I'm sorry, son."

Jake could only stare at the older man, trying to process the information. "A mine?" he echoed at last. "Ours or theirs?"

"German. They're making our final push as tough as they can."

"But he was trying to help them! And damn it, we were so close!"

"Close?"

"To sanctuary, sir. Artie's big plan."

The colonel didn't respond, eyeing Jake oddly, wondering if he'd run off the rails.

"Losing a friend is hard, Captain Abrams, but we've all been through it. Take a few hours to get your head around this, but then I need you back on the line, Jake. Artie's gone, but in the time it's taken me to tell you, a dozen more inmates have probably passed. This place is—" He looked away, because he had no words that could describe the camp. But Jake knew exactly what he meant.

He tried to arrange a proper ceremony for Artie, but when he told the sergeant in charge of the burial detail he wanted to sit *shivah* with his friend, the harried NCO just stared at him blankly, baffled.

"Sir, my burial details are interring a dozen camp inmates a day, and more are dying every hour," the sergeant said, speaking slowly, as if explaining to a child. "As an American officer, Captain Weiss got priority, of course. A proper Christian burial with full military honors, a bugler for 'Taps,' a volley from a rifle squad. He was laid to rest among friends, in a section of the cemetery reserved for American troops."

"A Christian burial?" Jake echoed, dumfounded. Until he realized what must have happened. Artie's bogus dog tags. Jake was so stunned he couldn't rage or even laugh. Because the only man in this world who would have truly enjoyed this amazing joke had just received a proper Christian burial in the last place on earth he would want to be.

Jake stayed on at Buchenwald through the last months of the war, treating wounded GIs, trying to undo the horrors perpetrated by the camp's medical staff, and doing what he could for the prisoners, which wasn't much. The inmates were so physically depleted they continued to die long after their liberation.

Pooch was shipped stateside as soon as he was well enough to travel. Jake stopped to say goodbye, though that was really all they had to say to each other. And soon, Jake followed him. Troopships heading home needed doctors to tend the wounded, and Jake had more than enough battlefield credits to qualify for an honorable discharge and even a promotion.

"Congratulations, Major Abrams," his colonel said, shaking his hand. "You're going home."

But he wasn't. Because Columbus wasn't home anymore. His father's shop was still in the same old neighborhood, the same mean streets, but the war had ended the Depression. Stiffs who never had two nickels had steady jobs now. Friends were glad to see Jake home in one piece, but nobody cared where he'd been or what he'd done. The war was old news, the last thing anyone wanted to talk about. They'd moved on to cheerier topics: the Oscars, the end of rationing, the bombsight hood ornaments on the new Studebakers.

Even at home with his family, Jake felt alien, like a golem who resembled their son, but wasn't. Not anymore.

Their home was so quiet he couldn't sleep. Nights, he would prowl the house in the dark, double checking the doors and windows. Then an hour later he'd check them again. Until the night he blundered into his father and almost brained him with a poker.

They didn't go back to bed. No point. Instead, Isaac made a pot of sweet tea, and they sat at the kitchen table in the dark, smoking Luckies and sipping in silence. Isaac had grown thinner while Jake was away. Stringy sinews in his arms, his dark hair going gray, thinning out. He'd always had high hopes for his only son, he'd gambled his business to see him through school. But now? Jake could read the concern in his eyes.

"What do you *want* to do with your life, son?" Isaac asked, at last. "Do you have hopes or dreams?"

"I'm almost thirty, Pop, and I've seen more of death than life. All I really know is war. If I had any hopes, Buchenwald erased them. And the only dream I've ever had wasn't even mine."

"What dream?"

Jake explained Artie's dream of finding sanctuary in Viking heaven, Valhalla. "It was only a fantasy, Pop, every soldier has one. We were seeing so many terrible things every day. We were drowning in them. We needed something else. Anything else. To talk about. To *think* about."

"But your friend, this Artie, he believed in this place?"

"With his whole heart, but that's how Artie was about everything. He always expected happy endings. So, Valhalla? It was a beautiful idea, but that's all it was. Just another pipedream."

"Perhaps so, but that doesn't make it wrong. I have a good life here, with your mother, and my shop. But if I were a younger man? Alone? I would consider such a dream."

"You want me to go, Pop?"

"I want you to stay, Yakov. But yeah, I think you should go. There is more to life than war and these streets. Go. If only to honor your friend."

Packing was no problem. Everything Jake owned fit into the duffle bag he tossed in the trunk of his father's prewar Packard.

The drive north was a good seven hours, west to Naptown, up through Fort Wayne to Grand Rapids, then a scenic run up Michigan's north shore.

A hundred miles out of Valhalla, Jake burst out laughing, when it dawned on him that, except for a few postcards, Artie Weiss had never actually *seen* this place. Only dreamed of it.

But as it happened? Artie's dream wasn't so far off.

Valhalla was much as the brochures had described it, a quaint resort village on the shores of Lake Michigan. An artsy-craftsy downtown district, mostly antique shops and boutiques that sold fudge or original art. The heart of the village was its harbor, filled with motor launches and sailing craft, sleek as greyhounds. The surrounding hills were pine forests, with rippling streams and shadowed trails for hiking and biking. Jake could almost hear Artie's smug voice in his inner ear.

"*Told you so,* boychik. *Sanctuary. We can wear our Mogen Davids on our fucking hats.*"

Settling in was surprisingly easy. One of the town's few doctors, an elderly GP, had been waiting out the war to retire. Jake expected some pushback because of his faith, but the old timer welcomed Jake as a partner in a state of the art clinic with a seasoned staff and surgical privileges at the local hospital. Compared to the godawful conditions in French cow barns? Or the camp? Valhalla actually *felt* a bit like Heaven.

It was too good to be true, of course, and Jake didn't buy it for a minute. He'd been too far, seen far too much, to accept good fortune as anything but temporary. He settled in, but down deep? He was waiting for the other shoe to drop . . .

And then it did.

A few months after the move, Jake made his first real commitment to Artie's dream. He put a down payment on a home, a cottage on a hundred-acre plot with its own inland lake, as far from other humans as he could reasonably get. He fenced in his land, and posted it as private, no hunting, no trespassing.

His first visitor wasn't the welcome wagon. Hector Baptiste, a back-woodsman who lived a few miles up the dirt road, came to bitch about the new fence. He was a big man, Baptiste, bearded, in a faded flannel shirt and grimy coveralls, hunting boots.

"Old Chris, who owned it before you, always gave me permission to hunt his property. Half your land is a cedar swamp, Doc. Deer feed on them cedars in winter. If you don' keep their numbers down, they'll chew up your trees and kill 'em, then the whole herd will starve out before spring."

"Sorry," Jake said, "I've seen enough killing for this lifetime. I want no hunting on my land, Mr. Baptiste."

"If not the deer, what about the critters? Coons, possums, coyotes? They'll raid your garden, attack your animals—"

"I don't have a garden, or any animals. I'll make it simple, Mr. Baptiste. You stay on your side of the property line, I'll stay on mine, we'll get along fine."

Hector Baptiste glared at him a moment, then muttered something under his breath as he turned away. Kike? Or Yid, maybe? Definitely something. Jake smiled tightly at the epithet, relieved to finally hear it. He'd been expecting it ever since he came to this place. A reminder of how the world really is.

He got another reminder later that same week. Baptiste had three boys, grown men really, as feral as their father. Jake was pulling into his driveway, when they went flying by in their rattletrap pickup truck, passing him on the right, whooping like wild Indians, flashing him the finger as they passed.

Welcome to Viking heaven, he thought. But again, he let it pass. There was trouble enough in this world without looking for more. But sometimes trouble finds you, whether you're looking or not.

In the coffee shop the next day, Jake noticed an older man sitting alone by the front window, wearing a long black coat and a yarmulke. Meeting Jake's glance, the old timer motioned him over, gesturing toward the empty chair.

"Sorry for staring," Jake said. "There aren't many of us in this town."

"I'm Rabbi Asher," the old man said, offering his hand. "Retired now, just visiting. Mostly, I come for the high holy days. I have not seen you at temple."

"I'm not religious."

"You were in the war," the old man said. It wasn't a question, but Jake nodded. "You must have seen terrible things. The camps?"

"Buchenwald," Jake said.

"And you think God abandoned us? Or was never there?"

Jake didn't bother to answer that one.

"It is right and just to blame God for that war," Asher said mildly. "He made this world so marvelous that men always want more of it, when all the land a man really needs is six feet by three. From his head to his heels. What brings you to this . . . backwater?"

"A friend thought we could find sanctuary here. It was his dream."

"A noble one," the old man nodded. "And have you found it?"

"I don't think it exists for us. Anywhere."

"Have you met hatred here?"

"Not yet," Jake admitted.

"Then perhaps your friend was right."

"My friend is dead, rabbi. Killed by people he was trying to help. And his dream—well, it was just a dream."

"I'm sorry you feel that way. I think the Nazis' vilest sin was making us believe that all the world hates as they do. It's not so."

"Isn't it?" Jake said, rising, offering his hand. "I have to get back to the office. Nice meeting you."

"And you," the old man nodded. "As to your sanctuary? Perhaps it's not a place one finds. It's a place we make for ourselves. I wish you luck, my young friend."

"Thank you. Have a good day, Rabbi Asher."

"Not so good," the old man said with a wan smile. "We bury Isadore Sobel today. You should come. I promise the service will be short."

"I'll pass," Jake said. "I've seen all the Jewish graves I care to."

Perhaps the old man was an omen, or a magnet for the hatred Jake had seen in the war. Because that day it followed him home.

Dusk was falling when Jake pulled into the driveway of his little country cottage, but even in the twilight, he could see the place had been vandalized. His garbage cans had been tipped over, some stomped flat, trash scattered around his yard in mindless destruction.

He felt an instant surge of rage, mixed with an odd satisfaction.

He wasn't really surprised by the carnage. He'd been expecting it, or something like it. In Columbus, vandalism was commonplace in neighborhood feuds. A neighbor giving you grief? Scatter trash around his stoop. Garbage cans were favored targets for street kids, dump 'em in the dark, run away laughing. And in a world that would kill Artie Weiss, what else would you expect? There were no swastikas daubed on his walls, but that would be next, if he let this pass.

Which he would not.

He mulled it over as he cleaned up the mess. His suspect list was short. His surly neighbor, Hec Baptiste, and his thug sons.

He found Hec in the front yard of his swaybacked shack, splitting firewood with a double-bitted ax. Shirtless, the hair on his chest and back was matted with sweat, thick as a pelt.

Hec glanced up as Jake climbed out of his car, but kept splitting the wood, each blow a savage strike.

"Somethin' you want, Doc?"

"Somebody trashed my place, Mr. Baptiste, scattered my garbage cans around, made one helluva mess. Would you know anything about it?"

"Sure," Hec said, pausing to wipe the sweat off his forehead with the back of his hand. "It was likely a boar coon or coyotes. Or maybe a chief's son if he's hungry enough."

"Chief's son?"

"It's what the Anishnabeg call black bears. They mostly avoid folk, but if one gets old or injured, they'll raid garbage. Put them cans inside your garage. And be watchful around your place. You don't want to meet no chief's son in the dark."

"Or your roughneck sons either. You need to understand, I won't be a victim. In the war, I saw where that goes. Starts with Kristallnacht and vandalism, ends up in the camps."

"Doc, I got no fucking idea what you're talking about."

"Then understand this. Keep your boys off my land, Hec. I will not be pushed."

"You're the only one pushin', asshole. This ain't the big city and we ain't alone in these woods. Leavin' garbage cans out is like hangin' up a big sign sayin' free lunch, come get it. All you can do now is move 'em inside, though it's probably too late."

"Why too late?"

"Because you've been teaching whatever it is to raid your damn cans! If you put 'em inside, he'll likely go after 'em there."

"And if it's the neighborhood punks? Will they go after it?"

"Ain't no punks in these woods but my boys, mister, and they got better things to do than paw through your precious garbage. You don't belong out here. You shoulda stayed in the city."

"In the ghetto, you mean? With the rest of the Yids?"

"Yids?"

"I'm Jewish, Mr. Baptiste. I'm guessing you have a problem with that."

"The only problem I got is you, pal," Baptiste said, straightening up, hefting his ax. "I work two jobs to keep this place up, I hunt in the fall, trap all winter. You'd be amazed how little I time I spend worryin' what church you go to."

"Temple."

"Whatever. So if you're done bustin' my balls, you'd best move off before we *do* have a problem. Neighbor." He split another log, one handed this time to underscore his point.

Baptiste's annoyance seemed so sincere that driving back, Jake halfway believed him. Until he pulled into his yard to find his garbage cans strewn around again and saw that the side door of his garage had been forced open.

Baptiste had admitted it. The only punks in these woods were his boys. And Jake could still hear them crashing around in there. All three of them? He was past caring.

The door had been torn half off its hinges. Furious, Jake kicked it open and charged in, flicking on the lights as he came, hoping to take the raiders by surprise. But in the sudden glare, it wasn't Baptiste's roughneck boys who whirled to face him.

It was a chief's son! A five-hundred-pound black bear that could take his head off with a single swipe of his great paws.

And in that stunned instant, Jake realized the rabbi was right. He'd been so eager to face the haters, assumed his neighbor was one of them, and ignored his warning. A huge mistake.

The bear was no bigot—he hated all men equally, and Jake could read his death in the bruin's eyes. With a savage roar, the bear swept the garbage cans out of his way, scattering them across the garage like tenpins, clearing the killing ground. Rising to his full fighting stance, he shambled forward, feinting with his paws like a prizefighter. He'd pull Jake into a death hug, crushing his bones, then tear him to pieces with his slavering jaws.

Jake could only back away, casting desperately about for any kind of a weapon—his fingers touched the door opener, and he pressed the button. The sudden rumble of the garage door rising froze the bear for a few seconds, offering him an obvious escape route.

But the bear didn't take it. Instead, he resumed his murderous shuffle, coming straight on, slashing the air with claws the size of switchblades.

Jake backed up another step, but only one. And then he stopped.

Enough!

This wasn't just a garage, it was *sanctuary*. Artie's dream, and now his. Their six feet of earth. Together. And he knew to a stone certainty that Artie wouldn't cede one inch of it. Not to this bear nor to anything on this earth.

Groping behind, Jake's fist closed on the handle of a shovel, the only weapon within reach. Whipping it around, he brandished it at the bear, thrusting it into the brute's chest. Hard.

"Get out!" Jake shouted into the face of the startled bruin, the cowed German villagers, their Nazi overlords and all the haters in the world. Jabbing the chief's son again and again, he forced the brute back, driving him toward the open door.

"*Raus!*" he roared at the baffled bear. "*Raus mit uns!*"

The Cost of Something Priceless

Elizabeth Zelvin

When you read this, my darling granddaughter, I will be dead, and this necklace will be yours. It has been in our family for close to five hundred years. You can have it appraised, if you like, but it is priceless. It belonged to a great lady: Hürrem Sultan, wife of Suleiman the Magnificent of the Ottoman Empire, where the Jews found refuge when we were driven out of Spain. Your many times great-grandmother, Rachel Mendoza, was her friend.

The documents too are now your responsibility. The brownish stains you see on them are blood. Only a fool can expect the cost of acquiring treasure to be payment in full. Blood has a tendency to leak and go on leaking. So do reputation and deceit.

Nobody cares about history anymore. Then they wonder why the world keeps making the same mistakes. At least the Jews are not surprised when someone has it in for us. It's been happening for thousands of years. We celebrate the Seder every Passover so we won't forget. The only surprise back then was how well the Jews were treated in the Ottoman Empire—a Muslim empire—after Christian Spain kicked us out.

The Mendozas, the Sephardic side of the family, left Spain in 1492, on the same day that Columbus sailed west into the unknown. Family legend says Rachel's brother shipped with him on the *Santa Maria* and that both Rachel and her brother accompanied the Admiral on his second voyage in 1493. We believe Rachel spoke and wrote Spanish, Hebrew, Italian, Turkish, French, Portuguese, and Arabic. Our Sephardic ancestors were prodigious linguists. They had to be.

The rest of the family fled to Italy. But Europe was in turmoil, and the Ottoman Sultan offered the Jews a home. He's supposed to have said publicly that the king of Spain was a fool to throw out such skilled and worthy citizens: scholars, artisans, doctors, merchants.

So the Mendozas settled in Istanbul, and Rachel found employment as what they called a *kira*, Jewish women who acted as purveyors to the harem. The Sultan's concubines and female relatives never left the palace. They needed someone to perform errands and carry messages for them. Such a woman had to be discreet and completely trustworthy. Rachel had been a *kira* for many years when Hürrem commissioned her to carry an extremely valuable necklace as a gift to the Queen of France. That's right. The story the family knows is that the Sultana's necklace was a gift to Grandmother Rachel. It was not. You now inherit the necklace and two true stories: our foremother Rachel's and my own.

𐡀

"Just marry a nice Jewish boy," my mother said. "That's all I ask."

That must sound crazy to you, my precious little twenty-first-century Rachel. You learned about sex in a middle school classroom, and your mother sent you to high school sleepovers with condoms in your backpack, just in case. But did they care if you brought home a Jewish boy or a Christian, a white boy or a black one, as long as he loved you? Did they care if you brought home a girl? Of course not. And neither did I.

Jewish boys were useless to me, and I to them. When they looked at me, they saw their mothers and sisters, who nagged and guilt-tripped them. To Jewish boys in the 1950s, sexy and attractive meant blond *shikses*—an uncomplimentary term from the Ashkenazic side of the family—with short noses, long legs, and slender thighs. But I was a good girl, and good girls obeyed their mothers. I tried. And it didn't work.

The first time a tall *goyisher* boy with blue eyes and smooth fair hair said he found my looks exotic, I couldn't believe my luck. They found the stereotypical Jewish package hilarious and charming: the *zaftig* body from the Ashkenazic side, the frizzy dark brown hair that had more bad days than good, and the kind of profile the Sphinx might have had if the desert winds hadn't given her a nose job. Do you even know what a nose job is, my Rachel? You kids may stick rings through your nose and walk around looking like Clarabel the Cow, but thank God you don't think you'd look prettier with half of it chopped off.

So tall, blond, blue eyed, and anything but Jewish became "my type." In due course, I married one. If you'd told me that the stars in Foster Gale Bentbridge IV's eyes were merely reflections of the Sultana's necklace, I wouldn't have believed it. My own parents' union was considered a mixed-marriage by their respective Sephardic and Ashkenazic Jewish families. But that didn't stop them from giving me and my chosen WASP a hard time. His family was none too keen on his marrying what they called a *Jewess* either. My parents thought that should have given me pause. But when did her parents' opinion ever stop a young woman in love? I wasn't *that* good a girl.

If one generation were capable of learning from the mistakes of the one before it, the world would be a very different place. Every girl thinks she's so smart. And every girl is so naive, so willfully blind. That's how she gets her heart broken, a sad but boring tale. More interesting: What does she do about it? What kind of woman does she become? The grandmother you knew and loved was very different from the woman who did what she did when her husband betrayed her.

❧

The ambush caught them off guard. If their company had been bigger, they would have sent scouts ahead and kept a lookout on either flank. It was twilight, and vines and trailing branches overhung the rough track through a wood thick with shadows when they paused briefly. Rachel had dismounted and stepped a few paces off the track for privacy. She was returning when she heard shouts and the clash of steel.

What a fool she was! She had left her bow hanging at her saddle and had not so much as a throwing knife at her waist. At least she kept the necklace on her person at all times, in a shawl bound around her breasts. She ran toward the clatter and cries of the conflict, scooping up a couple of rocks as she ran. They had known they might encounter brigands. Lawless men who preyed on travelers would find just such a wood hospitable. But there were so many of them. And they were skilled in arms. The janissaries were down, soldiers trained to defeat the best troops in Europe. The others, her husband, son, and brother, still fought fiercely. If someone would throw her a sword, she might be of some use!

Where were their horses? Had the attackers scattered them? Even if they prevailed, it would be a long walk to Paris. At least she had the necklace. As she reached to give it a reassuring pat, she felt a blow to the back of her head, and then darkness.

🦋

People say so glibly that two people come from different worlds. Everyone said it about Foster and me. I laughed it off. I had no idea what it meant. Take "going to Princeton." When a Jewish boy from New York went to Princeton, it meant he was exceptionally smart. He'd competed successfully in academics, athletics, and an array of showy "extracurricular activities" to make the extremely small quota of New York Jews the university was prepared to tolerate. When Foster Gale Bentbridge IV went to Princeton, it meant that Foster Gale Bentbridge I, II, and III had gone to Princeton. Period. I had similar unassailable and completely wrongheaded beliefs about Foster's whole history and the life he continued to live when he kissed me goodbye every morning and walked out the door of our cute apartment (yes, it was small) in the East Sixties.

"Why didn't you Google him, Gran?" I can hear you say. Today's children need history lessons not only on the sixteenth century but also on the twentieth. In the 1950s, Google did not yet exist, and neither did the internet or cell phones or personal computers. Do I wish I had asked Foster at least a few sensible questions about himself before I married him? Of course I do. But in those days, girls *didn't* ask a lot of questions. We only cared about the answers to a few crucial ones: Will he call me? Will he ask me out again? Does he love me? Mind you, I didn't *ask* these questions. I discussed them endlessly with my girlfriends and tried to figure out the answers.

Boys only had to ask one question. And when Foster "popped the question," my head spun and my heart thumped and I could hardly wait to say yes. Whether *I* loved *him* or even liked him didn't come into it. Did I trust him? What do you mean? He loved me. He had asked me to marry him, hadn't he? Did I think he would make a good life partner? I wouldn't have known what you were talking about, and not only because we said "husband" in those days rather than "life partner."

If Foster had been Jewish, my father would have made some attempt to intimidate him on general principles. He would have asked about his ability to support a wife, his career plans, and his thoughts on starting a family. But Foster's WASP demeanor intimidated him, so their one frank talk was awkward and yielded no useful information. Foster didn't seem to have a job, though he sat on the boards of several corporations and foundations, and he was a member of several clubs. He also took an interest in the arts, especially old documents as well as several categories of antiques. He would go to auctions and come home with some find. I quickly learned not to ask what it had cost. That was vulgar. I was eager to hear more about the clubs, a term that in my world meant an organization composed of people with a common interest or activity: a chess club, a hiking club, a glee club. Not in Foster's world.

Before I stopped asking questions—because it turned out that Foster considered all my questions stupid ones—I gathered that in WASP society, a club was a place where men like Foster went to sit in comfortable chairs, read the newspaper, smoke, drink in a gentlemanly fashion, and sometimes dine among others of their own kind. His favorite was the University Club in the East Fifties, an easy walk from our apartment. When he described it, he got quite animated in what a friend who had begged me not to marry him called a vanilla kind of way. It had a library with pillars and arches like a cathedral; a long banquet hall, sparkling with chandeliers, that resembled Versailles, though of course without any vulgar mirrors; even a swimming pool. I could hardly wait to see it. That turned out to be stupid too: neither Jews nor women were admitted.

How could I have possibly missed that billboard-sized neon warning sign of Foster's ingrained anti-Semitism? you ask. When a woman has chosen an irrevocable course and desperately wants to believe she has chosen love, clarity flies out the window. I missed other signs because I didn't want to see them. The expression of distaste on his face when my uncles on the Ashkenazic side told Yiddish jokes. His refusal to take a turn at reading from the Haggadah during the Seder, even with the Mendozas, the Sephardic side, whom the Ashkenazic uncles called "Jewish Episcopalians." *When we were slaves in Egypt* was never going to pass those thin lips. After the first few years, he found excuses to skip Passover with the family. He had no interest in Jewish philosophy or principles or ethics. We attended charity benefits, but the term "social conscience" was not in his vocabulary.

Foster had no interest in Jewish history. In retrospect, I'd say that if you gave him truth serum and asked him to say in three words what he really thought about the Holocaust, he'd say, "In poor taste." Nor did he care about my family's history—with one exception.

The Sultana's necklace was not a secret. It was the basis of our family's fortune. It had been written about and photographed and occasionally lent to museums for exhibitions of Ottoman art, though never for long. There was a family legend that the piece had once been larger and even more magnificent, but no expert had ever been invited to take a closer look. So no one could either claim or deny that it showed any sign of having been repaired.

Foster was avidly interested in the story from the start. In retrospect, I can remember how many questions he asked about the necklace itself and the documents that proved its provenance. These were a letter in Turkish and French from Hürrem Sultan, wife to the Ottoman emperor known to history as Suleiman the Magnificent, to Eleanor, Queen of France; and a letter from Queen Eleanor thanking the woman she knew as Roxelana for the gift. The documents had never been photographed or displayed, though various experts had examined them, so his interest seemed innocent at the time.

The children, your father and your Aunt Miriam, were still babies when my grandmother was diagnosed with lung cancer, and I was not yet disenchanted with Foster. So I let him console me in the first big sorrow in my young life, and against the oath I had sworn on my grandmother's deathbed, I told him the family secret: we had a *second* set of documents. It was the worst mistake of my life. I bitterly regret the consequences.

I knew that Foster was a forger for a long time before I allowed myself to know. He was good at calculating precisely what to say to keep me quiet depending on what I had seen, what hidden knowledge I had stumbled on, at any given moment. The first time, he was a copyist, practicing the beautiful penmanship of a seventeenth-century document on ancient vellum with an ink-dipped quill. Then he was a "gentleman forger," as if there were some virtue in that. The provenance of some antique or other was solid, but the documentation, which the owner, a good friend of his, had kept carefully for many years, had sadly been lost in a fire, and now he had fallen on hard times and had to liquidate some of his inventory, so you see? A gentleman had to stand by his friends, and it wasn't *really* forgery if the provenance was authentic.

You are probably thinking that this doesn't sound like your savvy, tough old Gran with her doctorate and her short way with fools. I changed. I had no choice. Once he realized I had witnessed him forging the provenance of an antique, he stopped working at home. In fact, he spent hardly any time there. We had a bigger apartment by now, and we no longer shared a bed. I had long since fallen out of love with him. The children barely knew him. I had mixed feelings about that.

Foster claimed that social climbing was vulgar, but he had certain ambitions. The most persistent of these was to become a member of the board of the Metropolitan Museum of Art. If you were rich enough to fund the expedition that found King Tut's tomb or had stolen the Parthenon from the Greeks, I gathered, this was easily done. In other words, potential board members had to have something desirable to offer. Foster was convinced that the Sultana's necklace was the key to a coveted invitation.

Of course, I said no. The necklace wasn't mine to give or lend. I was its custodian but, by family tradition, any decisions regarding it were made by an informal family consensus. Besides, why should I do Foster any favors? By this time, he had reached the lipstick-on-the-collar stage of our crumbling marriage. I thought he must want a divorce as much as I did. I suspected he was hanging on in the hopes that he could change my mind about the lending the necklace to the Met. There was also the matter of the Mendoza money. Foster had always been tightlipped about his finances. It had finally dawned on me that perhaps the Bentbridge trust fund was not the bottomless well he had always made it sound. I couldn't tell him to go to hell, because who knew what would happen if it came out that the Mendozas had had no right to the necklace in the first place? Worse, that we had known all along?

You may ask why the secret you are inheriting today is still important. Is there a statute of limitations on such a theft? It *was* almost five hundred years ago. But the Greeks still want the pieces of the Parthenon in the British Museum back. The German and Austrian Jews still want their Nazi-looted art back. The Mexicans want their pre-Columbian art back. And although I am not proud to say it, what selfless gesture by a Jewish family of today would change by one iota the attitude of today's Turkey toward today's Jews? We must continue to protect the Mendoza family, as our ancestors have done for so long.

I went into therapy. I told Foster he couldn't stop me, though he thought that therapy was bunkum—a favorite word of Foster Gale Bentbridge I, II, and III. I used Mendoza money. I made no mention of forgery or historical necklaces, but I told the therapist about the lipstick and the loneliness and the bourbon on Foster's breath. I hoped she would tell me whether or not I should get a divorce.

"Only you can make the big life decisions," she told me. "But first, you need to get in touch with your anger."

"I'm not angry," I told her. "I know I should be, but I'm not. I'm never angry. That's just the way it is."

"It only takes one therapist to change a light bulb," she said. "But the light bulb has to want to change."

"I do want to change," I said.

"*Desperately* want to change," she said.

It irritated me no end that she didn't think I was desperate. But I didn't get angry—not at her, even though she assured me it would do me good, and not at Foster, until the day I had no choice.

❧

Rachel felt like a cracked eggshell when her captors finally rolled her off the horse. One of them handed her a waterskin and a hunk of bread hard enough to loosen teeth. He would not meet her eyes, but she noted that his beard was neatly trimmed and his face clean under the grime of battle, not smeared with months of brigandry. He pushed her roughly toward a nearby stand of scrub, making signs that she could relieve herself in relative privacy there.

"Now," said the one the others called Captain, "let us unwrap this package and see if it contains the pearl we have been commissioned to retrieve."

He had a pockmarked face, battle scars, and an air of competence. He spoke Spanish. It had been a long time since Rachel had heard her native tongue unmixed with Turkish, Persian, Arabic, or Hebrew. Not brigands, but Habsburg soldiers, enemies of the Sultan and King Francis, sent to intercept her mission.

Rachel held herself rigid, enduring with clenched teeth the stripping away of her voluminous robes. The younger officers bantered about seeing a "Turkish harem girl" for the first time, wagering on whether a jewel would be found in her navel.

When they yanked off her veil, the youngest, disappointed, cried, "Oh! She's an old lady!"

They fell silent then, their attention growing keener as the sash that bound the necklace to her waist was unwound. All gasped as the leader snatched it and held it up with a cry of triumph. It sparkled in the firelight, for night had fallen. For a moment, Rachel was forgotten.

Then an arrow took the leader in the throat. The necklace fell from the captain's hand. Rachel caught it before it could land in the fire. Seizing his dagger, she slit the throat of the soldier who had called her an old lady. Her brother Diego rushed forward, fighting two-handed with sword and dagger. Her son Moshe was close behind, whirling like a dervish as his scimitar flashed left and right. Diego dispatched two of her remaining captors. Moshe's scimitar disposed of the fifth. Rachel's husband Ümit sent an arrow through the heart of the last.

"You look very beautiful, beloved," he said. "But I suggest you clothe yourself. And bestow that cursed necklace safely while I retrieve my arrows. We must get away quickly."

Rachel rebound the necklace around her waist and tucked enough cloth around herself for decency. For a moment she clung to her menfolk.

"You are safe! I thought you were dead!"

"Enough, Mama," Moshe said. "Papa is right. We must go. We still have a mission to complete."

"If no more ill luck attends us," Diego said. "All may still be well."

Ill luck, however, did not leave them in peace. On the second day, Rachel stopped to loosen the necklace around her waist.

"Go ahead," she told the others. "I'll catch up in a minute."

She caught up at a gallop, urging her horse past the others. The mischievous glance she cast over her shoulder cost her any warning of the rabbit hole directly ahead of her mount's speeding hooves. The horse stumbled and pitched Rachel over its head as it went down itself, legs flailing. The precious necklace went flying. The horse twisted its back and stamped its hooves, squealing with distress, as it attempted to rise. After a struggle, it stood shivering and snorting: two legs sound, one bent at an unnatural angle, and one iron horseshoe planted firmly on the Sultana's necklace.

"The horse?" Rachel asked without opening her eyes.

"It must be dispatched, Mama," Moshe said. "It cannot walk."

"And the necklace?"

"A master jeweler might be able to repair it," Ümit said. "But not quickly. And it is no longer a gift fit for a queen."

"Now what?" she asked.

"What can we do but return home?" Diego said.

"To report to Hürrem Sultan that I failed her?" Rachel asked. "Hand back a broken piece of trash, saying, 'This was the priceless jewel you bade me guard with my life'? And how do I answer when she asks, 'What have you done with my beloved Sultan's janissaries?'"

"You say, 'They died protecting us, which was their duty,'" Moshe said.

"And then she says, 'Then why are you alive and the mission not accomplished?'" Rachel said. "How can I go back to Istanbul at all? I risk disgracing the whole family."

"Mama, this is not like you," Moshe said. "You have brought us up always to hope and never to accept defeat."

"Or to accept defeat without losing hope," Diego said ruefully. "Some would call that the very definition of being Jewish."

"I want to go home," Rachel said. "But I can't see my way."

"There is a solution," Ümit said. "You must keep the necklace."

"You mean, cheat Hürrem Sultan?" Rachel said.

"It's just a bauble," Ümit said. "Since the embassy will never reach Paris, Queen Eleanor will never know that the Sultan intended to send her a necklace."

"But what do I tell Hürrem?"

"You will tell her that you delivered the necklace," Ümit said, "and bring her a letter from Queen Eleanor telling her it's the best gift she's ever received."

"It is a brilliant solution," Diego said. "Rachel, you and I between us can write as many letters in as many languages as needed to give the scheme verisimilitude. In our youth, we were Admiral Columbus's scribes, and you write all the Sultana's letters yourself except her love letters to the Sultan. We both know how to write to kings."

"I do not like lying to Hürrem Sultan," she said. "Her trust is precious to me."

"It is necessary, Mama," Moshe said.

"The Ottomans have been good to us, my love," Ümit said. "But they are not renowned for making allowances."

"And my integrity?"

"If God did not wish the Jews to survive," Diego said, "He would not have given us the wits to deal imaginatively with so many threats to our survival. I would rather keep the necklace than see you bound and thrown into the Bosphorus in a sack weighted with rocks for failing to deliver it."

"Oh, I think I would be strangled with a silken bowstring," Rachel said. "Hürrem is quite fond of me."

"Of course she is," Diego said. "She is bestowing a magnificent necklace on you as a token of her regard. We will write a letter to prove it."

❧

It never occurred to me that Foster would actually steal the necklace. Perhaps I was still befuddled, against all reason, by the idea that a tall blond guy with Mayflower crossings and signers of the Declaration of Independence in his DNA was a "gentleman," and that this elevated him to a mysterious standard of integrity beyond the ken of mere immigrant Jewish stock. I would have done better to forget "gentleman" and concentrate on "forger." Foster's plan was a clever one. First, he made copies of both the authentic documents and the ones my ancestors had faked, one by one. Of course, I kept them under lock and key. But Foster was my husband, and it was still the 1950s. He had no difficulty finding, removing, and returning them without arousing my suspicion. That is, he removed the originals and returned impeccable forgeries. To approach any museum or private collector, he needed the real thing. He might have lacked ethics, but he had great skill at his craft.

Without his ability to forge documents, I doubt Foster would have put the scheme in motion. As you can imagine, any time one crook has to trust another, he becomes vulnerable to blackmail. But creating a convincing replica of what the art and antiques world would call an "important" sixteenth-century Ottoman necklace was beyond his powers. For that, he needed an accomplice. He must have decided that an accomplice who had made a previous, let us say, deposit of lipstick on his collar presented less risk than most. If not for that, I never would have caught him.

But, Gran, I hear you say, what about the jewels? The Sultana's necklace is loaded with rubies and sapphires and diamonds. If he stole the real ones, how could he fool anyone with fakes?

Ah, Rachel, you see, he never had to fool anyone but *me*. I looked at the necklace only once a year, and I certainly never examined it with a jeweler's loupe. I had taken the necklace out into the sunshine to admire its full fire only once: when I first became its guardian. Foster knew that. I suggest you do the same and that you do *not* talk about it with the man you eventually marry, no matter how much you love him.

I was not looking for a jeweler. I was looking for my husband's partner in adultery, because when I finally broached the subject of divorce, Foster first refused to consider it and then, when I persisted, threatened to take the children with him. Since several Bentbridges were senior partners in a white shoe law firm—a white shark law firm, according to its competitors—this was no empty threat. Although mothers were considered children's natural guardians back then, an anti-Semitic judge who belonged to the same clubs as my in-laws might award him custody. I needed any ammunition I could get. So I hired a private detective, who identified a beautiful and sophisticated woman who had not only been having an affair with my husband for the past year but also appraised and restored antique jewelry. I paid off the detective and traveled several hundred miles to have another appraiser confirm my suspicion that the necklace in my possession was a fake. I went through the same process with each of the documents my family had held since 1536.

My husband had replaced every one of them with his own forgeries.

I planned carefully. I took my time. Foster wouldn't act until he stopped seeing the jeweler. I was sure he kept his stolen treasure at the University Club. It was someplace I could never go.

I worked out an alibi. I would leave the city for the weekend and sneak back undetected. I sent the children to my mother's. I bought men's clothing I thought would fit me at Gimbel's a couple of weeks beforehand. I went on a sale day. Women shopping for their husbands and sons were practically climbing on each other's shoulders, clawing their way toward the counters to get at the bargains.

No women at the University Club? Very well. I would not be a woman.

I gave the name of someone to whom Foster would be eager to show his secret acquisitions at an hour when the club would be empty. I had done my homework well. He had the necklace and the papers out. His smile crumpled into a puzzled frown as he registered, first, that I looked familiar, and then, who I was.

I demanded the return of the Sultana's necklace and the documents he had stolen. He refused. I said I wanted a divorce with no absurd demands for Mendoza money or custody of the children. I said that if he behaved reasonably, he could see them, since, being innocents, they loved him. He refused. I stepped forward, reaching out to take what was mine. If he had raised a hand to stop me—blocked my arm with his or struck me across the face—I don't know what I would have done. Would I have slapped him? Burst into tears? Turned and left without a word?

But a gentleman did not raise his hand to a lady. Instead, Foster spoke.

"That's right, grab it. That's all you kikes know how to do. Grab, grab, grab at anything shiny. Money-grubbing, vulgar, loud—my parents were right about you. I should have listened to them in the first place. Look at you with your big nose and your fat thighs and your greasy skin. I can't imagine how I ever found you attractive."

My hand rose without my volition. It held a slim Ottoman blade. It was said to have belonged to one of Grandmother Rachel's many great-granddaughters, passed down among the girls in the family and kept sharp by tradition. As the dagger sliced across his pale neck and the blue eyes glazed, for a moment it seemed to me I heard the thudding of hooves and the crash of waves upon the shore, smelled the smoke of a wood fire and the tang of sweating horses. When I came back to myself, Foster lay at my feet. I wiped the dagger. The kitchen would be deserted at this hour and the service exit not yet locked for the night. As I said, I had done my homework.

"I was never here," I said to the red grin of his throat. "No Jews are admitted to the University Club."

The Black and White Cookie

Jeff Markowitz

He was a city boy, born and bred, but when his wife told him he was going to be a father, he made a decision. His son would grow up in the suburbs. It didn't take him long to find what he was looking for, a three-bedroom, one-bath ranch house, one of a thousand identical ranch houses sprouting in the fertile soil that had, until recently, been a potato farm.

He told no one of his plans. When his wife went into labor, he called the doctor, took a last look around the apartment and drove her to the hospital. Three days later, he put his wife and baby son in the car and drove them to their new home.

It was the suburbs, but just barely, 1.55 miles from the city's easternmost border. And every day, he made the commute from his home in the suburbs, through the outer boroughs, to his job in the city, traffic getting heavier, day by day, year by year.

He didn't mind the commute. It was, he knew, a small price to pay so that his son could grow up with a backyard. Well, not *so* small a price, he decided, when he thought about the toll. You see, there were thousands of men just like this one, tens of thousands, with their job in the city and their home in the suburbs.

The tollbooth went up at Mile Marker 1.

If you wanted to get to your job in the city, it would cost you a dime. If you wanted to drive back to your home in the suburbs at night, it would cost another dime. He did the math. Ten cents a trip, twenty cents a day. That's a dollar a week. Fifty dollars each year (accounting for his two-week vacation).

And so, every morning, he would bypass the highway entrance at

Mile Marker 1.55, working his way through the neat little neighborhoods, getting on the highway one exit closer to his job in the city. And every evening, coming home, he would get off the highway one exit early, and make his way through those same neat little neighborhoods.

א

My earliest memories are of my father coming home after a long day on the job. He would pull his car into the driveway, and walk into the house, a briefcase in his right hand, in his left, hidden behind his back, a simple brown paper bag. He would pretend that he had forgotten, and I would play along, knowing that my father would never let me down. It was a ritual that played out through my childhood. Some days the anticipation was almost more than I could bear. But with a flourish, my father would pull the bag from behind his back and reveal the treasure within, the near perfect combination of shortbread and icing known as the black and white cookie. As the name suggests, one icing was not enough for this bakery masterpiece. Black icing and white icing, side-by-side. You could write a doctoral dissertation on how people ate the cookie. Me, first I ate the shortbread off the bottom, leaving only icing. Next, I ate the white icing, delaying gratification, before savoring each bite of the remaining black icing.

I was approaching my thirteenth birthday, studying for my bar mitzvah. Dad continued to bring home the brown paper bag, but he would make me wait until I had completed my lessons before he offered up the cookie.

בָּרְכוּ אֶת יְיָ הַמְבֹרָךְ. *Bar'chu et adonai ha-m'vorach.*

And then one day, he didn't.

I don't mean he didn't bring me a cookie. I mean he didn't come home.

That was the worst night of my short life, until the next night and the night after that and every night that summer. I grilled my mother. It was cruel, but I had learned in school about the five w's and I was determined to make good use of my education. I knew the who, but the what, where, when and why were a mystery to me.

"Where's Dad?"

Mom didn't waver, saying only, "He'll be home soon." And then she went about her routine, struggling to maintain the appearance of normalcy. The cooking, the cleaning, the shopping, the laundry. She threw herself into housework. Our clothes were always clean, our pants neatly pressed, our shirts with just the right amount of starch in the collar. Well-balanced meals were served on time and it seemed like the dirty dishes washed themselves. That was the summer Mom's hair started to fall out, just a few strands at first, but, by the end of the summer, in tangled gray clumps. That was the summer Dad missed my bar mitzvah. That was the summer I outgrew black and white cookies.

בָּרוּךְ יְיָ הַמְבֹרָךְ לְעוֹלָם וָעֶד. *Baruch adonai ha-m'vorach le'olam va'ed.*

Two months later, as I walked home from school, I turned the corner on Meadowbrook Lane and saw my father's Holiday 88 parked in the driveway. It looked so normal there in the driveway that its reappearance didn't register right away. Then it did. I sprinted home, threw open the door, and barreled into my dad. He was standing in the front hall, a confused look on his face. I could tell that something was not right. That some*one* was not right.

Mom was determined to maintain the appearance of normalcy and Dad was willing to try. Every morning, he got up and dressed for work. He bypassed the highway entrance at Mile Marker 1.55 and made his way through the neat little neighborhoods, getting on the highway one exit closer to his job in the city. Only, he didn't bother taking his briefcase and he didn't return with a brown paper bag.

I didn't need the five w's to determine that my father no longer had a job in the city.

He'd been home for three uneasy months when I was awakened in the middle of the night by screaming. Cautiously, I bumped open my bedroom door. I stared at my father. He stood at the far end of the hall, hitting himself in the head and screaming. My mother did her best to help him calm down. He looked at her—no, he looked *through* her—and I could tell that he didn't know who she was. My father didn't recognize his wife. Don't ask me how I could tell. If you'd been there, you would understand. His gaze shifted to the crack in the bedroom door. When I saw his eyes, I didn't know what to do. After all, I was only thirteen.

No, I promised myself this would be a true account. It had nothing to do with being thirteen. I'm in my sixties now.

If it happened today, I still wouldn't know what to do.

I locked the bedroom door.

The next morning, Dad was gone.

A week later, I got into my first fight at school. I was in gym class when Nick started teasing me about my dad. I pushed him to the ground.

We rolled around in the dirt until Mr. Bellamy pulled us apart. The best thing I can say about our gym teacher is that he didn't think it was a bad thing for boys to settle their differences physically. So, he never reported the fight to the assistant principal who was in charge of discipline.

The next time Nick made a crack about my father living in the loony bin was in French class. I smacked him across the head. The French department had a decidedly different attitude about physical violence. Mademoiselle Choffard sent us both to the office. An hour later, my mother arrived.

"Everything we have, we owe to your father. He is a good man and he deserves your respect."

Anything I might have said would only have gotten me deeper in trouble, so I stared at my hands and said nothing.

"I know that your father embarrasses you. I pray that one day you understand just how wrong you are."

❧

My father never did come back home. And I never talked to him about his disappearance. I'm married now and have a son of my own. We don't talk much, but I'm pretty sure I embarrass him, much the way my father once embarrassed me. I tried to discuss it recently with my mother. I asked her about Dad and her face lit up, but she couldn't give me an answer. At least, not an answer that I could understand. She has Alzheimer's.

Her doctors tell me that it's time to place her in a facility. So, I'm going through the house, identifying the things she will take with her when she moves. The social worker suggested I include a few small items that have strong emotional value. Things that would connect her to happier times. I struggle with the task, wondering whether I am making the right choices.

Mom stands there watching and says nothing.

Finally, I give up. I throw a few items into her suitcase. It's time. I walk Mom to the door. She grows agitated. "The box," she says, by way of explanation. "The box."

I'm tired. I hate the hint of aggravation in my voice. "What box?"

"The box," she repeats. Her agitation fills the space around us. She bangs on the sofa. "The box." And she is silent.

I don't know what I'm looking for, but I start looking anyway. The house is filled with a lifetime of boxes. I pull out boxes at random and show them to Mom. "This box?" I ask.

She pushes the box away. "The box," she repeats and walks into her sewing room. She reaches into the closet and sweeps the sewing boxes off the shelf. Fabric spills out on the floor. Buttons and thread and yarn and mostly pins and needles. Thousands of pins and needles and Mom stands there in bare feet.

"Be careful, Mom." I take her by the arm and sit her down in her old sewing chair. "Is the box in the closet?"

Mom doesn't answer.

I take a closer look. In the back corner of the closet, buried beneath a pile of sewing books and magazines filled with patterns, I spot an old cardboard box, musty and decrepit. I lift it carefully from the closet, fearful that the aging cardboard will disintegrate at my touch.

"Is this what you want?"

Mom doesn't answer.

I open the box slowly. It's filled with old newspaper clippings. The *Herald Tribune*. The *Daily Mirror*. The *World Telegram* and *Sun*. I forget all about my mother, about Alzheimer's, about the care facility. I sit there in my childhood bedroom, reading the ancient newspapers.

In 1961, men and women, at great personal risk, were challenging segregation at lunch counters, water fountains and especially on interstate busses. On May 24, 1961, twenty-seven Freedom Riders were beaten and arrested at a bus station in Jackson, Mississippi. I find all twenty-seven mugshots in a yellowed folder at the bottom of the box. Young men and women, black and white—one of them, my father—sentenced to two months in Parchman, guilty of violating the Jim Crow laws.

I force myself to dig deeper into the ancient cardboard box. I find more clippings scattered in the bottom of the box. Beatings. Lynchings. Black and white bodies hanging from trees, side by side. I peer at the photographs, searching for my father, a prayer at my lips.

I find a letter addressed to my mother.

My dearest wife,

I believe by now you have seen the news reports. Do not worry. I am fine. It appears that I may not be home in time for our son's bar mitzvah. I trust he is still doing his nightly lessons. He is a good boy. I deeply regret the delay, but it cannot be helped.

Your loving husband

I can't begin to imagine the horrors he had to endure during his two-month stay at the Mississippi State Penitentiary. I wish I could find the words that would let my mother know that I understand.

"The box," Mom says.

I look up. Mom is smiling. There's a brown paper bag in her lap. She reaches into the bag and hands me a black and white cookie.

"We were once slaves to Pharaoh in Egypt. Now we are free."

SCATTERED AND
DISPERSED

Islands

Gabriela Alemán

This is what my job is like: You skirt the edge of a bottomless whirlpool of papers, conjectures and distractingly colorful spangles. You toss out a line. If fortune strikes, you get more than just a nibble. Sometimes it's a two-hundred-pound marlin. Other times, your line snaps on the high seas, taking hours of fruitless struggle with it.

The Baroness was a big, slippery fish. The first time I told her story, I slapped together a fake, rubber fish for the official photo. I didn't write what I wanted to say, I wrote what they wanted me to say. Sometimes it's like that too. You barely manage to fight to a draw. You do your job, but without much satisfaction. I managed to entertain the readers with gossip about a movie they made, an artsy film the Baroness appeared in. That was when the ten-inch fish turned into a whopper. I never forgave myself. Not because I wouldn't have done her justice—I wasn't really attracted to her personality—but because I could never tell the other story, the one that really interested me. The story of why the Ecuadorian government gave carte blanche to a woman who claimed to be all kinds of things and promised even more. It was the story of a European press hungry for scandals that would distract people from the miseries of the Great Depression. It was also the story of the prelude to World War II.

Chinese puzzle boxes, Russian dolls, stories within stories, whatever you want to call them, that was the article I never wrote. What I did write about, paying particular attention to the juicy details, was the legend that revolved around the eight inhabitants of Floreana Island

Translated from the Spanish by Kenneth Wishnia

in the Galápagos Islands between 1930 and 1934. Everything I said was based on speculation. The few available documents were long-winded, rambling interviews and articles from the period. There wasn't a single photograph for the record. The only thing you could say for sure is that the inhabitants made up an unusual group.

The story starts in 1930, when a couple named Dora and Friedrich Ritter arrived on Floreana. Dr. Ritter was a dentist, a vegetarian, a defender of nudism and of Nietzschean philosophy, who had removed all his teeth and replaced them with a steel plate before voyaging to the archipelago. He regularly wrote pseudoscientific articles for various magazines, offering a sort of self-help guide for his followers. The world would be saved, according to the doctor, by living an ascetic life plagued by physical difficulties, which would separate the great men from the masses. He had traveled to the Galápagos Islands to put his theories into practice, and had complete faith in his project. His companion Dora, twenty years younger than he, appears only rarely in his notes. For example, he never mentioned that he made her pull out her teeth and replace them with a steel plate as well. Nor did he mention that the volcanic island they had chosen to live on had very poor soil for growing vegetables, and that during the dry season, there was barely enough water to drink and none for the crops. That his "vegetarian" diet consisted of wild pigs and goats left over from the days when pirates plowed the seas around the Enchanted Islands. I wrote about how all this changed in 1932. The Ritters stopped being the sole inhabitants of the island when another German couple arrived, the Wittmers. They came in search of a healthy climate for Heinz Wittmer's asthmatic teenage son. They were Bavarian country folk. Margaret, Heinz's second wife, was pregnant. I wrote about how the Ritters kept their distance, fenced off their land and ignored the newcomers—which is pretty hard to do on an island that's only sixty-six square miles, but they tried. The Wittmers built their house near the only freshwater spring in the hills of Floreana Island, about a mile from the other couple. They didn't want to bother them but they were also practical, and thought that having a doctor nearby (even though he was a dentist) would be a good idea if there were any complications during the delivery. Relations weren't very cordial, but there weren't any confrontations.

Halfway through the year, such cordiality was no longer possible. The Baroness came ashore with her three lovers—Valdivieso, Lorenz, and

Phillipson—and as soon as she did, she drew the hatred of the other inhabitants. The main reason for the dispute were her baths: she soaped herself up in the freshwater spring high on the hillside, contaminating everyone else's water. Water wasn't the only problem she had with the small group of inhabitants. The Baroness decided to build her house next to the one functioning pier, across the water from the Devil's Crown, and in doing so turned it into her own private property. She collected a tax from the other inhabitants when boats pulled up to deliver supplies. After much resistance, they had to give in. The rest of the island was surrounded by a riot of rocks and reefs that made coming ashore impossible. Then came the complaints about the noise, the loud music, the visitors, the orgies. There were rumors that, thanks to the use of pen and paper, turned into absolute proof against her. When I was researching the article, I came across a letter from Ritter to the local authorities in which he denounced her: "This woman's conduct in no way corresponds to that of a normal person; she undoubtedly suffers from a spiritual imbalance, whose presence in a place as isolated as ours presents a real threat." This damning piece of evidence came from the vegetarian with the steel dental plate, and appeared in my article as the absolute truth against the Baroness, when in reality it was the kind of information that should have been handled with tongs.

While writing my piece, I gathered some other bits of information: that in lieu of payment for using the pier, Margaret ended up working for the Wagner woman; that the minimal contact they had didn't keep them from developing an irrational resentment toward each other; that Valdivieso (the only Ecuadorian) escaped in a rowboat within a month of arriving; that Lorenz abandoned the Baroness sometime in early 1934, alleging physical, psychological, and spiritual abuse, and ended up in the Ritters' house; that the Ritters' marriage wasn't the most solid; that Margaret didn't particularly care for her stepson Harry; that Harry was an introverted boy who, after helping his father with the chores, was given to vanishing into the surrounding forests and scrubland. But—the editors insisted on this—I described in minute detail the wild parties that Ritter carelessly referred to. Let's just say that I took a little factoid and chewed on it until it became soft enough to stretch. In fact, let's say it wasn't even a factoid but a rumor that eventually became part of the legend. People said that the Baroness, who was by then the undisputed Empress of the Enchanted Islands, had starred in a pirate movie directed by her friend, Captain Hancock, and that he came up with the perverse displays for certain scenes in which the Wagner woman appeared in the nude. I described them and, while I was at it, took the opportunity to include a few choice details about her pearl-handled pistol and the whip that never left her side. I summarized the film as a faithful portrait of an unstable Baroness with a flair for dirty tricks. I really played up the dirty tricks. That was my big, fake rubber fish. I barely mentioned the true crisis in this story, that in less than four months in 1934, half the island's inhabitants died or disappeared. That barely got a line in the final article. And once it was published, I forgot all about the Baroness and the other inhabitants of Floreana Island. Until one day, several years later, I received an invitation from the Association of Naval Historians to present a paper on the Galápagos Islands at their annual gathering in Puerto Rico. It seemed like a strange invitation, but I accepted it. They wanted me to give a short presentation on the US occupation of the archipelago during World War II. Since I hardly knew anything about it, I read some books and prepared my presentation. I never made the connection between the Baroness and the US occupation of Baltra Island. It wouldn't have occurred to me.

When I finished my talk, a few people came up to congratulate me, mostly military men. One in particular, with a lazy eye, insisted that I should drop by the Naval Archives in San Juan. He gave me a business card and told me to present it to the librarian, who would help me. I thanked him but told him that I was only in Puerto Rico for a few days, but he said I wouldn't regret it, that I would find documents that would make me reconsider my portrait of the Baroness von Wagner-Bouquet. I was unmoved. What could a naval historian, a navy man, know about the frivolous Baroness? I started to reply, but the man had disappeared. This is where the story starts getting a little twisted.

I left the Casa España on Ponce de León Avenue, where the conference took place, and headed to my hotel, but halfway there, I stopped. An enormous moon hung over the island, and I wanted to look at the sea, so I let myself get pulled along by the warm breezes. I stopped at Paseo de la Princesa, where the foam sparkled and I could hear the waves crashing against the pier. A guard stopped me from heading to the port, saying that civilians were prohibited from entering the US Naval Base. With all the attention I got during the conference, I hadn't realized that the Puerto Rican Navy was really the US Navy. I hadn't even thought about what country I was in, but it was now clear that the archives that man had invited me to visit belonged to the US military. I decided to pay him a visit the very next day, which is exactly what I did. But when I presented his business card to the receptionist, nobody recognized his name. So I dialed the telephone numbers on the card, but they were out of service. I gave up trying, and went upstairs to the library and gave the card to the clerk. He showed me to a table and asked me to wait while he went looking for the files I needed. He came back with a file box, placed it on the table, and left. The room was empty except for me.

I emptied the contents onto the table. Three bundles. The first was full of business envelopes, the second held a hardcover notebook full of writing in German and a bunch of loose pages written in English, the last one held a batch of photos of the Baroness and a newspaper clipping. I had never seen a picture of her and was overcome with curiosity. She wasn't at all what I expected. The descriptions from the period talk about a woman of singular beauty: the picture before me was of an ordinary woman with a jaw like a horse. There were passport-sized photos of her face and others of an ocean voyage. Information about the photos was written on the back. They were all dated June 1932, the date she arrived in Ecuador. The photos must have been taken on the cruise ship she took to Guayaquil. By the time I finished, it was past three in the afternoon.

The librarian reappeared and handed me an envelope. Inside was a single sentence written on a piece of paper: *If you brought a camera, you better use it.* I did so immediately. It seemed like a signal that I wouldn't be allowed to see this material again. When I finished, I returned the fifteen archived sheets to their separate envelopes. They were reports about the Baroness. Someone had traveled with her from France to Ecuador. The first document spoke of their departure from Marseilles, the last one about her arrival in Guayaquil. The man (or woman) who wrote them didn't seem to have any special feelings for her. There were unnecessary details (though I was grateful for their vividness), thanks to which I felt I could practically touch the lady Eloisa. I didn't trust my camera to cleanly capture the handwritten texts, so I transcribed the last report, the one that included the most intimate details.

Report #15
She supervised every detail of her arrival. Two hours before sailing into the port of Guayaquil, she put on some perfume, makeup, and a long pearl

necklace that hung between her breasts all the way down to her hips. She wore a diamond tiara on her head to draw attention away from her beast-of-burden-sized jaw. It didn't work. Her jaw was the first thing people saw. But the Baroness knew how to create illusions: with powders, base, and the right angle (she had it down to a science), she could pass for a woman of tender age. She stayed in a first-class cabin by herself. She sent Phillipson, Lorenz and Valdivieso to the third-class quarters, where she found a stateroom for the three of them. In reality, only the last two shared the stateroom. From the night they sailed from Panama to the night before their arrival, Phillipson slept with her. I'm sure she was hoping to make a grand entrance, with lots of commotion over her valises, and her plunging neckline, and if that wasn't enough, she was also carrying forged letters of introduction in her purse. Her plan was that, once she came ashore, the reporter who covered the port would fall prey to her charms. At least that's what she imagined would happen. The Baroness had never been to Ecuador, but I had.

I don't know how dangerous she is or her traveling companions. One of the waiters tried to approach her on numerous occasions. But he was so inept, he kept trying to speak to her when she was entertaining the first-class dinner guests. He was so obviously interested in her that I went up to him to ask what he wanted with the Baroness. I took him by surprise, but he readily confessed that he wanted to warn her that one of the inhabitants of Floreana Island, where she was headed, was a Nazi sympathizer. He didn't seem to know anything about her, but I didn't say it out loud. He might have been a Jew or someone who witnessed the horrors of National Socialism up close, because his fear was genuine. You could see it in his eyes. But I didn't ask any more questions. I'm recording it here because I saw him finally make contact with her on deck, near the railing, early one morning after a long, sleepless night. I never saw him again.

The ship docked around noon, and the cloud of mosquitoes that welcomed her as she left her cabin was even thicker than the cloud of horse-flies darkening the horizon, expanding infinitely as it advanced toward her. You couldn't even hear yourself think. She couldn't get the smell of rotting fish out of her skin, even using two pots of honey that Lorenz brought to her room nightly so she could smear it on her body before submerging herself in the hotel's bathtub. Sweat stains the size of continents formed on her clothes, and her usual composure didn't even last half an hour. She lost the tiara when a dockworker carrying four sacks of cocoa on his head bumped *into her as he passed by. She didn't stop screaming about it till the three men accompanying her appeared by her side. She sent the Ecuadorian to find the offices of the city's most important newspaper, ordering him (while glaring at him with a predator's eyes) not to come back without the reporter who covered the society pages, and to do that only after making sure he knew who she was. She sent Phillipson to find a hotel, while Lorenz stuck by her side like a guard dog. If he did a good job, maybe he'd get to sleep with her on their first night on land. (The look on her face confirmed this.) But all that waiting made her feel heavy and slow.*

By late afternoon, when Valdivieso returned with the reporter, the Baroness had gotten Lorenz to turn her extensive luggage into a sitting room. A group of children held the edges of a mosquito net around the Baroness, reclining on a steamer trunk while her servant fanned her. The fishermen told their wives to come down to the pier to get a look at her. The scene would surely be a source of commentary for weeks. Who was this woman? Opinions were divided between those who thought she was a movie star and those who were convinced she was just some rich gringa. *The second group was made up of people who had seen her up close.*

"She's got the face of a mule," said more than one fisherman.

I burst out laughing when I finished reading the report. The Baroness had suddenly become a real person. She stopped hiding behind the veil of lies that kept her at a distance. It was like meeting a childhood friend that one had completely forgotten about. The photos and documents didn't just make her appear more real, they brought her into the present, casting her in a new light. The report was written in a professional style that allowed me to see another side of her. I pounced like a greedy child on the yellowing press clipping guarding the envelope full of photos, hoping it would be something by the same reporter. It was from the *Telegraph*, a Guayaquil paper, dateline: June 1932. Bingo!

She's a mixture of every Western culture, leaving her with deep traces of profound sweetness and grace. She speaks proudly of her ancestors. Her grandfather was the last of the noblemen who belonged to the Order of Maria Theresa. Her grandmother was a Prima Donna at La Scala in Milan, where she sang with Caruso. She's the sensitive type.

I read the whole article. It didn't once mention her jaw, her tangled hair, or her sweat-stained clothing. The reporter had been hypnotized by her and had forgotten why he was there. He couldn't have done a better job if the Baroness had paid him to write the article.

> *This trip to the beautiful land of Ecuador is a voyage of discovery. . . . I'm looking into the possibility of building a grand hotel or compound on one of the islands, where there won't be any problems regarding prior ownership, to bring tourists and immigrants of the best races. . . . The hotel will be devoted to providing every comfort for a short stay or a permanent one by millionaires, tourists, artists, and anyone yearning to breathe fresh air.*

So said the Baroness. The reporter didn't ask any follow-up questions. He didn't think of following the most obvious line of inquiry: How would the tourists get to her marvelous hotel, where would she find the construction materials, who would build it, who would invest in it, and what would the visitors spend their money on? No, the piece closely followed the line laid down by the Baroness. And not just the reporter. The authorities also succumbed to her charms and her promises to improve the race—the dream of so many leaders. They felt like applauding her. She was a master of deception. She wasn't a movie star; she wasn't even rich. But something about her convinced people, something that left no doubt that she was *someone*. She had the gifts of a snake charmer. On top of that, her intelligence was as reliable as a clock. She calculated which words to use and the precise moment to use them. She must have been widely read, and surely was familiar with the words of the most famous anthropologist of the day: *Toads must think other toads are paragons of beauty.* The mixed-blood authorities with noble titles who received her, upon hearing her promise to improve the race, imagined a country populated by themselves. How could there be any doubt of that? They gave her carte blanche and all the esteem she needed.

I wanted to talk with someone about what I'd just read and stretch my legs a bit after being seated in that room for too long. I was also a bit confused, as if I'd finally hooked a giant marlin and wasn't sure I could reel it in. There was also the story of the business card and the disappearance of the man with the lazy eye. But by then the sunlight was fading and night about to fall.

I stopped speculating when I heard a sound like the paws of a rodent scampering across the polished wood floor. I looked down: an enormous carpet lay under my feet. I lifted my eyes just in time to glimpse a shadow disappearing behind a bookcase and slipping out of the room. I walked over to the bookcase but nobody was there. Looking out the window at the roof of the building across the way, I saw some white sheets hanging on a line, floating in the late afternoon breeze, as if pulling the building forward. I felt like I was standing on the deck of a ghostly ship. When I turned, a silhouette was retreating from the writing desk where I'd left my things. When I got there, my camera was missing. Who on earth cared about making sure those photos didn't leave the room? I checked my watch. I didn't have much time left to go through the materials. I forgot about the theft and picked up the second bundle. I can't read German, but I recognized the tiny scribbles as the sloppy handwriting of Harry, Wittmer's teenage son, Margaret's stepson. I looked through the loose pages, which were a translation of the diary. I read them from beginning to end (it began in 1932). All two hundred pages were about the Baroness. The kid was lovesick. The first thirty pages described the Baroness's voluptuous, nude body in considerable detail, many of them concentrating on how the boy's hands explored every part of her body and lingered there awhile. The next twenty pages described the places he would go to wank off where nobody could find him, followed by thirty pages of his thoughts and feelings while he was hiding from the world. I smiled as I thought about whoever had been hired to do the translation. Did he take those photos of the Baroness, and follow in Harry's footsteps?

What happened next, of course, shattered the romantic images that usually accompany the legend of the Empress into a thousand pieces. According to the diary—the diary of an awkward teenager who barely spoke and whom no one paid any attention to—Ritter was transmitting information to the Nazis about naval movements around the islands via shortwave radio. His father was sending it, behind his stepmother's back, to a branch of the German army that wasn't pleased with Hitler's rise to power. He knew about it and had written about it, because Lorenz, his only friend on the island, had confided to him that the Baroness was a spy for Japan. He also wrote that when the Wagner woman's radio stopped working, she went to Ritter to borrow his. Harry had seen them meeting at night on more than one occasion, and he knew that Dora could have eaten the Baroness alive, that the front she maintained with the doctor was just a façade.

How could I have missed it? It was only five years before the start of World War II. The various factions got along, but were already marking their territory. On this side of the Pacific, what the Japanese were doing mattered as much as what Germany planned to do. The Galápagos Islands were the gateway to the Panama Canal, the archipelago closest to the coasts of North and South America, where fake fishing boats dropped anchor and submarines of many nations lurked beneath the waves. If you had a taste for adventure and easy money, that was the place to be. And there was Eloisa von Wagner-Bouquet. Why didn't I see it before? Because I let myself be convinced by the other story, the scandalous story that the newspapers wanted to fix in the minds of their readers during the 1930s. The story of millionaires and magnates and Hollywood stars, which I repeated like a parrot in the piece I wrote. But this other story, highlighted in these crumpled pages, was the key to the mystery of the strange deaths and disappearances on Floreana Island.

Someone turned on the lights. I couldn't see who. When I heard distant footsteps, my heart started racing. I felt a pressure in my chest but turned back to the loose pages and concentrated on the final part of the diary. I wanted to see what Harry had to say about the disappearances of Phillipson and the Wagner woman, of Dr. Ritter's poisoning, of the death of Lorenz and the discovery of his mummified body on a distant island. Based on the reading, I understood that Margaret lived to complain about the boy to his father. She didn't love him; she thought he was an idiot—so much so that she didn't even try to hide it when she went down to the Baroness's property the day before her disappearance. And she didn't even try to invent a better lie than the one she used: that the Baroness had gone into the house to tell Lorenz that she was going to Tahiti on the yacht *Sans Souci*, and when she couldn't find him, that was the last word on the subject. Harry spent the whole day in a locust tree and didn't see the Baroness step outside once, or the arrival of a yacht to carry her away. Harry also wrote that he saw a submarine two nights before the Wagner woman's disappearance, around sundown. (Could it have had something to do with the message the Baroness sent with Ritter's radio? Were they coming to pick her up? To bring her a new transmitter?) Then, putting it very plainly, almost in passing, he said that Margaret murdered the Baroness. That she did it with a hoe, from behind. That his stepmom was strong as an ox and when Phillipson came near, she turned on him with the same savagery and sliced his throat. That Lorenz knew something was wrong when he went looking for the Baroness the next day, and found Margaret trying on her jewels. Fearing the worst, he fled to avoid the same fate, but even that couldn't save him.

A strong current pushed his little vessel toward Marchena Island, where he died of thirst.

Harry also wrote that the only thing he wasn't sure about was if Dora poisoned Ritter's food, though she certainly had good reason to. Before finishing his narrative, he described how his stepmother wrapped the two bodies in a blanket, dragged them to the pier, and loaded them into a dugout canoe. He said she didn't row but just let the current carry them along, and when they were far enough from the coast she tossed the bodies into the sea. There was a bull shark sanctuary near the island, so Margaret knew the bodies wouldn't sink to the bottom in one piece. After that, Harry's story loses some of its passion. Nothing seemed to make much sense, so the rest is nothing but facts: that when they learned the Baroness had disappeared and that Dr. Ritter had died, reporters came flocking to tiny Floreana Island; that Harry escaped with one of the reporters; that he stayed on the mainland, working on a cocoa plantation, hidden in the groves for more than a decade so they wouldn't deport him; that's where he was when he learned that his father had died on the island, and that Margaret had inherited all his property, built a hotel and, later on, kept a fleet of fishing boats. That she was the only survivor and thus the universally acknowledged heiress of the title, Empress of the Enchanted Islands. A title, she once told the press, that she never sought. There it was, the part of the story that nobody spoke about, the part that had nibbled at my fishhook.

It was nearly midnight when I finished reading. The librarian was gone for the day, and the doors must have been locked. Who could be spying on me behind the bookshelves? If somebody wanted me to read these documents, clearly somebody else didn't want me to (if not, then what happened to my camera?). I didn't want to pursue the matter. I gathered my things and tiptoed out of the room. The hallway was dark. I turned on the light and waited. Nothing. I went downstairs. My face must have been stamped with fear and fatigue like a watermark, but somehow I felt lighter. I had pierced the veil of an ancient secret with the help of a horny teenager who didn't know how to hide his feelings, which made the world seem more transparent to him. When I reached the door to the street, it was open. I heard somebody laughing behind me. I controlled myself and didn't turn my head. I went out to the street, where the suffocatingly humid night air slammed into me, as strong as the breath of life.

On the way to the hotel I had a thought—it was only a moment, then it passed—that all this had something to do with what I knew. But, as I said, it was only a moment and then it vanished, like a line snapping on the high seas.

Datura

Joy Mahabir

I open my eyes and for a moment the sunlight through the hospital blinds fools me into thinking I'm back in my bedroom in Princes Town. There, my window opened to the back of the house, and every morning I saw the white flowers tinged with lilac that grew in abundance in Sanjay's garden. If only I had married Sanjay instead. He was so gentle.

The nurse comes in to check my vitals, a stern Trinidadian woman. She says to herself, "Fell down the stairs. Hmm." She stares at me in a disapproving way and I discern that she knows the truth. I don't want her to think I'm just another blond-haired American girl.

I say weakly, "I'm Trinidadian like you. From Princes Town."

She motions her head toward the three arrangements of white and yellow roses and states, "Your husband send plenty flowers. Too much."

Then she walks out.

When the Jamaican orderly comes in I immediately tell her where I'm from. I don't want her to see me as another privileged white girl. I'm like my great-grandfather now. Papa, which was what we called him, hated that Jews like him, refugees to Trinidad, were so quick to assimilate into white Trinidadian society, embracing the descendants of plantation owners who had fled from Haiti and Martinique during the Haitian revolution. Even in the twentieth century, these families refused to raise their glasses in toast to Haitian independence.

The Jamaican orderly smiles at me and I feel better. I am being discharged from the hospital. It's not the first time. The last time I told the nurse I fell off a ladder—Jason had banged my head into the wall and my hair was matted with blood. Although I was bleeding, I was sad for Jason, for his remorse, for his inability to control himself. I thought it wouldn't happen again.

The Trinidadian nurse returns and reads my chart. Then she says, "Sophie. Listen to me, Sophie. There is always a way out. You just have to find it. You hear me, girl?"

I nod.

When Jason picks me up he is in a good mood, apologizing profusely. He has chocolates and a blue Tiffany's box. I am silent in the car. I don't know how our relationship changed. Everything started off so well. Even my mother liked Jason, although he wasn't Jewish or the kind of husband she had imagined for me. She thought him strange and introverted, but liked that he could provide for me. Before the wedding, he promised to help with my education because I wanted to become a doctor like Papa. Then the promises stopped.

When Papa landed in Trinidad in 1939 he set up his practice in St. Clair. His passion, however, was medicinal plants, and he spent his weekends wandering through south Trinidad, speaking to locals and making notes in his old brown leather notebook. He had started studying plants and alternative methods of healing in Germany, and his notebook was so precious to him that when he and Mama had to flee Berlin it was the only thing he packed. Poor Mama had to make decisions about everything else: documents, photographs, clothes, and one or two precious items including a blue musical jewelry box with a ceramic ballerina in pirouette inside the lid.

Mama's jewelry box was passed down to Grandma Rachel, then to my mother, and then to me on my wedding day. It once stood on the center of my dressing table, but one day Jason flung it to the ground in fit of rage and the ballerina broke off. I had come home late after strolling about our neighborhood. I apologized, but he was enraged. While he was calling me an inconsiderate and selfish bitch, I was half-listening. I was looking down at the box and saw that the delicate ballerina was broken at her feet, so she could be easily repaired. I felt a sense of relief. All I could think of was gluing the pieces of the jewelry box together again.

Mama was delicate, like the ballerina. Some years after landing in Trinidad she become confused, slipping in and out of reality. Papa must have noticed, but few in the Jewish community around St. Clair did, since Papa had alienated many by constantly declaring, "When did Jews start thinking of themselves as Trinidadian whites?" He was perhaps one of the few refugees who could not tolerate how carefully the local whites protected their circle. It bewildered him that white skin was valued more than education and manners. When invited to dinner parties, he didn't understand the sudden anger at the table when he mentioned the legacies of slavery and indentureship. The other refugees rarely took his side, frowning at him for offending the host. After a couple of years, Papa realized that many established white families had secrets of lineage: African or Indian female ancestors. This was when he came up with his favorite phrase, taking any opportunity to declare, "Who's white in Trinidad? Damned few." After that, the dinner invitations stopped.

Despite the ostracism, Papa kept his practice in St. Clair and taught a Hebrew class on Saturdays for the children of refugees who all called him "Papa" too. He only moved to Princes Town when Mama developed a mild kleptomania. She started picking up items in expensive shops and asking herself, "Take it or leave it?" Fortunately, Stecher's, the store she frequented, was owned by an Austrian Jewish refugee who never pressed charges when Mama walked out with a china teacup or a pair of gold earrings. He just informed Papa discreetly and Papa paid for whatever Mama took.

Princes Town, named so because two British princes once visited this small bustling place, became home. Every morning there was a line outside Papa's office of patients who had heard of the Jewish doctor on Tramline Street who accepted plants, herbs, fruits, or cooked food as payment.

Papa's daughter, my Grandma Rachel, had many friends up north, and soon she was married to someone from her circle. Grandma Rachel and Grandpa Pierre spent their weekends going down-the-islands and partying with the local whites whom Papa hated.

The time came when refugees with relatives in the US were given the opportunity to migrate. Papa's brother wanted the Trinidadian family to join him in New York, but Papa refused. He had fallen in love with the island and its wealth of medicinal plants. Grandma Rachel and Grandpa Pierre migrated to New York, but their daughter, my mother Hannah, loved the wild greenery of Princes Town and spent all her vacations there until she eventually inherited the house from Papa.

Years after Papa died, my neighbor Sanjay and I were playing hide-and-seek in the spare room near the kitchen. As we were running, a box tumbled and Papa's notebook fell out. Sanjay picked it up ever so carefully and began to turn the pages, examining Papa's drawings of roots and leaves. The first pages were written in German, but the rest was in English.

I snatched the book from him. "It's mine. I'm going to be a doctor like Papa."

"Me too," Sanjay said quietly.

He started to plead with me to lend him the book. He would keep it safely and study it. He wanted to be like Papa too, learning about plants and herbs.

I ran to find my mother, who was reading in the living room. She said that Sanjay absolutely could not have the book and that he was only eight and would not understand what Papa had written there anyway. Sanjay stood barefoot in his white T-shirt and blue shorts and tears filled his eyes. I had never seen him crying. My mother softened and said he could borrow it for a few days.

I am thinking of Sanjay as Jason is driving me home from the hospital. I want to go home to be with him. I want to leave Jason and New York, this man and this city, both foreign to me.

"I want to visit my mother in Trinidad. Just for a week."

A mistake. Too soon to ask. He knows what I'm thinking.

"Right now you don't seem ready to travel by yourself. You seem confused."

"I'm fine. I want to see my mother."

He is already two steps ahead. "I spoke to her today. Remember you had a nervous breakdown when you were sixteen? It may be happening again. You don't understand that I'm trying to save you. Save you from yourself. Sometimes I go overboard, and I'm sorry. So sorry."

I am silent. When we are back in our apartment on Third Avenue, I look at New York City through the window. Outside the night is blue with twinkling lights. People are walking around, enjoying the evening. What would it be like to be outside, walking freely? I don't know. Soon after I met my New York relatives, they introduced me to Jason. I got married, stepping into this prison. I remember what the nurse said. Was she right? Is there a way out?

I move from the window and see my reflection in the glass. At first I don't know who this person is. She is thin and tall with curly hair and large blue eyes. Then I realize it's me, and I'm surprised at how young I look, as if I'm still sixteen, exploring Papa's notebook with Sanjay.

Sanjay and I met up on Saturday afternoons when my mother and his grandmother took their naps. We walked down the hill to the river. Neighbors called out to us along the way, noticing me first because I was the only girl in the area with curly blond hair and blue eyes. On the way was a small shack where Nari lived. He was a man in his thirties, an outcast. As soon as he saw us he would shout, "White girl, I going tell your mother." I had the perfect retort: "Who's white in Trinidad? Damned few." Sanjay and I would burst out laughing and run down the hill while Nari stood scowling at us.

Down the hill was a stream with smooth blue and gray stones. We waded until the bend where the stream suddenly widened. Here, curving black bamboo covered the sky, sheltering us. Thin blades of sunlight fell through the green leaves. We sat on the riverbank with our feet in the flowing water. Sanjay would open his satchel and pull out the plants he collected during the week. He had never returned Papa's book. It was his holy text, consulted for every plant. Papa had copious notes on the wonder-of-the-world leaf, which could cure any skin condition as well as dissolve tumors when warmed and applied topically. Soursop leaf tea was used by locals to cure cancer. Some plants were poisonous, though, and Papa had a special section on these.

At times in the bamboo there was a different sound, a slight rustle. We knew it was Nari peeping at us. Nari was tall, clumsy, and unkempt; it was impossible for him to hide in in his old red T-shirt and gray sweats. We always made a joke of it. Sanjay would say loudly, "Look, a red and gray bird in the bushes," and we would laugh and whistle.

We never paid attention to Nari stalking us, but we should have. Sanjay and I both turned sixteen in July, and we went down to the river to celebrate. My mother's bagels were fresh, and Sanjay had a small jar of his grandma's homemade guava jam. We spoke of our future. Sanjay was a step ahead of me because villagers believed he possessed the gift of healing, and they had already started coming to him to cure their ailments.

"I'm jealous," I said, playfully rubbing his short black hair.

Sanjay held both my hands. He was thin and lean, and many assumed he was physically weak, but his grip was strong.

"You have healing hands Sophie," he said, tracing the lines in my palm.

"Thank you, Sanjay."

Sanjay said that he wanted to kiss me. "Not with your guava-jam mouth," I laughed.

"But you like guava," he said. My heart was racing and we kissed for the first time. We spoke of the future again, of how he would take me to Curaçao for our honeymoon and show me the Snoa, the oldest synagogue in the Americas. He had started reading up about Jewish culture, and knew that the synagogue was built in the seventeenth century by Jews from Spain and Portugal who were fleeing religious persecution. Sanjay wondered if there were no secret forests like our bamboo refuge where one or two Jews in Europe could have hidden, and perhaps survived like maroons? I promised to ask my mother.

As we sauntered happily back to our homes, holding hands, I saw my mother standing at the doorway. Her hair was tied back and her arms were folded across her white shirt. From her posture I knew she was angry. Across from her, in the next-door house, was Sanjay's gray-haired grandmother. Her arms were also folded, and she seemed to be anticipating something unpleasant. Nari stood on the side of the road, smirking.

I wasn't sure what was happening. Surely my mother was not going to reprimand me for a kiss. Suddenly my mother screamed accusingly to Sanjay, "Thief! You stole my grandfather's book! I'm calling the police!"

Completely embarrassed, Sanjay took the book out of his satchel, threw it on the ground and trampled over the white datura flowers as he ran into his grandmother's house. I started crying. I couldn't believe that my mother would do something so cruel. This was the last time Sanjay and I spoke. Sometimes I saw him going down to the river alone. I knew that if I ever wanted to see him, I could wait for him there.

I am realizing that I married Jason because he is tall and lean and has open, brown eyes like Sanjay. Perhaps I too am to blame for the abuse in our relationship. Perhaps I knew that he wasn't for me, yet I went along with the marriage, deceiving him. I should call my mother and tell her the truth, tell her that I need to come home. Right now, though, Jason is in his happy phase. He even let me use his credit card to purchase some plants, He encouraged me as I tended the lovely white flowers on the windowsill. He didn't see me copying his card number, expiration date, and CVV code.

I have been going to the park to read Papa's book. It feels as if I'm sitting with Sanjay at the river, and he is encouraging me in his quiet way. I often lose track of time. I'm walking into the apartment later than usual and Jason is home early.

"Ah, Sophie, you have that glazed look in your eyes. Where were you?"

He is angry, but not shouting. I think it's a good sign that he is not in a rage as yet. Perhaps I can calm him down.

"I went to sit in the park," I answer.

"You've become so distant, Sophie. Have you been meeting someone in the park?" Now his voice is rising. "Who have you been meeting? Tell me!"

"No . . . no one, Jason."

I can't think. I know I must say something because he becomes angrier when I say nothing. When his fist connects to my cheek I fall. I remember what the nurse said to me. While I'm lying on the ground my face is stinging. I'm in pain, but I'm crying mostly from relief. Relief, because I finally know the way.

Today is the day. As soon as Jason left for his office I went online and bought a ticket to Trinidad. It was three times the usual amount because of the late purchase. The taxi would be coming in twenty minutes and for the first time in my life I understand Mama and see her swirling about her Berlin home thinking, "Take it or leave it? Take it or leave it?" It is my dilemma now. I decide on two things only: the ballerina jewelry box and Papa's notebook. Both fit in my tote. I have my airline ticket and some cash that I have accumulated little by little from Jason's wallet.

I tell the taxi driver that I'm late for my flight and he gladly weaves in and out of traffic. At JFK, I check in and go through security quickly. By now, Jason will be feeling the effects of the white flowers I have ground into the coffee he takes to his office every morning. In his spidery writing, Papa noted:

> *The indentured Indians brought the datura plant to Trinidad, and they sometimes refer to its solution as "joy-juice." In villages in south Trinidad where it grows in abundance, it is taken as a hallucinogenic, especially during Hindu worship devoted to Shiva or Kali. When ingested, users claim they encounter shadow entities sent by Kali to steal their energy. If taken in excess the seeds and flowers are poisonous (tropane alkaloids).*

I used every single petal of the flowers on the windowsill. Jason will see the shadow entities; he has so many trapped inside. It will take the doctors some time to determine the cause of his psychotic behavior and intense vomiting. Most likely he will not survive.

Now, in the boarding area, I make the phone call to my mother. I know that she will be extremely happy to hear from me. I'm shouting into my cell phone, "Mom! I'm coming home today."

"No, Sophie. You can't come back, honey. You're not well. It happened to Mama too. But Jason will help you. You'll get the best treatment there. "

"I should have married Sanjay."

"Honey, no. Sanjay is not here anymore. Remember what happened when you were sixteen? Remember what that man, Nari, did to him in the bamboo forest? Terrible things. Remember they found Sanjay's body near the river?"

I am silent.

She continues, "Sophie, just stay there. What did you do? Tell me. The police just called. They said the New York police contacted them in case you arrive in Trinidad."

I say nothing.

She says in an exasperated tone, "*What did you do?* Please stay there. Remember you can't hide here. You stand out because you're white—"

I fling my cell phone into the trash. I should have done it sooner, in case the police tried to locate me. I should have never called my mother.

The airline makes the announcement, saying to remain seated until each group is called. I stand with some anxious passengers, just in case we can board earlier.

Waiting, I look outside and see sunlight flashing on the metal wing of a plane. It makes me think of the white trumpet flowers outside of Sanjay's home, how iridescent they will be at this time of the morning. Down the hill the river will meander slowly round the bend. The thick bamboo, with its black stalks, will create a dark, solitary space for whoever ventures there.

Rhododendrons

Xu Xi 許素細

Eventually, even the rhododendrons in the corridor could not mask the smell emanating from B3. We hadn't seen him for days, but that was not unusual, not since his wife passed away earlier in the year. Letitia, the Liebermans' Filipino domestic helper was away for her annual four-week Christmas holiday in Manila, and the morning she returned home, on December 30, she let out a shriek so loud it resonated throughout our building.

"Didn't you notice the smell?" The police asked when they came to interview us that afternoon. Apparently, Mr. Lieberman had been dead at least a fortnight, if not longer. We live in 12-A1, on the west wing of our floor facing south, and at first I was tempted to say, no, we didn't, just to stay out of the whole affair. But Mum piped up. "Stinky! Always so stinky." She glared at the policewoman, an English speaker with the red stripe on her shoulder. "That woman never throws anything away, so there are dead cockroaches and dead geckos in her piles of junk." Mum blinked, and I knew she had forgotten that Mrs. Lieberman was dead. "She's half-Japanese you know. They're those Jews of China."

"Come on, Mum," I said, "it's time for your bath," and I motioned to Rosa, our helper, to take my mother away. Turning to the policewoman I switched to Cantonese. "My mother's very old and she's a bit forgetful, so don't mind what she says."

The policewoman nodded. "Did you know Mr. Lieberman well?"

"Not really. He kept to himself most of the time."

Our south facing neighbors next to us in A2 had been garrulous about an incident in early November and the police wanted to know if I knew who this other woman was, how they could get in touch with her and whether or not I'd seen her around recently. No, no, and no, I replied. I was glad when the hubbub finally died down that evening and we all went back to our lives behind closed doors. Now that I've crossed over into my sixties, I find too much excitement irritating, and a dead body, especially in a flat locked from the inside, is such a nuisance.

The next morning, Letitia was at our flat, jabbering away with Rosa. "Oh ma'am," she said, when I came out of my room, "it was so horrible. He was purple. And the smell! I used up two whole bottles of Dettol and it still won't go away. Even worse than sweeping up all the dead cockroaches and insects after Ma'am Lieberman died."

The police returned again, and visited all the flats on 10, 11 and 12. I gazed jealously at A3, the flat to the left of us that faced west. It was currently empty, because the Lo family were all away in California on holiday. Mr. Lo was the last corpse to leave our floor, just four months earlier, but he died of an aneurysm and there was no mention of foul play. Mrs. Lieberman had expired at home in B-3 after a long illness, and was the corpse back in March prior to Mr. Lo. And B-1 and B-2 were not really part of our floor, because those were the upstairs of the joined penthouse flats on 11, so their doors remained perpetually locked. I'd never seen them once in the decade since they moved in. This left the Chans in A2 next door to us. Their dog barked furiously every time I came home and had been barking even more furiously in November during the incident of the woman in the corridor.

She was from China, surnamed Zhang, Rosa said, and was Mr. L's current lover. Now, with both Rosa and Letitia having tea in our living room, I heard the entire story again.

"I bet she murdered him, ma'am, because he wouldn't sell the flat and give her the money. A million dollars he gave her already, and still she wanted more. You should have heard her, screaming away outside our door. Mr. L refused to let her in and she finally went down to the lobby. After he went out, she came back up and forced her way in past me and broke those porcelain pigs and rabbits Mrs. L brought from their home in Shanghai." Letitia took a deep breath. "Poor Ma'am L, those were her favorites. Mr. L didn't even wait for his ma'am to die to take this woman as a girlfriend. They've been together at least two years. I warned him she was trouble. His son in Shanghai also warned him, but men . . . what can you say? And now he's dead. Murdered!"

It didn't seem likely to me, but by now, the whole building was talking about the murdered Jew in 12 A-3.

Rosa chimed in. "I thought Jews were very smart. How come he was so stupid to fall for this crazy woman?"

I refused to fuel further speculation and murmured something about Jews being people like everyone else—some were smart and others not. The building was as abuzz as it had been years earlier in 1973, when Bruce Lee died here, on 3, if I recall correctly, although it wasn't a murder that time, just cerebral edema while he was with his lover. I wasn't so sure it was murder now, but with the police traipsing in and out of the flat down the hall, it was hard not to be swept up by all the talk and excitement. Letitia had worked for the Liebermans for twenty years, but I remember their arrival, thirty years earlier, when Dad was still alive and chatted with them regularly, although Mum remained guarded and suspicious, the way she was with everyone in our building. Dad and the Indian family on 10 were probably the only ones, besides the Filipino domestics, who spoke to the Liebermans, and somehow, I didn't think it was murder, even if the evidence, or rather the gossip, pointed to that possibility.

❧

Our family had moved to Hong Kong from Jakarta in the late 1960s when I was in high school. We used to rent over on the island, in Causeway Bay, close to the Indonesian Consulate. We bought our flat in this building when it was first built back in 1970, on this hilltop in Kowloon Tong, and this has really been my home in Hong Kong. Back then we and the Indians on 10 were the only foreigners here. So when the Liebermans arrived, I welcomed the added diversity. By then I had graduated from university and was working for the Hong Kong & Shanghai Bank. It's HSBC now and is where I still work in private banking.

"The Jews of China," Dad had declared over dinner one night, "are like us *wah kiu* in Southeast Asia. The professionals and the traders, we Chinese Jews make money and believe in education." It was shortly after the Liebermans moved in. Their son was around ten or so at the time, a likable boy and who had, like his parents, reddish hair.

Mum ignored his declaration. "How come they have red hair?"

"They're Ashkenazi Jews," I said. "Some have red hair."

"And how come she's part Japanese?"

By now, Dad was fiddling with the television channels and was no longer paying attention to anything Mum said.

"People marry and have children, Mum. Even the Japanese and Jews."

"They're so strange."

Dad didn't find them strange at all, and he often came home with stories about Mrs. L's rhododendrons. There were at least a dozen pots of the colorful fragrant blooms in the hallway and even after her death, Mr. L kept them there and Letitia watered each pot faithfully. Mrs. L had originally asked Dad if it was okay for her to place her rhododendrons in the corridor, for the southern light from the windows at the lift, she said, to which Dad said, "Why not?" Mum was livid and nagged him for weeks after that, saying our Cantonese neighbors wouldn't like it and why did he have to tell her that? Later, she complained to me that Dad was flirting again.

Back then, Dad worked from home, while Mum and I went out to work. It was true that Dad was very friendly with Mrs. L. They both liked music and talked about opera all the time. Sometimes I would come home from work and find them both listening to opera on Dad's stereo. Our large crystal vase in the living room would be full of rhododendrons whenever she visited. I wondered if Mr. L minded, but whenever I saw him, he was always pleasant and complimented my appearance, asking, why I didn't have a boyfriend. He definitely had an eye for Chinese women. He gave me a pretty porcelain vase as a gift one Chinese New Year. I still have it.

I remembered all that now in the wake of Mr. L's demise. It was all hearsay, but he apparently had choked to death, although it wasn't clear if someone strangled him. But the crazy woman who created the huge ruckus didn't have a key to the flat, of that Letitia was absolutely positive. Even if she was jealous of Mrs. L, and later, even Letitia, it didn't necessarily mean she killed him, especially if she had no way into the flat. Rosa heard some talk among the other Filipino helpers about a fish bone, but later that turned into a chicken bone, and still later someone said he had coughed up a lot of blood.

Yet the police were in and out of our building for days.

Madam Policewoman and a young assistant showed up a week later with more questions for me. "There aren't many Jewish people living around here, are there?"

I wondered what the point was but simply assented, saying nothing.

"Why did they live here so long?"

Here it was again, the local attitude about anyone different. I passed as local because I spoke Cantonese and, these days, even Mandarin fluently, although my parents had never quite mastered the local languages and defaulted to English. But it was tiresome, how much the locals missed. About everything.

"It was their home. Mr. Lieberman had an import and export business in Chinese porcelain, and their son went to school here in Kowloon Tong." She looked dubious, so I added, "They're from Shanghai but have been in Hong Kong since the fifties."

"Really?" She looked sincerely startled.

"Really." Hoping to deflect further questions, I asked if they'd found the Chinese woman, surnamed Zhang.

"Yes. She says she hasn't been near the building in days. Have you seen her around?"

In fact, I had seen her lurking in the lobby a couple of days earlier, and wandering around the car park where she stopped next to Mr. L's car. Letitia said she often waited around, hoping to catch him when he went out.

"I don't recall," I replied.

"He had red hair. It's strange, don't you think?"

Enough, I thought. I made some excuse about having to see to my mother and dismissed her as soon as I could.

※

This year has been unusual, with all these corpses leaving our building. The elderly Indian lady on 10 passed away at the beginning of the year as well. She was one of the last, besides my mother, who made it into their nineties. Mr. Lo was an aberration, an undiagnosed abdominal aneurysm, his daughter said. He was in his sixties, like me. Most of our neighbors now are younger families, like the Chans next door with their noisy mutt. The Liebermans were in their seventies. She had been a packrat for some time, and when she died, the mountains of newspapers and magazines she hoarded disappeared even before her body was cold. I couldn't blame Mr. L, though. From what Letitia told us, it was all she could do to eke out a pathway between the heaps of rubbish in order to do some semblance of cleaning. It was no wonder he stayed out so much, and I could almost even forgive him his woman from China, surnamed

Zhang. She was crazy but sexy, with wild hair and eyes. And Mrs. L had been ill for almost three years, virtually bedridden.

It was different when Dad died ten years earlier. By then he flirted openly with Mrs. L, and every afternoon, they took a walk together before dinner in the park below. So I had to listen to Mum berate him at dinner every night, on and on—how could he behave like that, how could he humiliate her like that—until I learned to tune it out. By then, Mum's memory was in partial decline, and Mr. L was screwing around although that was a different woman, from Taiwan, surnamed Chao. She was at least sane and didn't show up at our building. Letitia told Rosa that he kept her in a flat on the island.

The police came the time Dad died as well, because his death occurred at home, so that was standard procedure. By the time they arrived, I had flushed the remains of the mixed-up medication Mum fed him. She had been a pharmacist, and even though her memory had begun to fail, she still knew what she was doing. Dad had a weak heart and took a whole bunch of different medications, which Mum administered, so it was easy for her to give him too much of something to trigger the attack. I could never be sure but I'm more inclined to believe that if there was a murder in our building, it was Dad who was the victim and not Mr. L (or Bruce Lee for that matter, because that's been thoroughly picked over by history). Mum was so distraught. She found Dad in bed, dead, when she came home after morning mass. I spoke to the police for Mum and they only came to see us twice, and at the hospital they simply wrote it off as death by heart attack with a preexisting condition of a weak heart.

So why is it that the police are still here two weeks later, hounding us with endless questions about these Jews in our building? What is it they really expect to learn? Can't they just let Mr. L rest in peace? You'd think they'd never seen a Jewish person before, but . . . that might well be the case. I suppose it helps that we look Chinese, despite our mixed Indonesian blood. Maybe it's the red hair. Really, it's all just too strange.

Mosquitoes over Bamako

Yigal Zur

Omar laughed.

I hated that laugh.

He laughed again.

I hated it even more.

Omar's full name was Omar Al-Hajji, formerly of Jounieh, Lebanon.

I didn't hate Omar because he was from Jounieh. I didn't hate him because I'd killed his older brother, his father, his uncle, and probably two of his cousins. I hated him because he laughed.

I was sitting in his bar in Bamako in Mali, West Africa, hating every syllable of laughter he emitted. We were drinking beer, Carlsberg Green, the cloudy piss sold throughout Africa. It's the swill you drink when you're dying of thirst, or done in by the heat, or high as a kite.

"What hotel did you say you're staying at?" Omar laughed.

"Beau de Lac, beautiful lake," I answered.

Omar laughed so hard he nearly fell over the bar.

"You could have stayed here," he said.

"I didn't know that when I got here," I said. There was something apologetic in my tone. Apologetic? That merely intensified my hatred for Omar. "Ahmed took me to Beau de Lac."

"Ahmed?"

Omar is a chubby guy. I was afraid his heart would give out right then and there. In any case, whatever came out of my mouth sounded

Translated from Hebrew by Sara Kitai

like the funniest thing in the world to him. I was getting increasingly irritated, and I hated him more and more.

We were in Bamako. I didn't have an M16 to take him out like I did his brother, his father, and I don't know who else. I don't remember the whole list of motherfuckers I polished off in Jounieh. It's long. But who's counting?

"You're telling me that Ahmed took you to Beau de Lac?" Omar said, roaring with laughter.

I nodded.

"What's it like there?" he asked, doubled over. He was holding his bulging stomach, which was dancing in time to his laughter.

"Why do you want to know?" I asked suspiciously.

"What about the walls? What are they like?" His tone was crafty. "And the mosquito netting?"

"You bastard," I said. "Believe me, if I had a tank I'd aim it straight at the cunt of your mother in Jounieh."

Omar laughed even harder. He thought I was kidding, which goes to show that he'd been away from Jounieh for a long time, too long. He bent down and pulled out two more beers. The drops of ice water on the bottles winked at us.

"Asshole," I said. "Where did you get the Heineken?"

"You see," he answered, "even in Africa you need connections."

I thought to myself that it's much more important to belong to the right tribe, but I'd let Omar find that out for himself.

We clinked bottles and sucked on the beer thirstily. He reached for the stereo system and turned the dial to the right, ramping up the volume. We listened raptly to Ali Farka Touré, Mali's legendary singer, performing African blues.

"Now tell me about the mosquitoes," Omar said, not laughing.

I looked around, although I knew there was no one there. The bar was empty. And not because of the hour. No Westerner in his right mind comes to Bamako at the height of summer. Just me and a few Americans from the Special Forces Counter-Terrorism Unit.

"They're not mosquitos," I said. "They're bugs the size of airplanes that line up in formation on the wall and attack."

Omar looked at me skeptically.

"You don't believe me?"

The expression on his face said "whatever."

"You don't, huh?" I took a quick sip of beer. "You remember when our planes came in on a bombing strike?"

"Yes." His tone was serious.

"Aah," I said. "I finally made you remember your shitty past."

"Did you expect me to forget?" he complained.

"We were talking about mosquitoes," I reminded him. "The planes were just an analogy. There's no reason to make any more of it. Just a visual metaphor, a literary device, all that shit."

"I'm trying to keep my cool," he said. "But don't forget I'm Omar Al-Hajji, from Jounieh, Lebanon."

"Don't worry," I said. "I haven't forgotten."

Our bottles were empty. We lined them up next to the others. They were shorter, but you can't always go by size. Omar is also about eight inches shorter than me.

"It was late when Ahmed took me to Beau de Lac," I said, defensively. "His taxi didn't show up. The sun was setting by the time we left the airport. And then he had to stop on the way to pray. When we got to Bamako it was dark out. Nobody's in the mood to start looking for a hotel in the dark."

"So he left you there and took off?"

"Yes."

"That's Ahmed for you," Omar said.

"I checked in and went upstairs. Room number six. I saw them as soon as I opened the door, but by then it was too late."

"And?"

"I went to sleep," I said. "I was exhausted. The whole trip from Gao to Timbuktu, and from Timbuktu to Djenné. And then they leave you waiting there on the tarmac for the plane to Bamako to do you a big favor and land. I tossed and turned all night because of the fucking mosquitoes."

"There wasn't any netting?"

"Sure there was. The kind that has more holes than anything else. The mosquitoes made sure to get me out of bed before dawn. After a night like that, even a humane man like me discovers he has an urge for revenge. I walked around the room squashing the bugs on the wall. They were so full of my blood they couldn't move. I tried to take a shower in the drizzle of cold water that came out, all the time doing my best not to step on the filthiest spots on the floor."

Omar laughed.

"I've seen a lot of red spatters on damp walls in my time," I went on, "but these were the most disgusting. I figured the Beau de Lac was as good as you get in Bamako."

Omar couldn't stop laughing. "You think the Americans sleep there?"

"I didn't know there *were* any Americans in Bamako. Who knew the long arm of Uncle Sam reached as far as West Africa?"

"It does. One of them already asked me if I'm a member of Hezbollah."

"What did you say?"

"I asked him how he wanted his hamburger. That was enough to make him chill."

"Yes," I agreed. "Two Americans meet in the middle of Africa and all they have to talk about is how bad the hamburgers are."

"They have nothing to complain about here," Omar said. "I buy the best cuts of beef from the Omranis."

"They're fucked in the head, those Americans," I said.

"They're fucked all over," Omar agreed.

John and Mike came in. Two hefty Americans. John was dressed in Bermuda shorts that revealed his bulbous knees. Mike was in faded jeans. They were both wearing green army-issue T-shirts and Chicago Bulls caps.

"What's up?" John asked.

He lifted his huge ass onto the stool next to me. Mike stopped opposite the dart board and threw a single dart. Bulls-eye.

"We were just talking about you," I said. "Omar says the Americans are fucked up."

"Omar said that?" John asked.

"I said I buy the best cuts of beef from the Omrani clan and you want it ground up and well-done. Don't you think that's a waste of good meat?"

"No," Mike said, sitting down.

"So how did you spend the shitty day?" I asked.

"Like every other shitty day in Africa," Mike answered.

"And it's not over yet," John added. "After we down a few of Omar's nasty beers, we have to go back to the office and write it all up. What they like to call a report."

"What's it gonna say?" I asked

"That the long arm of Hezbollah has reached as far as Mali," he said, pointing to Omar.

"Stop with the bullshit," Omar said. "You trying to put a target on my back?"

"Maybe," Mike said, winking at John and me.

John lifted his right buttock off the stool and let out a major fart that went on for at least thirty seconds. It sounded like he was firing a round from a machine gun. When we were kids, we used to call it an Abdallah, stretching the *l* sound.

"You've picked up the habits of the locals," Omar said.

We all laughed.

"You like beans?" I asked.

We laughed even harder.

The high point of any dialogue in Mali is the accusation that the other person is very fond of peas and beans, a reference to his farting, which the locals find hilarious. They're not the only ones. We couldn't stop laughing. John and Mike started exchanging greetings in the native language, Bambara.

"*I ni sògòma.*" Good morning.

"*Nba, i ni sògòma.*" Good morning to you.

"*Nba, hira sira weh?*" Did you sleep well?

"*Nba, N'sira hèrè_la.*" I passed the night in peace.

"*Nba, i ka kènè.*" How are you feeling?

"*Nba, toro si te.*" I'm fine.

"*Nba, I muso_ka kènè wa?*" How is your wife?

"*Nba, Tòorò_si t'a la.*" She is very well.

A lot of *nba*'s, a Bambara word that basically means, "I hear you." Whoever has the most *nba*'s wins. Whoever utters the last "*nba*" wins it all.

We were laughing like lunatics. Omar got the hamburgers from the kitchen and put a plate down in front of each of us. He brought over the set of ketchup, Worcestershire sauce, and Tabasco and put more cold beers on the bar. We set to work. After our mouths had been occupied with the food for about fifteen minutes, John suddenly asked me, "Did you go to that place in the Grand Marché I told you about?"

"I did."

"And?"

"Hold on a minute," I said. "She gave me something."

I made of show of looking through my pockets although I knew exactly where it was. Finally I pulled out the small package wrapped in newspaper and tossed it toward John's plate, which was now stained with remnants of ketchup and fries. The paper came off in midair, and the black shrunken head of a monkey baring its teeth rolled across the bar. John burst out laughing. He grabbed it and pitched it to Mike like a baseball. Mike caught it in one hand and called out, "Hey, Omar." Omar, bent over the refrigerator, straightened up. He must have been startled, or maybe he wasn't paying attention. In any case, the head hit him in the chest. The blood drained from his face and he leaned back against the bar, gasping for breath.

"Don't be such a sissy," I said, going behind the bar and picking up the monkey head, which was rolling on the floor. Then I took out my gun and put a bullet in Omar's head. That's what I was here for, after all. I came out from behind the bar and laid the monkey head beside the cash register. Mike was still chewing on the last of his lettuce.

"Wanna go get a beer?" I asked.

The two Americans nodded. John raised his buttock and farted one last time in parting.

In Africa, the only thing that matters is the tribe you come from.

A SHANDEH FAR DI GOYIM

(YOU SHAME US IN FRONT OF THE WORLD)

Wishboned

Jill D. Block

I can't remember the first time I heard the expression "split the baby."
It's one of those things I feel I always knew, like maybe it was congenital,
which means present from birth. It comes from the Bible story about
the very wise and respected King Solomon. And my name is Solomon,
so maybe that's why I feel a connection. Anyway, the story has always
resonated with me.

For example, it really bugs me that people use the expression "split
the baby" when they are talking about a compromise, like they think that
"split the baby" means the same thing as "split the difference." But that's
wrong. It's not at all what it means. The Bible story has nothing to do
with compromise. In fact, the splitting of the baby doesn't even actually
happen, which is pretty much the whole point. King Solomon uses the
threat of chopping the baby in half to find the truth, to figure out which
mother is lying. The prospect of splitting the baby was so horrible to the
real mother that she would rather give up her baby to the imposter than
see her baby killed. But that, of course, assumes that the baby would die.

Certain kinds of lizards can regrow a leg or their tail. And the human
liver can regenerate itself after resection. So maybe we shouldn't be so
quick to assume that splitting a baby would necessarily be fatal.

I'm just saying.

❧

Time stopped. I mean that literally. As you will see, I choose my words
carefully. It is sometimes hard for me to understand nuance, especially
when people don't actually mean what they say. So, I am careful with

my words, just in case other people are like me. Anyway, as I was saying, time had quite literally stopped doing what it is that time does.

You know the clocks they have at school? The ones hanging on the wall, usually by the door? They're big and round, super easy to read, with a white face, black numbers, and a red second hand. Where you can actually see the second hand move—tick, tick, tick—while you're staring at it, waiting for the bell to ring. It was that same kind of clock. Over by the door, right next to the glowing red Exit sign. That sign drove my mom crazy. She had wanted them to cover it up because she said it was going to ruin the pictures.

Anyway, I checked, and the second hand had actually stopped moving. Everything was still, silent. Like everyone but me had been caught in a giant game of freeze tag.

Up until that second—the second when time stopped—everything had been happening at once. It was all so loud and colorful. It was a cacophonous pandemonium. A pandemonious cacophony. The band was playing, people were getting up out of their chairs, circling the dance floor, moving first to the left, then to the right, clapping, kicking, stomping their feet, shouting to be heard over the music.

I tried to stay centered by focusing on just one thing, one person, one object, one conversation.

"Did you have some sushi?"

"What?"

"Sushi! Did you get some of the sushi?"

"They have sushi? Where?"

"Not in here. Before."

"What?"

"Out there! Before! During the cocktail hour."

It was a shame that she'd missed the sushi. We'd paid extra for it.

As promised, we were in the big room, the Grand Ballroom, according to the contract my mother had read and reread at least a hundred times. "Because your father, the lawyer, is apparently too important to be bothered with something as trivial as this." She'd made me read it too, which was obviously ridiculous. I am thirteen years old. Well, I was only twelve at the time. Yes, it is widely acknowledged that I am very bright, extremely well-read, and endowed with an impressive vocabulary, but what did I know about what a catering contract should or should not say?

What it said was that our event, the Felder bar mitzvah, would be in the Grand Ballroom, which has a maximum capacity of two hundred. There would be fifteen round tables, for ten people each. Plus, the two kids' tables. Everything would be set with white linens and blue and silver accents. There was to be a dedicated staff of waiters, busboys, and bartenders dressed in black pants and white, long-sleeved, button-down shirts, twenty in all. And that wasn't even counting the band. Or the dancers.

"Dancers?" my dad had asked. "Is that really necessary?"

"Only if you want people to actually enjoy themselves," my mother snapped. "Do you want to have a goddamn party, or do you want to save money?"

That was his cue to say, once again, that paying for a bar mitzvah is like buying a brand-new sports car and driving it straight off a cliff. Depending on her mood, my mom would sometimes respond by rolling her eyes with an indulgent smile, smug in the knowledge that they could afford this ridiculous expense. Or else she'd snap back.

"Do you not want to do this? Because if you don't want to do this, let's not do it. This isn't for me, you know. We could have just taken him to Israel like the Grossmans did. Or, you know what? Even better. Let's just cancel the whole goddamn thing." And if she really got going, "Do you think this is fun for me? Do you have any idea what's involved, what I've had to do? It's like a full-time goddamn job. And for what? So I can listen to the two of you complain?"

And on that note, I would leave the room. Quietly. Hopefully without her even noticing. It was bad enough when she was just pissed at him for complaining about the money. But when she got started on my lack of appreciation? That was a whole different thing.

I couldn't understand what she was so stressed out about. It's not exactly like we were making it up as we went along. In fact, I'd already been to nineteen bar and bat mitzvahs this year. And twelve of them were kids from Hebrew school, which means my mom and dad know their moms and dads, so they were there too. The other seven were kids I know from school or from camp, and my parents don't know their parents, so they weren't invited. Take my word for it, bar mitzvahs are way more fun when your mom and dad aren't there.

Anyway, maybe that was the pressure. I have a late birthday, so mine was one of the last bar mitzvahs in my Hebrew school class. Which means there were a lot of Joneses for us to keep up with. And even though there was a certain sameness from one to the next, it seemed like each successive event had to have at least one feature that hadn't already been done before. A chocolate fountain, a photo booth, a caviar bar, a game room for the kids. Our thing was a martini luge, this giant ice sculpture with some kind of alcohol running down through a winding carved channel. I wasn't allowed anywhere near it, so it seemed like an odd way to commemorate my becoming a man. It obviously wasn't my idea.

Anyway, after years of preparation, months of planning and untold thousands of dollars, the big day finally arrived. It started out just like you would expect. My mom made my dad and me get up way too early, and she was already slightly hysterical. She was utterly fixated on what I was eating for breakfast, and then getting my dad to shine my shoes. When he told her that she should have just taken them to the shoeshine place near the post office during the week she got so mad I'm surprised our neighbors didn't call the cops.

Once my shoes were properly shined, or as my mom said, good enough, she turned her attention to my grandmothers, Nan and Gran. They hated being called Nan and Gran. But it really shouldn't be up to them. In fact, I'd pointed out to each of them that you don't get to pick your own name, and especially not your own nickname. I mean, obviously. Does anyone honestly think that I chose to be called Solly Felder? I've always thought that Han Solo would is a much better nickname for me—Solomon, Solo? But I never could get it to catch on. My dad said I should give it up, because you can't pick your own nickname. Anyway, Nan and Gran hate being called Nan and Gran, mostly because they hate being referred to together, like they are a unit. So we only refer to them as Nan and Gran when we talk about them behind their backs. Which we actually do, kind of a lot.

The plan was that Nan and Gran would meet us there, but my mom was so worried that they would be late, she wouldn't put down her phone. She just sat there, staring at Google Maps, like maybe if she concentrated hard enough she would be able to control traffic.

Oh boy, I thought. Here we go again. How many times do I have to tell her that telekinesis is a skill. It's like a muscle that you have to develop. She is really unbelievable. I mean, come on. Look at me. I'd read every book there is about telekinesis, every article I could find on the internet. I'd been practicing since I was nine, doing exercises every single day, working on my breathing, improving my focus, and I still wasn't even able to move a marble. Actually, though, it is starting to feel like I'm getting close.

Mom said we were leaving in fifteen minutes, so I waited in my room, practicing the Torah portion I'd be reciting about the revolt of Korah against Moses in the wilderness, when God unleashes his wrath and the earth opens up and swallows Korah and all his people, and reading over my speech one last time. The original version had been better, but my mom told me that I had to change it. She said that no one was going to want to hear me talk about time travel at nine in the morning. The speech comes toward the end, so it would actually be more like ten thirty by then, but she was probably right. Especially because everyone was already going to be thinking about food, and wondering if we'd sprung for the deluxe Kiddush package.

We had.

֍

The service went exactly as planned, and none of the terrible things my mom had been so worried about happened. Everyone arrived on time. The flowers on the bimah looked substantial without being ostentatious. Rabbi Silver managed not to offend anyone. We had a nice turnout and, if I may say so myself, I performed beautifully. Needless to say, I set a high bar, pun intended, for my five cousins.

You see, I was the first-born grandchild on both the Felder and Berenson sides of my family. Solomon Asher. A gift from God. The answer to my grandmothers' prayers. So precious. Such a good sleeper. Oh, that appetite. Those eyelashes. What a strong grip. So smart, so tall, so handsome. What a good boy.

I know. It was a lot.

Anyway, in the beginning, back when I was the only grandchild, everything was a competition with Nan and Gran. Everything. For them, it was like my birth was the gun they shoot to start a race—the race to be the best grandmother ever. Who could be the most helpful? Who could give the best gifts? Who would be my favorite? The most cherished? The best loved? For a long time it didn't actually bother me, since I was almost always the beneficiary.

I guess it started the day I came home from the hospital, when they both showed up at our house with the same gift, the same perfectly thoughtful, useful, practical-yet-still-somehow-extravagant baby swing. One of them would have to go back, of course. But whose? It was apparently a really big deal. And from there, it had gotten worse. To the point where now it's like they are mortal enemies.

A long time ago, when my Zaza was still alive, Nan once said to Gran, "What do you have to complain about? At least you still have your husband." Nan's husband, my dad's dad, had died before I was born, pretty soon after my mom and dad got married. Gran was like, "What do *I* have to complain about? How about my whole family being killed by the Nazis? Can I complain about that?"

"Oh, for God's sake. Again with the Nazis? Honestly, I can't wait until Marty dies and you're all alone. Then maybe you'll understand what it's like for me."

"Did you just—did she just say she can't wait until my Marty dies? She's an animal!"

Zaza died a couple years later. While we were sitting *shivah* at Gran's, it felt like it was somehow my job to keep Gran from going completely bonkers, maybe because I was the oldest grandchild. She made me stay next to her practically the whole time, and she wouldn't stop touching me, rubbing my back, touching my face, holding my wrist tight in her two hands, like she was afraid if she let go I'd float away. Her skin felt cool and soft and powdery. She kept asking me to give her a hug, because she said no one was ever going to hold her again. That made me sad because she was going to be lonely, but the idea that I was filling in for Zaza kind of grossed me out too.

I remember thinking now that Zaza died, Nan and Gran could be friends. Or roommates. Like on that show *Golden Girls*. But of course that didn't happen. They hate each other. My mom says it's because they are so much alike, but my dad says it's because they are so different.

He once said that if Gran and Nan were Spice Girls, Gran would be Sporty, and Nan would be Posh. Gran lives in Katonah, in the same house where she and Zaza had lived together, which my mom says is way too big for just her. My mom wants her to move into an independent living place but Gran says that when she moves out of her house it will be feet-first. She is pretty much always outside in the garden, planting flowers or pulling weeds. Or else she is in her kitchen, usually with her arm shoved up inside a raw chicken, pulling out the giblets. She has crazy curly white hair and she wears pastel-colored sweat suits practically all the time. My dad thinks it's hilarious when she wears pants that say "Juicy" across the butt. She listens to Howard Stern on the radio in her car.

Nan would *never* listen to Howard Stern. She probably doesn't even know who he is. She always only ever wears dresses and stockings. Her hair is what my mom calls "bubby blond," and she goes to the beauty parlor every week. She lives in Great Neck, in a fancy building with a doorman. Her apartment has white carpet and her dining room chairs are covered in silk, which makes my mom very nervous. She likes to take me to Broadway shows, and concerts at Lincoln Center. She's madly in love with Yo-Yo Ma, the cellist, and she knows every single thing about him. We once sat in the first row in Carnegie Hall to see him and I swear, she got tears in her eyes listening to him play.

Anyway, the whole thing with Nan and Gran was starting to get weird. Like their competition was becoming really aggressive. In the weeks leading up to my bar mitzvah, Nan and Gran had each called me a bunch of times to ask me what I wanted for my birthday. And I was like, "I don't know." But they were really insistent that I tell them something, and it was pretty clear that it could be, should be, something special, something big. The bigger the better.

🦋

Our cocktail hour was held outside on the terrace. As my mother said over and over, thank God the weather held up. There was also a separate area for the kids during the cocktail hour. There was a big sign that said "The Screening Room," and it was full of couches and beanbag chairs and computers and game consoles and a big TV, all loaded up with games and Netflix, and a waitress who kept bringing in trays of snacks for us. It was a bit much, but my mom firmly believes that the best indicator of a successful bar mitzvah is if the kids had a good time.

After about an hour of cocktails, sushi, and pigs in blankets, the waiters started ushering everyone into the ballroom. My mom and dad and I waited, sort of hidden out of the way, until just about everyone had gone inside and found their table. Then the band guy tapped on his microphone to get everyone's attention.

First he introduced my mom and dad, "Your hosts for the evening, Laurie and Jeff!" The band played music and everyone clapped as my mom and dad sort of ran into the room, holding hands and raising them up in the air, like when a sports team runs out onto the field before the game. Then he introduced me, "The star of the show, Solomon Asher Felder!" and two of the dancers sort of danced me into the room and across to where the band guy was, standing with my mom and dad. Then someone rolled out a table with a giant loaf of bread on it, covered with a napkin, and the band guy, talking into his microphone, asked Nan and Gran to join us up front to recite the *hamotzi*, the blessing of the challah. I knew from the looks on their faces that they didn't like having to do it together, but what choice did we have? If it was just one of them, the other would be mad.

While the challah thing was going on, I looked around the room, especially at the two tables of Dad's work people. One was people from his office, most of whom I'd met, and the other was mostly clients, whom I didn't know. Some of them seemed a little uncertain, not sure what was happening. Was it really possible that these fortysomething business-people had never been to a bar mitzvah? Or maybe this particular brand of northern New Jersey bar mitzvah was somehow different from the ones they'd been to. Anyway, it seemed rather strange to me.

But maybe what we were doing seemed weird to them. Like the candle lighting ceremony. It was pretty standard for the bar mitzvahs I had been to, but I guess it might seem kind of strange. The bar mitzvah kid calls people to come help him light the candles, one at a time, on his birthday cake. And for each candle, he recites a poem about the person being asked to come help. After the poem, the person gets up and walks across the dance floor to join him, and they light the candle together while the photographer takes a couple pictures. There are thirteen candles, so it goes on forever.

Lots of times the mom writes the poems but, as you might have guessed, I wrote mine myself. And I must say they were quite good. I actually was thinking I could have a business writing candle-lighting poems for people who can't write their own. I still might do it, so I don't want to just give them away, but here's one, as an example:

> Candle number four is the next to need lighting
> For help, Nan and Gran are who I am inviting
> When it comes to grandmothers, you two are the best
> I am so very lucky, I feel bad for the rest

For my birthday this year you asked me what gift
Would be something special, would give me a lift
It took me a while, but I finally decided
We'll do something together, one family, united
This year for my birthday, I'm thinking a cruise
A trip to Alaska for Mom, Dad, me, and both of you.

I had to use a little poetic license there at the end, but all in all I thought it was inspired. I mean, an Alaska cruise. What a great idea, right? Well, you should have seen the looks on Nan and Gran's faces. They were not happy. If I thought they were mad about having to bless the challah together, that was *nothing* compared to this.

❧

It took only about four notes from the band for my friends to recognize the "Hava Nagila Medley." All the kids kicked off their shoes under the table, and the girls stopped to put on the bright white socks they pulled out of their bags. Then they all raced onto the dance floor, sliding across the parquet. The adults got up from the tables around the dance floor, slowly, one by one. First up and out of their seats were the Moms. These were the Jewish Center moms, the moms from the neighborhood, my mom's friends, the moms of the kids I went to Hebrew school with. The Moms were followed somewhat reluctantly by the Dads. It was always the same ones who had to be coaxed, cajoled, glared at by the applicable Mom.

This was routine, standard stuff. There was a core group of seven families, eight, including us. The Moms and the Dads were all always invited, and they all always attended. Even the petty squabbles—about who had said what about whom—were ignored when it came to who to invite, and whether or not to attend. The Moms and Dads all knew exactly what was expected of them, and they did not disappoint. They could count on each other; they had each other's back. And that meant, once the band started to play, they would get up and dance. It's just what they did. After all, the second-best indicator of a successful bar mitzvah is a boisterous and unrestrained hora.

So, as I was saying before, it was a sensory overload. It was fast and loud and colorful. Everything was moving at once. It was hard for me to focus on any one thing, because everything blended together, and it was impossible to separate the talking from the singing, or the singing from the music, or the music from the dresses, or the dresses from the dancing. And I was in the middle of it, literally. All of a sudden, I was alone in the middle of the dance floor with all of this noise and color swirling around the perimeter. I guess I just stood there, trying to remember what I was supposed to do to calm myself down when I feel overwhelmed, when all of a sudden there was this tugging on my arm. It was Gran. She came out onto the dance floor, hooked her right arm through mine, and started dancing me around in a circle. I could see that people were clapping and that the band was playing, but all I could hear was buzzing in my head. Just breathe, I remembered. Deep breaths in and out. Not easy to do when your grandmother is spinning you around in a circle. And then, when I finally started to feel a little bit settled, like it all might be okay, all of a sudden there was something else in front of me. Nan was standing there on the dance floor. Gran and I almost crashed right into her. And then it was like everything was in slow motion. Nan reached her left arm toward mine and danced me away from Gran, spinning me in the opposite direction.

After what felt like forever but was probably not even two minutes, I slipped my arm out of Nan's. I just needed everything to stop for a minute. I was sweating. I was breathing hard. I tried to pick a spot to look at, to focus, to ground myself. But the room was spinning, and I couldn't hear anything past the buzzing in my head. All I wanted was to sit down. I took a step, but it was like the floor had disappeared. I stretched my leg forward, foot extended, but I couldn't stop leaning back, and there was nothing in front of me to step onto.

There were Nan and Gran, right in front of me. They both looked mad, so serious. It's what I imagined grim determination looks like. I could tell what they were thinking.

"Move it."

"Get out of the way."

"It's my turn."

Nan hooked her right arm into mine, and Gran took my left. And they pulled me in opposite directions.

In that moment I saw a flash of light, and then everything started to get dark. My field of vision got smaller and smaller, and the buzzing in my ears got louder and louder. There was a loud clap, like thunder.

It was suddenly silent. It was still. I wasn't sweaty anymore. I wasn't out of breath. Everyone around me was frozen in place. That is when I looked up at the clock.

Time had stopped.

Perfect. It was just what I needed. A moment to calm down, to gather myself, to focus.

Whenever I heard the expression "split the baby," I always imagined the baby being sliced in half, right down the middle, split into two equal pieces, each with one eye, one ear, one arm, one leg. Mirror images of each other. But in my case, it was actually more like a wishbone. Nan had gotten my head, my neck and my right arm and shoulder, and Gran had gotten the rest. As you might imagine, I was very surprised to see my left arm, still hooked to Gran's, and attached to my torso and legs, all the way over there. Even more interesting to me, though, was that there was no blood. Which surprised me. I mean, after being so violently ripped apart, you would think there would be blood. But, no. None. Which is what made me think about salamander tails. And hepatic regeneration.

I was also surprised by how tired you get when your grandmothers literally tear you into two pieces. I had never been so tired. So, even though I was extremely interested in seeing what was going to happen next, I couldn't—

I had to—

I just—

I needed to close my eyes. Just for a minute.

❧

"Stand back."

"Did someone call 9-1-1?"

"Watch out. Give him some air."

"Someone should call 9-1-1."

"Go get Jordan. He's a doctor."

"Oh, please. He went to med school in the Cayman Islands."

"Who, Jordan? Yeah, I wouldn't take a dog to him."

"Where's my phone. I should call 9-1-1."

"We don't need 9-1-1. Everybody calm down. He just fainted."

I fainted? I'd never fainted before.

"Is he waking up?"

"Look. I think he's waking up."

"Here. Give him some water."

The medical term for fainting is vasovagal syncope. I didn't know that then, but I looked it up. It occurs because your body overreacts to certain triggers, such as the sight of blood or extreme emotional distress. The vasovagal syncope trigger causes your heart rate and blood pressure to drop suddenly.

"Sweetie? Sweetie, can you hear me? Solly, open your eyes."

It was my mom. She was next to me, kneeling down on the floor. My dad was on the other side of me.

"Hey, Han Solo. You okay?" Han Solo! He called me Han Solo. *That* made me open my eyes.

I lay there for a few minutes, at the edge of the dance floor, with someone's jacket folded under my head. I didn't say anything. I just let my mom keep running her fingers through my hair. Intellectually, I knew it had been some kind of a dream, but still had to make sure. Very slowly, I lifted up my head and looked toward my feet. One, two. Two feet. Two legs. One torso. Two arms. Two hands. I wiggled my fingers. It seemed that everything was still intact and working.

I laid my head back down, closed my eyes, and listened. I could hear people whispering, fragments of conversation—how scary it had been, that they'd known I'd be fine, how it was so stuffy in there, that they should have had the air conditioner turned up higher, and about that time Miriam Abrams fainted outside the Stop & Shop because of her low blood sugar. I heard five different people say how no one will ever forget Solly Felder's bar mitzvah.

The band guy came over and my dad got up to talk to him. The dancers were directing the guests off the dance floor and back to their tables. I started to get up too, but my mom told me to wait. That's when I heard them.

"Oh, so you're saying this was my fault?"

"He was dizzy. He was overheated. You should have let him rest a minute."

"Oh, for God's sake. If he was dizzy, it was because of the way you were spinning him around. Like a maniac."

"Now I'm a maniac?"

"Yeah. A maniac."

"How dare you? You—you *bitch.*"

"Who talks like this?"

"Are you kidding? Look at yourself. Look at how you are behaving at your own grandson's bar mitzvah."

I looked up at my mom. From where I was, still on the floor, I was looking right up her nose. Her nostrils were flaring, like a horse, and her lips were pinched together. I knew that look. I wasn't sure if she was mad or sad, but something was happening, and it wasn't good.

We got up and went over to where my dad was standing, watching Nan and Gran. They were standing face to face in the middle of the dance floor. I looked at them, and then at my dad. I could tell that he was getting angry. His hands were clenched into fists. He opened his mouth and then closed it, like he didn't know what to say.

"You're impossible."

"*I'm* impossible?"

"Yes. You're impossible."

"I'll tell you what's impossible. Being stuck on a boat with you. *That* will be impossible."

"There isn't a cruise ship big enough."

"That's the truth."

"And one thing is for sure. I will not be sharing a room with you."

"Absolutely not. Over my dead body."

That was it. I had to do something. They'd been doing this my whole life, and it was getting worse and worse. This was my bar mitzvah, my big day, my rite of passage. They were upsetting my mom, and my dad was getting mad. I couldn't just let them ruin everything, right there, in front of our 189 guests. Now that I was a man, it was up to me. I had to make them stop.

I thought of the books I'd read, all the exercises I had done. I realized this was it, the moment I'd been working toward, and I was ready.

I slowed my breathing. I stilled my thoughts. I relaxed my jaw, and let go of the tension in my neck. I cleared my mind and concentrated, focused, thinking only about the molecules. I breathed slowly in through my nose and slowly out through my mouth. And again, slowly in through my nose, slowly out through my mouth. I took one more deep breath in, and I held it. Keeping my body relaxed, holding perfectly still, using just my mind, I squeezed. I pushed. I flexed my mental muscle.

I felt something. Something was happening. Like the wrath of God in the wilderness.

Standing there with my mom and dad, I saw a jagged line appear across the dance floor. We watched together as the line became a crack in the parquet. People around the room began to notice what was happening. They got up from their chairs and stepped away from their tables so they could see. They stood silently at the edge of the dance floor, watching, waiting to see what would happen next. Slowly, the crack opened up. It got wider and wider, the dance floor falling away. Nobody moved. No one said a word. The only sound was the collective gasp as Nan and Gran disappeared, sucked into the abyss of black nothingness.

The Shabbes Goy

Craig Faustus Buck

Esther Gutterman raced the sinking sun, shuffling down the sidewalk as fast as her eighty-six-year-old arthritic hips would allow, dragging her rolling shopping basket behind her. She watched her shadow grow longer in her path as if stretching the distance ahead just to taunt her. She tried to pick up her pace, but a sharp sciatic pain shot down her leg. It being Friday, she'd be screwed if she didn't reach her elevator before the sundown ushered in the Sabbath. God forbade Orthodox Jews like Esther to do any work on Shabbes.

To Esther, work meant sweating over an ancient Singer sewing machine eight hours a day. She had to work in a men's suit factory to support her beloved granddaughter and her no-goodnik husband's useless life of religious study. Her deceased first husband had loved his work as an electrician. But Esther experienced work as something unpleasant you did to put food on the table, a sacrifice you made for family and tradition. It was a mystery to her how Jewish scholars, through some byzantine interpretation of ancient Talmudic writings, had determined that work included pushing an elevator button on the Sabbath.

Somehow the rabbis managed to confuse the completion of an electrical circuit with the act of starting a fire, which Exodus proclaimed a Shabbes sin. So, if Esther didn't get home before sunset, she would have to schlep herself and her groceries up fifty-one stairs. Never mind that she'd probably plotz from the exertion and keel over dead. Why not just kill herself in the lobby and save herself the climb?

❦

Holly Hockenbeck stripped the flapper dress off the shapely mannequin she displayed in the Spanish-arched front window of her apartment. The sun would go down in another few minutes, marking the start of the weekend. It was time to get nasty. She took a slug of vodka and Coke Zero, then grabbed a steel-studded leather corset—bright red, like her hair this week. She painstakingly hooked the corset around the mannequin's slender body, adjusting the circular cutouts to fully reveal the nipples she'd so lovingly painted. No point in a depraved display if the anatomy was unrecognizable from the street below.

Once night fell, she'd light her salacious model with a low spot to make sure the display was visible to nocturnal passersby. But her true target audience, the holier-than-thou Jewish fascist next door, wouldn't get his eyeful until he walked to temple in the morning.

She turned her stereo speakers to point out the window and canted them toward her neighbor's apartment. She planned to wait until dark to blast her rap because she knew the Orthodox creep couldn't use his phone on the Sabbath to call the cops.

Holly stepped back and reconsidered her mannequin. Something was missing. A prop of some sort. Scanning the room, her eye fell on a black leather flogging whip. Perfect. But how to attach it? As she pondered this, she heard a knock.

Holly opened the door to the Pizza Pronto delivery boy. She wasn't sure if it was the smell of pepperoni or the way the guy's Angels jersey draped from his shoulders, but her mouth started to water. He looked eighteen or nineteen—a few years younger than she—with long, sexy blond hair, and tight-ass joggers that would have intrigued her if her attention hadn't been drawn to his shoes. His Air Jordans sported long, black leather shoelaces. Perfect for strapping the whip to her manne-quin's hand.

"Come in," she said. "I'll just get my purse."

She turned away, knowing his eyes would be glued to her smooth bare waist as it flowed into the delectable half-rounds that molded her tight white skinny jeans. With her back to him, she popped open the top two buttons of her blouse to let her breasts play a little peek-a-boo with the boy. She fished her wallet from her purse and turned back to him.

As expected, his eyes flew to her cleavage.

"I really like your laces," she said.

He looked confused. "What?"

She leaned forward, leaving nothing to his imagination. "Wanna trade 'em for a blowjob?"

She watched his eyes grow large.

"Wow," he said. "Is this a trick question?"

She punched his chest, causing him to stumble back into an old, leather club chair whose arms were scarred with cigarette burns.

"Just do what I tell you to do," she said, yanking his joggers down to his knees.

He swallowed hard. "Yes, ma'am."

She smiled. "That's what I like to hear."

א

Moishe Gutterman sat at his ball and claw foot dining table, twisting his gray *peyes* around his curling iron, molding the sidelocks into ever tighter ringlets as he agonized that it was almost sundown and Esther still wasn't home. He knew there were things he could be doing to prepare for Shabbes, but he was too *farmisht* to think straight.

Should he light the Shabbes candles? It was supposed to be done eighteen minutes before sunset, but it was a woman's job. Esther's live-in granddaughter Becca was in her room, allegedly writing her master's thesis in psychology, but Moishe suspected she was procrastinating, probably on the internet violating some commandment. He thought about asking her to light the candles, but Becca was so resistant to his Talmudic wisdom that she might as well be Gentile. He doubted she even knew the prayer.

He was permitted to do the lighting if a woman wasn't present, but what if Becca came out or Esther got home midceremony?

And what about the switch in the fridge? Should he tape it so the light can't go on if someone opens the door? He wasn't sure he even knew where the switch was. Another one of Esther's neglected duties. Maybe Becca wouldn't mind taking care of the fridge. No prayer required there.

But, no. If he took care of one of Esther's chores, she'd expect him to take care of another. And another after that. He'd never get his studying done. Better to leave the candles unlit and the fridge off-limits. That way, when Esther arrived late, he could spend the whole twenty-five hours of Shabbes castigating her about it. The prospect brightened his mood.

א

Becca adjusted her cropped tube top in the mirror until she could see the bottoms of her breasts peek out beneath the clingy fabric. She smiled at the thought of what her dickhead step-grandfather would say if he could see her now. She pulled the top down to see how it would look at its intended latitude and imagined a tattoo on her belly, maybe an iguana with its tongue flicking into her crotch. She'd always wanted a tattoo. She had plenty of piercings: lower lip, eyelid, three in each ear, and she was considering her nipples but had yet to summon the courage. But tattoos were another matter. Out of respect for Nana, she refrained, knowing they triggered unimaginably grim Holocaust memories. It seemed cruel to add a tattoo to her grandmother's burden when the woman was already afflicted by a bloodsucking tyrant of a husband.

Becca was her grandmother's only source of love and emotional support, even though Becca's presence was a painful reminder of her deceased mother—her grandmother's only child. Becca's parents had both died when her father drove their car off a mountain road while loaded on prescription drugs. At the time, Becca was four, the age when a child's mind begins to grasp the irreversibility of death. But Becca's sense of loss didn't really kick in until her early teens, when her Grandpa Ben died and her nana was required by ancient Jewish law to marry Ben's brother Moishe. According to that law—*yibum*, a three-thousand-year-old tradition that very few Jews still observed—if a man dies without living children, his oldest brother has an obligation to marry the widow. With her only child deceased, Esther qualified.

Ben had been an Orthodox Jew, but not nearly as extreme as Moishe. Ben studied the Talmud, but he did so in his spare time, spending his days doing electrical subcontracting, sometimes taking Becca along as his assistant—grandfather time that Becca cherished. While the family kept Kosher, Ben was easygoing about tradition, cutting Esther and Becca a lot of slack in their compliance with religious rituals. If Esther accidentally broke a Sabbath rule, Ben would simply roll his eyes and ask God to forgive her. Moishe liked to refer to his little brother as a Reform Jew in Orthodox clothing. He meant it as an insult.

Moishe's devotional expectations spread a pall over the household. The slightest Sabbath faux pas would unleash a vicious response, ranging from verbal abuse to physical intimidation. Though Becca had never seen Moishe actually hit Esther, Becca feared that he only restrained himself in front of witnesses.

Becca was sixteen when Moishe moved in, and his only contribution to the household seemed to be gloom and domination. When he married Esther, Jewish law gave him control of his brother's estate, and his first fiduciary move was to stop supporting Becca. He saw no reason to finance her sacrilegious single life when she was of marriageable age. He would gladly pay for a matchmaker to arrange a suitable marriage, but he refused to support Becca's philistine lifestyle, even though the money came from her grandfather's estate.

Becca was in the first year of her master's at UCLA. She was forging a career, molding a future. Esther wanted, more than anything, for her granddaughter to be free and independent, to live a happier life than Esther's ever was. But Moishe was determined to quash Becca's dreams. Esther was distraught. She had survived the Nazis, but she was afraid to confront the totalitarian that God had commanded her to marry. So, she got a menial job to pay for the room and board that Moishe demanded of Becca. Esther rose before dawn to spend every day but the Sabbath sewing hundreds of left sleeves onto men's suits. She'd come home exhausted, eyes red from strain, hands aching. Ben would have been mortified by Esther's sacrifice. It broke Becca's heart. But her grandmother was adamant that she focus on school.

Moishe hardly earned the right to complain about Becca freeloading. He spent his days studying ancient Jewish texts in his *kollel*, a yeshiva or seminary for married men. Most *kollel* students stayed for a year or two after their marriage before leaving to pursue a career. But Moishe chose to make religious study his life's work. He'd been hard at it for more than two decades, and for his efforts, he brought home a paltry stipend of $200 a month. Hardly enough to pay for his kosher matzoh balls.

"How can you put up with him?" Becca asked her nana.

Esther didn't respond. Becca realized she hadn't heard. Becca raised her voice.

"How can you put up with him? You could have your own life. Be happy for a change."

"Who am I to argue with the Torah?" Esther replied. "The rabbi said this marriage was decreed in Deuteronomy."

"Nana, no one practices *yibum* anymore. Not even the Hasidim."

"Well, Rabbi Goldman does."

Becca knew she was fighting a lost cause. Rabbi Goldman had been her grandfather's best friend since childhood. The two of them had met Esther in Auschwitz when all three were barely teens. The trio banded together in the camp and somehow managed to survive. They remained close-knit after the war, and immigrated together to the United States. Ben and Esther went on to marry, and their third wheel went on to become a respected religious scholar. As far as Esther was concerned, Rabbi Goldman was as close to God as a man could get. His word was gospel, his opinion sacrosanct.

🌸

Esther's left hip was killing her as the sun set a good ten minutes before she reached her block. She felt her shopping basket bump over a crack in the sidewalk and looked back to see an overpriced kosher brisket bounce out. It took enormous effort for her to stoop for the six-pound roast, and when she stood up, her heart was hammering. As a two-time cardiac arrestee, she was already dreading the chest pain she'd have if she managed to survive the stairs. Almost as much as she dreaded her husband's wrath when she walked in late.

Passing the building next door, Esther looked up to see her *shikse* tramp of a neighbor in her front window working on this week's smutty display. The girl was tying some sort of whip to her mannequin. A memory slammed Esther like a head-on collision—a Nazi guard, in front of the disrobing barracks in Auschwitz, flogging her mother's naked body with his belt.

As Esther's anguish roiled, the door to the girl's building opened, and a lanky young man in a sleeveless shirt and a Pizza Pronto cap came bouncing out like a toddler who'd had too much birthday cake. She wondered what sort of *goyishe* fashion craze had prompted this boy to wear such fancy athletic shoes without laces.

🌸

Jason Jarvish was reliving the soft pressure of Holly's lips when the old lady blurted, "Hey, you!"

Startled, he stopped in his tracks. "Me?"

"Yeah, you," she said. "I live next door. But I can't push the elevator button now that it's Shabbes. It sure would be nice if some person should just happen to push the fourth floor."

"You want me to push your elevator button?"

"That I can't ask. It's forbidden. But it sure would be nice if some person just happened to be passing by."

Her tone made him smile. Even at her ancient age, she had that same flirty lilt in her voice that reminded him of his beloved grandmother, may she rest in peace.

He watched a dollar bill seem to fall from her pocket and flutter to the ground.

She acted surprised. "Whoops. Oh well. I can't touch money on the Sabbath. You should just keep it."

He looked at the dollar, then back at her.

"The Sabbath?"

"It starts at sundown every Friday."

"Okay," he said, snatching the bill.

As Jason accompanied the old lady into her building, he was still thinking about the babe who'd just devoured him. He'd seen lookers like that come on to pizza delivery guys in online porn, but he never thought those things happened in real life, especially not to nobodies like him.

Ever the practical businessman, Jason had called his manager at Pizza Pronto and begged out of deliveries for the rest of the night, claiming his car had broken down. With Holly commandeering his blood flow, he envisioned an evening—okay, maybe a half hour—of pure porned-out bliss. Little did he know she could suckle him to climax in less time than it took her to delace his shoes. The lady had talent, even if it cost him an evening's tips, which he could ill afford to lose.

"You waiting for a bus?"

Jason realized he was standing in the elevator, staring into space. He'd zoned out on the old lady.

"Sorry," he said, and punched the fourth-floor button.

"You know, I had a dream last night," she said. "A nice *goyish* boy came into my kitchen and turned a back burner on low. Then he covered the range with a metal sheet I keep there."

He wasn't sure how she did it but, out of nowhere, a ten-dollar bill drifted, like a feather, to the elevator floor.

❧

Moishe frowned at the smell of his own armpits. He'd been so preoccupied with Esther's absence that he'd forgotten to take his customary pre-Shabbes shower. Now he was stewing in his own stink, and if he wanted a shower, it would have to be cold. No hot water on Shabbes.

Esther's key finally clicked in the lock, derailing his train of thought. For maximum effect, he twisted his face into a glower, but the well-practiced expression faltered when he saw a blond-haired boy follow his harried wife into the apartment.

"The traffic you wouldn't believe," said Esther. "I could have baked this brisket by the time my *farkakteh* bus got to Fairfax. In fact, I could have raised the cow."

"Never mind the cow," said Moishe. "What's with the boy?"

"Who, him? I was running so late, I found us a Shabbes goy."

❧

Jason reacted hesitantly to Esther's descriptor, wondering whether he'd just been insulted. "A what?"

"Someone who's not Jewish," said Esther. Then, suddenly worried, "You're not Jewish, are you?"

"Evangelical Lutheran," he said. "Lapsed. My mother—"

"Mazel tov," interrupted Moishe, clearly uninterested in the boy's life story.

"Good," said Esther. "Because if you were Jewish, this wouldn't work."

"What wouldn't work?" said Jason.

"Being a Shabbes goy," said Moishe. "A non-Jew can do things on Shabbes that we can't, according to our laws, which are ancient, by the way."

"That's what the elevator was about?"

"Clever *boychik*," said Esther.

"What's wrong with pushing a button?" said Jason.

"The rabbis have spoken," said Moishe. "If a person completes an electric circuit it's the same thing as starting a fire."

"A biblical no-no," said a young woman's voice behind him.

Jason turned to see a prim, twentyish girl in a modest gray dress that cloaked her from her neck to midcalf. Thick black knee socks completed the cover-up. Her only nod to fashion were some small gold-hoop earrings, though in the poor light, he thought he saw some unoccupied piercings. She looked plain, yet he found her strangely attractive, as if her modesty veiled a buried treasure.

"According to the book of Exodus," the girl continued, "if you make a fire on the Sabbath, it's punishable by death."

"You kill people for calling an elevator?"

"We don't," said Moishe. "God does."

"If he decides to," added Esther, "which he usually doesn't."

"Does the goy have a name?" the girl asked Esther. "Or didn't you ask?"

Jason was amused by the way she teased the old woman. Esther let slip a coy grin—another reminder of his grandmother.

"I'm Jason," he said.

"Becca," said the girl.

The conversation was suddenly overwhelmed by the pounding intrusion of bass-thumping rap music.

"Oy," said Moishe. "That *farshtunkeneh shikse* again."

"I know her," said Jason. "I can try to talk to her if you want."

"No," said Becca. "I'll go. You've got things to do here."

𐤎

"You didn't start the *blekh*?" asked Esther.

"Don't look at me," said Moishe. "You're the one who came late."

"So we should eat cold food all Shabbes?"

"What do I know about the blekh?"

"What's to know? It goes on the stove."

"But for setting it up you need an advanced degree," he said.

"Oy." Esther shook her head. "You put a burner on low, then you put the blekh over the top so no accidental cooking can go on." She looked pointedly at Jason. "Am I right?"

"You want me to . . . ?" Jason started to ask, but she held up her hand to cut him off. Then she nodded toward the metal sheet by the stove.

"I study the Talmud, not the kitchen," said Moishe, watching Jason approach the stove. "You want I should defile the Sabbath to make up for your neglect? God forbid I should make the blekh too hot and violate the rules."

"What kind of rules?" asked Jason as he selected a knob on the stove to ignite a back burner.

"Don't ask," said Esther, then proceeded to answer. "You can leave a pot of cooked liquid, like soup or tea, on the blekh before sundown, but you can't *put* one on after. If you have a pot already on the blekh, you can't pour cold liquid into it. You can warm a pot on top of another pot that's already on the blekh, but only if it's got liquid in it that's already cooked, not solid food like chicken or kugel. You can't put solid food on the blekh, but you can put it on the counter next to the blekh to take the chill off, as long as it doesn't get to a hundred thirteen degrees. How you're supposed to measure a hundred thirteen degrees, I wouldn't know since you can't use a thermometer unless it's the old-fashioned kind. But if you have to shake the mercury down, you can't. You want tea? Don't pour hot water on the leaves because that would be cooking. So you can pour water that was heated before sundown into a dry cup, then pour that water into a second cup, then finally onto a tea bag in a third cup. And after all that, it's forbidden to lift the tea bag out of the cup."

"Holy moly," said Jason. He lowered the blekh onto the stovetop, making sure the lip covered the control knobs.

"I get a headache just keeping it all straight," said Esther. "Some *meshugene* day of rest. The rules are more work than the work they're supposed to forbid."

"Now you question the Rabbis?" said Moishe.

His voice was edgy. A warning shot. Jason felt hackles tingle on the back of his neck.

"What do you know?" Esther shot back. "You study the Talmud all day and don't even know from lighting the stove."

"What do I know?" His voice rose in fury. "I know you failed God and your family. That I know. And you failed to light the candles eighteen minutes before sundown. You failed to put up the blekh. You failed to put our food up to warm. You failed our daughter by raising a grandchild who comes home reeking of bacon. You failed our family by wasting money on luxuries like a Shabbes goy. Those things I know. You should grovel in the filth of a pigsty for the failure you bring on this house!"

She turned from Moishe to face Jason. He could see her tearing up.

"Wouldn't it be nice," she said, "if someone would put some tape on the automatic light switch inside the fridge?"

Jason suspected she'd turned to him to hide her hurt from Moishe, and the intimacy of the moment felt awkward. At the same time, the depth of sadness he saw in her eyes infuriated him, reminding him of his grandfather, who used to fuel himself with Jim Beam and keep his wife in check with his fists. Jason had always dreamed of pounding the man into a pool of bloody sludge, and now his fists cramped from the urge to do the same to Moishe.

❦

Becca had flutters in her belly as she rang Holly's doorbell. When the door opened, Holly greeted her with a poker face.

"We're trying to make a Shabbes dinner," said Becca. "Do you really have to crank the music again?"

Holly's broke into a grin. "It's my way of getting to see you earlier on Fridays."

"Bullshit."

Holly reached out and stroked Becca's cheek. "I don't get enough of you."

Becca took Holly's hand and kissed it. "I'll come over after the grandies turn in. Should be around ten, assuming your music doesn't keep them up."

"The music's done its job." Holly crossed the living room and lowered the volume. "Your Nana doing any better?"

"She'll be depressed until he stops grinding her down. It just kills me to watch. I worry about her health. Her heart's not in great shape."

Holly pulled Becca into a hug. Becca lowered her head to Holly's shoulder dejectedly.

"Baby, don't worry," said Holly. "We'll do it. Soon."

She stroked Becca's hair.

"I saw your Nana talking to the pizza guy today," said Holly. "What was that all about?"

"She brought him up to the apartment."

"Shopping for a new husband?"

"I wish."

"Well I hope she's not after a good fuck. The pizza guy's not too long on stamina."

"You slept with him?"

"Baby, I wouldn't do that to you," said Holly, gently brushing a black curl out of Becca's eyes. "I only gave him a blowjob."

"Jeez, Holly." Becca was torn between feeling hurt and amused. She knew sex was merely recreational when Holly toyed with boys. But that didn't stop Becca from wrestling with jealousy.

"You shoulda seen his face when I offered." Holly laughed.

Becca fought the urge to say something catty.

"I think he's going to be my grandmother's new Shabbes goy," she said.

"What's that?"

"It's a non-Jew who can do forbidden chores on the Sabbath. Turn on lights, change the TV channel, stuff like that."

Holly mulls this over. "This is like a weekly thing? He'll go to their apartment?"

"Yeah."

"Shit, Becca. He could be the guy we've been talking about."

"You think pizza boy could . . ." Becca struggles for the right words. "Take care of Moishe?"

"Why not? We've been trying to figure out a way to get somebody access. This guy's already in their apartment. In their lives."

Becca struggled with the concept. She'd had an image of "the guy" from old movies—a jaded, mature man, like John Garfield in *The Postman Always Rings Twice* or Fred MacMurray in *Double Indemnity*. Jason didn't fit the part.

"He seems kind of . . . too nice," she said.

"Nice?"

"Like the kind of guy who would be shocked and disgusted if we asked him to do this. Maybe even call the cops."

"That could be true of anybody," said Holly. "We just have to cultivate him. At least I've already got my hooks in this guy. And don't forget, he's got access."

Becca reflected on the moral hedging she'd already done to get to this point in their planning. It wasn't easy for either one of them to move beyond their aversion to the act of murder. And once they managed that, it became a question of who would actually do the reprehensible deed. While neither woman had an issue with whipping a guy, or working him with oversized sex toys, taking a life was another matter altogether. Especially when they contemplated the aftermath: dealing with the body, dealing with the cops, dealing with the courts, dealing with the relentless memory.

In the classic noir movies, femmes fatales always found a fall guy, a willing man with a broken moral compass and a weakness for immoral women. But this was real life. What if they propositioned the wrong guy? A guy with a moral compass that worked?

꙳

Jason smelled something foul before he even opened the door to his apartment. His roommates had been cooking while stoned again. Last time, they'd had to buy two new pans to replace the ones they'd burned beyond salvation. Another twenty bucks down the drain.

He walked into the stench. His landlord, a short, round man who called himself Rambo, was standing by the counter in the kitchenette, staring at a sink full of dishes that had sat unwashed so long that the bottom of the stack sprouted green mold.

"This place is a pigsty," said Rambo.

"You're supposed to give twenty-four hours' notice to come in here," said Jason.

"And you're not supposed to have roommates, but the place looks like a crash pad."

"They're just visiting."

"I'm not an idiot, Jason. You think I don't hear what goes on from the other tenants? I've had it. You've got sixty days from the first of next month to get out."

"You can't do that. I have a lease."

"Yeah, well, your lease says no one lives here without my written consent. I never approved anybody but Sharon."

Her name hit Jason like a cluster bomb. He still couldn't fathom how the one girl who'd ever claimed to love him had left him. Not that he didn't get why she split. He just couldn't comprehend what had taken her so long to see through him, or why she'd even fallen for him in the first place.

"Your lease is as broke as you are," Rambo continued, then stomped out without waiting for a reply.

Jason felt like someone was trying to bust out of his head with a jackhammer. He opened a kitchenette cabinet and grabbed a bottle of aspirin.

When he'd leased the place to live with Sharon, her parents had paid the rent, thinking she was subletting. They had no idea that her boyfriend was living with their daughter on their dime. When Sharon dumped Jason, he found himself stuck with a lease for a rathole that was far beyond his means. But if Rambo kicked him out, he'd have nowhere else to go. His deadbeat dad had died years ago and his mother lived on Social Security in a VA nursing home. His only other relative was a cousin so far removed that Jason hadn't heard from her in more than a decade, and his few friends were worse off.

Jason shook four aspirin from the bottle and swallowed them dry. He crossed the living room to the claustrophobic bedroom he used to share with Sharon but now shared with a Chicagoan named Friedrich who snored like a chainsaw. Jason flopped onto his saggy bed and one of his shoes fell off. He smiled at the memory of Holly relieving him of his laces.

As improbable as it seemed, according to Esther's straight-laced granddaughter, Holly actually liked him. Maybe he could see her again. Mrs. Gutterman had offered him ten dollars a week to come every Friday evening and do whatever Shabbes chores might need doing. Ten bucks wasn't much, but he liked the old lady. She reminded him of his grandmother, and he liked the feeling. He also felt a protective urge, having witnessed her humiliation at the hands of her jerkwad husband.

Besides, if he got to see Holly, the ten bucks was gravy. The idea of a woman who could be so nonchalant about sex was infatuating in and of itself. Maybe the committed relationship he'd had with Sharon—which had gone down in flames anyway—wasn't the only way to fly. He hadn't given it much thought. He'd just assumed it was the way of all flesh. But why couldn't flesh be an end in itself?

Jason reached into his pocket and pulled out the Post-it from Holly that Becca had given him. Holly's penmanship had a graceful, curvaceous precision that reminded him of the love notes his first girlfriend used to pass him in eighth grade English. He imagined Holly's pen dancing across the page in her soft hand. The vision made him hard.

For the first time since he'd dropped out of high school, Jason felt like something was going his way. He dug into his pocket for the 1901 Indian Head penny that he'd found on the floor of a McDonald's restroom when he was fifteen. His good luck charm. He gave it a kiss.

꠸

Jason was determined to wait until the following day to contact Holly. He knew he'd seem like a loser if he called or texted right away. Instead, he killed ninety minutes streaming a classic Stormy Daniels film. Seven minutes after the movie's climactic ending, his determination crumbled.

"Hi, it's Jason."

"Oh, hi." He strained to catch anything in her tone that might indicate that he'd blown it but she sounded pleased to hear his voice.

"Is it cool that I called?" he asked.

"I was hoping you would," she said. "I felt a little guilty the way I rushed you out when you were here. I was kind of focused on my work."

"Work?"

"The mannequin. She's an art project I'm journaling for school."

He knew nothing about art and had no idea what journaling was. "Well, don't feel bad. I had a fantastic time. Not that . . . I mean, it was great to meet you and everything. Even though . . . I gotta say I felt a little guilty about not, you know . . . giving back."

"I'm free right now. What are you up to?"

She was too good to be true.

❦

Holly stared at the horse-tail butt plug in the online catalog and wondered how she might attach it to her mannequin without drilling a hole. If she cut the plug part off and stuck the tail on with some sort of adhesive, would it still be a butt plug? And would that lack of veracity undermine the conceptual aspect of her piece? She thought about Chris Burden crucifying himself to a Volkswagen bug and wondered if it would still have been art if he had used duct tape instead of nails.

Her ruminations were interrupted by the doorbell. Jason. Time to switch gears from art to artifice. She opened the door to find him holding a bouquet of flowers. Supermarket daisies, already drooping. But the gesture was sweet.

"Hey, handsome," she said. "Those for me?"

"Too corny?"

In response, she moved in and gave him a kiss that was so French, her tongue triggered his gag reflex.

"Wow," he said.

"Get your ass in here." She grabbed the front of his T-shirt and pulled him inside. He skittered in like an exuberant puppy on a slick floor and she knew he was hers to do with as she pleased.

She led him into the kitchen and settled him on a stool to watch her trim the flowers and arrange them in an empty pickle jar.

"Nice place," he said. "You live here alone?"

"Yeah. But I'm thinking about getting a roommate."

"Yeah?"

She ran some water into the jar.

"Cash is pretty tight," she said. "Why? You interested?"

"For sure. My landlord's kicking me out."

She opened the freezer and took out two iced beer mugs.

"What did you do?" she asked.

"Nothing. He's just an asshole."

She pulled an IPA from the fridge and popped it open. She wanted him to get used to her making choices for him, so she didn't ask him what he'd like to drink before she poured it. He eagerly accepted the frosted IPA.

"Let me show you my boudoir," she said, wondering whether he knew the word. "I've got just the thing to cheer you up."

❧

As he followed her down the hallway, Jason free-associated the names of sexual positions he'd seen on the web—cowgirl, reverse cowgirl, reverse cowgirl with a twist, reverse cowgirl double salchow—but nothing in his wildest fantasies prepared him for what he encountered in the bedroom.

The room was dominated by a ceiling-high, black steel frame that looked like a thick line drawing of a cube. It surrounded a king-size platform bed upon which, looking strikingly alluring, wearing nothing but a red sheet draped over her legs, lay Becca.

It took a moment for Jason to register that this sexpot was Esther's observant Orthodox Jewish granddaughter, the unassuming young woman he'd met a few hours earlier during the observance of Shabbes. When he'd last seen her, she'd been modestly clothed from head to toe, according to the ancient laws of Judaism. Now she lay naked, according to the ancient laws of nature.

Holly smiled at Jason. "Do you mind if my friend joins us?"

Visions of threesomes danced in his head. Jason was unaccustomed to dreams coming true, especially twice in one day, and this was one he'd harbored since he was twelve, when his friend Danny's older brother introduced him to porn.

All he could think to say was "I thought you kept kosher."

❧

The two women transported Jason to heights of rapture that racked him from head to soul. They opened new worlds for him, exploring intimacies he'd never known, sensations he'd never felt. When the three lay fully depleted, exhausted, drenched in each other's sweat, entangled in each other's arms, it felt like heaven on earth. It seemed like they couldn't get enough of each other, and after three or four more ecstatic sprees, he'd fallen wildly and completely in love with them both.

Over the next two months, the three lovers managed to rendezvous three or four times a week, including every Friday following Shabbes dinner, after Esther and Moishe retired for the night.

When Jason was forced out of his apartment, Holly invited him to move into her spare bedroom. Though the arrangement was supposed to be temporary, they shared a tacit understanding that he could stay as long as the relationship between the three of them continued to flourish.

Meanwhile, the Gutterman Shabbes ritual was becoming second nature to Jason. And as he became accustomed to the proper setup of the blekh and various other chores that Esther would occasionally neglect, he realized that her serial oversights were not accidents, but passive aggressive expressions of the frustration and heartache she suppressed.

Moishe seemed impervious to the pain he inflicted. In fact, his transgressions were increasingly flagrant. When he'd first met Jason, he'd affected a pretense of civility, but it waned as he grew inured to the Shabbes goy's presence. The more time Jason spent with the Guttermans, the more brazenly Moishe mistreated Esther. His sadistic arrogance turned Jason's stomach, increasingly grating on the limits of the Shabbes goy's tolerance.

※

Becca and Holly continued to ravage Jason with every sexual technique in their arsenal. He had been understandably nervous about their more adventurous forays, but the women were patient with him, and things that had alarmed him at first became activities that his lovers trained him to enjoy. In the process, they also trained him to obey.

Before long, he'd become not only willing but grateful to do whatever they asked of him.

One night, as he was lashing Becca to the bedposts, she burst into tears. The erotic ambiance evaporated like a water-drop on a hot griddle. Jason was panic-stricken.

"I'm sorry," she said. "The ropes, the restraint . . . I started thinking about Nana, about the ties that hold her down. I mean, she escaped the fucking concentration camps. Yet, now she's back under some bastard's thumb. And that asshat control freak thinks he's doing God's work! I wish God would just smite him once and for all."

"You need to get out of there," said Jason, untying her hands.

"Move in with us," said Holly.

"She'd kill herself if I left. I mean, literally. Slice her wrists. I'm the one thing that keeps her sane." Becca broke down again.

Jason wrapped her in his arms and held her tight. Desolation rolled over them all like a fog.

"It's okay," said Jason.

"No, it's not," said Holly.

"You know I love you, Becca," he said. "I'd do anything to make you happy."

"Really?" She gave him a lingering kiss, washing his cheeks with her tears.

For days, Becca's spirits continued to flag, and her feelings proved contagious. Finally, one night over Ethiopian takeout, Jason hit the wall.

"I can't watch you suffer anymore," he said.

"Let's tell him," said Holly.

"Tell me what?"

"We have a plan," said Becca. "Nana thinks her misery is God's will. She'll never leave Moishe on her own. So, we need to emancipate her."

Jason wasn't surprised as she outlined their proposal. He had come to the same conclusion and had already primed himself for the sordid nature of the task. The details seemed almost anticlimactic in comparison, as if the means justified the end.

Their roles were clear-cut: Becca would distract Esther; Jason would do the deed; and Holly would corroborate Jason's alibi.

"I'll be at the table with Nana," said Becca. "Her back is to the hallway where she sits, so she won't see you do anything."

"What if she hears something?" said Jason.

"Are you kidding? She's deaf as a snail."

"Okay," he said. "So, I make an excuse to leave while you're still eating."

"Right. I'll wait ten or fifteen minutes, then pretend to hear him fall. That's when I'll find his body in the bathroom. Nana will think he died after you left, and that's what she'll tell the cops."

"What about the extension cord and everything?" asked Holly.

"When they ask who plugged the thing in, I'll say Moishe did," said Becca, "before sundown, so he could use it on Shabbes. It'll look like a suicide."

"You think the cops'll buy it?" said Jason, his voice aquiver with anxiety.

"I'll tell them you were with me," said Holly.

"And we'll have Nana to back up your alibi," said Becca. "Who's going to doubt an eighty-six-year-old Holocaust survivor?"

⅄

In her bedroom, Becca felt like the kindling was set. She just needed a match. Her thick woolen knee socks would do. She walked into the dining room just as Jason arrived. Esther was struggling, with shaky hands, to melt the bottoms of two Hanukkah candles, trying to glue them upright into crystal candle holders meant for wider candles.

"What kind of stupid idiot runs out of candles on the Shabbes?" asked Moishe.

"Leave her alone," said Becca.

Moishe turned to see that her lower calves and ankles were bare. He blanched.

"You let a goy see you dressed like this in my house?" he said, indicating Jason. "You look like a whore!"

"Moishe—" said Esther.

"Not one word from you!" he snapped.

His brow broke into a sweat as it always did when his temper flared.

He turned back to Becca, "You might as well walk in the street and sell sex like Jezebel."

She laughed at him, knowing the effect it would have.

"Jezebel never sold sex," she said derisively. "Is that the kind of bullshit they teach at your stupid *kollel*?"

Moishe's neck flushed and he lashed out, slapping Becca across the face, knocking her to the floor. Jason was mortified. If he'd had any second thoughts about dealing with Moishe, they were swept away by that one swipe of the man's hand.

Esther cowered in her chair, afraid to further antagonize her rabid husband. Becca picked herself up off the floor and defiantly sat down at the table. She glared at him as she calmly picked up a spoon and took a sip of soup.

Moishe took a napkin and wiped at the sweat on his forehead.

"Look how you got me worked up," he said.

"You should go shower," she said. "You stink like a pig."

He glowered at Esther, "You see the sacrilege you beget by being lenient with her in my house?"

"It's Nana's house. She pays the rent."

He wiped his forehead again, then extended the napkin for her to see his sweat. "You see the filth you've spawned before God Himself? I feel polluted. I need to cleanse myself."

"You can say that again."

He stood. "And when I come back, I expect you to be dressed with proper modesty."

❧

Esther maintained a stoic façade, quietly sipping spoonfuls of chicken soup. Pretending to double-check the flame under the blekh, Jason sneaked down the hall behind her. He saw Becca watching him from the corner of her eye as he opened the door to a utility closet across from the bathroom where Moishe was showering.

Beside the furnace, Jason found the old-fashioned fuse box. He'd never seen one before. He read down the handwritten labels until he found the one marked "hallway." Wearing food gloves from Pizza Pronto to avoid leaving fingerprints, he unscrewed the glass fuse and stuck his lucky Indian Head into the socket behind it. He used the eraser end of a pencil to seat the copper coin, then replaced the fuse to secure it in place. The fuse was now bypassed, the circuit unprotected from overload.

He listened to the water running in the shower and tried not to think about what he was about to do as he pulled an extension cord from his waistband and plugged it into an outlet in the hallway. As Becca had explained, they couldn't use the outlet in the bathroom, because the building code required it to have its own fuse—a ground-fault detector—which could have defeated the plan.

Becca came up behind Jason with Moishe's curling iron. Jason took it and weighed it in his hand, assessing how much heft it would add to the burden of his anxiety. As Becca returned to the dining room, he ran his finger down the crack in the casing where she'd loosened the screws to make sure water could get into the wiring. Ceding his qualms to resignation, Jason plugged the God-forbidden appliance into the live extension cord.

His heart was pounding like a low-rider's stereo. His hand, gripping the thick plastic handle, wouldn't stop shaking no matter how hard he willed it to.

He opened the bathroom door and stepped inside. The tiled room felt icy. He was struck by the conspicuous absence of steam from the cold shower. *In this bathroom, on this Sabbath,* thought Jason, *hot water would be the least of all sins.*

He steeled himself and whipped the shower curtain aside. The reality of Moishe's naked, hairy, overstuffed body took Jason by surprise, even though he'd imagined this scene many times, and even rehearsed it. But a flesh and blood human being cranked the moral magnitude to the max. Beset by unexpected misgivings, Jason froze.

Then Moishe shrieked. "Get out of here, you *goyish shtik drek*!"

Jason didn't know what the Yiddish meant, but he knew it was a gross insult, and his adrenaline surged. He thrust the iron against Moishe's fleshy chest, just above heart level. Even through the nonconductive handle, he could feel the jolt of current that surged through Moishe's heart, coursing toward the metal shower drain in the water by his feet. Moishe's eyes popped wildly open and his legs gave out. He collapsed like a dead weight to the tiled floor, grasping for the shower curtain as if it were a lifeline. The curtain and its rod came crashing down.

Jason smelled something foul and realized it was burnt flesh, an odor he'd never smelled before. He felt like throwing up.

א

Jason returned to the dining room looking ashen. "I don't feel too good," he said. "I think I'll go home and lie down."

"Feel better," said Becca, silently thanking God for her grandmother's hearing problems.

"*Gut Shabbes,*" said Esther.

After Jason left, Becca waited about fifteen minutes before saying, "Did you hear something?"

"No," said Esther. "Not just now."

Becca excused herself and headed down the hallway to investigate.

❧

Holly's stomach had started to cramp as soon as Jason left for the fatal Shabbes. For the hour he was gone, she sat clutching her belly, wondering when the pain would go away. Then she heard his key in the lock and her stomach unclenched.

"Well?" she said, impatiently. Then she saw his face and softened. "Oh, baby. Are you okay? Was it horrible?"

He closed his eyes and took a deep breath. "It was worse than horrible. But it's over."

She came to him and pulled him close, stroking the back of his head, as his tears silently flowed.

❧

Becca barely had time to pull on her modest knee socks before two uniformed policemen arrived. They herded her into the living room and instructed her to stay there.

Esther was already sitting in the rear of the room, rocking back and forth, staring vacantly out the window.

Though Becca had not been naïve enough to expect it, she had harbored the hope that Esther would respond to Moishe's death with joy and relief, as if she were reliving her liberation from Nazi internment. Becca had imagined her grandmother being a woman unchained, free to dress as she liked, eat what she liked, live her beliefs as she liked and, most importantly, enjoy her twilight years with her granddaughter.

But so far Esther was acting depressed, floating in an emotional limbo whose exit could be anywhere. This was not encouraging, but Becca prayed it was short-lived.

Becca's own state of mind was another story. When she was devising the plan for Moishe's elimination, Becca had been doubtlessly clear-headed. But in the aftermath, nothing seemed clear anymore. She'd felt confident that the police would buy whatever she tried to sell them. Now the prospect of an investigation filled her with fear. She'd anticipated a rush of relief when Moishe died. Now she felt haunted by the vision of his ugly, broken body, half in and half out of the shower, blood staining the floor tile where he'd fallen. And the last thing she would have predicted was guilt, yet she was swimming in it.

Becca sat on the couch and watched the shorter of the two cops head down the hall to assess the body. The taller stayed with her and Esther. After a moment, the shorter one returned, reporting that he'd called for detectives.

A half hour later, the doorbell rang. Becca was surprised to see Esther get up to answer.

The two detectives supplied names that Becca failed to register. She thought of them as "Holmes" and "Watson." She wondered what Watson's purpose was since Holmes did most of the talking.

Esther returned to her seat in the back of the room and resumed her blank stare out the window.

Holmes pulled a small notebook and a pencil from his coat pocket and addressed Becca. "Where were you when Mr. Gutterman had his . . ." To Watson, "Whaddaya call it?"

"Disagreement with the electrical system," said Watson.

"Yeah, that." Holmes swallowed a chuckle.

Becca was caught off guard by their tactlessness.

"I was at the dining table," she said, "with my grandmother."

Holmes glanced at Esther, who gave a confirming nod without turning to meet his eye.

"And that's when you heard him scream?" he said to Becca.

"Not scream," she replied. "More like someone crying out in pain. And there was this crash, I guess when he fell."

"The door was closed with the shower running, but you still heard him fall?"

"Yes."

"There was no one else in the apartment besides you, your grandmother and the victim?"

Before Becca could reply, Esther said, "The Shabbes goy was here."

Becca felt the walls come tumbling down. The entire construct of Moishe's suicide narrative depended on Esther buying into Becca's charade of hearing a commotion fifteen minutes after the actual death. Jason's alibi depended on it. And if Jason went down, Becca and Holly would surely follow.

As much as Becca loved her Nana, she thought the old woman was close to doddering, hard of hearing, and susceptible to suggestion. She never dreamed that Esther would be able to not only hear but also register Moishe's fall. Now her grandmother had taken an axe to the timeline they needed like a tent-pole to hold up their story.

"Nana," she said. "Jason had already gone home. Don't you remember?"

Becca shot her grandmother a pleading look. If Esther received the message, she didn't show it.

"Where can we find this Shabbes guy?" said Watson.

"It's *goy*," said Becca.

"It could be *gay* for all I care. Where do we find him?"

❧

"Esther's old," said Jason, terrified. "She forgets things. That's why they hired me. To do things she forgets."

"So where were you when Mr. Gutterman went off to shower?"

"Next door. The old man was still eating dinner when I left. I wasn't feeling too good."

Holmes started to jot this down in his notebook. "I think you're hiding something," he said without looking up from his writing.

"If Becca says he was gone, he was gone," said Esther.

They all turned, surprised. Jason breathed an inner sigh of relief. Then Watson walked into the room.

"Lookie what I found," he said, and held up Jason's Indian Head penny in his latex-gloved hand. "It was jumping the fuse for that plug in the hall."

Jason felt the truth closing in like a swarm of killer bees. He looked helplessly to Becca.

"That was my step-grandfather's," said Becca. "His good luck charm."

"I didn't know Jews believed in lucky charms," said Holmes.

"A locust's egg, a jackal's tooth . . ." said Esther. "It's in the Mishnah."

"The huh?" said Watson.

"If my Becca says it was Moishe's, it was Moishe's," said Esther.

"So you think he set this all up himself?" said Holmes.

"He was a very unhappy man," said Becca.

"Is that right, Mrs. Gutterman?" said Holmes.

"I don't know from what's happy," she said. "But my Moishe said many times he wanted to do this thing."

Holmes and Watson looked to each other askance, not sure what to make of this.

"You coulda mentioned this before," said Watson.

She shrugged. "I'm eighty-six years old. So is my brain."

Holmes checked his notes. "And you're saying he plugged the iron in himself and took it into the shower?"

"He would have plugged it in before sunset," said Becca, "and left it on."

"Why's that?" asked Holmes.

"Shabbes," said Jason.

"Come again?" said Watson.

"It's the Jewish Sabbath," said Becca. "Our religious beliefs forbid us from plugging in, turning on, or even adjusting electrical things. That's why Moishe was taking a cold shower. Using hot would have triggered the water heater thermostat."

"But if the curling iron was already on, he could use it," said Jason.

"This whole thing don't smell right," said Watson.

"Such is life," said Esther.

"So all three of you claim that he committed suicide," said Holmes. "And *you*," to Jason, "claim you weren't here. And *you*," to the women, "claim neither one of you plugged that thing in and threw it in the shower."

"We couldn't," said Esther. "The rules of the Sabbath are holy law. If we break them, we answer to God."

"It's inviolable," said Becca. "God Himself is our alibi."

℣

It was late by the time the detectives left. They seemed unsatisfied, but there was little they could do if all three witnesses agreed and no physical evidence contradicted them.

Though it was still Shabbes, Esther took down the blekh to make tea on the stove.

Becca asked Holly to join them and Esther didn't object. When Holly showed up with a bottle of cognac, all four of them spiked their tea.

"Who would have thought he'd take his own life?" said Holly. "Don't Jews think that's a sin or something?"

"The Orthodox do," said Becca. "Moishe would have."

"He was a vain man," said Esther. "He'd never kill himself."

The three conspirators exchanged glances.

"But, Nana," said Becca, "you said . . ."

"I know what I said. And I know what you said. And I know what you did."

"But . . ."

"Don't worry, *bubeleh*. There's one thing I learned in the camps: if you sin in the fight against evil, God looks away."

To Catch a *Ganef*

Lizzie Skurnick

It all began when they moved to Jersey City, and Markus began to poop his pants. It was not gradual. Markus had been trained since he was two—Mei and Arnold had been somewhat smug about this—and had since had only the occasional pee accident. But now he was five, or nearly so—an age when you were absolutely, unequivocally *not* supposed to poop your pants. And here he was, doing it. Repeatedly.

"Darling? Are you okay?"

That had been Mei's reaction the first time—when she did not yet know that the poop was not a one-time affair; that the poop would soon destroy twenty pairs of underwear, her confidence as a parent, and reshape the arc of her career.

The Taekwando camp where she had placed him for the three weeks before school started called. She rushed over, sure he must have caught some exotic virus from the unfamiliar East Coast germs. The camp director explained the problem in the lobby, as the smell rose. Mei tried to keep a polite smile on her face. Then she yanked him out, still smiling, as if pooping in your pants was a normal event, like splitting your lip or projectile vomiting.

She placed her hand on Markus's forehead. It was cool. "Bed," she announced.

At home, she washed him down in the shower, then put him in the bath. The new bathroom was massive, with gray plank tiles and floating sink, but it didn't have a window. She would have opened it.

"So what happened, bud?" she asked, scrubbing Markus's head. He was unnaturally quiescent—because he was sick, or because he was ashamed of the poop, Mei had no idea. His head was topped with suds. All he needed was a cherry on top.

"Can I watch trains?" he asked.

Markus had recently become obsessed with trainspotting videos on YouTube, particularly a channel that specialized in trains that were forced to go up and down gradients. Most of these were in India or Mongolia, countries with too much sheer space to dig a straight line from one end of the line to the other. She had instituted a rule that none of the videos could be of a train that actually tipped over.

"Not today," she said. She dumped a bucket of warm water from the bath over his head, something she would have blasted Arnold for doing. He screamed. She kissed his wet head. He slapped her off.

As Mei dried his hair, she could not help thinking again that, though he was hers, he was objectively a beautiful child. Markus's deep chocolate eyes and smatter of brown freckles were an improbably mix of her po po and Arnold's zeyde, but it worked. The compliments were endless. Even when he was six months old, on the street, a teenage boy had called to his friends, "Guys! I just saw the most awesome baby!"

"One show," she amended. She'd been letting him watch too much YouTube. But how else could she unpack the enormous stack of boxes still hanging out in the corner, ready to collapse on the couch at any moment? How else would she get a minute to consider what her life had become—and how she could get some of the old one back?

❦

What had brought them to Jersey City? Well, Arnold's job, because at this time, he was the only one who had one. When they met in San Francisco, Mei had been a jewelry designer of some acclaim, featured in glossy local mags and high-end shops, with the occasional piece in a Garnet Hill or Sundance catalog.

Then, Arnold had still been a lowly manager in his father's corrugated box company. But when she got pregnant—shockingly—in the first month of trying, Mei had to decide if she wanted to gestate their one (mutual decision) child while soldering in a respiration mask. They had budgeted at least six months of fertility problems to figure out her time off. Instead, she was forced to sell off her remaining stock at a steep discount to one of her least favorite clients, an online boutique that sold her $300 bracelets alongside herbal constipation tea.

But, just as she was planning to ease back into the business, Arnold's father had died. It became clear that his *zeyde* had purchased several valuable—*very* valuable—waterfront properties his father had let languish. Arnold plugged the money into production. This allowed them to expand what had been a very little box company to a minor player in the lucrative new world of online orders. Now, every time Mei ripped open a package from the Gap or Amazon Fresh, she knew it was possible (not very, but *possible*) it came from the stock of Muehler Corrugated.

Muehler Corrugated had, of course, provided all the boxes for the move.

Mei had not intended to stop working. Her whole life, her po po had told her the story of how, when she was widowed early, she'd attended San Francisco University's nursing program at night while she worked at a laundry in the day. She wore gawdy costume jewelry with her whites, clip-on earrings and bracelets winking far too brilliantly to be real. Mei often thought that's how she had become a designer—pulling off her po po's ugly earrings and seeing how to make them better.

Mei had given up her studio long ago. When they moved, her entire business had been reduced to one box. It wasn't a Muehler box. It was bright red silk, padded, embroidered. It had been a gift from her grandmother. In it was a bag of solder, her gold, a velvet bag of precious stones, sapphires, and diamonds.

The remnants of her career. When she finally unpacked it, she realized she hadn't touched it in five years. Combined with her work, with her artistry, the box was worth many thousands. Without that, it was worth nothing to anyone but her.

❦

And then, like a tiresome guest, the pooping set in. It happened the next day, while Mei was touring a school. The Taekwando studio's owner was less pleasant, less understanding. It happened again that night, right before bedtime. The third time, the director gently explained the camp's policy on toilet training. Mei knew she could not try a fourth. "So *what* happens?" she asked on her last try. She had changed Markus in their bathroom, finding the scratchy toilet paper unequal to the task.

"The teacher says he's in the corner," she said.

"He puts him in the corner?"

The director widened her eyes. "Mrs. Muehler, we don't put our campers in the corner," she said.

"Ling," said Mei.

"Pardon?"

"My name is Ms. Ling."

"Ms. Ling, when Markus is ready to return to camp, let us know. Of course, we cannot offer refunds . . ."

While Markus was in the bath, Mei Googled "five-year-old who still poops" and "boy goes in his pants." She became lost in a sea of comment threads involving iPad and M&M bribes, cutting holes in diapers, and precise descriptions of how to catch the kids before they went into the corner. (No one wrote how to get the kid *out* of the corner in the first place.) Many parents described straining and pain, something called "Holding." One father wrote, "It took us about nine months for Andre to completely become comfortable again—"

Mei slammed the computer shut.

Mei went into the bathroom. "Bubs," she said. "Does it hurt?"

Markus looked up from the boat he was dunking. He lifted it and placed it on his head, and the water streamed down over his face. "What?" he said, his voice muffled.

"When you go. Does it hurt?"

Markus dipped his head back and began to drink the water. Mei snatched the boat out of his mouth. She had washed him off first, but what were the chances his own bacteria had gotten in the water? Wasn't human shit the dirtiest thing in the universe? She had read that somewhere. "Are you going at camp because it hurts?"

Markus began to hum the bluegrass version of "I've Been Working on the Railroad," the song with which his favorite trainspotter ended all of his videos. "Can I get out?" he asked.

"Five more minutes," Mei said. Markus gave a small cry of dismay, but he quickly stifled it when she gave him a look. She l`ooked in the fridge, but she knew it was empty of carrots and hummus—she hadn't been shopping while he was at camp. That night, she decided, she would feed him Oodles of Noodles—which could not be constipating, *right*?— and lay off the cheese and yogurt. She would add dried seaweed.

By the time Arnold came home, it was ten, and Markus was sleeping. Since she hadn't been able to go to the Korean grocery on the corner, the one with decent roughage, she had ordered their week's groceries from

Amazon Fresh, paying $17.99 for a morning delivery. Which meant she would have to stay home all next morning.

"How was today?" Arnold asked, whipping off his shirt. He did not wait for an answer. In the bathroom, she heard him splash his face, repeatedly.

"Fine," she said. He came back and sat on the couch, still breathing roughly. He grabbed the remote. "Can I take a look at the game?"

She was watching *The Crown*. She paused it.

"Give it a sec," she said. "So, something is happening with Markus."

"He's pinching again?" Arnold said, frowning. Markus had spent three months two years ago pinching his best friend, and Arnold still wasn't over it.

"No," said Mei. She weighed how to put it. "He's going in his pants."

"One or two?"

Mei let out a breath of relief. He saw the possibility it could be two, which meant "Two" might not be insane. "*Two*," she said.

Arnold sighed, then scratched the back of his head, where his balding was beginning to give his pale red hair the appearance of chicken fluff. "He's probably just too excited to stop," he said.

"Too excited to stop pooping?"

Arnold laughed, then put his arm around her. "Whatever he's doing," he said.

"Did you ever do that?"

"Probably."

Mei found it unlikely that Sondra, Markus's imperious mother, always impeccably turned out in Eileen Fisher—who had never, it had to be said, put on one piece of Mei's jewelry, ever—would have tolerated something as disgraceful as pants-pooping in any of her four sons. Then again, none of them had ever done anything wrong.

"Also, remember, this is a lot of new stuff," he said. She had thought of that, of course, but she could not explain how at odds this assessment seemed to be with Markus's general air of relaxation. He ate healthily, went to sleep swiftly, had had zero tantrums since they'd arrived, despite the new home, unpacked boxes, gang of left-behind friends, his father's absence, and general air of chaos. All of the reasons Sondra had said they shouldn't move.

"Why don't you bring him to the doctor?" he said.

"I still have to find a doctor," Mei said. "I haven't had time to see who our insurance covers."

"Pay out of pocket!"

Arnold, she remembered, had never seen the emergency room bills for Markus's broken toe and one nosebleed: $4K and $2K each—which only took them halfway through the deductible. She wasn't going to tell him that now.

"It's just, school starts in six weeks," she said. "He has to be trained."

Arnold laughed. "He'll be fine!" he said. "It's not like he'll go in a room full of kids." Mei did not point out that he was doing that anyway.

"Let's watch and wait," he said. He picked up the remote and switched it to TiVo.

Mei could have told him that "watch and wait" was not really watching. It was more like panicking, scraping out shit in a small bathroom, throwing away underwear, then taking him home to wash him twice—then washing her own hands and arms like she was scrubbing for surgery.

But Arnold, she had to admit, had been doing an unbelievable amount of work himself. His expanding of the business had revealed a genius she was slightly amazed to realize he had. Their retirement accounts were fully funded. His mother's account had enough to support her through decades of elder care (not that she seemed to be slowing down anytime soon). He had been generous with the brothers, who unwisely had declined to take over the small company, splitting the proceeds of the waterfront properties though they were in the company's name. And now, look at him—expanding Muehler Incorporated to the East Coast, practically personally. Hadn't she agreed to all this? What was changing five shits?

It would be fine. "Is there anything to eat?" Arnold asked. Mei barely heard him. In the utility closet, Markus's *gi* turned in the new washer/dryer. The wash cycle was supposed to be silent but had a low grumble, like someone turning over in their sleep.

❧

So it was that Mei began to bring Markus to Hamilton Park instead of camp—which looked beautiful, but in the pounding August heat, was covered with a low cloud of mosquitos that exactly matched Mei's mood.

The same thing happened every day. After Markus was dressed and fed, she would put him on the toilet with the iPad. Soon she realized that unless she sat in the bathroom with him, he would squirm off the toilet and watch the iPad on the bath mat. Once she found him on the floor, with the iPad, a poop in his pants. So each day, she sat.

After half an hour of nothing, they would go to the park. Markus, who made friends quickly, would run and shout with a changing cast of kids. She would look away for a moment—to check her phone, to smack a mosquito, to chat with another mother. It did not matter how brief. Markus would be gone. She would race through the park and find him somewhere, on all fours, the poop that had eluded them the night before and that morning firmly ejected.

"Markus! What is happening?" she asked. She could feel the other moms looking. "You're a big boy! No more pooping in the pants!"

"I can't help it, Mom," Markus would say. "I can't feel it."

"But when you sit down, you must feel it then!" she said. "Otherwise you wouldn't sit down!"

Markus gave her a shrug. "I just can't," he said.

On the day she met Dora, Mei had finally given in and brought a plastic bag to the park. Markus's poops had become a solid brown mass so thick it could be pulled off in one piece, like fondant. When Markus went, she would do what she had seen the people in the dog park do: pull the bag over her hand, grasp the poop with the makeshift glove, then snap it back and throw it in the trash. If she took him into the bushes and did it quickly, no one but the other moms would see.

The distracting agent that morning was no less than a pair of police officers. In a park where the previous week an old man chewing a cigar had been bawled out by no fewer than three mothers, they were a ludicrous sight: a lean young woman and a hefty older man, each weighted down with enough ordnance to take down an elephant.

"Ma'am, can we ask you a few questions?" the lean girl asked. At least she looked like a girl to Mei, who had turned thirty-six in May.

"Is everything okay?" Mei asked. Around her, women and nannies were bundling their charges into strollers and heading off on scooters, as if arrest was imminent.

"Ma'am, everything is fine. We are simply questioning people to see if anyone has noticed anyone strange. There has been a string of robberies around the park."

"Street robberies?" Mei said, panicking. She looked immediately around for Markus. He was nowhere. She rose. "I'm sorry, I—"

"*House* robberies," a voice interjected. Mei looked over. A diminutive old woman rapidly pushing a stroller back and forth looked oddly merry at the prospect. "I saw it on NJTV."

The hefty man frowned, then turned back to Mei. "That's correct, ma'am," he said. "There have been several. We're asking if anyone has seen anything strange."

"You think the thieves are maybe playing on the monkey bars?" the old woman said.

The young police officer grimaced, as if she were trying to humor the woman, but something in her face suggested she'd rather arrest her. "No, ma'am," she said gently. "We don't know exactly what we're looking for. That's why we're asking you."

"Are they, like, robberies at gunpoint?" Mei asked. It might not be too late to move back to San Francisco.

The police officers looked saddened, as if that might be preferable. "No ma'am," the man said. "Mostly small items—phones, cash, Grandma's earrings, you know. Normally we wouldn't make that much of it, but we're talking over twenty robberies this spring alone."

The idea of someone creeping through her apartment while she slept, pocketing Donald's iPhone 11 Pro Max and the $300 they always left in the coffee table drawer, was terrifying. It seemed unlikely, though. The building was a modern high-rise, with a doorman and its own security card. You needed a key card to get into the elevator, your hallway, to open the lock on your door so you could insert the key. You even needed a card for the dinky playroom, with its chewed-up Legos.

"You wouldn't make that much of it?" said the old woman at the same time Mei said, "We'll certainly keep an eye out."

"Appreciate it."

As the officers walked on, the old woman gestured pointedly at the young woman's rear. "Quite the hotsy-totsy," she said. "My sister wanted to be a police officer. Of course, she never would have filled out the uniform like that."

Despite herself, Mei laughed. "I'm sorry, I've just got to—"

"He's right there," the woman said, pointing.

And there was Markus, spinning on the tire, thank God, not on all fours in the corner beside the oak tree, the place he had successfully retreated to yesterday.

"Thank you," Mei said, deeply relieved. "Is this your—"

"I'm the babysitter," the woman announced. "Dora. Very nice to meet you."

"Nice to meet you too," Mei said. "I'm Mei."

The woman nodded, though something suggested she'd overheard this already. She was tiny—her feet barely reached the rubberized asphalt—but vigorous, keeping up an impressive pace with her withered claw on the handle of a carriage. "May I ask you something?" she asked.

Mei's heart sank. It would be about the poop. She had noticed them leaving each day, noticed Mei's checking his pants, her cry of dism—

"I have noticed something about the children when they are half-Oriental," Dora pronounced. Well, this was hardly better. Mei winced, looking around to see if there was a fellow mother to wince with. There was no one. "They all have this hair—this, what do you call it, color?"

Mei decided not to be angry. The woman was so teeny, so old, so small. She might be even older than Mei's own po po, who had gone out of her life calling her own nurses "colored."

"Auburn?" Mei said. Saying "Oriental," for Dora, might be progress. Dora had probably been alive when they still said "Mongoloid."

Anyway, Mei had quickly learned that the playground was an equal-opportunity place to offend. Most of the couples were interracial, and no children looked like their parent. A parent might not be easily placed either. A black parent might be from Haiti, Paris, or Cincinnati. An Indian parent could have just come from Delhi, or Denmark, or three generations deep in the suburbs of Pittsburgh. Parents might scream at their children in Spanish, but the Spanish could have been learned on a fellowship in Madrid or a life in the DR. Mei herself had almost certainly offended a Chinese woman raised in France last week.

"Auburn!" Dora said, pointing up at the air. "I always wanted that hair. Auburn." It was actually true—many of the half-Asian, half-Caucasian children Mei knew—and she knew quite a few—had Markus's auburn hair. Dora's own hair was sparse, fluffy, and white, bits of pink scalp peeking out where she'd put her barrette.

"Nap time," Dora announced, standing with some difficulty. It didn't seem to be a problem that the baby was already asleep. Mei leaned over to grasp Dora's elbow, but Dora shooed her away. "Oy gevalt!" she said. "You know what means oy gevalt?" She pronounced *what* with a hiss, like *voss*.

Mei did. "Like oy vey, she said. "But bigger."

Dora looked impressed. "Your husband's a Jew?"

"Yes."

"You didn't convert."

"No."

"I didn't know if Orientals can convert."

"Sometimes."

"Didn't you want to?"

"My husband didn't want me to."

Dora smiled, and Mei smiled back. "Feh," said Dora. "*Nisht geferlekh*. You know what means '*nisht geferlekh*'?"

"No," Mei said.

"No biggie," Dora said, and smiled. "*Nisht geferlekh*. When I was a girl, there was no Torah for us either."

࿐

It was true that Arnold had not cared one way or the other if she had converted. But it was also true that Mei had no intention of putting herself through whatever it would have been to try.

She had gone to school with a woman—a half-Jewish, half-Korean woman—who looked entirely Korean. She had become a cantor, then a rabbi, and now led one of the chief congregations in New York. Mei also knew from news stories over the years how she had suffered, how many rabbis had rejected her, had told her she could not study Talmud. She had been an object of curiosity, hostility, derision. It was, she had said, only her faith that had sustained her.

But if Mei was off the hook, Markus was a different story. Grandma Sondra had already paid for his lavish bris—and an equally expensive surgeon to perform it. It was she who bought the tickets for Yom Kippur services they attended as a family, even while Markus was in a sling. Each Passover, they sat around her Seder table as the four Muehler boys and their children chanted, washing and dipping and eating and singing. On Rosh Hashanah, they blew the ram's horn. Yom Kippur, they fasted.

The other Muehler wives, two California Jewish, and a Minnesota Lutheran who had converted—seemingly adored these events. They would gather in the kitchen around Sondra, resplendent in caftan, checking the brisket, chopping the *kharoset*, whipping egg whites, and shooing away children.

Mei had tried. She had really tried. And it wasn't that Sondra was racist, necessarily. Mei thought she could tell that she just wasn't that interested.

Had Sondra started it, or had she? Did it start at Markus's Hundred Days party, which Sondra begged off because "they had already done the bris"? Or was it back when Mei brought her moon cakes from one of Chinatown's best bakeries, and Sondra forgot to serve them? Mei's own mother invited Sondra to the large party she threw every Chinese New Year. Without fail, Sondra said she didn't like to go to Chinatown. Mei's mother didn't live in Chinatown. She lived in a large condo she had wisely purchased right before the boom, with a back deck and spotless white carpeting.

And Sondra had never invited her mother once—not once—to Shabbat.

Arnold liked to joke that Mei and Sondra didn't get along because Jews and Chinese were "too alike." "We're cheap, overbearing, and we know how to load on the guilt!" he would say. But Sondra was *anything* but cheap, and it wasn't guilty she made Mei feel.

Here's how she made her feel. One day, when he was three, on the way to see Sondra, Markus asked Mei how to say "grandma" in Chinese. Markus ran up to Sondra, yelling, "Ma Ma! Ma Ma!" Sondra reminded him that *Mei* was his Mama, not *her*.

"You're *Ma Ma* in Chinese," Markus said, jumping from side to side in excitement. "You're *Ma Ma* in Chinese!"

"Cantonese," Mei added.

Sondra gave him a stern look, then looked at Mei. "No. I'm *Grandma*, darling," she said. "Grandma."

❧

That night, Mei began to Google crime stats in Jersey City.

There had been break-ins in their old neighborhood, of course, but they had always seemed personal—the boosting of a Google employee's Tesla from his driveway, for instance. That a band of marauders were passing in and out of houses two blocks from where they lived, looking in on sleeping children like her own in the night, was unbearable.

Then, drawn by she knew not what, Mei Googled the name of the woman who'd bought her stock, the woman whose catalog sold her creations alongside vegan candles and fingerless gloves. The link was broken and, for a minute, Mei was glad. Someone besides her was a failure; her time, it seemed, had passed not only out of her life but also the world. But then she saw a second listing for the name, one on Instagram.

Mei had an Instagram profile that she'd created and never used. Now she clicked on the Google link, and it automatically logged her in. It took her a moment to recognize the woman. She had lost at least forty pounds and cut her hair into a half-Mohawk. She had 800K followers. Mei looked to see if she'd misread it.

The woman's page was stacked with perfectly posed photos of her products—the candles, the teas, the gloves—but it said the woman had expanded into other jewelry items, chunky rings, stacked bracelets, body lariats—

But wasn't that a lariat there? By *Mei*?

Mei was filled with disquiet. She opened the picture, and there it was—a lariat, designed by her. It wasn't hers but it looked exactly like her work—the same claw-like filigree, the waterfall of semiprecious stones, the distinctive triple loops.

It was just done *shittily*.

"Fuck you," Mei whispered. She began to click through the other photographs. She found herself in stacked rings, several necklaces, even a jeweled snood, something Mei would never had done in her life. And her prices were doubled, even tripled—though she could tell the stones were poor quality and it was a cheap alloy, not gold or platinum.

How had the woman done it? Had she simply hired some designer and shown them her work? Told them to copy it? What kind of jewelry designer would do that?

Probably no one in San Francisco. But it would be easy enough to get it copied elsewhere.

Before she could stop herself, she clicked on "Message." A box popped up. The words flew from her fingers. "Nice jewelry," she wrote, and hit "Send."

❧

Mei had already gone through a rageful cry on her own, then a despairing funk by the time Arnold came home. Markus was again sleeping.

"How's the pooper?" he asked. He had taken the tack of treating Markus's new habit as a mildly hilarious interlude in their otherwise uneventful lives.

"Someone stole my stuff," Mei said.

Arnold's head snapped around. "At the park?"

"No," Mei said. She felt tears rising again. "My designs. That bitch has them on her Instagram store."

"What bitch?"

Mei let herself sob. "That lady," she said. "The one who took the rest of my stock."

Arnold sat down slowly. "Oh honey," he said. "I'm sorry they haven't sold."

"What do you mean 'haven't sold'?" Mei asked.

"I thought you just said they're on Instagram."

Mei felt the rising impatience of someone who's being perfectly clear and not being understood by an idiot. "It's not my stuff," Mei said. "It's copies of my designs."

Arnold stood. "Exact copies?" he said. "That's illegal. Those designs are yours."

Mei wiped her eyes. "They're not exact," she said. "It's my style, really."

"What do you mean, your style?"

"You know," Mei huffed. She knew it was disgusting, but she wiped her nose with her sleeve. "My waterfall. My triple loop. My claw."

Arnold looked doubtful. "So, it's like a homage?" he said.

Mei exploded. "What the fuck do you mean, homage?" she said. "She's pretending she's me!"

"She put your name on it?"

"No, of course not."

Arnold looked sad. "Oh, honey," he said. "I'm afraid you have no case."

Mei was stuck between wanting to throw something at him or bury him alive. "I don't want a case!" she said. "I want you to care that someone is stealing my shit!"

Arnold sat and took her hand. "Look, honey," he said. "I know this has been difficult, having Markus all the time. But once school starts—"

"If he doesn't stop pooping in his pants," Mei said, the tears spilling down, "*he will not go to school.* And what then?"

"Honey, he'll stop! You know this!"

"*Nisht gefeyle,*" Mei whispered.

"Honey," Arnold said. "You are *not* a failure."

❦

The next day, Mei arrived at the park with two crumpled plastic bags, a full-sized bag of vegetable sticks, and three juices stuffed in her tote. Dora was sitting where she had been sitting yesterday, energetically pushing the stroller back and forth as if they had never left.

This time, Mei peeked in. She could only glimpse the child's bright-pink cheek and the rise and fall of her breath.

"Six weeks?" she said.

Dora leaned over as if it were a secret. "*Three*," she said. "A girl."

"She doesn't get too hot in there?"

"With a newborn, you have to keep them warm," said Dora.

It seemed to Mei that the swaddle might actually be putting the child to sleep, but maybe that was the point. "This is the only place she'll sleep," Dora said, seeming to read her mind. "At the park. Mine were the same." She waved her hand around. "It's the noise." *Noyce.*

"If you don't mind my asking," Mei said, "what is your accent?"

Dora looked amused. "You don't know this accent?" she said. *Ziss eksent.*

"We're from California," Mei said. "Is it New York?"

"I thought you said your husband was Jewish!" Dora exclaimed. "This is a Yiddish accent, darling." *Dahlink.*

Mei knew what Yiddish was, of course, but had never heard anyone speak it. There weren't many Yiddish speakers in San Francisco. "That's what *nisht gefeyle* was!" she said. "I thought it was German."

Dora looked offended. "German?" she said. She made face, as if to spit. "Ahhh, your relatives are German Jews," she said.

The Muehlers had been in the San Francisco area since the late 1800s. "I think so," she said. "I never asked. It's a German name, I guess."

"Those are high-class Jews," Dora said. "Not from the *shtetl*. You know what means *shtetl*?" *Voss.*

"Village, right?"

Dora looked impressed. "Smart girl."

"I think we have a similar word," she said. Mei's third-generation Cantonese was pretty spotty, but didn't her po po have a poem she recited about a village girl? "*Cun*, I think?" Mei said.

Dora looked pleased. "A podunk place?" she said.

"Exactly."

Mei realized she hadn't looked for Markus in some time, but there he was—on the swings. That made it very unlikely he had gone. She pushed down the panic. Breathe.

"I see our friends are back," said Dora.

There were the two officers again. As they made their way toward them, she straightened up and felt Dora straighten up too, as if they were about to be called on in school.

This time they were carrying a piece of paper. "You have something for us?" Dora said.

It was clear the policewoman had forgotten them entirely. "Ma'am, there has been a string of robberies—"

"Yes, yes," Dora said. "We talked to you yesterday. Forgetting is for old women, not you!"

Now the policewoman remembered. She reddened. "I think we may have a description of the individual."

Dora snatched it, and Mei looked over. On the paper was a sketch of a man. He looked neither black nor white, Hispanic nor Asian, young nor middle-aged, fat nor thin. His features were both all races and no races, his hair cropped short, so you couldn't tell its texture. His expression was thoughtful. He looked, Mei thought, like one of those mashups magazines sometimes did about what all humanity would like in the future.

"It's not a great sketch," the policewoman admitted. "The view was partial."

Dora handed it back. "Looks like my son-in-law," she joked.

Mei shook her head. "He doesn't look familiar," she said.

As the policewoman walked away, Mei suddenly remembered last night.

"I got robbed," she said.

Dora twisted around in her seat to face her. She looked alarmed. "They robbed *you*?" she said.

"No, no, not like that," Mei said. "It was someone I used to work with."

"Ach," Dora said. "I know about that."

Mei tried to keep herself from crying. "Before I came here," she said. "I was a designer. I designed jewelry."

Dora said. "They made off with your rocks."

Mei smiled despite herself. "No, not exactly," she said. "I just found out that—someone stole my designs. A woman I used to work with. She's selling jewelry that looks like mine."

Dora let out a thick, hearty laugh. A thin cry rose from the stroller. Dora didn't seem to hear it. Mei was confused.

"Oh, darling, I'm sorry," she said. "I wasn't laughing at you."

It didn't seem like anything funny had happened. "Okay," she said.

"I will tell you a story," Dora said. "When my husband and I came here, I worked in millinery. You know what means 'millinery'?"

This time Dora had her stumped. "Things for the military?" she said.

"*Hats*," Dora said, loudly, as if she were deaf. "Making hats." She turned to the baby and fussed at the blanket. "We had a company. The English Maid. I went to the stores, bought a woman's hat. Morris would make it. Then he'd sell it back to the stores—cheaper."

This story was starting to sound very familiar. "Knockoffs," she said.

"Yes!" Dora was lost in thought. "It was a very successful company. Not sweatshops." Mei didn't know if that was meant to be personal. She knew, of course, about the *gai-chongs* of her po po's childhood, but her job had been at a regular laundry. "No," Mei said to reassure her.

"But then he died," Dora said. "And now, people don't wear hats." *Hets.*

It sounded like a far more satisfying conclusion to the story than her own. "What happened to the company?"

Dora sighed and returned to the present. "Oh," she said. "The partner bought it. Cut-rate."

"I'm so sorry," Mei said.

It was clear Dora took that to mean the stolen money, not the death. "Well," she said, looking at the baby. "It could be worse." *Voys.*

Dora stood. "This one will be hungry," she said. She cast a gimlet eye at Mei. "You still have your jewels?" she said.

That made it sound as if Mei had a chest bursting with diamonds and rubies. "Not jewels," she said. "I do still have my stones." She felt outraged yet again. "*I* make my jewelry with real ones," she said. "Not like her."

"Well," Dora said. "I only know about hats. There were a lot of women who bought the knockoffs. But," she added, "there were a lot who bought only the real thing."

❧

And so it began that Mei and Dora settled into a routine, arriving at the park at 9:00 a.m., chatting about their lives and backgrounds.

Dora was particularly interested in the Chinese festivals and holidays—the mid-Autumn Moon Festival, the Chinese New Year, the Hundred Days ceremony for a child's birth. "Like a bris," Dora said, wondering. "But the boy doesn't lose his genitals!"

One day, Mei explained Qing Ming. "We go visit our ancestors' graves," she said. "We bring food, wine, incense. And we burn things, paper things that resemble things in real life. Like shoes, clothes, money."

"Why burn?"

"So they can receive them in the afterlife."

"We have different," Dora said. "The week of a person's death, we burn the *yahrzeit* candle. On the anniversary, we visit the grave."

"Do you do anything there?"

"We put rocks," Dora said. "Yours is better."

Midmorning, Dora would go to pee at the corner store. "I'm an old lady," she said. "I have to go every hour." She insisted on bringing Mei a coffee. Because she bought the milky, sweet stuff for a dollar—not the five-dollar cortados from the café on the other corner—Mei let her.

Mei offered to watch Olivia while she went, but Dora always refused. "The carriage is my walker," she would wink.

Dora was also interested in Mei's exposure to Jewish life. "You do Shabbes?"

Mei had only ever heard it as *Shabbat*. "Only at his grandma's," she said.

"His *bubbe*," Dora mused. "She is observant?"

Mei had never heard the word. "*Bubbe*?" she said.

"His *bubbe*!" Dora said. "His grandmother!"

"Is that what you call a grandmother?"

Dora sniffed. "That's what you call a *Jewish* grandmother!" she said.

Every day, Dora asked for updates on the thief. "I don't know what I'm going to do," Mei said. "She's blocked me."

Dora patted her knee. "I will come for any Chinese holiday," she said. "I will be your Jersey City *bubbe*."

❧

One day, Dora arrived carrying a plastic bag of her own. "Oy gevalt," she said, lowering herself onto the seat. "This is for you."

It was a plastic food container, the kind of you got at a Chinese restaurant—the kind with which Mei's mother had stored food her entire childhood. The food inside was beige. "What is it?" she asked.

"Homemade apple sauce," Dora said. *Epple.*

Mei didn't like or dislike applesauce, but she was touched. Was this a Jewish thing? "Thanks," she said. "We'll love it."

"It's not for you," Dora said. "Darling. This thing he does, is not good."

"I know."

"How will he attend school?"

Mei burst into tears. "I don't know."

"This is a problem sons have," Dora said. "I gave this to my son."

Mei wiped her eyes. "Your son had this?"

"The same thing," Dora said. "And I tell you. It was until he was *nine.*"

Mei was struck dumb. Such a thing had never occurred to her.

"We took him to doctors, psychiatrists, teachers, everyone," Dora said. "They would have thought he was a mongoloid, except he was already doing algebra."

There was "Mongoloid"—the slur in a surprising place. Well, Markus was beginning to read, and this too had soothed Mei. "And my Mama, God bless her and keep her, made him this."

"And it solved it?"

"It took a couple of weeks," she said. "But yes, then he went properly. And he never did it again."

Mei had grown up choking down disgusting concoctions—not only Chinese ones from her po po but also other items, like castor oil and garlic-onion tea. Apple sauce seemed a relatively benign ask.

"We'll try it," she said. This seemed an opportune time to ask Dora something she had been wondering for weeks.

"If you don't mind *me* asking," Mei said, "how old are you?" She considered adding *You look fantastic*, as she might for one of Sondra's friends. Dora, as tiny and wrinkled as dried apples, did not seem to require the compliment.

"Oh me," she said. "I'm an *alte kaker*. You know what means '*alte kaker*'?"

Mei was used to this routine by now. "Old?" She ventured.

"Old shit—" Dora began.

"But you're not a shit!" Mei said.

Dora waved that away. "No, not an old shit, an old *shitter*," she said. "A person who *shits*. Who is shitting a long time."

"Oh, who *knows how to shit*," Mei said. "Who is, like, practiced in shitting."

Both women began to laugh. They laughed and laughed until another bench of mothers turned to look.

❧

Things with Arnold finally came to a head, though not in any way Mei could have predicted. One late night, two weeks before school was due to start, he walked into the door, slipped, then lifted up his shoe to look at the sole. "What the *fuck*?" he said.

Mei had been unpacking some books and came to look. "Oh, God," she began. A chunk of Markus's poop must have fallen out. He had managed to silently go on the elevator. "It's—"

"I know what it fucking is!" Arnold yelled. "He's still doing this?"

Mei felt rage rising in her chest like the red on a thermometer. "Of course he's still doing it!" she said. "As you would know, if you ever got home before nine o'clock."

"You didn't take him to a doctor?"

Mei had tried to make an appointment, but the practice that took their insurance was booked until two days before school. She was supposed to call every morning to see if there was a slot, but she had given up after getting the answering machine for five days. "Why is this only *my* job?" she said. "He's your son too! Maybe you should be helping!"

Arnold looked incredulous. "Have you noticed I'm *building a business*?" he said. "I told you things wouldn't calm down for months. I'm trusting you to handle things!"

Mei threw the books she was still holding down. "Have you noticed this entire place is unpacked?" she said. "Have you noticed I have had Markus *every day*, since he can't go to camp? I am up from seven to nine with him. He doesn't nap, you know. I don't have any more time than you do!"

Arnold scoffed. "You're in a building with a playroom and a pool," he said. "You're at the park every day. You can order food. You're not exactly a pioneer woman."

"If you're such a pioneer man," Mei said, "then clean the shit off your shoes yourself."

"Mom?" Markus said. He was standing at his bedroom door. "Hi, Dad," he said. "You're here."

Arnold was caught. He wanted to come in, but he was afraid of spreading shit on the floor. Mei took pity. She went into the kitchen and wet a paper towel, then handed it to him. "Just clean them off and leave them here," she said. "I'm not washing them, though."

Arnold gave her a withering look. "We'll talk about this later," he said. "C'mon, bud. Let's get you back to bed." Oh, he made the big show *now*.

That night, Mei woke up suddenly. Markus's face was directly in hers. The clock said four o'clock.

"Mom, I'm really trying," Markus whispered.

"I know you are," Mei whispered back.

❦

A week before school was to start, Dora came to the park with some devastating news. "The family is moving," she announced.

Mei, who had been shoving Markus's vegetable sticks in her mouth for breakfast, uttered a cry of dismay. "Where's the baby?" she asked. Dora was alone.

"Oh, with Mama," Dora said, sitting down heavily. "I just came to bring you this." Dora handed her the last carton of apple sauce.

"But where will you go?" Mei asked. Already she was calculating if they could afford to use her as a nanny.

Dora's face split in a smile. "I'm not going out with the trash, darling," she said. "I'm going with them."

"Where?"

Dora shrugged. "Chicago, Los Angeles, London—who know with these people?"

Mei realized suddenly that she'd never asked Dora much about her work life—whether she lived with the family, what they were like, how long she had been a babysitter, or what she did with her weekends. She had simply taken her as she came—as company. All while Dora had listened to her troubles, had given her advice, had cooked for her son. Had been a friend.

"Why don't you come over for tea?" she said, struck by a sudden impulse. In the back of her brain, she realized, she had been planning a get-together for a long time: to bring Dora to dinner for the moon festival, maybe, and cook the cakes from scratch. She could have even had her for Shabbes.

"Oh darling, it's a busy day," Dora said. "I don't think I—"

"I know you need to pee," Mei said, determined. "Don't pee in that horrible corner bathroom! Just come to the house."

Mei reached over and grasped Dora's hand. It was stubby and dry, as white as a peeled potato, but not unpleasant to hold. Dora grasped hers back, then touched her face. "*A sheyner punim!*" she said. "You know what means '*punim*'?"

At the house, she seated Dora at the coffee table, then put Markus on the iPad. He would poop or not poop; it didn't matter. "Just give me one second," she said. She ran into the bedroom and pulled out the box from under the bed. She thrust her fingers into one tiny bag. Not there. She looked in another. Finally, she remembered. There they were, taped to one corner, so tightly wrapped, they looked cloudy. She put the bag to her teeth.

"Is everything all right?" Dora called.

"Fine!" Mei said. She walked back in the room, her hands behind her back—grasping her one holdover from her stock, the one thing she had never sold. Slowly, she put the gift on the table.

The earrings were sapphire with diamond chips, drops, a bit less baroque than Mei's usual style, but still uniquely hers. Dora's hands flew to her cheeks.

"I can't take these!" she said.

"I want you to have them," Mei said.

Dora reached out and touched one, then pulled it back, as if it might break. Mei laughed. "It's diamonds!" she said. "It's not going to break."

"I thought you only worked with semiprecious."

"These were for a special client." They had been indeed. "The lady I wanted to give them to died," she added.

"They're clip-ons," Dora said.

"This lady only wore clip-ons. You do too."

"Smart girl," Dora murmured. Her ears were bare today. Slowly she clipped one on, then the other. She preened, like a young movie star, and fluttered her eyelashes.

"How do I look?" she said.

"*Sheyne*," Mei said. "*A sheyne punim.*"

※

"Finished!" said Markus. He put the spoon down.

It was a week later, and Markus had finished the last of the apple sauce. Not only did he like it—which was remarkable—he sometimes asked for more. But Dora had forgotten to give her the recipe. And she didn't even have Dora's phone number.

Mei had come to some decisions. The first was, she was not going to do anything about the lady selling her designs. After all, those were old designs, old work—out of style and not worthy of her artistic range. She would develop a new style and sell that. She would string those diamonds on materials she had never used: wood, leather, amber, silk. She might branch out into clothing, shoes. Arnold was not the only one who could build an empire.

She would also tell Arnold her plans, but whatever he said, she would not step aside anymore. Muehler Incorporated had taken up the family's time for the past five years. It had done well. It had done marvelously well. But Mei didn't intend to play second fiddle to it her entire life.

She was also going to try to be less ashamed of the pooping. After all, Dora's own son had had it, hadn't he?

"I think the applesauce is working," Mei had told her as they said goodbye.

Dora smiled patiently, as if she knew better. "It takes time, darling," she said. "Remember. All this will pass. Soon, you'll be watching *his* children."

"*Nisht gefeyle.*"

"That's right," said Dora. "*Nisht geferlekh.*"

Today was Markus's Well Child appointment. She would deal with the pooping then. Whatever happened, she would be ready.

"Markus!" she yelled. "Toothbrush!"

She headed over to the bedroom. She could start sketching today, but she had to check her inventory. She pulled the box out from under the bed and opened it.

It was empty.

"Mom," called Markus. "*Mom!*"

At first, she didn't know what she was looking at. Had she moved them, half-asleep? Could Arnold have touched them? That wasn't like Arnold—

165

"*Mom*!" Markus yelled.

Then she knew.

Mei remembered those trips—those endless trips to pee, for coffee, always bringing the stroller. She remembered how Dora had whipped her hand out for the artist's rendering of the thief, had seemed so shocked when Mei said she had been robbed.

She remembered that before Dora had left that day, she had used the bathroom. The one in the bedroom.

And who, she thought, wouldn't open the door buzzed for an elderly woman with a baby, one with broken English, who had just happened to ring the wrong buzzer? A lady who just happened to know the house of every mother and nanny at the park, knew their precise comings and goings, because she saw them every day?

Sure—people had nanny cams, door cams. But a nanny hauling her charge in—wouldn't the police have sped by that particular shot without even looking? Especially if that nanny came out and simply returned to the park? No wonder they couldn't figure out who was breaking in. It didn't look like a break-in.

Hell, half of the people probably helped her carry the carriage.

That meant, Mei realized, she had sat among the spoils. Dora had returned to the park after each robbery with the jewelry, sitting placidly among the moms with their diamond earrings, tennis bracelets, and iPhones. Where had she put them? The diaper bag? The snack pack? Within the bottles themselves?

That thing that cried sometimes—was that even a real baby?

"Mom! Get in here!"

A laugh came bubbling from her lips. She slapped her hand over her mouth, but it continued.

Poor Dora—if that was even her name. How she must have held off, never asking for an invite, never wheedling her way in, even though she knew what was inside! How tempted she would have been! The last trip to the bathroom—it was Pavlovian. She had to take Mei's valuables— though the most valuable of all had been freely given.

Mei knew she should be angry, should feel panicked. But she could not help it. She was filled with understanding, even gratitude. She didn't need the diamonds or the garnets to start her new business. She needed to leave them behind.

"*Mom*!"

"*What?*" Mei screamed back. She went to the bathroom. "Why are you making such an infernal racket?"

Markus could only smile and point at the toilet. Mei looked in. She smiled. There, finally, was the poop, curled and shining—as perfect as any jewel.

Inheritance

Terry Shames

"Hi, Grandma. How's it hanging today?"

"Don't call me 'Grandma.' I'm not your grandma. And the only thing that's hanging is my tits, as you well know." She smirked.

"Feisty as ever, I see." Hands on his hips, Jacob surveyed Mrs. W's room. Walker near her chair? Check. TV remote where she could reach it? Check. Uh-oh, dirty dishes on the side table. He picked them up and marched them into the cramped little kitchenette, where he cleaned them and placed them in the drying rack. Most of the residents at the Jewish Home for the Aged didn't use the kitchenette, but Mrs. W liked to cook. Jacob was scared one of these days he was going to come in to work and find out she had burned the place down. With a lot of them, he wouldn't have cared one way or the other, but he got a kick out of her.

"All right, Mrs. W, you got any instructions? Wash your fine lingerie? Make you a martini?

"Oh, you." She flapped her hand to shoo him away. "I never liked a martini even in the old days. It was gin fizz for me." Even with her saggy old body and wrinkled face, he saw in her bright eyes and fine bone structure the good-looking woman she must have been. Plus, she had a few pictures of herself around the apartment that told her story. A few years of being a jazz singer, and then married to a rich man with steely eyes. In the photos she was well dressed, in furs, back in the day when women could wear them. You could tell by the way she preened herself when he commented on her hair or the way she was dressed that she appreciated being admired.

Some of the old people didn't care how they looked, but even push-ing ninety, she got herself dressed up every day as if somebody might want to take her out for a nice meal. And she wasn't one to mope around the place. When they had a program downstairs, she was there. She liked the young singers. She'd tell Jacob the next day how cute the guy was, and that he had been singing Sinatra hits. She might reminisce about a time when she went to a club and heard some famous singer that didn't hold a candle to Sinatra.

He grinned. "I bet you liked your gin fizz. So, nothing you want me to pick up at the store? Prescriptions? Depends?"

"Depends! Don't get fresh. I'm got my daughters to do that for me, or Mark," she added with a lift of her chin.

Jacob frowned. He wouldn't say anything to Mrs. W, but he didn't like her grandson, Mark. Too smart for his own good, if you asked Jacob. Not that anybody asked him. His job was to make the rounds every day to do little errands for the residents of the home. He did everything from picking up their mail, to bringing them a chicken sandwich from Arlo's down the street, to getting their prescriptions. The pay wasn't much, but it wasn't a hard job either, and at sixty-three with his prison record, he was glad to have a job at all. And sometimes you got people like Mrs. W who slipped you a little extra cash on the side.

He bade Mrs. W goodbye, did the rest of his rounds, and spent the rest of the afternoon completing the errands. When he got back to the building with his bag full of pills and products, books and magazines, about three o'clock, he almost ran right into Mrs. W's grandson, Mark. With his hair slicked back like a matinee idol from Mrs. W's time, Mark wasn't bad looking, but there was a weasely cast to his eyes.

"Jacob, what up?" he said. Trying to sound like somebody from the hood. Kid like Mark, maybe thirty years old . . . put him in the real 'hood, and he'd last about five minutes before somebody took him down a peg.

"I'm fine, Mark. Did you go visit your grandma?"

The kid looked uneasy. "Nah, I needed to talk to somebody."

Now what could that mean? Why would he be here to see anybody else? Jacob saluted Mark and got on the elevator for the fifth floor.

It took an hour to distribute all the goods, what with having to stop long enough to chit chat. Some of these old people were lonesome. He figured it was no skin off his nose if he stopped to visit. But the whole time he was uneasy, and when he was done he stopped back by Mrs. W's apartment.

He knocked on the door and was oddly relieved when she called out, "Who is it?"

"Jacob. Can I come in?"

When he stepped in, she said, "You getting dementia? You already stopped here once today."

"Just checking back. You have any visitors this afternoon?"

"Visitors?" Her wrinkled old face sagged for a split second before she said, "I don't know what you're talking about. Who has time? We're having a program before dinner. I had to get dressed up."

Jacob was embarrassed to realize that he hadn't noticed she was all gussied up. "And you look terrific," he said. "Remember, it's not how you feel—"

"It's how you look," she finished the line.

"And you look mah-velous," he retorted. "I see you're all set to go. Can I escort you downstairs?"

"Jacob, that would be very nice of you," she said. "Not that I can't make it on my own."

"I know, I know, you could tap dance your way down there, but admit it, it's nice to have company."

Even after he got her settled near the action and went on his way home, Jacob was troubled. What had her nephew been doing in the Jewish Home for the Aged if he hadn't been there to see her?

The next morning Jacob had one of his frequent stomach issues and had to call in sick, so it wasn't until Friday that he got back to JHA. He had a routine which put Mrs. W near the end of his visits. That way he got the whiners and the truly sick residents taken care of early, saving Mrs. W and her humor for later. But all day yesterday his thoughts kept coming back to her and his low-level worry about her grandson, so today, he planned to visit her earlier.

Jacob didn't know exactly why he had a soft spot for her. It wasn't as if his own grandmothers had been dear to him. His grandmother on his mom's side had had a tongue as sharp as a blade. And his dad's mother had faded away and died at the age of sixty-two, leaving little impression. Maybe deep down he wished he could have had a grandmother he could kid with. Who knows how he would have turned out if he'd had someone to prod him the way he saw her get after her daughters, when they came around? Which wasn't often.

He didn't know why Mark bothered him. He didn't truly think the kid would hurt Mrs. W, but he had a furtive way about him. To tell you the truth, he reminded Jacob a little of himself at that age, and that hadn't turned out so well.

Midmorning, he tapped on Mrs. W's door. There was no answer. She might be in the john, or maybe even still in bed. Since he never came to her apartment this early, he didn't know her habits. He waited a good two minutes and tapped again. He thought he heard a faint voice, but he couldn't make out what she said, whether it was, "Come in," or "Give me a minute." He waited another minute and then used his passkey. He eased the door open and without looking in, called out, "Mrs. W? It's Jacob."

This time he heard a distinctive groan, so he stepped inside. "Mrs. Weintraub, are you okay?"

"Jacob?" A faint voice from her bedroom.

She was still in bed, her face barely visible above a mess of covers. "Mrs. W, what's up? Shall I call downstairs and get you some medical help?"

"No, no," she said. "I'm all right. Just tired."

He didn't see any water on her bedside stand so he fetched a glass and helped her up. She drank greedily. Maybe she was dehydrated. He hated to say it, even to himself, but she looked bad. Maybe it was because she didn't have any makeup on, but her face was gray and her eyes looked dull. "Tell you what, I know you just need a little rest, but I'll feel better if you get checked out."

"No, that's . . . well, maybe so."

He was glad not to have to argue with her. He went to the house phone and called downstairs. "I don't think it's an emergency," he said. "But she's usually pretty perky."

"Oh, I know she is," Zerlene said. She was a big, black woman who commanded the front desk. "I'll get the nurse up there right now."

The nurse was the pretty one, Rachel. With a dark mop of hair and flashing blue eyes, she looked so young that it was hard to believe she'd been through nursing school.

"Let's see what's going on with you, Mrs. Weintraub," she said. He was glad she didn't use that smarmy tone of voice that a lot of young people used with the elderly.

Jacob waited in the living room while Rachel checked out Mrs. W. Nobody would have blamed him if he'd left, but he wanted to stick around in case he was needed. While he waited, he puttered around straightening up the place. His flaw was that he'd always been restless. That's what had gotten him into trouble as a young man.

He slipped on a pair of latex gloves that he always used when he was cleaning the old peoples' places. He washed the couple of cups in the sink, dried them, and put them away. He fluffed the throw pillows and put the magazines in a stack. There was a plastic prescription bottle on the table next to the chair where Mrs. W usually sat and watched TV. He was going to take it to the counter and put it with her other medications, but then he saw that it was a prescription that belonged to Mrs. Epstein up on floor six. She must have come down to visit, had the bottle with her and forgot about it.

He set it back where it had been, next to a photo that usually sat with the others on the chest near the door. It was a picture of Mrs. W and Mrs. Epstein. The two women flanked the bandleader that Mrs. W had sung with in her twenties. The bandleader was in a white suit and holding a trumpet. The women were dressed in flashy dresses. Mrs. W's was all sequins, low-cut and figure-hugging, and with a boa slung around her neck. Mrs. Epstein's dress was a little more conservative but still nice.

Just then Rachel came out. She was frowning.

"How's she doing?" Jacob said.

Rachel smiled at him. *Oh, Lord, to be thirty again.* He'd make a play for her, that's for sure. "You like her, don't you?" she said.

"I do. She's got a lot going, even at her age. You think she's going to be okay?"

"I think so. I can't see any reason for her to be so tired. But . . ." she shrugged. "Unfortunately, at her age we have to expect some physical ailments. She'll probably snap out of it. I'll check back in tomorrow morning and if she's not up and around I'll call the doctor in."

Jacob wasn't sure what good that was going to do. Dr. Goodman was a nice enough man, but he seemed vague, and Jacob wondered if he was playing with a full deck. Maybe he ought to call one of Mrs. W's daughters. He shuddered. The question was, which daughter? The older one, Susan Perry, was a shrew who reminded him of his first wife, Janet. But the other one, Marsha, was a nervous wreck. If she had the slightest hint that something was wrong with her mother, she'd go to pieces. He'd wait until he had to call them.

He thought about Mrs. W several times that evening, and almost went back to check on her, but then he realized that was a little too pushy. After all, she wasn't kin. He was an employee, no matter how much he liked her.

But the next morning when he arrived at the center, it was just in time to see the ambulance arrive. Mrs. W's two daughters were huddled in the doorway. He saw the still form of Mrs. W and wanted to rush to her side and make sure she was still alive, maybe say something funny, like tell her she looked mah-velous. He took it as a good sign that her face wasn't covered. At least she was alive, although she was lying awfully still.

The director of the home, Evelyn Cruikshank, a tall, angry-looking woman, rushed to Jacob. "Don't stand there and gawk," she said. "The family won't appreciate you making a spectacle of their beloved mother."

He crept inside, seething and sad all at the same time. He should have decked that bitch, or told her to mind her own business. He should have at least stopped and told the daughters that he was sorry their mother was ill.

Heart heavy, he did his rounds and then went off to take care of errands. That afternoon, after he finished dropping off people's orders, he was just passing Mrs. W's door when her older daughter, Susan, stepped into the hallway. "Oh, there you are, Jacob. Can I ask you to come in here for a minute?" Her voice was always like cracked glass.

"Sure thing." Inside, the younger daughter, Marsha, was sitting on the sofa, her face a mask of misery.

"Have you heard anything more about your mother's condition?" Jacob asked. He wondered what they were doing there instead of at her bedside.

Marsha said, "The doctor told us they'd be keeping her overnight. So we came back here to pick up her medicines and get a nightgown."

Susan sneered. "Why would *you* care?" She was rail-thin, the bones in her face so prominent that it looked like a skull barely covered with skin. Her hair was jet-black, except you could see the white roots. She was dressed in an expensive jogging suit. He doubted that she jogged, since she was probably older than he was. But it sometimes surprised him what some women would do to stay thin.

He had known women like this his whole life, who couldn't find a good word for anyone. "I like your mother," he said.

"I'll bet you do," she spat out. She was holding some legal-sized papers. She walked over to the little round kitchen table and slapped them down on it. "Come over here."

"Susan . . ." Marsha stood up.

"Oh, don't start," Susan said to her sister. Jacob hadn't moved and she said, "I want you to tell me what this means." She pointed to the document.

Jacob's impulse was to tell her to go to hell. It's what he would have done years ago. But he needed this job, so he made his feet move to the table.

She jabbed her finger onto the paper. "Are you responsible for this?"

Jacob picked up the paper. It was Mrs. W's Last Will and Testament. He looked at the part Susan had pointed out. He had to read it twice before he understood for real. Mrs. W had left him twenty-five thousand dollars. Twenty-five thousand! It might not mean much to everyone, but to him it meant not having to worry about every dime for a while. "I . . ." He couldn't think of what to say. Mrs. W frequently tipped him handsomely, but it never occurred to him that she had that kind of money, much less that she would leave any of it to him. "I had no idea."

"I seriously doubt that. I'll bet you sweet-talked her and then stood over her while she signed this. I've seen how you fuss over her."

Jacob took a deep breath. He may need this job, but he didn't have to take this kind of talk. "I resent your implication," he said quietly. "I fuss over her because I like her. I didn't have any idea that she was planning to leave me money."

Susan snatched the documents out of his hand. "I'll get to the bottom of this. I've always been suspicious of you, the way you sneak around like you've got something to hide. I'm going to find out what it is, and you'll be out of here." She came so close to him that he could see the pores on her face. "And I'm going to see to it that mother's lawyer amends this. It's a travesty. Taking money away from her family and giving it to some . . . toad like you."

Marsha gasped. "Susan, you don't have to be so rude." It was barely a whisper.

Susan turned on her. "Oh, really? Somebody has to keep this family's best interest at heart. You'd give a handout to every bum on the street."

"If that's all, I'll be on my way," Jacob said, hating the tremble in his voice. Okay, so he wasn't the world's most handsome man, with his sallow face and the weight he'd lost, but she had no right to talk to him like that. Back in the day it would have been *her* trembling, not him. As he opened the door, he turned, "And I'm not a bum on the street."

By the time he got to the house van that he used to do errands, he was practically sick with rage. He was glad he didn't have to take anyone to an appointment this morning so he could nurse his grievance in private and do the coulda-woulda-shoulda thing about what he should have said to Susan Perry. God, he wondered what kind of pussy her husband was. By the time he got to the pharmacy for his first errand, he had cooled down enough to think about what $25,000 dollars would mean to him. If he ever saw it, that is. Which he doubted.

Zerlene called him the next morning before he left for work to tell him that Mrs. W had slipped away during the night. "Rachel said you had a soft spot for her, and I thought you'd want to know."

He thanked her for calling. He had to sit down for a few minutes and collect his feelings. Dear Mrs. W. How had she gone so quickly? He knew it was sentimental, but he wished he could have said goodbye. He wondered if there was some way to pay respects to her. The family would have the funeral right away, of course, and he surely wouldn't be welcome there. But they would sit *shivah* for a week. He hadn't been to services like that since his grandma died, but imagined it was about the same as always.

If he had been an old friend of the family, he would have gone by the house to sit and reminisce with them, but he could imagine the kind of stink Susan Perry would make if he showed up. She'd probably bring up the matter of the money. To be honest, his heart did a little leap at the thought. He told himself not to get his hopes up. The likes of Susan Perry would probably find some way to make sure he didn't see a dime. Besides, maybe Mrs. W didn't actually have *that* much money. Some of the elderly people boasted of riches that they had in the past but that they had forgotten no longer existed.

By Monday, he had decided it was too risky to go by and pay his respects, but when he got to the JHA he had an idea. He liked Mrs. W's friend, Mrs. Epstein, just fine. She was nice enough, although she didn't have the gift of humor that Mrs. W did. Still, she and Mrs. W had been friends and he thought it would be a nice gesture to ask if she would like him to take her to visit the family during *shivah*.

When he got to her apartment, he found her in a tizzy. It seemed she had been waiting for him to come by. As soon as he knocked on the door, she pulled him inside. "I'm so glad you're here. I'm missing one of my pill bottles, and I need you to go right now and get the prescription." In contrast to Mrs. W, who had had a little meat on her bones, Mrs. Epstein was as thin as a waif. Her dark eyes were huge in her sunken face, which was flushed from being upset. "I don't know how I could have misplaced them."

"Hold on," he said. "I know where your pills are."

"Where?"

"I saw a bottle of them down in Mrs. W's place on Friday. I bet that's them."

"How in the world did they get there?"

"You probably had them with you the last time you visited and left them there."

"But I haven't been down to her apartment in *weeks*."

These old people sometimes forgot what they did. "Did she come and visit *you*?"

She shook her head, her expression so bleak that he asked, "Was there a problem?"

She nodded. Her lower lip was drooping. "The last time I saw her, we argued." She looked up at him with miserable eyes. "She liked you. She said she liked to talk to you. Did she say anything about being mad at me?"

"Never. I'm sure she knew it was just a spat and that it would blow over."

"You think so?"

"I know so. Neither one of you is one to hold a grudge." He leaned in to whisper in conspiratorial voice, "Not like some I know around here."

She pursed her lips. "I know who you mean. That Mrs. Jordan." Her eyes snapped. "You know, I don't really think she's Jewish. I think she lied about it so she could live here cheap."

Jacob snickered. "Now don't let me hear you talking like that. You're of a better class of person than to repeat that kind of gossip."

"Humph. Maybe so, but I've got my thoughts on the subject."

Jacob clapped his hands together. "Let me see if I can get into Mrs. W's apartment and bring your pills back."

"Jacob, you are wonderful."

But when he let himself into the apartment, he found that it had been cleaned out. The furniture was all there, but every picture, every knickknack, all the toiletries, the clothes, and the prescriptions were gone. Susan Perry had certainly lost no time. It seemed disrespectful to be in such a hurry. But maybe the manager had told her they needed the apartment.

With a heavy heart he reported back to Mrs. Epstein.

"Oh, I wish they hadn't done that. I would like to have had the picture of me and her back in the day."

"I know the one. The one with you two and the bandleader."

"That's the one."

"You don't have a copy?"

"I did, but I don't know what happened to it. Seems like I lose everything these days."

Jacob saw his chance to get to pay respects to Mrs. W. "I wonder," he said, "would you like to go sit *shivah* with the family one day? That would give you a chance to find out if your pills are there. And maybe the photo too."

Mrs. Epstein thought about it. "I would, but my daughter is out of town and I don't have any way to get over there. I guess I could hire a car, but . . . well, the money."

"What if I took you over there? I was fond of Mrs. W, and I'd like to pay my respects, but . . ." he sighed. He didn't know if he ought to tell Mrs. Epstein why didn't feel comfortable butting in.

Her eyes narrowed. "But you think that daughter of hers will cause a fuss if you show up, is that it?"

He cocked his head. "How did you figure that?"

"That girl thinks she's the cat's pajamas. She wasn't very nice to me either. Thought because I was in a nightclub act back in my day, that I was a floozy. In fact, that's what Eileen and I were fussing about. I was miffed because her daughter was mean, and Eileen said I was being too sensitive."

To be perfectly honest, Mrs. Epstein *had* been something of a floozy according to Mrs. W. The nightclub act she was talking about was being a cigarette girl and a dance hall girl. He admired Mrs. W for telling him that it hadn't mattered to her one bit. She liked Mrs. Epstein and had remained friends for the decades after they were no longer at the club. Mrs. W had married a rich man, but Mrs. Epstein had not fared as well, marrying a salesman who turned out to be a philanderer, and was too fond of his drink. "Just between you and me," Mrs. W had said, "I sometimes had to slip Glo a little money to tide her over when her husband drank up the paycheck." She had also told Jacob that Gloria Epstein always managed to pay the money back. "Wouldn't hear of letting it be a gift." He wondered, now, if Mrs. W had left her friend anything in her will.

He winked at Mrs. Epstein. "If you and I go over there together to pay our respects, Susan Perry will probably keep her mouth shut. Strength in numbers, you know."

She shrunk back into her chair. "I don't know. I hate asking anybody for anything. If I ask about the pills or the photo, she might say no, and then I'll feel like a fool."

He sighed. "I know what you mean." His fingers were tingling. What was that all about? They hadn't tingled like that in twenty years, not since he got sent away for robbery. Multiple robberies, truth be known. And then he realized why his fingers were tingling and his brain was fizzing. He felt a sheen of sweat on his upper lip. "But who said anything about asking?"

"What do you mean?"

"Don't you worry."

She dimpled. "Jacob, what are you getting up to?"

"Never mind. How about if we go over there tomorrow? What time?"

She fussed around for a few more minutes but finally agreed to ten in the morning.

"Now what about those pills?" he asked. "Are you all right without them?"

She said she had two more days' supply in her pillbox.

❧

Mrs. Epstein was wearing too much makeup. She looked like one of those Japanese geishas. Jacob wished there was some way to tell her without hurting her feelings. She had on a burgundy wool suit, too hot for the season, and her blouse had a smudge of makeup on the collar. He had brought his car to take her to Susan Perry's house, instead of taking her in the van. When he asked Mrs. Cruikshank, the director, for Mrs. W's address, she quizzed him as if he was planning to rob the place. She only gave it to him when he said he was doing a favor for Mrs. Epstein. "Don't spend too long there," she said. "You have your rounds to make."

He was happy not to spend much time there—just long enough to think a few parting thoughts about Mrs. W, and to get hold of Mrs. Epstein's medicine and the photo. He was looking forward to that.

As he expected, the house was a grand sprawl, located on the bay. The landscaping alone must have cost a bundle.

It was a great relief to find that Mrs. W's younger daughter, Marsha, had been left in charge while Susan had gone to pick up her son Mark.

"It's so nice of you to bring Mrs. Epstein, Jacob," Marsha said. She kissed Mrs. Epstein on both cheeks. She showed them a memorial that Susan had set up, some old photos of Mrs. W's life. "I just wasn't up to it," she said. "Susan has more energy than I do."

Jacob noticed there weren't any photos of Mrs. W. as a singer.

Marsha served them cookies and punch. Jacob tried not to be impatient. He was afraid Susan would come back before he could do what he'd come here for. But soon a couple of other people came to visit and they took up the conversation with Mrs. Epstein and Marsha. Jacob excused himself for a "bathroom break."

He made his way upstairs, careful not to make any noise. All but one of the doors were closed. From years of poking around in people's houses, he knew something about the way people organized their lives. He figured if Mrs. W's goods were here, Susan wouldn't bother to keep the door closed. Sure enough, the open-door room was full of bags. His heart sank. A lot of stuff to go through. Well, nothing for it but to get started. He pulled the door closed to muffle any noise he made. If anyone caught him in here, he'd tell them that he was looking for Mrs. Epstein's pills and didn't want to disturb anyone.

He picked up each bag in turn and shook it. The third bag rattled. Sure enough, it contained all the pills from Mrs. W's apartment. There must have been thirty bottles. He tossed through them until he found the one he was after and slipped it into his pocket.

Next, the photo. He was in luck. It was near the top of the bag that had the living room stuff in it. Just as he secured the frame in his inside jacket pocket, he heard voices outside the room, including a man's voice and the piercing voice of Susan Perry. Old instincts kicked in and he darted into the closet just as the door opened.

"Here we are," Susan was saying. "I don't know if this will help, but these are the bags we took out of the apartment."

A rumbly male voice said, "Do you know which one has the pills?"

Jacob would have recognized the command of a cop's voice anywhere.

"Well, of course not, officer. As you can see, I just had everything packed up and hauled over here. We haven't had time to go through them yet. And it's just as well we haven't because we probably would have thrown away all the prescriptions."

Jacob wondered what they were looking for. He heard bags rustling and the same rattling sound that he'd identified the pills with. Another man said, "Here we go. Here's the pills." There was the rattle of one bottle after another. "I'll leave you," Susan said. I have to go down and entertain these . . . people." The way she said "these people," it sounded like a bunch of riffraff.

The pill rattling continued, and after a minute a rumbly voice said, "Sheesh, she's a harpy."

"Ah, go easy. She just found out her mother was murdered. Gotta be tough."

"I guess."

Murdered? Jacob's gut clenched. What the hell? He hoped they'd say more, but they continued working in silence. After a while, rumbly-voice sighed. "Jimmy, I don't see anything. These prescriptions are all hers. Whatever killed her, it isn't here."

When the cops left, Jacob was reluctant to go back downstairs. Still, he had been gone awhile. If the cops were still there when he returned, and somebody commented on it, he'd have to come up with one heck of an excuse. He didn't like being around cops, even if he hadn't done anything. Anybody knew that once you were in the system, even after you had done your time you were a prime suspect for anything that happened around you. There was no reason for them to suspect him of killing Mrs. W. Everybody knew they got along well. But then there was that $25,000 . . .

He crept downstairs and sneaked around the corner to the bathroom. He went in, flushed the toilet, and washed his hands. When he went back into the living room, he waited outside the door, looking at an array of family photos on the wall. When he heard someone telling a lively story that had people laughing, he eased into the room and went to Mrs. Epstein's side. There were a half dozen people here now, and no sign of the cops.

"Where have you been?" Mrs. Epstein asked him, loud enough for everyone to hear.

"I stopped to look at some photos of Mrs. W before I went to the john," he said.

"Why are you here at all?" Susan Perry asked. "You weren't *friends* with my mother. You were an employee."

"Marsha—" Her sister whined. He wished she'd grow a spine. She was standing, and Jacob saw that she had given up her chair for her nephew, Mark.

"I'm here to say my goodbyes. She was a good person, funny and friendly, and I'll miss her."

Mark snickered. "He thought Mima liked him," he said.

In Jacob's day he would have wiped that smirk off the kid's face.

"I bet that $25,000 you think you're going to get will ease your pain," Susan said with a vicious smirk.

A couple of people gasped. One woman said, "Susan, I know you're upset, but you need to calm down. Remember what the doctor said."

Jacob perked up. If Susan Perry was sick, it was fine by him.

"I told you, I didn't know anything about that," Jacob said. He wanted to slap her. What made her so nasty, so different from her mother? "I came to bring Mrs. Epstein and took the chance to pay my respects too."

"What $25,000?" Mrs. Epstein asked, frowning at him.

Susan said, "In her wisdom, my mother decided to leave this man a bundle of money in her will. We'll see how far that goes. I have my lawyer looking at the will." She turned to Mrs. Epstein. "Don't worry, Gloria, she took care of you too."

"Jacob, I think I need to get back to my apartment," Mrs. Epstein said. He saw that she was pale.

"Let me bring the car around, and I'll come back in and get you," he said.

"Very nice," he heard someone murmur.

Susan Perry jumped up and followed him out the door. "Wait a minute," she said.

He turned to see her standing hands on hips, her face rigid with fury.

"How dare you come here and gloat about my mother leaving you money in her will? I'll be talking to Mrs. Cruikshank about this. Don't think I won't."

Jacob sighed. "I'm sure you will."

When he had Mrs. Epstein in the car, she said in a shaky voice, "What did Susan say to you when she came outside?"

"Just making her point about the money again," he said. "She's got plenty of dough. What's a measly $25,000 to her?"

"She's always been greedy. For somebody like her, there's never enough. She wasn't nice to Eileen either. But Eileen just took it. Do you know Susan had the nerve to come to my apartment last week and tell me she thought I had taken something from her mother's place? I told her in no uncertain terms that I hadn't been there in a month and that even if I had, I didn't need anything bad enough to steal it."

She was quiet for a moment. "By the way, you were gone a long time. Did you manage to find my pills?"

"I did. They're in my pocket. And the photo too." He drew the framed photo out of his jacket pocket and handed it to her.

The rest of the way home Mrs. Epstein talked about how much fun she and Mrs. W had had back in the day. She forgot to ask him for the pills, and he was glad. He had some thinking to do about them.

Mrs. Epstein was tired and said she wanted to have lunch in her room. Jacob said he'd pop down and bring it up to her. When he got back with it, she eyed it with distaste. "The food here sucks," she said.

Jacob was startled. He thought to jolly her along. "What do you think this is, the Ritz?"

She stared back at him with cold eyes. "I could have had the Ritz if it hadn't been for Eileen Weintraub."

Jacob was uneasy. "What do you mean?"

"You know why I wanted that picture?"

He shook his head.

"Because it was the last picture I had of Manny before he threw me over for Eileen."

"I thought she was married to a businessman."

"She was. Oh, you thought she was such a lady? No sir. She had *two* men on the hook. All those years she was married, she carried on with my beau on the side. I got stuck with a schlemiel. She was just plain selfish."

Jacob didn't know what to say. "Life is funny," he said. Lame. But he remembered that Mrs. W told him she had slipped money to Glo Epstein.

"Not so funny when you're on the bad end." She cocked her head. "But you know about that, don't you? You may kid yourself that you'd be fine without that $25,000, but you want it. I can see that. You'll be lucky to see a dime of it with that witch of a daughter of hers pulling the strings."

She was probably right. "She said Mrs. W took care of you too. You know how much?"

"She said she was going to leave me a bundle. I doubt it, but she should. She owes me."

"I thought . . ."

"I know what you thought. You thought what she told you. She probably told you she was helping me out, am I right?"

He nodded.

"Well." She poked at a limp carrot. "I don't want to turn you against her. All I'm saying is that I deserved better." She frowned. "By the way, do you have those pills?"

He nodded, but didn't take them out of his pocket. He was reluctant to hand them over. Were these pills responsible for Mrs. W's death? Had Mrs. Epstein killed her?

"Don't look at me like that," she said. "I didn't give those pills to her. I don't know how she got them."

Jacob's mind was working furiously. If she hadn't killed Mrs. W, who did? "You said Susan visited you recently. Could she have taken the pills from your apartment?"

Mrs. Epstein grew still and thought. "I don't know."

"How about her grandson, Mark?"

Her mouth fell open. "He came to visit me last week. I couldn't figure out why. He said he hadn't seen me and he wanted to say hello." Her face clouded. "He's just like Eileen. What a sneak. He could have killed her, you know. I'll bet she left him sitting pretty and he wanted that money. Well, he'll see his inheritance, but I imagine after Susan Perry's lawyer gets done, you and I will be out in the cold."

"I wouldn't be so sure," Jacob said slowly. For the second time in a week, his hands were tingling. He hadn't realized how much he missed that feeling.

A smile started tugged the corners of her mouth. "What are you cooking up?"

He told her.

In the afternoon, he went to ask Zerlene if he could have a word with Mrs. Cruikshank.

"I wouldn't if I were you," Zerlene said. "She's on the warpath."

"What happened?"

She looked to make sure Mrs. Cruikshank's door was closed. She beckoned Jacob closer and whispered. "The police were here. Apparently, Mrs. Weintraub had been poisoned. The doctor said she had a dose of the wrong medication. You know how Mrs. Cruikshank is. She took it personally. 'Oh, it couldn't have happened here, blah, blah.'"

"Oh, dear, that's awful! I loved that woman. Who could have done that?"

Before Zerlene could reply, Mrs. Cruikshank's door opened and she strode over. "Just the person I wanted to see. Jacob, in my office, please."

Mrs. Cruikshank sat down behind her desk, but didn't tell Jacob to sit. She got right down to business. "I had a call from Susan Perry. You have some nerve! She said you coaxed Mrs. W into leaving you money. That is completely frowned on. She wanted me to fire you."

"I didn't coax Mrs. W into anything," he said. "We were pals. Everybody knows that. I hope you don't fire me. I need this job."

She glared him. "The only reason I'm not firing you is that Rachel stood up for you. She said Mrs. W cared for you. But don't think I'm not watching. If you make one false move, you're gone." She stood up.

"Uh, Mrs. Cruikshank? I wanted to ask you something."

"What's that?"

"Every time I think about Mrs. W I think about her in that chair of hers. I know I'm being sentimental, but do you suppose her daughters would let me buy that chair?"

She looked surprised. "You're in luck. As matter of fact, Susan asked me if any of the residents would like to buy the furniture."

He had figured as much. Which fit right into his plan. They agreed on a price and Jacob said he'd have the chair moved tomorrow after work.

꙳

Sneaking into Susan Perry's house that night wasn't the hard part. Either time. It took only a few minutes to find a bottle of pills in her medicine cabinet like the one that contained Glo Epstein's pills. And it also wasn't hard to get the label off Mrs. Epstein's pill bottle because it didn't matter if he smeared the prints that were already on it.

The hard part was getting the label off Susan Perry's without disturbing her fingerprints. Delicate work. It was important that the cops could get a good set of prints. It took longer than he thought, but eventually he got the label off and switched it with Mrs. Epstein's. He poured Mrs. Epstein's pills into the bottle that he had taken from Susan Perry's house—the one with her fingerprints on it, and put her pills into Mrs. Epstein's, which now bore Susan's label. At 4:00 a.m. he sneaked back in and placed Susan's pills back in the medicine cabinet. Nobody would ever know the bottles and labels had been switched.

The next day, midafternoon, he called the police. He and Mrs. E waited for them downstairs in Mrs. Weintraub's old apartment.

"And you found these pills where?" He was the grumble-voiced cop who had looked for the bottle at Susan Perry's house.

"It had rolled under the chair," Jacob said. "I'm buying the chair, and I came to pick it up. When I moved it, I saw the pill bottle there. I had heard that somebody had dosed poor Mrs. Weintraub with the wrong pills and that's what killed her, and that you guys were looking for the bottle the pills were in." He pointed at it lying where he had positioned it, in the dust bunnies under the chair. "I don't know if that's the one you were looking for, but I didn't want to touch it in case there were fingerprints."

The cop picked up the vial of pills with his latex-gloved hand, and read the label. "Gloria Epstein," the other cop said. "That's you?"

"Yes," Mrs. E said. "Jacob called me as soon as he saw them. My pills went missing last week. I told Jacob a couple of days ago I didn't know what had happened to them." She grabbed Jacob's arm as if she needed him to steady her. "Somebody took them and brought them . . . oh, my goodness. I'm afraid somebody used them to kill my dear friend. Who could have done that?"

Jacob patted her hand. "We're going to leave this to the police. They'll figure it out."

"Hold on," the cop said. "Mrs. Epstein, do you have any idea who might have taken them?"

"I don't want to say." Mrs. E's distress seemed so real that Jacob was proud of her.

"Ma'am, we need to know."

She gave a little whimper. "Well, it could be either of two people. But I'm sure they couldn't have meant her any harm."

"What two people?"

With a little coaxing she told them it could be either Susan or her son Mark. "They both had a chance to take them."

When they found Susan's fingerprints all over the vial, the cops would find their culprit. It was too bad she had made such a fuss about his $25,000. She should have just considered it an inheritance tax.

THE GOD OF MERCY

Brother's Keeper

Eileen Rendahl

I knew something was wrong the second I pulled up. Zach's gray minivan should not have been parked in front of his place. It should have been parked forty-five miles away in Tracy, California, in front of a single-story ranch house owned by a County of Alameda employee named Gregory Murray. Zach should have been inside the van, camera set and ready to tape, when Murray came out and mowed his lawn or cleaned his gutters or went for a jog or did any of the hundreds of things he could do to show that the knee injury he was claiming made it impossible for him to work anymore wasn't nearly as bad as he wanted everyone to believe or possibly didn't exist at all.

Instead, the van was still here in Concord, parked at the curb, blackout curtains in place around the back and sides.

The front door to his place was tucked behind a Rose of Sharon hedge, still green and full in October in Northern California, though without blooms. I went around it and up the walk. When I saw the front door hanging open, I slipped my phone out of my pocket, ready to call for help. I stepped inside and the smell immediately hit me. I pulled the front of my shirt up over my face to mask out the worst of it but could still taste that coppery tang in the back of my throat.

I only went three more steps in because that's when I saw Zach. Or what was left of him. I crouched down to touch him to be sure, but I knew the second I saw him he was dead. I wasn't a medical professional, but I'd never seen a live person's eyes stare like that. Plus I didn't think anyone could survive whatever had been done to his skull. I stood up, backed slowly out of the house, trying not to touch anything, and called the cops.

Then I sat down on the curb, put my head between my knees, and tried not to hyperventilate.

❦

I huddled in the back of the police car with one of those weird aluminum foil blankets wrapped around me. When the cops and everyone else had shown up, I'd been unable to stop shaking. I'd barely been able to give my name through my chattering teeth. A white paramedic with French braided blond pigtails had wrapped the blanket around me. "Shock," she'd pronounced, glaring at the cop who'd been trying to question me.

He'd rolled his eyes and gone away, but he was back now, sitting in the front seat of the cop car while I remained in back. "Your name again?" he asked. I ballparked him in his late thirties. Latino Hair starting to thin on top. He was doing a bad job of hiding it by gelling it up into spikes. He wore too much cologne, but I was okay with that for the moment. It was getting that other smell out of head.

"My name is Leah Rabinowitz." I spelled it for him. "What's yours?"

"Detective Díaz. Raymond Díaz."

We went through a bunch of my particulars. Age. Address. Phone number.

"Tell me again how you came to find Mr. Milburn," Díaz said, head cocked a bit to one side.

"He's supposed to check in when he gets to an assignment. He didn't. I came over to see what was going on."

"And you work for a PI?"

I nodded. "Howard Investigations. We specialize in workers' compensation cases."

He made a face like he'd bitten into an apple and found half a worm. Plenty of cops filed workers' comp claims because plenty of cops got hurt on the job. That didn't mean that they all were as hurt as they said they were.

Díaz rubbed his chin. He'd missed a spot when he'd shaved. "When was the last time you spoke to Mr. Milburn?"

I squinched up my face and thought. "We texted back and forth yesterday afternoon a few times. Does that count as speaking?" I mean, who called anyone anymore?

"What about?" Díaz asked.

What had we been texting about? A Netflix show we disagreed on. Who would fire our human resources director when she was finally fired since firing people was usually her job. Whether Dutch Brothers coffee was superior to Peet's. "Stuff."

He cocked his head. "What kind of stuff? Work stuff? Personal stuff?"

"A little of both I guess." Heat crept up my neck, which was better than feeling like I was freezing, but still uncomfortable.

"You were just coworkers?" he asked with an arched brow.

"Friendly coworkers." So maybe one of Zach's girlfriends had called me his work wife. So maybe I'd kind of liked that. Díaz didn't need to know any of that.

"Would Milburn have had a lot of equipment in his place? Cameras? Stuff like that?" Díaz asked.

My phone buzzed. I glanced at the text and put the phone in my pocket.

"You need to get that?" Díaz asked, pointing his chin toward my phone.

I shook my head. "No. It can wait." I crossed my arms over my chest.

"Okay, then. Equipment? Would he have any in the apartment?" He scratched the side of his head with the end of his pen.

"Lots. A couple of laptops. Several cameras. Tripods. Beanbags. DVD burners. External hard drives." I hadn't looked around for any stuff while I'd been inside. I had a slight recollection of things being tossed around, but mainly all I could see in my mind's eye was Zach. "Is it all there?"

He popped a piece of gum in his mouth and started chewing. "Nope. None of it. Place is a mess too. They wanted to make sure they got everything worth taking, I guess." He sounded like he was impressed with the thieves' work ethic. "You know what he had? Do you have serial numbers and stuff like that?"

"Back at the office."

"Swell." He flicked his notepad shut and watched me for a second. "Looks like he surprised someone robbing the place and confronted them. Things went wrong. Real wrong."

Zach would not have confronted anyone over Howard Investigations equipment. He didn't love the company so much he was ready to go down in a blaze of glory for it. Besides, he knew everything was insured up the wazoo. He wasn't really a confrontational type of guy either. That wasn't the way a detective specializing in surveillance did things. He was sly, cunning, a little crafty. It was part of the gig. "Are you sure? It doesn't sound right. It wasn't even his stuff to worry about."

Díaz shrugged. "Maybe he didn't confront them. Maybe he had bad timing. Walked in when they were taking the stuff. Either way, the stuff is gone and he's dead."

I shuddered and my teeth chattered again. My brain still wasn't willing to process that information. Zach dead. Of all the things that didn't sound right, that sounded the least right.

A look of compassion crossed Díaz's face. It was the first expression I'd seen that I wouldn't have categorized as annoyed. "Sorry. He was your friend. I didn't mean any disrespect." He looked away. "Occupational hazard."

He handed me his card. "Send me that list of equipment. I'll probably have some follow-up questions for you. I'll be in touch." He left the car.

I stared down at the card, then gathered the foil blanket tighter around me and went back to my own car.

⁂

Dean, our boss, sent me home early. Probably a wise move. I wasn't functioning well. I kept trying not to cry just to realize that everything looked blurry because my eyes were full of tears. I'd already processed the videos from the previous day before I went to check on Zach. Everything else could wait a day.

I walked up the stairs to my third-floor apartment, glancing through the mail I'd picked up on my way into the building. I slid the flyers and catalogs and other junk to the back of the stack. Then my fingers stopped on a padded envelope. Not too big. Not too fancy. Not something anyone would notice. Except it had Zach's address in his scrawling handwriting in the upper-left-hand corner.

He'd done it once before, sent me a couple of thumb drives, a key, and a burner phone at my apartment, asked me to hold on to them for a few days, then picked them up from me the next week.

Once I got inside, I slit open the envelope. Yep. A thumb drive. Just one. A key on a key ring I recognized, a polished stone with the word TRUST engraved into it. It had been one of the cheesy items in the gift bags our human resources director gave out at the holiday party. Zach and I had had a lot of fun mocking it, but otherwise it was pretty useless. Then there was a burner phone and a note also in Zach's distinctive spiky handwriting. "Hold on to this for me, kiddo. Thanks, Z." The "kiddo" set my teeth on edge, but there wasn't much I could do about it now or, if I was being honest with myself, ever. I had tried in my own way. I set the drive and the note down carefully on the counter in my kitchen. My apartment's a studio. One big room with a galley kitchen and a little bathroom decorated in what I thought of as early Poverty Barn. A futon. A rocking chair I'd pulled out of a dumpster. A bed curtained off in the corner with a bunch of shawls I'd sewn together.

My phone buzzed again. I glanced at it, but didn't respond. Instead, I pulled some leftover spaghetti out of the fridge and popped it in the microwave and poured myself a big glass of red wine. It was five o'clock somewhere, right? When everything was ready, I sat down crisscross applesauce on my couch, wrapped myself up in an afghan, powered up my laptop, slid the thumb drive in and hit play. A scene timestamped 5:45 a.m. lit up my screen. Nothing special. A typical grounding shot that all our detectives took when they set up in the morning, panning over the neighborhood, then zeroing in on the most likely place our subject would exit a home or a business.

It was kind of hard to see much. Dawn hadn't quite broken as Zach set up. That was part of the point. When whoever you were watching got up, you were already there. They didn't see anyone arriving.

So why put it in that envelope and send it to me? I leaned back, red wine in my hands and watched as nothing happened. Like seriously nothing. There wasn't even enough of a breeze to make the limbs of the Crepe Myrtle in the front yard sway. A car drove through—a gray Ford Fusion, I thought—maybe going a little fast, but that's what passed for excitement.

My phone buzzed again. An actual call this time. I sighed and answered this time. "Hi, Davey."

"Where have you been?" he asked in that distinctive tone, the one most people would recognize right away. If they didn't recognize it in his voice, they'd recognize it when they saw his face and those unique features.

"At work. Now home." I picked at the edge of the afghan with a fingernail.

"Why didn't you text me back?" He sounded hurt.

I sighed. "I was busy, bud. You know I can't always answer."

"But I sent two selfies! You didn't send me even one!"

I rubbed at my forehead with my thumb. "Sorry." I was, actually. It was one of our rules. We always answered each other.

"Are you coming this weekend?"

"I'll try," I said.

"Please? Can we go to services?"

I don't make it to Friday night services every weekend. I could probably be happy never going to services at all, but Davey liked the Oneg at our parents' temple, Congregation Ahavath Achim. They get their babka from Bakery Ayelet and that's pretty much the best babka in the Bay. I tried to get Davey there at least once a month. Maybe I'd say kaddish for Zach. He wouldn't have known what that was, but I would.

"I'll do my best."

There was a pause. "Please?"

"I can only promise I'll try."

I was three when my brother was born. There are almost no photos of my mother or my father holding him. They're all of me with him. I helped him take his first steps. I potty-trained him. Later, I'd give him his bath and read bedtime stories to him. As far as I was concerned, he was mine. At three, I hadn't understood what Down syndrome was or what it meant. I'd thought those distinctive features made him cuter than all the other babies.

My parents both have PhDs. My mother is a tenured professor. My father works at a research lab that requires a security clearance. A baby with Down syndrome was not in their plans. They're not monsters. Davey was always fed and clothed and got anything and everything he needed. There just always seemed to be some distance. Now there was even more. Davey was sent to live in a group home at about the time I left for college.

I had fought them. I had screamed and cried and kicked walls until they'd pretty much threatened to send me to a group home too.

In the end, it was fine. Sort of. Most of the time, Davey was probably better off there than living at home. Things were set up for him there. He had a job bagging groceries and went to the gym and had lots of social activities. He was less isolated than he would have been if he'd still lived at my parents' place. He also had no privacy, and the last time I picked him up to go to the movies, he had a bruise on his upper arm that he refused to talk about.

Plus, the drive to Castro Valley where the group home was from Vallejo where I lived was about an hour, if there was no traffic, which is a pretty huge if in the Bay Area. I needed to move him closer. There was a place in Benicia close enough that Davey and I could have lunch together. It wasn't even a group home. It was a community living situation where Davey could have a little apartment of his own but still have all the advantages of help with shopping and transportation. My parents said no, though. It was way more expensive than the place they had him now and he'd been fine there for years. I'd badgered them enough that they'd said they'd move him if I could pay the difference.

Honestly, it was just a ruse on their part. There was no way I could afford it. Despite my degree in criminal justice, Howard Investigations wasn't exactly paying me the big bucks.

"You know, if you'd accepted that spot at Hastings, you'd be a lawyer right now and you'd be making more than enough money to cover that," my mother had said.

"Yeah, but I'd be a *lawyer*, Mom," had been my reply.

She'd sniffed. We'd had the argument enough times that we didn't really need to have it anymore. Then she'd turned from the sink where she'd been finishing up the dinner dishes. "You know, you aren't your brother's keeper, Leah."

I wasn't so sure about that. If I wasn't his keeper, who was?

"I gotta go, Davey." I took a selfie of myself on the couch wrapped up in the afghan, sticking my tongue out and texted it to him.

I heard the ding of it going through to his phone. He didn't say anything for a second. "You okay, Leah?"

"Sure. Why?"

"You don't wrap up in Aunt Miriam's blanket unless you're sad."

Well, that was more perspicacious than I'd expected. "You're right. I'm not all the way okay. Something bad happened to a friend."

"But not to you, right?"

"No. Not to me." Not really. A bad shock. A slightly dented heart. Nothing big.

"But you're still sad?" he asked.

"Yeah. Same as I would be sad if something happened to you." I fingered the edge of the afghan.

"But I'm your brother. Your friend wasn't a brother."

"Sometimes it feels like everyone is my brother." Which would make me everyone's keeper, I guess.

❧

Sleep came and went that night, leaving muddy footprints in my brain of Zach's sightless eyes staring up at his ceiling, of the mess on the floor of his apartment, of the crazy pile of things strewn around his apartment. I woke, feeling neither rested nor refreshed. I dragged myself out for my morning run anyway. Dawn was breaking, the light a filmy gray that washed over everything, softening edges and leaching color.

It was probably only a few minutes later in the day than when Zach shot that video of the Ford cruising down the street. What had made it worth burning to a thumb drive and sending to me for safekeeping? Cars cruised past me now, looming up out of the gray remnants of an overnight Tule fog and disappearing away. What would have made one of them interesting enough to bang tape of, download it, burn it, send it to me?

Back at the apartment, I showered and dressed. I couldn't come up with a good reason to stay home, so I packed a sandwich and an apple and headed into work.

I punched in the code to turn off the alarm and let myself into the office. I was the first one there, which was normal. I got the morning emails to clients ready. When they came home at night, the guys—and they were pretty much all guys—would upload a bit of video. If they'd gotten good tape of someone on a dance floor or carrying moving boxes for a friend, they'd send that. If they hadn't gotten anything, they'd send a grounding shot. I scanned through, picked the best stuff, turned it into a clip, wrote a little description, and filled it into a boilerplate email to whatever insurance adjustor had ordered the surveillance.

I started the downloads, each labeled with the name of the subject and the date. I tagged each one with the name of the investigator as they popped up on my screen and checked my log against who had been working the day before.

No one had removed Zach's name from the list. He was still listed as being in Tracy. I deleted his name with shaking fingers. He wasn't in Tracy. He'd never be in Tracy again.

On the other hand, he'd been *somewhere* when he'd taped that Ford Fusion. Where?

I opened up our case management system. Zach was supposed to have been in Livermore that day, set up on Claudette Spurlock, who hadn't so much as twitched a curtain for days on end. There was no mention in his report of any other vehicles he'd followed or had been significant, so why the hell had he bothered to tape that Ford Fusion and send it to me? It still didn't make sense. Someone should look into it. The cops seemed the obvious choice.

I called Díaz.

"Yeah?"

Dude was a total charmer. Whatever. I explained about the thumb drive and the phone.

"And?" he asked.

"And *what*?" I responded, confused.

"And what does it mean?" That annoyed look he'd had on his face definitely transferred to his voice.

"I don't know. I thought maybe you could figure that out."

A gusty sigh came over the line. "You mean in my copious spare time?"

"Not your spare time. Your work time. What if it has something to do with why he was killed?"

"Why would it?"

"Why wouldn't it?" I countered.

Another sigh traveled through like a desert wind. "Because it seems kind of random. I think it's much more likely that someone figured out he had a few thousand dollars' worth of video equipment in an apartment that wasn't too hard to break into and Mr. Milburn had the bad timing to walk in while they were still there. A struggle ensued and, well . . . your friend got the worst of it."

"And that's it?"

"Most likely."

"You're not going to look further?"

"Of course we are. We took prints. We're talking to neighbors."

"What have you found?"

"Look, Ms. Rabinowitz," Díaz said, not answering me. "What happened to your friend was tragic and most likely random. Our best bet is to get a hit on the video equipment when someone tries to hock it. We got the list out to the usual suspects. I'll let you know if we hear anything." He hung up.

Because I come in early, I leave early too. I was heading to my car by three o'clock. Maybe Díaz was right. Maybe the thumb drive and the phone had nothing to do with what happened to Zach, but maybe it did. Maybe it would tell us who had killed my friend. Maybe it would tell us who had taken away the guy that maybe, *maybe*, one day I could have gotten to look at me as something other than a kid sister. But it wasn't going to tell us anything unless someone did a little detective work. Díaz wasn't going to look into it, so that apparently left it up to me.

❦

I pulled my Toyota Scion up to Claudette Spurlock's house. I brought up Zach's video on my laptop and checked it against my surroundings to be sure I was positioned in the same spot, around four houses down from the house on the opposite side of the street.

I'd folded the back seat flat before I left the office. Now I squeezed between the two front bucket seats into the larger space in back. I'd cut lengths of black material a little larger than the dimensions of my windows and with a credit card, I tucked the edges of the material tightly into the rubber gaskets around the windows, leaving one section of one window uncovered so I could see out how Zach had taught me the one time I went out with him. Within minutes, I'd be totally invisible to anyone walking by and casually looking into my car. All they'd see was dark windows as long as I didn't create any light inside.

I settled into the stadium seat I'd brought with me and watched the street where the Fusion had come from. Nothing.

Well, not *nothing*. A few cars went by. A kid on a bike, a mom pushing a jogging stroller, and an old guy walking with ski poles.

No Ford Fusion, though.

It didn't take long for me to get antsy. I was bored.

Our investigators spend a whole lot of time sitting in the backs of increasingly hot vans and SUVs waiting for something to happen. It was boring. Some read. Some watched movies on their computers. Some listened to music.

Zach had texted. A lot.

I generally received a running commentary of what was on his mind over the course of a day. I grabbed my phone and scrolled back through the text messages Zach had sent me until I got to the day he had taped the Fusion.

I'd gotten a text from him at six thirty that morning: *Set up at Spurlock residence. Blue Camry parked in the driveway. Looks like it hasn't moved since yesterday.*

Nothing for a while. Fifteen minutes later: *Hearing sirens nearby. Hope they're not for me.*

I snorted. It wasn't unheard of for someone to call the cops on us. De'andre, one of our other detectives, had gotten made watching someone who lived near an elementary school. Apparently, an unfamiliar van with blacked out windows sitting near a bunch of little kids made someone suspicious. The cops pulled him out of the van and had him face down on the pavement for twenty minutes before we got everything straightened out.

I sighed. Maybe it was something. Maybe it wasn't. I texted Davey a selfie of me holed up in the back of the van. He texted back a picture of his feet in a very clean new pair of sneakers. I took a quick photo of me pretending to stick my finger up my nose and texted it back along with a note about his new sweet kicks.

He texted a GIF of Carlton from *Fresh Prince of Bel Air* dancing.

At a little before six, I pulled the blackout curtains down, climbed back into the front seat, and drove away. The sun was going down. I wasn't likely to see much once it got dark. I was two blocks away from Charlotte Spurlock's house when I went past the roadside memorial, one of those little shrines you see on the side of roads, usually a cross, to mark where someone has been killed in a car accident. They come in all shapes and sizes. Elaborate and simple. Piled with flowers and stuffed animals and tokens of love and respect or only a few faded mementos scattered in the dirt.

I almost passed it. It was pretty modest as far as memorials go. A small cross with three wilting bouquets and one teddy bear at its foot at an intersection where there was no crosswalk. I pulled over, parked down the street, and walked back. A car went by, its horn's blare increasing and decreasing in volume with the Doppler effect as it barreled past me. I jumped back into the weeds on either side of the narrow dirt path that ran alongside the road, nearly losing my balance. The name on the cross was Abner, and the ribbon across the chest of the teddy bear read, "We love you, Daddy."

❦

I got home and entered "Abner accident Livermore California" and the date on Zach's footage of the Fusion into the search engine and got a raft of articles. The top one was:

HIT AND RUN KILLS LOCAL MAN

The Livermore Police Department is looking for a suspect after a hit and run left an area man dead.

Officers responded to reports at the intersection of Shasta Drive
and Cornell Street around 6:00 a.m., according to a news release
from the department. When they arrived, they found a man who
had been struck by a vehicle.

The next three articles were virtually identical. The last one identified the
victim by name. Abner Hendrix. I chewed my lip. I knew I was stretching here, but I backed up the tape and slowed it down when the Fusion
drove through. Did it have any dents? The front fender didn't look great.
It was crumpled. The driver's face was an oval blur. I stopped the tape
and enlarged the image, but there was a limit to what I could see at that
resolution. It wasn't like on TV where they could say "enhance that" and
it would magically enhance. Pixels were pixels. There was no way around
that. Dim light, through a window on a moving car, I wasn't going to get
much. I backed up the video again. I didn't think I could get much more
detail on the face, but I might be able to on the license plate.

I enlarged it. I sharpened it. I played around with color and contrast.
In the end, I managed to get the first number, two letters, and then maybe
the last number. 7LS???5. California license plates for cars start with a
number that's followed by three letters and then three numbers, unless
it's a custom plate. I needed one more letter and two more numbers. I
slumped down on the couch and sighed. It was too many variables to
figure out the rest of that plate.

As a licensed private detective agency we have access to a database
that lets us run plates. It's handy when we're trying to figure out which
car parked along the curb or in the driveway our subject might get into
after exiting a home. Or what might come out of a garage. But that wasn't
much of a help if I didn't have the whole plate.

I pulled Aunt Miriam's afghan closer around me. I could call Díaz
again. I was pretty sure a cop could run a partial plate. Then I imagined
the way he'd sigh and decided against it. I wasn't sure if what I had now
would be enough to interest him. Maybe if I could find another connection. Something that would tie the Fusion to the hit and run.

I shook my head. What did any of it mean, anyway? Even if that
Fusion was the one that hit this guy, why would Zach send that thumb
drive to me? Why not send it to the cops? Or report it?

I picked up the burner phone. The phone's screen was locked, but
Zach always used the same set of passwords. I'd been accessing his stuff

for two years. It took me four tries, but I got it open. I checked the list of recent calls. There were three. All to the same number. I did a reverse search on it but came up dry.

I liked Zach. Maybe even loved him a little. That didn't mean I didn't know who he was. A year or so ago, he'd been following a regional sales manager who claimed he'd strained his back moving boxes of auto parts. He'd picked up a woman at a train station, drove her to a scenic overlook where they both got out of the front seat of the van and climbed in back. Then the van started to rock. A little while later—really, an embarrassingly short period of time for Mr. Sales Manager—they'd gotten out of the back of the van, back into the front seats, and he'd dropped her back off at the train station. Needless to say, the lady was not his wife.

A couple weeks later, Zach had paid off his car loan. I knew what had happened. I could see who had accessed videos on my system. I had started to ask once and he'd stopped me. He'd ruffled my hair and told me to stay trustworthy, that it made me unique.

If there was some connection between the car and Zach's murder, I was pretty sure it wouldn't reflect well on Zach. If he could pay off a car loan by blackmailing an adulterer, what could he do with someone who'd committed vehicular manslaughter?

❧

We had access to the database to run plates, but those plates had to be tied to a case. We couldn't run stuff for fun or for personal reasons. The threat of an audit hung over us. At any time, the records company could demand our records and we'd better be able to justify every plate we ran. Mainly, we tagged the plates we ran with a case number as we ran them, but sometimes things got a little fast and furious and a few searches would fall through the cracks. I fished them out of the cracks and set them on the straight and narrow by matching license plate requests with case numbers.

It was my first task after I got my emails out. Most of them were pretty easy. Joe had run like five plates at once trying to figure out which of the platoon of cars parked in front of an Eichler in Martinez belonged to the claimant. I tagged them. Anton had followed the wrong car and had figured it out by running the plate. I found the case he'd worked and tagged that. Then I found four plates from the days after Abner Hendrix had been killed. Each one started with a seven that was followed by an L and an S and ended with a five. They all were listed as having been run using *my* login and password.

I hadn't run those plates. I didn't remember every single plate I ever ran, but I was pretty sure I'd remember running a sequence like that. That meant someone else had used my login. It didn't take a brain surgeon to figure out who that someone was.

For security reasons, we all had to change our passwords every three months. That was true for the records research site as well as our email and our case management system and the video archive. I had a good memory, but no one's is that good. I kept a log of my current usernames and passwords on a piece of paper in my top desk drawer. We're not supposed to do that, but we all do. Otherwise no one would ever be able to log into anything.

Zach would sit at my desk on those occasions he'd come into the office. I'd walk in and find him tipped back in my desk chair, feet propped up on a console, at least once a week. He could have easily copied my passwords on one of those visits. All he would've had to do is take a quick photo with his phone and he'd have them all for the next few months and he'd know right where to come to get more when those stopped working.

I looked through all four of the requests. The first one came back to a Toyota Celica. The second one came back to a Subaru Legacy. The third to a Nissan Altima. The fourth came back to a Ford Fusion owned by Resource Property Management.

I rubbed my hands together like a piano player getting ready to warm up.

My phone buzzed. A call this time. Not a text. I picked up. Davey was talking so fast and so loud I could barely make out what he was saying. "Slow down. Breathe."

It took him a few minutes. "He took my shoes!"

"Who took what shoes?" I wasn't tracking.

"Henry. He took my new shoes. My new running shoes. The ones I got for the gym with my birthday money." He was near tears.

"Okay. Henry took them. Can you ask for them back?" I was pretty sure this problem was solvable.

"Of course I did." He sounded offended.

"And?"

"He got them all dirty and muddy. They're not like new at all anymore." I heard sniffles.

"I'll help you clean them up this weekend."

He gulped a little. "It won't be the same. I hate it here. Henry always takes my stuff."

It was true. Henry did take his stuff. To be fair, Davey usually had nice stuff. Remember, our parents weren't monsters. A little self-involved but not monsters. "Did you talk to Marna about it?" Marna was the supervisor at the group home.

"She said I should keep my stuff locked, but there's no place to lock anything."

In that sweet place in Benicia, he'd be able to keep anything and everything locked up. He'd never have to worry about someone taking his shoes. Especially not Henry who was considerably bigger than Davey and seemed to have a bit of a mean streak.

"Maybe Mom and Dad would buy a trunk for you. One with a lock. I'll ask. Okay?"

"Okay." He snuffled a bit. "You're still coming Friday, though, right?"

"Right." We hung up and I closed the Secretary of State site and opened a browser window.

Not everyone realizes how much of their information is out there and a matter of public record. Sometimes it's a matter of a simple internet search. Other times, you have to know where to look. I started with the easy stuff, putting his name into a general search.

After the obituaries, the usual stuff came up. A link to a Facebook page and a LinkedIn profile. I went to LinkedIn first. He'd been some kind of analyst with the state until about two years ago. Then he'd gone to work as a property manager for Resource Property Management, the company that owned the Ford Fusion in Zach's video. What. The. Hell.

Then I popped over to Facebook. It was public, which was a boon to anyone who wanted to snoop in his life. There was a stream of rest-in-peace messages, most pretty generic but a few more specific. A few that weren't so nice. One guy posted, "I guess I'll never get back the money you owe me." Ouch.

I scrolled down, watching his life in reverse. Most of what was there were things other people had posted to his Timeline, things where he might be in the back of a group photo or something. In the most recent photos, he was thin. Stringy, even. Going backward in time, he plumped up. Not too much, mind you. He was what we in California refer to as fit. It's a step down from buff, but a step up from Dad Bod. There was a post with a photo of a guitar, asking if anyone wanted to buy it. It looked like Abner also sold his bike, his golf clubs, and his skis as I made my way backward through his life. Based on the number of times he asked if anyone had a room to rent, he went through roommates pretty quickly too.

The progression to better-than-a-Dad-Bod ended with a photo from nearly three years ago he took of his own leg in a cast. The caption read: "Fell off the damn ski lift. Don't even have a good story to tell."

Before that he'd been quite sporty. There were photos of him with kids in a family run for charity and another with him on a bike. A lot of him with a pretty brunette. All of those had stopped appearing about a year after the leg-in-a-cast photo. I was loath to leave the place I'd scrolled, to—it takes those damn Facebook photos time to render—but there was a trove of information to check. I clicked "About."

No job listed, but a degree from CSU-Sacramento. That fit well enough with the job. Under family relationships, no wife and no kids. I put the brunette's name in the search bar. There were about five to pick from. It didn't take long to figure out which was her. Her profile was private, but there was a photo of her looking a little older with kids who quite well could be the ones in the other photos, also a bit older. There was a guy in one of the photos, a guy who wasn't Abner.

I went back to Abner's "About" to look for some more family relationships. A father and a sister, Caitlin. Dad's profile was also set to private. His profile pic was him with a fish. What is with old guys and fish?

I popped over to Caitlin's page and went through the same backward progression. There were photos of her with Abner presenting their dad with a birthday cake with a shit ton of candles on it and a selfie of the three of them at a picnic and a photo of the three of them at a ceremony where Dad was being given a special quilt to commemorate his service in the army. Lots and lots of photos of the three of them. A few of Caitlin with friends, but mainly always family. Family was Abner and Dad, and Dad didn't look like he was doing so great.

I knew that feeling. You'd probably see something similar on my Facebook page. Me and Davey. Davey and me. Occasionally a photo with Mom or Dad or both. You could tell from my page that family was what was most important to me and that family for me was Davey. My guess was you could tell what Caitlin thought from her page too.

Caitlin's page listed her as the owner of Resource Property Management, the company that employed Abner and had leased the car Zach had filmed. That could not be a coincidence.

I did a search on Resource Property Management. They were exactly what they sounded like: property managers. You own a property and want to rent it out and don't want to deal with being a landlord? Don't want those middle-of-the-night calls about stopped-up sinks? Don't want to evict people who don't pay the rent? You hire a property manager.

There was a link to a Yelp page for them. Seriously, did everything have a Yelp page? I was beginning to think the kid's lemonade stand down the street probably got reviewed. "One star. Our server picked his nose while he poured our drinks."

Resource Property Management, or RPM, as they were referred to, only had three stars. Ouch.

I scrolled down, like on the Facebook page, reading the reviews in reverse chronological order.

"One star. Don't rent from RPM. Took them two weeks to fix our clogged toilet and I think the guy stole money from my purse while he was here."

"One star. RPM sucks. Kept our security deposit to shampoo the carpets. I thought that was normal wear and tear."

"Three stars. Only deal with Caitlin. Everyone else there is worthless."

But if you went back farther. Things were pretty good.

"Five stars. Prompt and courteous. Does repairs on time."

"Five stars. Professional and friendly. I felt like I was renting from a friend."

The ratings had all started to drop around the time Caitlin hired her brother Abner. Until then, she'd been running a successful business. People check those reviews. I certainly would stay away from a three-star firm if there were five-star firms available.

I got the burner phone again and checked the number he'd called against the number for RPM. Bingo.

Just for giggles I plugged Abner's name into a county records request. A DUI.

A drunk and disorderly arrest.

Possession of a Schedule 1 drug.

All of them in the last year and the very last one from the day before the accident.

Zach could have easily figured all this out. It might have taken him a little longer to find the information. He was more of an in-the-field guy than a sit-at-the-desk-and-investigate-on-the-internet guy, but it wasn't that hard when you knew where to look.

What would Zach have done, then? I pulled up the GPS on Zach's van, out of curiosity. It might not tell me anything. He could have used his own car for whatever he was up to, but it was worth a shot. I pulled up his assignment list from the past two weeks. I clicked through the maps generated by the GPS from day to day. One day he was on Maya Newsom in Fremont. He'd spent most of the day sitting in front of the woman's house. She made a trip to the grocery store and the post office and he was on her that whole time. At six thirty, he headed back to his place in Concord. The next day, he was on Carter Headley in Lathrop. That guy had gone to the bank and a Target where he bought socks with Zach shadowing him. Again, Zach went right back home after he packed it all in.

Then he spent three days sitting in front of Teena Vo's house in Hayward. She went nowhere and nothing happened. For three days. On day four when Zach's written report was identical to the three days before of absolutely nothing, his van had taken a few trips. There was one trip to Oakland and another to Livermore. I plugged the addresses into the search bar. The Oakland address was the federal bankruptcy court, and the other was a salvage yard in Livermore.

Well, okay then. I pulled up the website for the federal bankruptcy court in Oakland. It took a few minutes of clunking around to figure out the right information to put in to get a record, but there it was. A year ago, Abner Hendrix had filed for Chapter 7 bankruptcy, the kind regular people file when their world collapses rather than the ones that businesses file.

The picture started to come clear. The weight loss. The trouble with the law. The trouble with money. The trouble with his wife. Losing his job. Going to work for his sister. Ruining his sister's business. All of it seeming to start not too long after he fell off the ski lift. Unless I missed my guess, not having a good story to tell about his injury was the least of his problems. Abner Hendrix was what news reports kindly refer to as a person who misused prescription drugs.

Howard Investigations specializes in workers' comp cases. Workers' comp comes into play when someone gets hurt on the job. Sure, there are some mental distress claims, but the majority of the claims that are squishy enough to have an insurance adjustor pay for us to follow someone involve a physical injury.

Do you know what doctors do when someone has an injury and is in enough pain that they can't work even for a day or two? They give them painkillers. Now things are starting to change, but two or three years ago? Doctors were handing out Vicodin prescriptions like they were coupons for free hugs.

Most people who throw out their back or break a leg or get their wisdom teeth out can take Vicodin for a few days until the worst of the pain passes then return to their regular lives like nothing has happened.

Other people? Not so much. Other people start to notice that nice floaty feeling they get when they take their painkillers. They decide it would be okay to take an extra pill on the weekend or after a hard day or because it's Thursday. Maybe they realize it's getting to be a problem and stop and experience the joys of withdrawal. No one wants to go through that. They do what they have to do to avoid it. It progresses from there. It's shocking how fast they go from regular people with jobs and families to people trying to score heroin on the street because heroin, a Schedule 1 drug like whatever Abner Hendrix got popped for before, is so much cheaper and easier to get than Oxy. They exhaust their family, emotionally and financially.

Still, running him over? I gnawed on my fingernail, trying to imagine what it would feel like to have a brother who went from best friend to a constant suck of my time and my energy and my money. Not everyone understood that addiction was an illness. From the outside, it looks so much like a choice. Stop taking that drug. Show up for work. Keep your hands off other people's belongings. How hard could that be?

Really, really hard, it turns out. Hard enough that people all across the country were ruining their lives and the lives of everyone around them.

Hard enough that your sister maybe had to bail you out of jail? Hard enough that maybe, when she dropped you off on that foggy morning and started to drive away, she might change her mind, turn around, and run you right down?

Which brought me back to the car, the Ford Fusion. Where was it now? What had she done with it? If she'd taken it into a shop with a suspicious dent, someone could very well have called the cops.

I went back to the report on the license plate and got the VIN, then bopped over to a website that let you search for vehicles by VIN.

The Fusion was listed as totaled. No way did it have enough damage in Zach's video to be totaled. That made no sense. Maybe I'd follow one more step in Zach's footsteps before I handed it all over to Díaz. I had a sneaking suspicion I knew where the car was: the salvage yard that Zach had visited.

I looked up at the clock. No way I'd make it there before the yard closed. It would have to wait until tomorrow.

Later that night, I took a selfie of me pretending to sleep and sent it to Davey with a caption that said "zzzzzz."

He texted back one of him with his head on his pillow, eyes closed. I peered closer. Was that a bruise on his cheek?

❧

The next morning, I called Detective Díaz again. "Yes, Ms. Rabinowitz," he said, sounding weary before I'd even said more than hello.

I told him about the car and the makeshift cross and flowers and what I'd found out about Abner Hendrix and how a car registered to his sister had been in the area.

"Uh huh," he said.

"That's all you have to say? 'Uh huh'?"

"None of what you're telling me means anything. It barely even qualifies as circumstantial evidence. No way the DA is going to bring charges based on that."

I could hear him shuffling papers on the other end of the line. It felt like I was being dismissed. Again. "So that's it?"

"For now, yeah. That's it."

I hung up feeling like steam was coming out of my ears. Fine. I'd see what more I could find out. Maybe I could find something that would jar Díaz out of his lethargy.

❧

By three thirty, I was talking to a remarkably clean looking guy at Double J Metals.

I flashed my Howard Investigations ID card at the salvage yard guy. "I'm here to take some photos of . . ." I made a big deal of looking at the clipboard I carried—Zach had once told me you could get into a lot of places just by having a clipboard—to check what car it was. I acted like I did this all the time and couldn't remember one car from another, and said, "A Ford Fusion. License plate 7JSY524."

"Let me take a look." He gestured for me to follow him into the office. He sat down at his desk and started tapping on his computer. "Yep. We got it. Should be right here." He took out a photocopied map of the lot and made an X where row thirteen and column D intersected.

"Pretty slick," I said.

He shrugged. "Nothing else to do here but my job. Might as well do it right."

Chalk one up for the rule followers. I waved goodbye and trudged out into the yard.

The Fusion was right where he said it'd be, although I didn't recognize it at first. The front end was an accordioned mess. The deflated airbag hung like a sad sack off the steering wheel. It had definitely been through something bad after Zach had filmed it. I wasn't sure that mattered, though.

I watch enough *Law & Order* and *CSI* and *Forensic Files* reruns to know that somewhere underneath that mess there was probably something that would point to how Caitlin Hendrix ran over her own brother. Because he had ruined his life and seemed hell bent on ruining hers.

Davey texted me a selfie making a funny face and I felt a wash of relief. Maybe everything was fine and I was borrowing trouble.

I found a car with an intact side mirror and took a photo with my phone's screen facing the mirror and got a trippy little image of me looking in a mirror with a picture of me looking in a mirror inside it.

Davey texted back a shocked-faced emoji.

What had happened to the Fusion to turn its front end into the car version of a pug dog's face? You have to be a Party of Interest to get hold of an accident report. That means driver or property owner or passenger. I was none of those things and I wasn't sure I could BS my way into convincing someone I was. Police blotters, however, are extremely public. Sometimes you have to know how to decipher them, but you can get there.

Three hours later, I found it. Police had been called out to a one-car accident on Alum Rock Road. Driver swerved to miss a deer, lost control of car, hit embankment. Minor injuries to driver. Paramedics at the scene released her. Car likely totaled.

So, she swerved to miss a deer but not her own brother.

Or had she? After all, she was the only one who saw a deer. There were no other witnesses. Having a second, much worse accident could be a very handy way of covering up an earlier dent. Anything anyone saw—blood or hair—they would quickly ascribe to the deer that she might have grazed on her way to the embankment.

That would all hold up fine under quick cursory glances, the kind an insurance adjustor would give to a totaled car driven by a nice middle-aged white lady. If a police lab got hold of it, though? Well, that might be a whole nother story.

That story was going to have to wait. If I was going to get Davey and me to services on time, I needed to put on a dress and hit the road.

It was six o'clock when I pulled up to the halfway house where Davey lived. It was a typical McMansion in a NorCal housing development. Pink stucco. Red tile roof. Arched windows in the front. One of the occupational therapy activities the people who lived there did was gardening. Lamb's ear dotted the front yard punctuated by lavender and salvia. Pampas grass waved its fluffy head. I rang the doorbell. Henry answered.

"Is Davey here?" I asked.

"Yeah," he said, but didn't move.

Henry was a big kid, so it felt menacing. I wasn't sure it was, though. Davey didn't always pick up on social cues. Henry might not either. "Could you let him know his sister is here?"

He stared at me for a second or two and then stepped back, yelling up the stairs, "Davey, your sister's here."

I heard footsteps thumping overhead then Davey appeared on the stairs. A smile spread across his face and I felt my lips turn up in a mirror of his. Then just as fast his smile faded as he looked to the side. I looked too. Nothing there but Henry. My bad feeling got a little worse. I glanced at my watch. We'd have to talk about it after services.

We got to the temple and filed in, choosing the pew we normally chose. Davey liked it because of the view of the stained-glass portrayal of Adam and Eve leaving the Garden of Eden. Plus if Hannah Geller was there, she usually sat directly across. He had a little crush. I straightened his yarmulke for him so he'd look spiffy. He batted my hand away and frowned at me. I held up my hands in a peace gesture and left him alone.

Rabbi Abrams came in and we all stood. Then we started through the familiar rituals. I did what I usually did: I zoned out. Standing. Sitting. Chanting. I'd done it so many times I didn't have to think about it.

Then we hit the sermon.

"The story of Cain and Abel is probably one of the most well-known stories in the Torah," Rabbi Abrams said. "After all, it's pretty near the beginning before most people have lost interest."

The congregation laughed a little.

"Plus it's got a true-crime element to it, and who doesn't like a bit of mystery?"

That got a slightly bigger laugh.

"It's not much of a whodunit, though. We're told who did it and why. Cain killed Abel out of jealousy. Yahweh had accepted Abel's sacrifice, but not Cain's, so Cain slew Abel. Some say he did it with the jawbone of an ass."

Davey turned to me, his mouth in an O. "Rabbi Abrams said a bad word," he whispered.

"It's okay. He used it in a different way than you're thinking," I whispered back.

He gave me a skeptical look.

"I'll explain later." I patted his leg and looked forward.

"Here comes the true crime section of our story," Rabbi Abrams went on. "Yahweh looks for Abel. Then he interrogates Cain. He asks him where his brother is. Cain answers Yahweh's question with another question. He asks, 'Am I my brother's keeper?'"

I took in a sharp breath. Hadn't my mother said something nearly identical? Cain sounded pissed in the story about being responsible for his brother. It seemed highly likely that Caitlin Hendrix wasn't too thrilled about being Abner's keeper. If he'd hit the point where he was getting popped for possession of Schedule 1 drugs, which include things like heroin, he had probably run through the family resources. Who wants to be responsible for an opiate addict, after all?

The rabbi was still talking. "The Torah goes on to list all the generations between Adam and Noah—with the notable absence of Cain. Since we are all descended from flood survivors, all of us, except Cain, are brothers and sisters."

Davey turned to me. "All of us?" he whispered, his forehead creased.

I felt my own crease in return. "Yeah. All of us."

Davey and I were both pretty quiet as we drove back to his place. We were almost there when he said, "Henry hit me."

I turned toward him so quickly I almost swerved the car. "He did *what*?"

"He hit me when I told Marna that he stole my shoes. But then he gave me ten dollars to not tell about hitting me." His fingers twined around themselves in his lap.

"I'll talk to Marna," I said, feeling the steam building up in my head.

"No. He might hit you if you do that." He rubbed at his eyes with his fists, a sure sign he was about to cry.

"I'm going to get you out of there, Davey. I swear it."

"How?" he asked.

"I don't know yet, but I will."

❧

Back at my apartment, I laid all the items from the envelope Zach had sent me on the counter. The thumb drive, the phone, the key with the TRUST keychain. He had sent this all to me for a reason, for safekeeping. But maybe for more than that? Maybe for a bit of insurance? That if something happened to him, someone would be able to figure it out?

And I had. I'd figured out why what was on the thumb drive was important and who he'd been calling on the burner phone. That left the key.

I picked up the key on its stupid key ring. I got mine out of the junk drawer and compared them to see if Zach had altered anything on it. If he had, I couldn't find it. They looked identical. I couldn't help but feel there was a message there to me. Trust. Zach trusted me. He told me to stay trustworthy. That it made me unique.

I opened up my laptop and searched for "trust + key" and got a lot of gibberish. Then I searched for "trust + lock."

Trusted Storage Solutions was the third item on the list. It was located five miles from Zach's place. It was dark already, but I didn't think I could sleep until I saw what might be there.

❧

Trusted Storage Solutions looked like every other storage place I'd ever seen. Lots of anonymous lockers of various sizes arranged in rows. It was easy to get in, but once I was there I was faced with the next hurdle. Which one of these hundred or so lockers was Zach's?

I parked the car and walked up and down a couple of the rows. Everything looked the same. There was nothing decorating the doors or the locks on them. No big flashing arrows pointing to a door with a sign saying, "Leah, look here!" But everything else in that envelope had been something I could figure out, something Zach knew I would be able to figure out. This had to be the same. So what was it?

I tried Zach's birthday as a sequence, but the numbers didn't go up that high. I tried adding the numbers of his birthday up. There was a locker for that number, but the key didn't fit into the lock.

I stood in the middle of the road, looking up at the huge October moon and thought. It had to be something I'd know. Dead leaves skittered around my feet as the breeze picked up. What would Zach know that I knew?

I hit my head as if I could have had a V-8 and added up the numbers of my own birthday and came up with twenty-eight. I found the locker and put the key in the padlock. It turned and the lock sprang free. I lifted the door. Inside, there was one gym bag sitting in the middle of the floor. I felt like a light should have shone on it and angels should have sung.

I knelt in front of it and unzipped it. It was stuffed with cash.

❦

The bag held $20,000. I'd brought it back to my apartment and counted it. It stood stacked up on the coffee table in my living room. This would be more than enough to move Davey to Benicia. Hell, it might even move *me* to Benicia for a bit.

It might also be the last bit of proof I needed to get Díaz off his ass to investigate Caitlin Hendrix for the murder of her brother and then the murder of Zach after he apparently blackmailed her. I took Díaz's now well-worn card out of my wallet and set it next to the money.

Caitlin Hendrix hadn't wanted to be her brother's keeper so she did exactly what Cain did when he got jealous of Abel. She'd killed him. Zach had figured it out, and rather than contact the police, he'd blackmailed her. She'd clearly paid up at least some. Maybe he'd decided to hit her up for more. There were three calls on that burner phone, after all. Maybe Caitlin decided that the only way to be free of him was to get rid of him or get the evidence. Maybe she'd planned to kill him. Maybe it was like Díaz said. Maybe she'd been trying to steal the evidence in his apartment and he'd come home at wrong time.

I totally wanted to be my brother's keeper but didn't have the cash to do it. Now, however, I was pretty sure I had Caitlin Hendrix's cash. There was a certain symmetry to taking the money Caitlin had paid to keep Zach quiet about murdering her brother and using it to take care of mine. There was also a certain symmetry to turning this all over to Díaz. There had to be enough here now for him to investigate for real. It would take the forensic guys no time at all to get what they needed from that Ford Fusion.

Caitlin had killed twice now. I bet it got easier each time she did it. Which meant she'd found it to be a pretty groovy way of solving her problems. Who might get in her way next? Maybe the next person wouldn't be an opiate-addled brother pulling his family down or someone trying to blackmail her. Maybe the next person would just be some kind of inconvenience.

Then again, Cain hadn't killed again. He'd gone off and started over, lived a good life from what we could tell. I could imagine the kind of desperation it would take for her to kill her brother. She probably hadn't planned it. She'd probably been blinded by her anger and her hurt and her worry and pushed that pedal down without even thinking. Rabbi Abrams said we were all brothers and sisters. Could I have compassion for Caitlin? Could I let her go? Could I be her keeper?

I fingered the TRUST keyring. Davey trusted me. He trusted everyone. How much longer would that last if he had to live with a bully? Was I his keeper? Was that my problem?

Zach had trusted me. He had trusted me with evidence. Maybe he'd trusted me to figure out what had happened if something happened to him. He'd definitely thought I was his keeper.

I looked from the card to the cash and back again.

Whose keeper was I?

If It Doesn't Kill You, Just Wait

D.M. Evans

Pomonok Housing.

I wondered about the omission of the word "projects" as I entered the immense Queens apartment complex. The brick maze of seven-story elevator buildings and three-story walkups spread out over fifty-two acres. Years of my life spent running through every hidden corner allowed me to find my way to the right court of apartments without thinking hard. The image of *yente*s lined up in their lawn chairs during the summer months superimposed themselves onto now-empty sidewalks.

I entered through a heavy steel door into an alcove of three apartments. The hallway smelled like cabbage. It always smelled like cabbage. I hate cabbage.

"Bubbe? Bubbe Rosen?" I said after a few knocks, like some other *bubbe* might answer. Thirty or so years ago, that could've happened. Yetta Rosen was the last Jewish inhabitant in her walkup. An old *mezuzah*, hung decades ago, shook in the corner of the doorframe with each knock.

My adoptive parents and I had lived next door. For years, my best friend Shari and I played in the hallway with our respective Barbies, mine black, hers white. A smile tried to push its way across my face.

I tried the handle. The knob turned and I let myself in. She told me she would be home all day. Perhaps she was in the bathroom.

"Bubbe? It's me, Pearlie."

The small apartment's living room was partially visible. Shelves, lined with old photos and knickknacks normally ordered and tidy, were on their backs or the floor. The little red tin where she kept her IOUs had fallen, and jagged slips of colored paper were all over the floor.

Mine wouldn't be among them. I had paid it off when I competed my undergrad.

"Bubbe?" I called again, becoming concerned.

It didn't feel right. I shoved my hand into my shoulder bag's side pocket where Gravel had convinced me to keep the .22. I kept the safety on just in case. Hope withered when I saw the soles of two little pink Keds.

"Bubbe!" I screamed and ran toward her, dropping to my knees.

She was face down. I needed to turn her over. I tried to keep myself from breaking into hysterics but felt the tears flowing down my face. I needed to check for a pulse. I needed to do CPR. My heart raced. I couldn't see. I couldn't make out whether Bubbe had a pulse or I just felt my own heart racing.

Something rustled behind me. Startled, I turned. Pain exploded in my head. Then, nothing.

※

Twenty-four hours prior

Dr. Riley began her normal check-in.

"How are you sleeping?"

"Shitty."

"How are you eating?"

"Shitty."

"Exercise?"

"No." The fifty or so shoulder-length twists in my hair shook with the response.

"Pain?"

"Always." The question of pain made my leg pulse a few times. It was always in the background, waiting.

"On a scale of one to ten, how depressed are you feeling?"

"I plead the Fifth."

Doc's brow furrowed with that response. My replies were all irritable. I'm sure she'd write it all down in the mental status section of her little notes.

"Does this shit ever end, Doc?"

"What do you want to end?"

"The pain. Not my leg. It feels like someone carved a hole in my heart five years ago and the knife is still there." It was that time of year.

The Doc was used to my shit. She sat there—kind, understanding, and empathetic. Why did I want to slap her?

"I feel so pathetic." Perhaps if I slapped her, she'd slap me back and wake me out of my f'ing zombie mode. My medication was somewhere in the sewer beneath Manhattan. She had warned me a long time ago not to abruptly stop taking the antidepressants. They made me feel disconnected. I threw the pills in the toilet. Now I felt even worse.

"Are you having thoughts about killing yourself?"

"Of course, but I'm not suicidal. I'm not planning anything."

She didn't look convinced, and with good reason. I'd survived twenty-five hydrocodone and a fifth of vodka a little over two years ago.

She sat silent, a tactic to which I'd grown accustomed.

"I want to drink. I want to take a pill. Maybe we can do that box thing again?"

"Box thing?"

"You know, put the memories in a box. Put the box on a shelf?"

"Is that how you're coping? Keeping the memories in a box?"

"Exclusively." My defiant tone unnerved even me.

My cell phone buzzed. Doc frowned. But I looked anyway. It was a text from Gravel: "COME QUICK PETE DYING"

I left the office with more than thirty minutes to go in the session. Talking about the panic attacks would need to wait, again.

❦

Gravel stood about six-four, easily. A reddish-blond afro blended with his ruddy beige complexion and slanted yellow brown eyes. He always wore two pairs of dog tags on the outside of his clothing. His shirt was off today. A Star of David, normally kept under his shirt, was also visible. The dog tags were the mementos of his past Marine buddies. Now Gravel only had two friends—me and Pete.

When I got home, Pete was on his favorite blue blanket in the middle of the living room. I thought he was sleeping, but Gravel's face read differently. He was on his knees, Buddhist prayer style.

"Pete's gone."

I noticed swelling around one of his eyes. A split lip said the swelling was not from crying. He'd been in a fight again. I focused my attention on the dog.

The little mutt never weighed more than ten pounds but had wasted to half that because of some kind of blood disease.

"I'm so sorry, Gravel." I put my hand on his bare shoulder once I'd made it to the floor. He flinched a bit. I couldn't recall the last time we actually touched. It wasn't necessary to ask if he was sure Pete was dead. Gravel had the distinction of having been an infantryman and a medic in Afghanistan. He did five or so tours in various war zones. We never talked about it. We both lived in the present, like two psych patients in a fugue state. Our past stayed behind us, at least until it crept on top of us and we shattered. We sat there, silent for several minutes. My thighs were killing me.

"I'm gonna have him cremated tomorrow. I saw an urn for him online."

It was always interesting to see which Jewish traditions Gravel would adhere to.

"I'll go with you," I said. I did not want to go to anything related to a funeral. But he was one of my two friends. Now, I would need to head to Bubbe Rosen's in Flushing from the pet crematorium. She had left me a cryptic voicemail to come see her ASAP and, for Shari's grandmother, I would drop everything and do anything. I felt as if she was my grandmother too. Her wisdom and checks got me through undergrad, after I was orphaned a second time at sixteen years old.

Gravel's unkempt eyebrows knit themselves in to one entity. My lips burned to give him another lecture about the fighting.

"Don't you have court?" he asked.

"Yeah, I know," I lied. My list of to-dos sometimes escaped me. Great excuses for skipping AA meetings. I needed to be in court in the morning to work out two plea deals. One battery, the other drunk and disorderly. Both longtime petty offenders. Shari had stuck her neck out to give me the opportunity to manage the public defender contract we had secured before the "Before." Fucking up my caseload was not an option.

❧

The smell of burnt rubber and blood—my blood spattered all over. I needed to check the back seat of the car. I couldn't move. My legs burned with pain.

"Kierra? Kierra!" I could hear my daughter crying somewhere behind me in the back seat, but I couldn't see her. "Kierra!"

Silent screams emerged from my throat as I forced myself awake from another nightmare. I thought about getting some water, but I was too tired to move. I just lay there, looking at the ceiling and hoping the nightmares had run their course.

※

"I said, get the *fuck up*!"

"Damn. Do you need to be so rude in the morning? Am I late?" I snatched the cover from over my head. Gravel stood near my bed with my big mug of coffee. Throwing away the antidepressant was screwing with me, like Doc said it would. I had tossed and turned all night after the first, second, and third nightmare. When I finally fell asleep, there was Gravel, awakening the shit out of me.

"Nope. But you don't want to be." He brushed past me. He was headed to the back porch to smoke his morning cigarette, the first of five that he parceled out in equal intervals throughout the day. It seemed like every day he added a new regimen to his life—and mine. He fixed my breakfast, tidied the house, ran errands, and helped investigate cases. I paid him a salary, which he had initially refused, plus room and board. It was the least I could do for someone who had saved my life.

※

Thanks to Gravel, I was showered and in my pantsuit—to cover the tats, the nose ring was already pushing it enough with Judge Alvarez—and at court early. Tod Riley was up first. He had a long history of exposing himself and pinching women's asses on the subway. At sixty years old, he still lived with his parents, both in their eighties. They showed up every time looking embarrassed and remorseful. It was obvious he had a disability.

When they brought him into the courtroom, his face was tearstained and bruised. He left with another misdemeanor and an admonishment to his parents to "keep a better eye on him" because next time could mean jail or the forensic hospital.

I kept my eyes on my watch. I had told Gravel I would meet him at home around noon. The wheels of justice were stuck in molasses today. Judge Alvarez declared a recess while she, an ADA, and the defendant's lawyer went behind closed doors. Then my cases were switched and I was now seeing Wallace Crawley. My stomach knotted. The charge was for selling opioids. The word "opioid" would occasionally flash me back to that night. Vodka bottle in my hand, limping down the street in the rain with no umbrella or coat. A homeless man I'd given a pair of socks to the prior winter got me to the ER and saved my life.

The waiting area, where public defenders could meet their clients, buzzed with low conversation. I turned around to see my defendant being led toward me in handcuffs and shackles. I held out my hand to shake his.

"A nigger? You're kidding me. I'm not working with no fuckin' niggers from a Jew law firm." Wallace Crawley turned his head to the side and made a spitting sound. "It's bad enough I got nigger hands on me," he said, nodding at his black police escorts.

Addicted, racist, and an asshole—what kind of fucked-up childhood did he have? The question helped me focus on my job.

"Yes. I'm here from Nigger and Jew, Partners at Law. And this nigga ain't dealing with your shit today. So, I suggest you shut your mouth, let me do my job, and you can get a court date. Or you can go back to your cell and fuck yourself until you get another attorney." Threatening extended stays in county jail usually engendered cooperation.

"I'm not guilty," he said once we sat down. "The cops planted that shit on me."

I gave him my "I give a crap" grimace. "You'll plead not guilty, then."

Crawley got his court date. I was out of there.

❧

In a rare moment, Gravel walked by my side, slower than his normal pace. My steps were shortened in an effort to hide a residual limp. Sweat began to form in the center of my back. I didn't have time to change. We made our way to the 7 train. I hoped we'd get an air-conditioned car.

The teal blue shopping bag Gravel carried rustled in sync with his steps. It looked brighter under a sunless sky. Pete was placed inside a shoebox, wrapped with his favorite blanket, and then inside a pristine Tiffany's bag. I guessed it was the one I'd had for years in a kitchen counter drawer—another stupid keepsake from my marriage.

❧

The 7 train jerked its way along the tracks from Thirty-Fourth Street. Gravel separated his self from me, like usual. He sat catty-corner across the aisle near the door with his dark sunglasses in place. Among his many self-appointed duties, his role included bodyguard. He'd positioned the Tiffany's bag next to him on the long bench-style seat that forced riders to squeeze themselves next to a complete stranger if they really wanted to sit. I had enough space on both sides of me at this point to sit comfortably.

"This is the number seven train. Next stop Vernon-Jackson Avenue," the conductor said. The announcement signaled the long period we would go under the East River. The doors closed. We clanked along ancient tracks. The lights flickered from time to time. A person plunked down next to me, way too close. Without looking up, I bristled with irritation and slid a few inches to the side so we weren't touching. The person slid close again. Now I looked up.

"What the hell's your problem?"

"Hey, girlie Pearlie." It was Richie B, an old connection to old habits. "Where you been? I've been trying to hook up wit'chu you for a while now."

"Richie." My tone was flat and unwelcoming. Richie was at least ten years younger than I. A putz, who still wasn't flossing. Halitosis prevented me from looking at him directly for too long. A wave of embarrassment and nausea sucker punched me in the gut upon recollecting an instance of drugged up, drunken, desperation fucking. I moved away another inch. He moved with me.

The lights flickered again. Between a flicker, Gravel now stood over him.

"Back off, muthafuckah." Gravel grabbed Richie by the collar of his jacket and wrenched it up around his neck, half lifting Richie out of his seat.

Richie gagged. I kind of smiled inside, but spoke up quickly before my companion-turned-Golem ripped Richie's head off.

"Fuck you," he managed to gurgle.

"Watch your fucking mouth," Gravel said.

"Let him go, Gravel." I felt the train slowing to a stop. People were staring now. I checked to see if anyone had pulled out a cell phone to video, but we were safe for the moment.

"When I let go, you get the fuck off the train."

Gravel released him. The doors had been open for a moment. The warning bell sounded. Richie leapt out the train door and grabbed the Tiffany's bag as they closed. He flipped us the bird and walked toward the exit stairway.

His victory stroll was short-lived. Gravel squeezed his meaty fingers between the closed doors' seam and pulled. They opened. He jumped off. The doors closed again. Now I was up, trying the same tactic. It didn't work. The train pulled away. Gravel looked back at me. I watched him speed away in the opposite direction as the train pulled out of the station. I banged hard on the door window. Too hard.

"Open, goddamn it!" People were looking.

Panic engulfed me. The air became thick. I couldn't get enough. My ears felt full of cotton.

Somehow, I made it to a seat and put my head between my legs. My heart raced. Sweat beaded on my forehead. I waited for the panic attack to subside. Three stops later, I sat up without feeling nauseous and dialed Gravel on my cell phone. No answer.

I texted him. "I'm going to Bubbe Rosen's."

🦋

I had no idea how long I'd been unconscious. My head felt like it weighed fifty pounds. The back of it burned and throbbed. It was difficult to move, so I lay there confused. I'd managed to raise my upper body into a half push up, when I stared directly into Bubbe Rosen's vacant eyes.

"What the—?" I shoved myself backward and scampered on all fours several feet away.

It all came back. I'd planned to try CPR, but now it was definitely too late.

"I'm sorry, Bubbe." I would need to call 911 and explain what I was doing in the apartment. As I contemplated next steps, I noticed a light blue sliver of paper protruding from her bosom. She and my mother had the same habit of using their bras as an extra pocket or two. It looked like one of the IOUs from the box. A tissue helped me extract the paper and lessen my guilt around tampering with evidence. I'd take a little peek and replace the paper—no harm, no foul. It was a typewritten note: *You will pay for your crimes you Nazi bitch!!*

It obviously wasn't one of the IOUs. Bubbe didn't even own a typewriter. I wondered who on earth would call her a Nazi bitch, and more importantly, why? And why would she be keeping such a note in her bra? I stared at the paper for a while. Something about it felt familiar.

The door shook as someone pounded against it. "Police!"

A dead white woman, a gun, a black person sitting over her, and the police.

"Fucking great," I mouthed. With no time to think about the consequences, I shoved the paper in my bra and threw my hands high in the
air a second before they flung open the door.

My heart banged in my chest as one of two white officers entered
the apartment. Upon seeing me, then the gun, he put his hand on his
holster. But neither he nor his partner drew.

I kept my hands up and tried to explain. "She was dead when I got
here, officers. So, y'all okay? Can I put my hands down?"

The tall one used his foot to push my piece a safe distance away.

"May I *please* put my hands down?" My thighs burned. If I didn't
get up soon I was just going to topple onto my side.

They looked at each other. I guessed my navy-blue pantsuit, white
oxford blouse, and sensible shoes rendered me a fashionless geek but
not a threat.

"Put your hands down," the tall one said. He checked Bubbe Rosen
for signs of life, shook his head "no" at his partner, and radioed for a
bus.

They searched me and my purse. A padded bra kept the note a secret.
It took less than ten minutes to tell them who I was, why I was in the
apartment, and what I encountered when I arrived. I showed them the
back of my head.

"You need to get that examined," the shorter one said. I heard sirens
growing louder.

"Yeah, I need my head examined. I've heard that plenty."

I was escorted out of the apartment to the street. A plainclothes
detective was already there questioning someone in handcuffs. As I got
closer I saw a robin's-egg-blue bag—the Tiffany's bag I'd held on to all
these years—torn and soiled, on the ground with a familiar blue blanket
exposed—Pete's last resting place. Then I realized it was Gravel, sitting
on the curb. A few of his knuckles looked raw and fleshy.

"He's gonna talk to you, now." The shorter officer left me with the
detective.

"This guy says he knows you. You're his lawyer?" The detective said.

"Yeah, he knows me. Who are you? Does he need a lawyer?"

"Let's not get ahead of ourselves. I'm Detective Martin Hanes with
the 107th precinct. Tell me. Who are you?"

I recognized the balding, plump man.

"Marty?" I looked at him hard in the eyes trying to jar his memory.

"It's me, Pearl. Pearl Johnson-Gates." I added my husband, now ex-husband's last name—pathetic. "Look at you—one of New York's finest, now."

He stared at me blankly. I felt the heat of embarrassment rising. I was sure he thought I looked like shit on a stick compared to the "Old Pearl."

"Oh, yeah! Now, I remember—Pearl Lee Johnson—voted best bullshit artist in high school. I knew you'd be a lawyer someday."

I worked up a smile. I'd heard his name at least twice from clients and during my time strung out on the streets. He was one of those cops who'd bust people and "lose" a bit of their drugs. We did the obligatory small talk for a moment before turning our attention back to a perturbed Gravel, sitting on the curb.

"Someone called the police about a weird guy lurking outside this apartment window." Detective Marty pointed to Bubbe Rosen's window.

"He works for me. He was just waiting for me to come out."

"So, why are *you* here?" he said.

I took another ten minutes explaining the situation, again. All the while the blue note in my bra poked at my right tit.

Thirty minutes later, Shari arrived.

"Pearl!" She said rushing toward me with her perpetual look of concern for me in her hazel green eyes.

I removed the ice bag someone had given me for my head. Gravel and I were a disturbing sight, banged and bruised, sitting there on the curb.

"What's happened? Why are you here?" she asked.

I stood up groaning. Before I could explain, they wheeled out Bubbe on a gurney. A sheet covered her from head to toe.

"Oh my God! Who is that?" Shari looked at me. I returned a pained expression. "Bubbe? Is that Bubbe?" She ran to the gurney and pulled back the sheet before anyone could stop her. A wail and her words pierced muggy, stifled air, "What happened?"

Detective Marty interceded. He pulled Shari to the side and began to explain his version of the situation.

Out of the eyesight of the detective, Gravel pulled at my arm. He bent to whisper in my ear. He *never* whispered in my ear.

"Her husband," he motioned his head toward Shari. "I saw him come out the building earlier."

"Jerry? You saw Jerry?"

❧

After another hour, the commotion dissipated. Shari regained some of her composure. She insisted I come home with her. I tried to decline. But she persisted.

"What about Gravel?" I wasn't going to leave him behind.

"I'm headed back to the city," he said. "Gotta take care of Pete. I'll catch up with you tomorrow."

Stunned, I simply said, "Okay." I really didn't expect him to leave me.

❧

I sat, trying not to throw up in the back seat of Shari's Mercedes. It was a hard sell for me to get into a car at all since the accident. Motion sickness was something new. We sat for over an hour on the Long Island Expressway with an occasional "How are you doing?" or "Doing okay?" passing between us. Anything more would've brought one of us to tears, so we said little.

The note in my bra and Gravel's news about Shari's husband bounced around in my head. Did that nitpicking fucker really hit me? I decided to keep the information and the note to myself for the moment. A jones for a martini worked its way into a massive headache, heightened by the lump on the back of my skull. The pain in my leg eventually beat out both. We arrived at Shari's house in Maspeth. I was a trembling, sweaty mess.

And, it was *Shari's* house. Jerry "the Gentile"—Shari didn't know Bubbe and I called him that—had moved in when they married. Bubbe and I didn't like him. I hoped he wasn't home. Shari had tried to call him a few times while driving, but he didn't pick up.

"There should be fresh linens and towels in your bedroom," Shari called after me. *My room.* When she bought the house, she promised I'd always have a place there, regardless of Jerry.

"Aunt Pearlie," Gabe's voice called out from the back of the house

"Hey, honey," I said with outstretched arms. After a hug, I gave the seventeen-year-old a quick but thorough once-over glance. He'd already been through two inpatient substance use programs. I always knew when he was back to smoking weed. I thought I was being stealthy, but he noticed my scrutiny and dropped his eyes.

"You gonna stay with us awhile?" He sounded enthusiastic about the prospect. To his stepfather's chagrin, I had stayed with them after my vodka and pill party fiasco. One night, I had overheard Jerry call Gabe a lazy bastard. I told Jerry I would fuck him up for verbally abusing the kid. I left after a week.

"At least for tonight, kiddo," I said.

"I want to do *shivah* for Bubbe," he said.

"What?" Shari said. Gabe had not been raised with any overt Jewish traditions.

"I want to sit *shivah*. Aunt Pearlie can help me cover the mirrors."

"You know," Shari put her hands on her hips. "Let's do it. Bubbe would like that."

We spent the rest of the evening together, hanging sheets, drinking grape juice, and sharing Bubbe stories with Gabe.

"She caught your mom and me smoking on the roof when we were fifteen," I said.

"Remember she tried to make us smoke the whole pack of cigarettes?" Shari added.

"But we barely finished one when she realized we would only be smoking up her stash," I finished.

"I liked celebrating Chris-Hanukkah. You were always there, Aunt Pearlie," Gabe said as we hung a tablecloth over the last mirror.

I recalled the controversial Hanukkah bush. Shari's granddad, Saul, put up with it. He loved his wife, Yetta. When he passed away over a decade ago, Bubbe Rosen refused to move to Maspeth with her granddaughter. Shari and I chalked it up to grief.

An image of the pink Keds interrupted my memories, and sucked the joy out of the moment.

"I'm about to pass out, I'm so tired," I said.

"I don't think you can go to sleep after being knocked unconscious," Shari said.

Gabe's eyes widened. "You got knocked out?"

"Would you go upstairs?" Shari interjected before I could give the question an adept brush-off. "And put some clean towels in Pearl's bedroom, please."

"The housekeeper already did that." But before Shari said another word, he retreated from the room. "Goodnight." After seventeen years of being around us, he knew when to leave the room for an adult conversation. He was good kid. I blamed Jerry for fucking him up.

Shari's face had returned to her now standard look of concern. Before she could ask about me, I said, "How are *you* feeling?"

She stuttered in her usual, semi-embarrassed manner. "You know me. I'm a trouper." I saw the tears well up in her eyes.

"Yeah, you are." A breast cancer survivor, single parenting, a philandering, fiscally irresponsible husband—she was a trouper. We hugged it out for a moment. It was late—too late to show her the letter or tell her about Jerry's visit to Bubbe's.

❧

I dragged my ass up a long flight of stairs to my room. I started to look at the letter again, but my eyes were throbbing. Still, I stared at it for a minute or so, attempting to imagine who—or what—would instigate such a note. My mind strained to put a reason behind the note's familiarity.

"Fuck it." I threw the letter on the night table and plopped on the bed after removing only my blazer and blouse.

❧

"Kierra!" I jolted upright after about a hot thirty minutes of sleep. Beads of perspiration covered my chest. The usual first nightmare had awakened me. I decided to get some water.

In the hallway, I could hear voices from downstairs. The conversation sharpened as I made my way toward the kitchen. Shari's voice carried into the dining room.

"I called you ten times. You could call and say you were alive."

"I said I was working." Jerry was home.

Shari slammed something that sounded like a pan. I walked in, attempting to appear as if I'd heard nothing.

"What's *she* doing here?" he said.

It didn't take much for Jerry to piss me off. The schmuck was cheating, again. I could feel it.

"Good fucking evening to you too, Jerry." I rolled my eyes at him and went to the refrigerator. In that moment I hated myself. Here I was adding to my friend's stress the day her grandmother died. It was shitty enough having a husband and a best friend that couldn't stand one another. I tried to smooth things over. "Hey, sorry for getting in the way. A little water, a little ice, and I'm gone."

"You need to be gone. You don't need to be here in the first place."

Shari's oversized custom center island counter stood between me and Jerry. He was too far to smack. I thought about throwing my glass at him. Instead I threw words.

"You dirty son of a bitch. I know you hit me in the head today."

"You're insane." He started fumbling in the liquor cabinet.

"It was him, Shari. He was at Bubbe's." I pointed at him. "Gravel told me he'd seen your husband, but I didn't want to say anything because it was bad enough with Bubbe."

"Oh, there's your reliable source," he retorted.

"Why were you at Bubbe's, Jerry?" Shari moved closer to him.

"So, you believe *her*? Why don't the two of you get married?" He grabbed a bottle of bourbon, a glass, and left me to explain to Shari why I didn't tell the police and then why I had a letter from her grandmother's bra. Shari stared at the note. Her face reddened, but she said nothing. I wondered if I'd lost another friend.

❦

I remained comatose for about six hours. No nightmares had broken my sleep. Fortunately, I had few items of clothing from past visits in the back of the bedroom closet. I showered and headed to get coffee. I dreaded the conversation regarding arrangements for the funeral. Perhaps Shari was no longer pissed with me.

Shari entered the kitchen as I was pouring my second cup and toasting a slice of bread.

"I don't know when they're going to release the body," she said. "Someone's supposed to let me know today."

The doorbell rang. It was Gravel, reporting for duty. I was only half surprised at his showing up. I saw an unfamiliar car parked in the driveway.

"Did you drive?" I asked as we both walked back to the kitchen. Gravel had managed to braid his hair into two plats and hairpin a yarmulke on the crown of his head.

"Yup."

"You're shitting me?"

"You hungry? I'll fix you guys some breakfast, if there's food," he said. I knew he was attempting to avoid more questions about the car. I let it drop.

"I'm sure there's something you can pull together." I felt out of sorts with the discovery he'd driven. Between road rage and thinking paper bags in the road were IEDs, he'd been in the same public transportation boat with me for years. I seldom had or even wanted to pry into his business. But when did he start driving? When did he get a car? I guess *his* therapy was working.

Gravel fixed us a giant frittata with everything related to a breakfast food in the refrigerator. Gabe, awakened by the smell, even joined us. Shari made phone calls for funeral arrangements and to the office to help reschedule both of us for the next two days. If she was mad at me, she didn't show it. For a minute, it felt like the old days, even though we ate in silence. Shari, a single mom with Gabe toddling around, and me, a kick-ass sistah in stilettos, starting our law firm.

Look at your tired ass, now, the mean girl voice taunted in my head.

We were halfway through our breakfast when Jerry came into the kitchen with his head in a newspaper.

"How long do we need to cover the mirrors?" he asked.

"A week," Shari said.

He shook his head. Somehow he missed seeing Gravel. Jerry froze midstep when he noticed the unsmiling face staring at him.

"Mind if I get some food in my own kitchen?" He examined the leftovers on the stove.

"Stop being such a drama queen, Jerry, and eat. Please. Just. Eat," Shari said.

The doorbell rang again. This time, Gabe ran to the door to answer. When he returned, Detective Marty accompanied him into the kitchen. He immediately noticed me.

"Pearl?"

"So, now she's bringing her friends here," Jerry said, stepping back into the kitchen.

The detective pulled out his badge.

"I'm here to give your family news about Mrs. Rosen," he said.

I expected someone to call on the phone and give news to someone else without my presence. He repeated my name. "Um, Pearl . . ."

"You can say what you need to say. She's family." Shari cut him off before he could ask whether the "family" was okay with my presence. Jerry rolled his eyes.

"We've concluded that Mrs. Rosen fell and hit her head." Detective Marty examined each one of our responses. He left a moment of silence which I broke.

"What about stuff all over the floor? The place looked ransacked."

"You're right. That's why we can't rule out that she was pushed for some reason." He pulled out a little notebook from his jacket pocket. "The neighbor who identified you," he said gesturing toward Gravel, "also said she saw 'the son-in-law' leave the apartment. Would that be you, sir?"

We all turned to Jerry. As much as I didn't like him, I didn't want to be the one to squeal on my best friend's husband. So, I kept quiet. I knew, well I *believed*, Gravel would do the same.

"We've been through enough, Detective," Shari interrupted. "If you want my husband or anyone in our family to answer questions, you can wait until you have a reason to do so. Right now, I just want to bury my grandmother according to our Jewish tradition."

He recognized lawyering up. Without hard evidence of a crime, the detective closed his little book and shoved it into his back pocket. He headed for the front door. Shari and I followed him out.

He turned. "Almost forgot, I wanted to let you know, we found some interesting information about your grandmother."

We stared at him.

"Well, seems she came up as a person of interest for war crimes."

"War crimes?" Shari and I said in unison.

"Helga Von Gertz, does the name ring any bells?"

Shari shook her head, "No."

"Apparently, that was your grandmother's real name. Somehow, she passed for all these decades as Yetta Rosen. I didn't get the impression there were pending charges—just ongoing investigations. I guess all that's a nonissue now, huh?"

Shari closed the door. We were both in shock.

"I don't believe it," I said.

"I won't believe it," Shari added. "Bubbe wasn't Orthodox, but she kept kosher, went to the synagogue. I mean she was *very* Jewish."

We returned to the kitchen to find Gabe crying and Jerry telling him to man up.

"It's my fault," he said between breathy sobs. "I should've called someone. Jerry told me he'd take care of it. He told me to leave because the police would think I pushed her or something because I have record. She just fell and hit her head. I don't know why. I swear!"

Shari rushed to her son. When she reached out to him, I thought she would give him a consoling hug. Instead she shook him.

"You were there? Why?" She caught herself and let the boy go.

"You *did* hit me, you shit!" I ran to grab the pan sitting on the stove. Gravel jumped up and blocked me. "I'm gonna let him know what getting hit feels like." Gravel grabbed the pan and easily held it out of my reach.

"You borrowed money from her again, didn't you?" Shari directed the question toward Jerry, but Gabe responded.

"You took away my allowance. I just wanted a few dollars to hang out with my friends."

Shari ignored Gabe. "Jerry, you borrowed money from her again."

"You think so little of me. I was checking on your son. I wanted to know what he was up to. It's more than you do."

"You're going straight to hell, Jerry," I butt in. "You sent Gabe away and let Bubbe lie on that floor, so you could snatch *your* IOU from the tin box on the shelf. That's why her shit was all over the place."

"You bastard," Shari interjected. "You were blackmailing Bubbe." Angry tears welled up in her eyes.

"You're both crazy."

"You're unbelievable. The paper, Jerry—the paper. You used your stupid, prissy office paper for the note." Shari pulled the blue note from her pocket and waved it around. "You knew her secret and you were blackmailing her."

"Fuck you, both!" he yelled as he left the room.

Frying pan or no frying pan, I was going to beat his ass. Gravel grabbed my wrist and held tight.

❦

Shari, Gabe, and I stood staring at the grave. Gabe had the daffodils, her favorite flower. I was spared going to two cemeteries in one week. Bubbe Rosen's body would be released after an autopsy. Who knew when that would be? Detective Martin Hanes smelled something rotten.

KIERRA RENE GATES

BELOVED DAUGHTER

Gabe handed me the flowers so I could place them at the foot of the grave. I saw her eight-year-old face as clearly as I saw the headstone. Exactly five years had passed since the car accident. I came every anniversary. This was my second year sober coming to see her. I stood there contemplating regrets and refraining from using profanity, even in my head. I still wanted to curse God and the world for my losses. I felt numb. I dropped to my knees and contemplated banging my head on the ground.

The sound of a car pulling up on the road behind me interrupted the thought.

I turned around to see an unfamiliar woman behind the wheel. I recognized the car from Shari's house. Gravel unfolded from the passenger side and joined me. The woman remained in the car. Gravel's therapy was definitely working.

He held out a thick hand to help me up from my knees. I remembered the cold day we met and handing him socks while he sat on a sidewalk grate.

"Thanks for coming out here, Gravel," I said.

He surprised me and put his heavy arm around my shoulder. "Of course. Whatever you need. I got you. We'll drive you back to the city if you want."

I squirmed from beneath his arm. I wasn't used to him being so . . . nice. That woman was ruining him.

His arm dropped and his affect flattened. He returned to being the Gravel I knew. I felt pretty shitty for that.

"Yeah. I need to work—keep busy. Thanks again for coming out," I said, trying to make up for the shoulder thing. He shrugged.

We stood silent for a few minutes, as I pretended to pray. Kierra's big brown eyes and beautiful smile stood out from the image of her face. I could hear her laughing and see her playing in the distance. It felt so real.

The sound of another approaching car interrupted my hallucination. The car stopped behind Gravel's ride. Detective Marty and another plainclothes guy got out and headed toward us. I expected to get some egregious news about Bubbe Rosen. I saw Shari's face brace for a mental slap. But Marty and the other guy grabbed Gravel and cuffed him.

Surprised, Gravel struggled. "What the fuck?"

"What the hell's going on?" I said, breaking my profanity rule.

"You're under arrest for the murder of Richard Benton," the partner said and continued to finish the rights up.

Gravel's companion jumped out of the car and ran toward him.

Gravel calmed down instantly. He'd had enough past experiences with what could happen if he resisted.

"I'll be fine," he said to her.

He looked at me. "Pearl. I didn't do it."

I couldn't help glancing toward his now scabbed-over knuckles.

They led him off to their car.

"We'll get this worked out, Gravel," I called. "And don't say shit to nobody till I get there."

Shari shook her head in agreement.

I had two new cases now to work on: Gravel's—and Shari's divorce.

The Almost Sisters

Ellen Kirschman

Rules to follow: Children shouldn't be frightened, parents should put their children first, anti-Semitism should go away, and old women should live in peace and comfort, minding their own business. This is what Nomi and I believed until the day I picked little Avi Putterman up at school. The day he was crying and wouldn't say why.

❧

As far as I'm concerned, Nomi and I, being sisters-in-law, are almost sisters. We had a good life, until our husbands, Herbie and David, died of heart failure in the same month, leaving us almost, but not quite, enough money to live on. This was why, at ages sixty-three and sixty-four, we moved from New York to the Alto Arms, an apartment complex on the central coast of California, where the rents are considerably cheaper and our grown children are considerably closer. Not that it makes a lot of difference where we live because our children are all too busy to visit.

It was a good move. Until the rent went up. Way up.

Different as we can be, on this subject, Nomi and I were of the same mind. We wouldn't ask our children for money and we weren't going to move into some cockroach-infested old people's home run by a charity and staffed with petty criminals and perverts. That's when I got the idea. We should go into business for ourselves.

Nomi was appalled. "We're too old to go into business."

This conversation, as I recall, happened in the back of the shuttle van that takes us to the megamall on Saturdays. As usual, the van was almost empty. Most of the other residents of Alto Arms drive brand new hybrid cars. Sofi and I own an eight-year-old sedan with cloth seats. In the interest of tightening our belts, we were taking the van to save on gas.

"Look at the putz driving this van," I said. "He's mean, nasty, doesn't like Jews or old people—but that doesn't stop him from trying to look down your blouse." I turned in my seat. "Nomi, how many years did we spend chauffeuring kids to school, to little league, to Hebrew lessons? We should start a taxi business."

"Taxi driving is one of the most dangerous jobs in the world. I read it in the newspaper."

I could have predicted her response. If there's a gene for pessimism it will be in Jewish blood. I heard it a million times, *keynehore*, don't relax, don't get too happy, something bad is coming.

"Nomi," I said, "just because something's in the newspaper doesn't mean it's true. We wouldn't take just any passengers. We'd keep the rates low, offer a senior discount. Only drive for people we know. We'd be almost a nonprofit, doing a mitzvah for the community. And we'd keep it simple, no records, no software." I barely know how to use the cell phone my children insist I carry. "I'm thinking a little home-based business, almost like a hobby."

Nomi, always with the better idea, said, "What busy people really want is a trusted person to watch their houses while they're away. Check the locks, water the plants, pick up the mail, feed the cat. Who's more trustworthy than two old widows with not enough energy to commit a crime? Plus, we're not interested in stealing stuff we don't know how to use, like computers. See how this could work? You take them to the airport, I watch their houses while they're gone." She leaned close, her mouth next to my ear. "I wouldn't advertise this part, and I would certainly charge extra if it happened, considering the risks, but should a traveler forget to leave me a house key, I could still get in. My Herbie was a locksmith, remember? Taught me everything he knew."

Nomi closed her eyes and gritted her teeth, the way she always does when she's thinking hard. "We're almost but not quite, sisters, right? And we're almost but not exactly, about to be homeless. Let's call the taxi service Almost There and the home care service—" she spread her arms for dramatic effect, "Bagels and Locks. L-O-C-K-S."

א

Three months later, we were raking in enough money to upgrade to a two-bedroom unit facing the pool instead of the garbage bins. The unadvertised side of Nomi's business was booming after she rescued the vacationing Mrs. Engelberg's precious cat, Brisket, from starvation. One of the perks of being legitimized house burglars was the secrets; we knew who didn't have a stick of furniture or a scrap of good taste, didn't cook, didn't clean, or didn't share a bed with their spouse.

My best clients were the Puttermans in unit 14A. A charming couple in their eighties, so small and wizened they looked like garden gnomes who had been left outside too long. Next to them, Nomi and I felt like giants. The Puttermans shared their condo with their daughter Rachel, her husband, Mordecai Goldman, and their eight-year-old grandson, Avi. Rachel and Mordecai were the founders of Jewish Justice. They traveled constantly combating anti-Semitism around the world in ways that left the Puttermans, Shlomo and Sarah, alternately bursting with pride and quaking with fear.

"They are targets for white nationalists, neo-Nazis, and radical right-wing groups." Mr. Putterman was whispering, even though we were sitting in his living room. "They can't be too careful."

I wanted to tell him that lesson number one is not be telling me, almost a perfect stranger, that his daughter and son-in-law have a price on their heads.

"Look at the awards Jewish Justice has won." He gestured at four framed certificates and three plaques shaped like shields. "Their work is recognized around the world. Anti-Semitism is on the rise in Europe, the Middle East and North Africa. Watching Avi, so his parents can travel without worry, without leaving him in the hands of strangers, is how we contribute to the cause. Neither Sarah nor I want to spend our last years making plastic lariats in an old people's home."

I could relate. Nomi and I liked the money we were making, but even more, we liked feeling relevant and being needed.

The Puttermans didn't drive, they walked Avi to school in the morning and I drove him home. Except on rainy days when I drove him both directions. Avi was a quiet boy. He preferred to sit in the backseat of my car playing games on his cell phone. So, one Monday, when he asked to sit in the front, next to me, I knew there was trouble.

"Tough day at school, Avi?"

He turned his head away, but not before two big tears plopped into his lap.

"Something bad happened?"

He shrugged and huddled closer to the door. I pulled away from the curb and in my rearview mirror I saw a boy, a little older and bigger than Avi, laughing and making obscene gestures in our direction. He had red hair, and I recognized him from our apartment complex.

"That boy with the red hair, did he hurt you?" Avi shook his head and didn't say another word. When I got home, I told Nomi. She told me to tell the Puttermans. I told her I was Avi's driver, not his therapist. This was his parents' and grandparents' concern, and we shouldn't get involved.

❧

Tuesday, the same thing happened, only this time Avi's face was scuffed, his bottom lip was swollen, and his T-shirt was torn at the collar. I didn't wait for him to ask to sit in front, I just opened the door and he slid in.

"Buckle up. Bet that lip hurts. What happened?"

Silence.

"I know something that would make it feel better." He looked at me from the corner of his eye.

"Ice cream. A big scoop of your favorite flavor. What do you think?"

"You'd have to ask my grandmother. She worries if I'm not home on time."

"No problemo," I said, just like I was a California native.

"We have to tell the Puttermans. I'll do the talking," Nomi said after I told her what happened to Avi. "Children are being molested and bullied at school. Every day in the newspaper I read about it. Just yesterday—"

"Stop with the news reporting," I said. "Let's go."

Mrs. Putterman served us hot tea in a glass and homemade sticky-sweet *schnecken* buns the likes of which I haven't tasted since moving to the land of blueberry bagels.

"So, you see, we think that Avi may be being bullied at school. We wanted to be sure you were aware, and maybe you should consider talking to his teacher." I had to admit, Nomi was pretty good at this.

Mrs. Putterman teared up. Mr. Putterman shook his head. "We saw his shirt and his lip. I asked what happened. He said he was playing and fell down. And then he asked if we were mad at him for ruining his shirt."

"Did you tell his parents?" I asked.

"No. We don't like to worry them when they're on the road."

Avi walked into the room. I think maybe he had been listening at the doorway. His grandparents moved apart and patted the space between them for him to sit. He looked at his grandmother's teary eyes and the hankie on her lap.

Mr. Putterman took Avi's hand in his. "I was just telling Mrs. Nomi and Mrs. Sofi what a good boy you are, how you never complain."

"Never complain?" I said to Nomi on the way back to our unit. "What little boy do you know who doesn't complain? My Irwin, always with the complaints, why couldn't he have this? Why couldn't he go there? I'm telling you, it's too much pressure for a little boy to be this good. How can the Puttermans help Avi? They look like they can barely take care of themselves. It's a *shandeh*, a scandal. The parents spending all their time helping people around the world, like there isn't enough anti-Semitism in the United States. Like their own son doesn't deserve protection." Nomi kept walking. "Cat got your tongue?" I said.

"I was just thinking," she paused. "About how you didn't want to get involved."

❧

On Wednesday, I got up my courage to ask Avi if he was mad at me for telling his grandparents about his troubles at school. He was in the backseat again, staring at his phone. I pulled to the curb and turned to face him.

"I'm sorry if you're angry, but we had to say something. Nomi and I can't let somebody hurt you and not do anything about it. If someone is hurting you, like that red-haired boy, tell me, I can help."

Avi looked at me for the longest time. I could almost hear the debate going on inside his little head. When he finally spoke, it was barely above a whisper.

"It was an accident. I fell."

❧

On Thursday it was raining. I went to pick Avi up to drive him to school. Sarah Putterman met me at the door.

"Avi has a stomachache. He won't be going to school today."

❧

It was still raining on Friday and Avi's stomachache was worse. Mrs. Putterman asked if I would drive them to the doctor.

"Mrs. Putterman, I'm sorry to be a buttinsky, but I think Avi is pretending to be sick because he doesn't want to go to school. Someone is bullying him. Have you talked to his teacher?"

Mr. Putterman looked up from his newspaper. "If someone is bullying Avi, better he learns early how to defend himself."

❦

On Saturday, Nomi and I found the word KIKE spray-painted across the trunk of our car in blue. For once, Nomi was speechless.

"I think I know who did this," I said, thinking of the red-haired boy, who watched as I picked Avi up from school.

"We should go to the police," Nomi said. "Anti-Semitism is on the rise in the United States. It was in the newspaper, third highest number of incidents since the 1970s."

"You mean talk to Officer Ortega, who interviewed me when I applied for my chauffeur's license?" She nodded. "The same Officer Ortega who wanted to know if I was ever convicted for a violent crime or a sex offense? You want to talk to that *dumkopf*, go ahead."

Nomi got rid of the graffiti with nail polish remover. Relieved that we weren't going to have to pay to have the trunk repainted, she calmed down and decided to wait for a repeat episode before contacting the authorities. We didn't have long to wait. Monday morning when I backed out of the carport, Nomi screamed and pointed at the passenger side door.

"What kind of animal would do this?" she said pointing at a jagged blue Star of David dripping in red blood and surrounded by swastikas. The words CHRIST KILLERS, splayed across the rear window, topped by a line of alternating red and blue crosses that spread over the roof like a line of neon ants. "Now?" she said. "Now can we go to the police?"

❦

As predicted, Officer Ortega said there wasn't much he could do under the circumstances. He dismissed our demands to fingerprint the car, install a surveillance camera, and post an officer at the carport 24/7. "Impossible," he said, given his department's limited resources. His dismissal was so forceful, I felt as though we had asked him to give us his firstborn son.

"Told you," I said to Nomi. "Now we'll do it my way."

The principal was delighted to see us until we told her why we were there. "You are not on Avi's list of emergency contacts. As such, I cannot talk to you about him."

"But he's being bullied, by a red-haired anti-Semite," I said. "You can't just do nothing."

"Red-haired? Big for his age?" She shuffled through a stack of files on her desk, found the file she was looking for and opened it. "As I thought. We have only one red-haired, big for his age boy in this school. I can't tell you his name, but he's a foster child, special ed, with behavioral problems. As of today, much to his teachers' relief, he's been removed from his placement and sent to a group home near Sacramento." She closed the file and gave a dramatic sigh. "All's well that ends well. I'm happy to say your troubles are over."

❦

I couldn't wait to tell Avi and his grandparents that his tormentor had been transferred to another school hundreds of miles away.

"We're happy too," I said. "He was a terrible boy. He was writing anti-Semitic slurs on our car. We even went to the police about him."

Avi looked puzzled.

"Bad words, Avi," I said. "Bad words about Jews."

"Against-the-law words," Nomi said, as if what I said needed further definition.

"Why did he do that?" Avi was shifting from one foot to another.

"To scare us," Nomi said. "Make us feel like we're in danger."

"If the red-haired boy is gone, thank God, you won't need these, except for practice," Mr. Putterman said, holding up a pair of boxing gloves, so new the price tag was still on them. "A pre-birthday present for the *boychik*. Congratulations, Avi. You stood up for yourself and the bully ran off with his tail between his legs." He looked at us. "I was beaten every day, twice a day, walking the gauntlet back and forth to school. I had to learn to defend myself. That's why I'm teaching Avi to do the same."

"Your parents will be so proud. You can tell them yourself, when they come for your birthday," Sarah Putterman pinched Avi on the cheek, then turned to us. "We're going to have a little party for Avi. Will you come, please? Rachel and Mordecai want to meet you. It's so hard for them to be away from Avi. And they don't say, but I know they feel like they are putting a burden on me and Shlomo. They are very grateful for the help you give us."

❧

The principal's prediction that our troubles were over lasted for exactly three days until I found the word KIKE spray-painted on the on the passenger side door of our car in lopsided yellow letters.

I called Nomi down to the carport. Instead, Sherlock Moscowitz showed up, holding the magnifying glass she used for her needlepoint in front of her face. All she was missing was the deerstalker hat.

"Call the principal," she said as she straightened up with a grunt. "Tell her the red-haired boy is back."

I did and he wasn't. When I asked the principal how she could be so certain, she said she had already received a call from the principal in Sacramento. The red-haired boy was sitting in his office after beating up a classmate.

❧

The vandalism continued. We settled into a routine. The vandal, always with the same word in the same color. Nomi, always with the magnifying glass and the nail polish remover. We waited, hoping the culprit would get tired and find another victim. At the end of a week, Nomi insisted she try for Officer Ortega's help. On her own.

"The quickest way to a man's heart is through his stomach," she said. The next day, she cooked a pot of Mexican matzoh ball soup she made from a recipe she found in a newspaper article about Jews who fled to Spanish-speaking countries after the rise of Nazi Germany. Ortega thought the soup tasted like his *abuela*'s pozole. He still wasn't willing to fingerprint our car or install a surveillance camera, but he checked for other reports of anti-Semitic graffiti. We were the only victims he found. "Be careful," he said to Nomi. "This sounds personal."

"Are you thinking what I'm thinking?" I asked her as we finished the leftover soup.

"Pretty tasty," she said.

"I'm not talking about soup. I'm talking about Avi. I think, maybe, he's the vandal."

She almost dropped her spoon. "Why would you think that?"

Answering a question with a question is one of Nomi's bad habits. "Because."

"Because why?"

"Because there are two vandals, not one. The first one used blue and red paint, this vandal uses only yellow."

"So he switched. Big deal."

"The red-haired boy is in Sacramento. You think he flies here every day just to torment us?"

For once she didn't have an answer.

"You, with the magnifying glass, haven't you noticed? The blue and red graffiti was better."

"Better how?"

"Better printing. More sophisticated, drawings, swastikas, crosses. The red-haired boy wrote all over our trunk and on the roof. Avi couldn't reach that high."

"Avi's a sweet boy. Why would he do such a thing?"

"He's sending *us* a message."

"What kind of message?"

"I don't know, but when I pick him up from school tomorrow, I'm going to find out."

※

I tried bribing Avi with an ice cream sundae. "So, Avi," I said. "Are things better now that the red-haired bully is gone? Is there anyone bothering you? Making you afraid?" He shook his head. "Somebody is bothering me and Nomi. Making us afraid." He held his spoon midair between the dish and his mouth, watching chocolate drip on the table.

"Remember, I told you and your grandparents that somebody was writing very bad, scary words on our car? We think it was the red-haired bully boy, but not that he's gone, someone else is doing it." The ice cream puddled between us. "We thought maybe you might know who." He didn't move. "If you did, you'd tell us, wouldn't you? We don't want to make trouble for anyone, we just want them to stop."

Avi clamped his lips around the empty spoon. When he opened his mouth again, he said the ice cream gave him a stomachache and asked me to take him home.

※

Normally, I don't take night fares, but two days before Avi's birthday, we couldn't resist the opportunity to meet Mordecai and Rachel Goldman alone, without Avi or the Puttermans present. We wanted to tell them we thought Avi was in trouble. That his grandparents, as much as they loved him and as hard as they tried, weren't up to the task of raising an eight-year-old boy. After a flurry of hellos, how-are-yous, and thank-yous for picking us up, Rachel and Mordecai fell asleep almost immediately in the car, their heads flopping like day-old tulips.

א

The Putterman's living room was decorated with balloons and streamers. A banner spelling HAPPY BIRTHDAY in colored letters hung over the archway. Avi danced around the room, his little hands hidden inside his boxing gloves, punching the air and yelling "Take that, take that" at his invisible opponents. Mr. Putterman gave us a wink.

"Finally, here they are, such sleepyheads," Mrs. Putterman said as Rachel and Mordecai entered the room wheeling a suitcase. The minute he saw it, Avi's face crumpled.

"*Tateleh*. We're not going away. This is *your* suitcase. See?" Rachel spun the suitcase around. Spider Man leered at us from the other side. "It's a surprise. We're going to Disneyland tomorrow, for your birthday. You, me, Daddy, Bubbe, and Zeyde." Avi's eyes darted around the room in confusion. Then he jumped to his feet and started jabbing at the air with his gloves.

"Such a good boy," his mother said. "Growing so fast." She looked at her husband and teared up. "We're missing so much. Sometimes I wonder . . ."

She didn't finish the sentence.

"No," Nomi shook her head. "I'm not going to break into the Puttermans' condo while they're at Disneyland."

"If you ask me," I said, "It's admirable to want to save the world from anti-Semitism, but they should have done it before they had Avi. He's the one who needs saving."

"We don't know for sure that Avi is the vandal. We have no proof. It's just your theory."

"That's because we haven't looked. If you would use your famous locksmith skills, maybe we could find some real evidence connecting him to the crime. We're in and out in a minute. If we don't find anything, what's the harm?"

The Putterman condo was remarkably low tech in terms of security. Nomi was expecting sophisticated electronics, motion-sensor lights and cameras that set off alarms and rang for the police. Instead, what we found were deadbolt locks on the doors and windows, and a sign connecting the condo to a security company that didn't exist. We walked to the front door, waving at the neighbors who were used to seeing us around. I fussed with a half-dead plant to distract any busybodies while Nomi did her burglary thing and opened the door.

"Upstairs first," I said. "If Avi has something to hide, he'll hide it in his room."

Wooden letters spelling "Avi" hung on the bedroom door. There was a Star of David quilt on his bed, a small dresser, a writing desk, and a toy box. An enormous map of the world covered the back wall. Blue and red pushpins trailed Avi's parents as they tracked anti-Semitism across Europe, the Middle East and Africa. Post-it notes fluttered at intervals, each one dated in Avi's childish handwriting. Nomi's eyes filled with tears.

"Pushpins for parents?" I said as soon as I could clear the lump in my throat. "At least they were trying to stay connected." I started digging through Avi's toy box. "My Irwin slept with his little button-eyed dog until he was ten. I think he still has it. Everything in this box—soldiers, Transformer toys—and in this room, especially those—" I pointed to the boxing gloves hanging by a hook on the closet door, "is designed for fighting, not comfort." I sat back on my haunches. "Look under the bed."

"You look," Nomi said. "You're already on the floor."

I reached under, hoping to find dust bunnies, missing socks and forbidden candy wrappers. Instead, I pulled out a wadded-up shirt and unrolled it on the floor. The front was streaked with color. Wrapped inside was a sticky can of yellow spray paint.

מ

I couldn't sleep that night. Neither could Nomi. We sat in the kitchen, eating toast and drinking tea.

"We could just forget we found those things. Maybe he'll stop on his own," Nomi said.

"We can't. He's looking for attention. First by being the best boy he can be and then, because nobody pays attention to good boys, he misbehaves, hoping to get caught."

"His parents are leaving again in a day or two."

"Happiness is more than a weekend in Disneyland," I said. "Avi deserves a real home. With real parents. Not pushpins."

"He'll hate us if we say something."

"He may hate us more if we don't."

"His parents are not going to quit traveling because we said they should. Jewish Justice is like a child to them."

"Isn't that the problem?" I said. "They may not listen to us. But maybe, just maybe, the one person they *will* listen to is Avi."

❧

Avi was unusually talkative on the way home from school, all smiles in his Mickey Mouse T-shirt. Nomi was in the passenger seat, holding a paper sack with Avi's dirty shirt and the can of spray paint. I pulled up in front of the condo. "We have something we'd like to show you," I said.

"Me first," Avi said." I have something to show you." He opened his backpack and pulled out two mouse ear hats embroidered with our names. "These are for you."

"For us?" we said at the same time as we put on the hats and fought back tears. "Thank you so much."

"You're welcome." Avi grinned at the sight of us and started buckling his backpack. "What did you want to show me?"

"It can wait," Nomi said, mouse ears riding high on her salt-and-pepper perm.

❧

"It can't wait," I said, as we pulled away from Avi's condo. "And take off those ears. I can't have a serious conversation with someone in a Mickey Mouse hat. The parents are leaving again in two days. We have to do something."

"Mañana," she said, just like a Californian. "It wasn't the right time, not after he gave us presents. He was so happy. We'll do it tomorrow."

The next afternoon Avi was back to his somber self, giving only the barest smile when we thanked him again for the mouse ears.

"You seem a little sad today," Nomi said.

He shrugged.

"Are you sad because your parents are leaving again?" He nodded. "And you'd like them to stay, wouldn't you? Have you ever told them how sad you are when they are away?" He shook his head. "Why not?"

"Because Grandpa told me that if Mommy and Daddy didn't go to work, people would get killed."

❦

That afternoon we asked the Puttermans whether we could drop over to visit with Rachel and Mordecai before they left town. Mrs. Putterman thought it was a lovely idea and promised to make her famous chocolate babka.

We all sat together in the living room. Rachel and Mordecai apologized for needing to run in and out while they were doing laundry and packing. "Avi's a big help," Rachel said as she kissed the top of his head and left the room for the third time.

Nomi and I stayed motionless in front of our plates of babka and glasses of tea. Mrs. Putterman asked if anything was wrong.

"Something else?" Mr. Putterman said. He turned to Avi. "You too? Maybe you would rather have something else. Ate like a horse in Disneyland. Not so much since we came home."

Rachel and Mordecai came back in the room, dropping into their chairs like they'd just run a marathon.

Nomi started. "Mrs. Putterman, Mr. Putterman, Rachel, Mordecai— we have something we need to tell you." Her voice was thin, like she couldn't get enough air to talk.

"Avi," I said, "come sit with us. We need your help."

Avi's eyes, big as saucers, moved from one face to another. First his parents, then his grandparents. He walked across the room slowly, dragging his feet over the carpet as though someone had tied weights to his shoes.

"Did you know Avi was being bullied at school?" I asked the parents.

"No," they answered in unison, then turned to the Puttermans. "Bullied? Pop, you should have told us."

"We don't bother you with such things when you're working."

"We talked to Avi's principal," I said. "The bully has been transferred to a school miles away."

"Thank you. That's a relief," Rachel said.

I started again. "The boy who was bullying Avi was also spray-painting our car, the car we use to pick Avi up at school, with anti-Semitic graffiti and bad words like K-I-K-E." I could feel Avi's body stiffen next to me on the couch. "We thought it would stop after this boy left town, but it hasn't."

"Have you called the police?" Mordecai said.

"We did. They couldn't help us. So, we did a little investigating on our own. We almost wish we hadn't. But, long story short, we found another vandal." I turned to Avi. "Is there something you want to say?" He shook his head. His parents were frowning, looking at each other.

Nomi shifted forward in her seat. "It breaks our hearts to say this, but we think the person who did the graffiti after the bully left town," she stopped to take a breath, "was Avi."

"Impossible." Mr. Putterman's face turned red as borscht.

Mordecai turned to Avi. "Son, is this true? Did you spray-paint bad words on Mrs. Sofi and Mrs. Nomi's car?"

Avi shrugged. "I don't know."

"What do you mean *you don't know*? Did you, or didn't you?"

Another shrug, this time with tears.

Mordecai turned to us. "You are making a very serious accusation. Do you have any proof?"

Nomi reached under her chair, pulled out the bag with Avi's stained shirt and the can of spray paint and emptied the contents on the floor. "We found these under Avi's bed."

"Under Avi's bed? What were you doing looking under his bed? Who gave you permission?" Rachel looked at her parents and then flashed back to Nomi. "Oh my God. Did you break into our house when we were in Disneyland? Momma said you were a locksmith, that you got paid for breaking into people's houses." She stood up. "Did you?"

Nomi nodded. "We had to. We didn't have any choice. We had to do something."

Mordecai stood up. "I don't know care what you thought you were doing or why, but you don't get to break into my house. Ever. I'm calling the police." He made a move toward the phone.

"I wouldn't do that if I were you," I said, also on my feet. "It would be bad for Avi. We already made a police report about the vandalism. When we show them the evidence, tell them that we found these things in Avi's room under his bed, it will be as clear to the police as it is to us that Avi is responsible. I don't think you want him to go to Juvenile Hall or be reported to Child Protective Services because he is left unsupervised."

"He is not unsupervised," Mr. Putterman scrambled off the couch. His wife was crying, tugging on his shirt sleeve. "We feed him, we clothe him, he has everything he needs."

"Except parents," Nomi said. "He got out of the house at night without you knowing it and walked to our condo. The authorities don't look kindly on an eight-year-old boy walking the street at night alone."

"We watch him all the time, never a minute unsupervised." Putterman's voice ratcheted high, like a guilty defendant pleading his case in front of a hanging judge.

"I don't want to go to jail." Avi jumped to his feet. I will never forget the look on his face. He was terrified.

"Talk to me, Avi." Rachel knelt in front of him. "Did you do this? Tell the truth. Did you write the word K-I-K-E on Mrs. Sofi and Mrs. Nomi's car?"

Avi nodded. His eyes filled with tears.

"How did you even know that word? We don't use that kind of language in this house."

"Grandpa told me. Because it happened to him. People called him names."

Mr. Putterman sank back on the couch. "I was telling a story, what happened to me. Not what you should do to someone else."

"I'm sorry, Grandpa and Grandma." Avi turned to his parents. "I'm sorry, Mommy and Daddy." Then he turned to us. "I'm sorry Mrs. Nomi and Mrs. Sofi."

Rachel and Mordecai dabbed at their eyes. Nomi put her hands on Avi's shoulders. "Can you tell us *why* you did it? We're not angry, we just want to understand. All of us."

Avi wiped his nose on his sleeve.

"Mrs. Sofi told me you were scared of the bad words that red-haired boy put on your car."

"Yes, we were," Nomi said. "Were you trying to scare us too?"

He nodded, tears bobbling off the bottom of his chin.

"Why? Why were you trying to scare us?"

"Because," he choked out the words, "I thought if you were scared to be in your car, you would stop taking my parents to the airport."

Rachel stifled a cry.

"Are you going to arrest me?"

"Of course not. We don't want you to go to jail. Nobody does," Nomi said. "Now that you've told us the truth, I think we can work something out." She turned to Mordecai and Rachel. "Avi needs you to stay home. He's just been too afraid to say so."

I couldn't see Rachel's reaction because she'd buried her face in her hands. Mordecai was staring at Avi, the corners of his mouth twitching with the effort not to cry.

"Anti-Semitism has risen to near historic levels in the United States," Nomi said. "Just yesterday, I read about it. You could fight anti-Semitism closer to home and be with Avi."

"You don't understand. We can't just quit," Mordecai said. "People depend on us in France, England, Germany, so many places where the Far Right is going mainstream."

"Like it's not going mainstream in the United States?" Nomi's face was turning pink and she was gritting her teeth. "I understand more than you think, Mordecai. These extremists, these racists, they do their business on the internet. Recruiting followers. Tweeting hatred. You have a laptop. You don't have to travel, you could fight anti-Semitism from your kitchen."

"Avi depends on you," I said. "It's not fair, putting your work before his welfare. Avi has problems. He's depressed. He has no friends. Look around. Nomi and I were the only guests at his birthday party."

"We told him, invite some friends to the house," Mrs. Putterman was speaking, tears gathered in the crevices around her eyes and mouth. "He's embarrassed because we're so old. He doesn't say, but I know."

I had a flash of memory, David, Herbie, Nomi, me, and our kids sharing a mountain cabin, taking hikes, playing hide and seek, hitting a tetherball. Laughing so hard we fell on the ground. We were young then. We could do things the Puttermans couldn't, no matter how much they wanted to.

"The Puttermans are trying, we can see that," I said, hoping for the right words. "But they are limited in what they can do. Think about what Nomi said. Anti-Semitism isn't going away, if you work for a hundred years, you still won't stop it all. Avi will be a grandfather and it will still be around. Avi needs to be a child. And a child needs his parents." Nomi was looking at me. Rachel was looking at Mordecai. The Puttermans were looking at each other, and Avi was looking at the floor. "Find a way to stay home with Avi," I say. "If you do, there's no reason for Nomi or me to go to the police."

We left the family alone to figure out what they were going to do. Stay home with Avi? Have us arrested for breaking and entering, or both? We still had the bag with Avi's shirt and the can of spray paint for insurance. A week went by, then two. Every day we waited to be arrested.

I panicked whenever I saw a police car near our condo. Nomi tried to find clues to our future by bringing more Mexican matzoh ball soup to Officer Ortega, despite the risk that he might arrest her on the spot. All he did was ask if the vandalism had stopped and could he have her recipe to give to his *abuela*. From this she deduced that the Goldmans had decided not to press charges against us.

❧

Three weeks later, we drove past the Putterman condo on our way to pick up Mrs. Engelberg's cat, Brisket, from the veterinarian. Mr. and Mrs. Putterman were standing on the sidewalk surrounded by packing boxes. We slowed down. They waved us over.

"Big changes. We're moving to the Riverdale. You know it?" Mr. Putterman said as we got out of the car.

Know it? Who didn't? A very classy senior residence at the other end of town. Lots of activities, discussion groups, theater trips, and museum visits.

"Mordecai, such a smart son-in-law, did a GoFundMe campaign. So many people appreciate Jewish Justice that they raised a pile of money—he wouldn't say how much, but enough for us to move and for them to buy whatever they need to run Jewish Justice from home."

The front door of the condo opened. Avi raced down the walk.

"I ride my bike to school now," he said. "And Mommy and Daddy are going to work at home, and Grandpa and Grandma are moving but not too far away so I can ride my bike to see them." His words tumbled out. "I'm going to the park now," he said. "Nice to see you." Mordecai and Rachel appeared in the doorway, calling Avi back for a goodbye kiss and instructions to be home before dark. They walked over to us. Mordecai extended his hand. "Thank you both," he said. Rachel leaned down and gave Nomi and me a hug. "I've been meaning to stop by and tell you what's happening, but we've been so busy. So many changes. All for the good, I think. We are grateful to you both. You taught us a hard lesson, but one we needed to learn." Then she hugged us again.

"It's your fault," Nomi said, dabbing at her eyes as we drove away. "You're the one who wanted to start the business. Now look at us. We don't just drive people around. We'll do anything to help them, including getting arrested. Almost." Then she leaned over and kissed me on the cheek.

Crossover

Zoe Quinton

Turns out, dying is easy. Living is the hard part.

This was what went through Jessica Ackerman's mind as she drifted down through the water. With unhurried ease, she looked up through the spreading cloud of her hair to the surface above. Her belly, protruding hard and round in front of her, finally felt lighter in these last, floating moments, the burden of gravity eased by the warm hands of the water.

The irony was almost enough to make her laugh. Or at least smile. But she was so tired, and either one seemed like so much work. Much easier to just close her eyes and let herself drift.

As she started to do so, faint noises started to reach her from above. Concerned faces peering down into the pool, mouths moving, voices muffled. She saw her husband, her sweet Adam, his eyebrows drawn together in alarm. For a minute, she wanted to rouse herself enough to tell him it was okay . . . she was just resting.

But again—so tired.

Finally, Jessica couldn't fight any longer. She closed her eyes and gave in to the languid embrace of the water.

❦

The day Beth found out her aunt had died was the worst day of her life. And even though she was young and had not yet lived many days, even though the hormones coursing through her teenage body regularly turned even the slightest mishap into total disaster—even so, she'd seen enough to know the bad from the worst.

On that particular day, Beth was in her room doing her math homework. The pink paint of her childhood walls was fighting a valiant but losing battle against her adolescence: a rapid onslaught of posters, drawings, movie tickets, and photos with her friends.

Though Beth's face looked calm—or at least resigned to the task at hand—the pencil point dug hard into the graph paper, leaving behind a deep trail on the page underneath. The paper was an unwitting victim of the fight she'd had with her mom after school that day, when she'd exploded under the weight of her mother's relentless nagging, pleading, scolding. So, when her mom came upstairs wearing those pound-dog eyes, Beth assumed she intended to kiss and make up.

Her mother, Miriam, stopped in the doorway and pointed at her own ears, mouthing, "Turn it off!" Beth sighed and removed first one earbud, then the other. She then gave a dramatic spin to her desk chair and crossed her arms, ready to face her inquisitor.

"What."

"Well, honey, I thought you should know . . . there's been some bad news."

Arms remained crossed. One skeptical teenage eyebrow raised in bare acknowledgement.

"Um, right. Well. I just got a call from Uncle Adam, and he said . . . oh God."

Despite her best intentions, Beth felt a finger of unease creep into her stomach. Her mom was actually crying. What was this? Where were the lame excuses; the half-berating, half-apologetic post-fight rant? This wasn't the way things usually went.

"Bethy. Your aunt Jessica. She had a horrible accident and . . . and . . . she's gone."

Incomprehension. The words didn't make sense.

"Gone. Where? Like, to the hospital? On vacation? Will she be all right? Is she having surgery or something?"

Then Beth felt the finger turn into a fist, a punch to the gut, a surgical incision straight to her heart.

"Wait. What about the baby?"

At last, her mom met her eyes, face scrunched into a rictus of grief and dread as she delivered the final blow. "No, honey. She's dead. The baby's dead. They drowned while Jessica was in the *mikvah* finishing her conversion process. They're both gone."

❦

The rest of this most horrible of days was spent in a haze of grief. Her beloved Aunt Jessica—the one adult who really understood her and heard her, the one who made her laugh and held her when she cried, the mother and big sister she should've had all rolled into one—was dead. How could this be? Just last weekend they'd gone to see a stupid chick flick together, making fun of it over mocktails afterward. How could she be dead?

After the initial wave of tears had slowed, after her mom had held her and made her drink a smoothie, Beth locked her bedroom door and curled up on her bed, creating a frothy pink nest of sheets and blankets around herself. She took out her phone and found the collection of photos that contained her aunt's face, relying on the magic of technology to let her probe the fresh wound at its deepest.

She started at the beginning, when Adam first brought Jessica home at Thanksgiving a few years before. To the rest of their observant Jewish family, the shock of a beloved scion of their proud lineage bringing home a tall, blond *shikse* was profound—and for some, unforgivable. But for Beth, right at the edge of adolescence, too quirky to be comfortable with her peers and too rebellious to want to fit in with her family, it was a breath of fresh air.

Just ten years apart in age, Beth and Jessica quickly gravitated toward each other, first at family gatherings, then outside of them. They found in each other comfort and companionship as outsiders in a world that seemed alien to them both. So their friendship grew until Jessica felt more like family to Beth than anyone actually related to her by blood.

The day Jessica married her uncle Adam and officially became her aunt was, by contrast to the day in question, one of the happiest of Beth's young life. Many of their more devout relatives refused to attend a mixed wedding, just as their local rabbi refused to perform it. Undeterred, the young couple formalized their love at a local state park, officiated over by a former army chaplain, his one lazy eyelid and long, sardonic anecdotes about marriage providing ample lightness to offset the missing relatives. Beth, by then too old to be a flower girl, was instead honored to be named as Jessica's youngest bridesmaid.

Beth glanced at her closet where her mauve bridesmaid dress still hung, clean and tidy, in its dry-cleaning bag. It was by far the nicest thing she'd ever owned, and hopefully would soon double as her prom dress—if she could just get up the courage to ask that geeky but kinda cute new guy in her English class . . .

Chastising herself for these disloyal thoughts, Beth redoubled her focus on her phone. Pictures of other movie dates, manicures, breakfasts together, a couple of amusement parks . . . Beth relived the past few years of her aunt's life and their growing friendship. After they discovered that they both loved getting a real letter or card in the mail, they relied on old-fashioned letter writing to cement their connection. Every missive Jessica had ever sent her sat in a shoebox in the closet directly above her bridesmaid dress, carefully preserved as a repository of adult wisdom.

All along, Beth and Jessica continued to discuss what had originally brought them together: the family they were both a semi-unwilling part of, the elderly aunts who still wouldn't talk to Jessica, the observant cousins who refused to hug or even shake hands with any woman other than their wife. It became a shared language for them, that of inclusion and ostracism, a mutual attempt to understand a world that was simultaneously mundane yet always just out of reach.

Then, Beth came to the giant collection of pictures and videos from her bat mitzvah two years before. As with any even remotely observant Jew, Beth had celebrated her adulthood in grand style, part of an extended arms race of ever-more-opulent extravaganzas put on by the wealthy (and those wanting to appear wealthy) families at her temple. She had studied for months beforehand, working to memorize the necessary scripture and get the pronouncement of the Hebrew words just right.

When the big day finally came, there were pictures of a thrilled but nervous Beth standing next to a tall rabbi, reading the Torah to a room packed full of family and a few friends. She wore a frilly purple dress, hair pulled back in a tight bun, voice high but unwavering. These segued into a nighttime of celebration—short, cream-colored dress; hair down, curls flying as she danced; photo booth shenanigans, delicious food eaten on the run, and too many cups of sugary fruit punch to count.

Then there was a video, one she had forgotten all about. It was of just her and Jessica, dancing together and mugging for the camera. A smile stole over Beth's tear-wet face as she watched her aunt, so full of life and unconcerned for the future ahead. The video was long, and just as Beth got impatient and started to skip to the next image, she noticed something in the background.

The rabbi. He stood nearby under a giant bunch of balloons, cup of punch in his hand, glaring at Beth and Jessica as they danced unwittingly before him. Beth's hand flew to her mouth.

It was the same rabbi who had refused to perform Jessica and Adam's wedding three years before because Jessica was not Jewish. Of all the people who did not condone their marriage, he had been the most opposed.

Could that have been reason enough for him to hurt her?

※

"Mom!" Beth caromed down the stairs two at a time, pushing her breathless way into the kitchen. "Mom. I need to know more about how Jessica died. Right now."

Miriam, in the midst of preparing dinner, looked pained. "Honey, really? Let's just drop it. It's too sad to talk about. That poor girl and her baby. I can't even think about it." She turned back to stirring.

"Mom, no. Don't bullshit me." Her extra-polite mother gasped at the profanity, just as Beth knew she would, but she went on. "This is important, and I need to know what they're doing about it. Was it really an accident? Tell me. Or I'll call Uncle Adam myself."

Miriam dropped the spoon, splattering bright-red spaghetti sauce all over the stove, and put her face in her hands. "Fine. Honey, fine, but only because I know you won't drop this till I tell you. And you can't torment that poor man with your impertinent questions now, when he's arranging funeral details and sitting *shivah*.

"When Adam called this morning, he said they think it was an accident. Something went wrong during the *mikvah* and she stayed under the water too long. She . . . she went down, but she never came back up."

A heavy sigh. Finally, she turned and looked up at Beth, tears heavy in her eyes. "They're saying it may have been suicide. I'm sorry love. I didn't know how to tell you."

Beth was too stunned to react. *Suicide?* No way. Jessica? While she was pregnant? *No.* Beth knew better than anyone how hard Jessica and Adam had tried for that baby, how long they'd held out hope. There was no way in the world she'd have done anything to hurt him.

Her mom came closer. "Honey, are you okay? I know that must have been hard to hear."

"No, Mom, I am not okay. *So* not okay! Are you kidding me? Jessica is dead. Her baby is dead. And now you're telling me she might have done that to herself? No way! Someone did this to her. They had to!" Beth pounded her hand on their wooden kitchen table, then immediately regretted doing so as electric shocks of pain reverberated up all the way up her arm.

"Oh, honey, no." Miriam shook her head. "That's not possible. Forget I said anything. It was all a horrible accident. Let's just leave it at that."

"Did Uncle Adam say anything about the police, Mom? Is anyone even looking into this? Does anyone even care?" Tears were streaming down her this face at this point, any valiant attempt to hold them back long gone. She needed to know the truth.

There was pity in her mom's eyes, which was almost worse than the pain she'd seen earlier. "No, love. Adam said that because it was either an accident or self-inflicted, there was no need for the police to stay involved. They are doing a tox screen just in case, but they don't expect those results for a few days."

It was Beth's turn to shake her head. "No way. That's ridiculous. In fact, I think it was that creepy tall rabbi from our temple. You know, the one who did my bat mitzvah at the last minute after Rabbi Shick got sick? He was the same one who wouldn't do their wedding because Jess wasn't Jewish. I bet when she finally did try to convert he took the chance and offed her before she could become one of us."

"But honey, why would he do that? It doesn't even make any sense."

"He hated her! I saw it in his eyes. I have a video from the bat mitzvah. I know it was him." Beth knew she sounded childish, but she couldn't help it.

Miriam sighed. "Why don't you go and talk to Rabbi Kovitz tomorrow? He's a nice man. Sure, he's a little more conservative than most, but he'd never hurt anyone, much less a pregnant woman. For now, can we please just eat dinner and have a quiet evening? Your dad is almost home."

"Mom, please. I can't eat. I need to talk to that rabbi, *now*."

Miriam got that gleam in her eye, the one that meant she was done with talking. "It's late. He won't be at the synagogue. You're exhausted, and you have school tomorrow. Sit. Eat."

Rolling her eyes in the age-old sign of a teenager giving in to an adult's outrageous requests, Beth sat. And ate. And strangely enough, she did feel a little better afterward—better enough to know that she needed to get a good night's sleep in order to get some real answers the next day.

༝

In the morning, Beth got ready for school as usual, trying not to alert her ever-vigilant parents that she was up to anything out of the norm. She grabbed her lunch and kissed them both as she walked out the door, but instead of waiting for the school bus at the end of her driveway as she normally did, she walked farther down the street to the city bus stop.

Sitting, waiting, jittery feet drumming silent melodies on the sidewalk, Beth tried her hardest not to keep imagining Jessica's last seconds of life—the water flooding into her mouth, the suffocation, the fear.

Or had she been calm? Did she even know what was happening? Did she struggle?

Beth closed her eyes and tried to clear her head of these horrible swarming thoughts. If she was going to figure out what had actually happened to Jess, she had to stay focused. Eyes open again, she at last saw the bus approaching. Then it hit her: what was she thinking? That she'd confront the rabbi who had possibly harmed—or even killed—her aunt all on her own? She was only fifteen. She couldn't even drive yet. What did she expect?

As the door of the bus yawned open in front of her, Beth sat frozen, undecided, terrified. But then she thought of Jessica's last seconds again and steeled herself. She had to find out more. She would ask the questions no one else was bothering to ask, because she alone cared enough to do so.

With the resolve of a knight errant going into battle, Beth boarded the bus, which would take her directly to the synagogue. She'd taken the trip many times during her bat mitzvah preparation, but never had she been this nervous before.

༝

Although the synagogue usually felt like a second home to her, today Beth walked through its sliding glass doors like she was venturing onto enemy ground. She'd even worn her biggest, most battered combat boots to boost her confidence, but still, she'd never felt more like a little girl.

Once inside the office, she marched right up to Rabbi Kovitz's door and knocked. Hard. At his brief but friendly, "Come in!" she opened the door.

Looking up, the rabbi recognized her. "Ah, Beth Speer. Sit down. To what do I owe the pleasure?"

Beth narrowed her eyes, not so easily won over. Was his tone a little too pleasant? Maybe he was being nice to hide something. Defiant as a fifteen-year-old could be, she remained standing, hands hanging awkward at her sides.

"As you please. But may I ask why you are not in school today?" the rabbi said.

Chin up, without preamble, Beth announced, "I'm here to talk about Jessica Ackerman."

"Ah, yes. So sad." Rabbi Kovitz—who genuinely did look upset—removed his wire-frame glasses and put down what he'd been reading. "A real tragedy. I'm still struggling to understand what happened, myself. It all went so fast. One minute I was reading the prayers with her, the next she was under the water . . . and then she didn't come up."

Despite herself, Beth was taken in by his air of genuine concern. She found that her knees were buckling, and she sank into the chair she'd declined a minute before. "Didn't anyone, I don't know, do anything?"

"Yes, of course. As soon as he realized what was happening, Adam jumped in after her, fully clothed. But it was too late. She had already stopped breathing."

"Wow. Just like that?"

"Just like that, I'm afraid. There wasn't anything anyone could do. It was like she just . . . gave up."

Remembering why she was there, Beth straightened up in her chair. "Are you sure, Rabbi? Because I don't see how this could have happened. I know—knew—my aunt." The correction caused Beth to pause for a second in pain, the reality of the situation hitting her anew.

"She was so excited about that baby. There was no way she would've 'just given up.' She would have fought for their lives. And zero chance she would've ended them herself. Nope." Beth shook her head, as if asserting her truth would make it so. "If she was that sad, she would've told me. I would've *known*. Something must have gone wrong, I know it."

"Look, Beth. I know what you're thinking." The rabbi looked tired all of a sudden, beaten down by the reality of what had happened on his watch. "I've gone over all of this with the police already. Everything went exactly according to plan . . . up until the minute it didn't. Nothing was out of the ordinary. It just happened."

"No!" Beth said, too loudly. Lowering her voice, she said, "I'm sorry. No. I'm not willing to accept that. Someone, somewhere, did something to her." Her eyes narrowed. "You're really convinced that it was just an accident, Rabbi? Do you have something you're hiding? I know how opposed you were to Jessica marrying Adam. I was just a kid then, but I remember you made a big deal out of it. Did you do something to hurt her, to stop her from becoming a Jew?"

The rabbi's eyes flew up to meet hers, wide with surprise. "Beth! My goodness, no! How could you possibly say such a thing? I may have been opposed to their marriage, but I would never hurt someone to stop them from becoming a part of our community. In fact, I was pleased that Jessica made the decision to convert before their son arrived. That meant he'd be fully Jewish from the moment he was born."

Unconvinced, Beth whipped out her phone, already open to the screenshot she'd taken of the video with him glaring at Jessica during her bat mitzvah. "Then how do you explain *this*? Why did you hate her so much?"

To her shock and outrage, the rabbi started laughing. "*That's* why you think I killed her? My dear, I didn't have my glasses with me that night. As you know, I had to stand in for Rabbi Shick at the last minute during your ceremony. In the rush, I left my glasses behind in my office, and I had a splitting headache from reading the Torah portion along with you. If I had to guess, I'd say in that picture I was just trying to see who you were dancing with so happily."

Beth immediately felt sheepish but pushed on anyway. "Okay, so then what's your alibi for the morning of the *mikvah* ceremony? Who's to say that you didn't give her some poison or something to make her drown?" She'd read Nancy Drew. She knew about these things.

The rabbi, still looking amused, said, "Beth, I can understand your concern. Jessica was very dear to you, and this must have come as a massive shock. But as I said, I've already talked to the police about this. I was training a junior rabbi on conversion practices that day, and he is happy to attest that everything went exactly according to routine. The tox screen will back me up when it comes in, but I promise you, she was perfectly healthy when she entered that water."

Beth looked down, her eyes filling with tears. "Okay, Rabbi. I believe you. But I do have one more question."

"What's that, my dear?" The rabbi glanced at his watch, his concern already fading as reality returned to the room. "I have a meeting with another member of the congregation in five minutes. Is it brief?"

"I don't know. But I promise it's important." She looked him in the eye. "If Jessica died during the conversion process, is she, well—*was* she Jewish? And . . ." Beth's voice faltered, unable to say the words.

"I'm listening." The kind voice was back as they returned to familiar ground.

"Was the baby Jewish?" Beth blurted out the unspeakable, the unmentionable, the horrible reality of the baby's death before it had even lived.

"Ah. A tragic but excellent theological question, young lady. If Jessica—and her baby—entered the bath Gentile, with the intention of converting to Judaism, and were fully immersed for the requisite three seconds, but never reemerged . . . hmm. My impulse is to say yes, they would still be considered Jewish, but I'm afraid it's an answer that we must ultimately leave in the hands of God.

"Now, if that's all I can do for you today, Miss Speer, I think it's time for me to take my next meeting." The question, and his dismissal, were clear on his face.

"Yes, Rabbi, that's all. Thank you for your time. I'm sorry to have doubted you," Beth said, rising from her chair.

As she turned to go, the rabbi added, almost as an afterthought, "You know, Beth. It wasn't just your family that was opposed to Jessica and Adam's marriage. If there was anyone who would've been against Jessica becoming Jewish, it was her own mother. If you want answers, I suggest you look there."

With that bomb dropped, Rabbi Kovitz waved her out the door and turned back to his paperwork, deep philosophical questions and matters of life and death already forgotten.

❧

Beth took her time leaving the synagogue, her combat boots now sounding a dirge against the linoleum. Once outside, she sat down on a bench in the garden to think. She'd been so sure of what she was doing, but the sudden reversals in her conversation with Rabbi Kovitz had thrown her off. Now she had no clue where things stood.

Jessica's *mom*? But she and Jess had been so close, almost as close as Beth had been to Jess. And Beth knew that Jessica's mom had been looking forward to the baby as much as everyone else.

Beth also didn't know what to do about it. She had a rough idea of where Jessica's mother lived, but it was somewhere up in the hills and therefore inaccessible by bus. Obviously, she couldn't ask her own mother for help getting there. But did she have a phone number somewhere?

She had to think hard to dredge up Jessica's maiden name, but finally it came to her: Spence. Encouraged, she searched her contacts, and sure enough, there it was. Barbara Spence. Beth felt a sharp pang of gratitude that she was such a digital packrat. Jessica must have sent her the number at some point when she stayed overnight at her mom's, and Beth had never gotten around to deleting it. Thank God.

Nervous again, not knowing what to expect, Beth made the call. Not surprisingly, considering she'd just lost her daughter, Barbara didn't answer. Undeterred, Beth left a message saying that she really wanted to talk about Jessica and could she please meet her at the coffee shop down the street from the synagogue in an hour?

࿋

That hour seemed like an eternity. Beth spent it sitting at a small table by the window, staring outside at nothing, an untouched cup of green tea cooling at her elbow. She didn't even know if Barbara would show, but she had to take the chance. And it had to be today, because she couldn't risk missing another day of school.

Finally, forty minutes in, just as Beth's stomach was starting to growl, she saw a tall white woman with elegant silver hair step out of a Mercedes that had just parked across the street. Barbara. Beth's heart sped up, her mouth dry. Would she have some answers? Had she done something to hurt Jessica before she could convert?

Beth followed Barbara with her eyes as she crossed the street to the café. Right away Beth could see that Barbara's normal thick coat of makeup was working hard to conceal the dark rings under her eyes and the pallor of her skin underneath. As if she could feel her stare, Barbara peered into the coffee shop window and smiled as she recognized Beth. Pulling open the door, Barbara sailed into the coffee shop, upright and regal despite the grief written on her face.

"Beth, honey. How are you?" Barbara threw her oversized purse onto a chair and pulled Beth into a huge hug. Caught unprepared, it was all Beth could do not to burst into tears. If anyone could understand her current pain, it would be Barbara. The possibility the rabbi had planted in her mind—that Barbara could have had something to do with Jess's death—gave Beth the edge she needed to hang on to her emotions, but only just.

"Hi, Barbara. Thank you for meeting me." Beth sat, buying time to collect herself—and to figure out what on earth she was going to say now that she actually had Jess's mom in front of her.

"Oh, my dear, I came as soon as I got your message. I've been trying to call you at your parents' house, but they always said you were in bed and couldn't talk." Barbara's eyes met Beth's, and she reached out to place a hand over hers. Beth always forgot how touchy Jess's family was. "I'm so glad you reached out. I can't imagine how hard this is for you. Is there anything I can do to help?"

Taken aback by this barrage of care and compassion, Beth found herself losing track of what she'd come here to say. "Um, yeah. I'm okay." Not knowing what to do with her hands, Beth picked up her stone-cold cup of tea and stared into it. Feeling rude—the woman had just lost her only daughter, after all—she remembered to ask, "Uh, how are you?"

To Beth's alarm, this simple question caused Barbara's eyes to fill with tears. As they threatened to overflow and ruin her carefully applied makeup, Barbara said, "I just don't know, dear. I don't know what to feel. I mean, it's horrible, obviously. No doubt about that. But at the same time . . ." She trailed off.

"But what?" Beth tried to maintain her concerned attitude, but inside she'd gone on high alert, heart pounding in her ears. Could it really have been that easy to get Barbara to talk about her objections to her daughter's conversion?

"Well, honey. You know I love your family. You've always been so kind to me, especially since Walter died, including me at your holidays and all. But I don't know, some of their beliefs seemed a little . . . extreme. I mean, to skip Jessica and Adam's wedding—Jesus Christ." Barbara's hand flew to her mouth. "Sorry. I mean, jeez."

"It's all right. I've heard the name a few times before." Beth smiled in what she hoped looked like encouragement instead of threat. "Go on."

"I just . . . I mean, we worked so hard on that wedding. And spent so much money. And then they wouldn't even show up. I couldn't believe it. Such a slap in the face, and for what? Because Jess wasn't raised a certain way—and I, her mother, wasn't raised a certain way? And to know that Jess was not only okay with being treated like that, but also would then go to such lengths to be included, let along bring my grandson up that way . . ."

Barbara shook her head so hard that a few strands of her just-so hair fell loose along her face. "Well, let's just say I was not feeling very good about it. I certainly never planned on attending Jess's conversion ceremony, whatever it was called."

Beth was stunned by this diatribe. She sat silent, cup still between her hands, legs pulled up onto the seat of her chair. Why hadn't Jess mentioned this side of her mom before? Was she trying to protect Beth from any outside criticism of their family?

Barbara's strident voice softened. "Oh, Beth. I'm so sorry. I didn't mean to attack your relatives. They're lovely people, I'm sure. I've just been questioning everything since Jess died. Looking for somewhere to place blame, something we could've done different. I keep thinking that if she hadn't wanted to belong so much, if she hadn't felt she needed to bend over backward to be accepted, she would still be alive."

Still in the same curled-up position, without making eye contact, Beth said in a tiny voice, "Did you hurt her?"

Now it was Barbara's turn to be stunned. "*What?*"

Emboldened by her reaction, Beth unwound herself and looked Barbara straight in the eye. "Did you do something to keep Jess from converting?"

"Goodness, no! How could you say such a thing? I loved that girl and her child more than anything else in this world. I may not have approved of her choices, but I'd have hurt myself before I did anything to hurt her or her baby." Angry now, Barbara stood to leave.

As a parting shot, she said, "Besides, like I said, I wasn't even here. As soon as she picked a date for that crazy ceremony, I planned a trip to Palm Springs with my girlfriends for that same weekend. I didn't want anything to do with it. What happened was a tragedy, and you know what? I blame it squarely on your family and that damn rabbi."

With that, Barbara turned on her heel and left the coffee shop. Speechless, Beth watched her retrace her steps across the street and back to her car, friendly smile now replaced by black spiderwebs of mascara running down her cheeks.

❧

By the time Beth left the coffee shop, she was crying so hard she could barely breathe. Her short-lived attempt to uncover the facts about Jessica's death had only revealed the truth that she was trying with all her might to deny: her aunt was dead, the baby was dead, and they were caught in some religious no-man's-land that even a rabbi couldn't identify.

Worst of all, if Jessica *hadn't* been murdered, then what? Could she possibly have been so unhappy as to take her own life without Beth being aware of it? Or could it just have been a horrible accident, like everyone was saying? She wasn't sure which was worse.

Knowing she would be unable to negotiate the city bus system in that state, Beth called her mom to come and pick her up, even though it meant admitting she hadn't gone to school. She was glad when her mom arrived with no scolding, and in fact the ride home involved very little talking at all, with hot tea and a cozy bed waiting for her at the end.

Beth spent most of the next two days in that same bed, buried in a cloud of blankets, grief, and pain. She knew that somewhere Adam would be sitting *shivah*, that his mirrors would be covered and his face unshaved, and some part of her wondered if his family would consider Jessica or their baby Jewish enough to join him in formal mourning. She knew she should go see him, but it seemed like way too much effort to leave the house.

Instead, Beth held her own personal *shivah* in her darkened room, barely coming out to use the bathroom. Her parents brought her food and schoolwork, which she for the most part ignored, preferring instead to sleep or binge watch old TV shows. Her friends called, texted, and left voicemails, but—thank God—her parents mostly left her alone.

The one clear interlude was when her mom came into her room to tell her that the results of the tox screen had come in. They were, as with the rest of her aunt's death, inconclusive: there was evidence of Xanax and some other stuff in Jessica's system, but not enough to have been lethal. In other words, she had probably taken some to combat her nerves in the hours leading up to the conversion ceremony.

After hearing this news, Beth remained silent. She turned over in bed, away from her mom, to face the wall. She was in a numb place, an empty place, a place without fear, where babies didn't die before they'd even taken their first breath. Nothing could touch her there. It was safe and quiet and predictable. She didn't want to leave. Ever.

※

The next time Beth's mom came into her room, it was with a letter in her hands. As she handed it to Beth, she noticed that her mom's hands were shaking. When Beth saw the return address and the distinctive, curly handwriting, she understood why: the letter was from Jessica. Beth's breath slammed into her lungs like she'd belly flopped off the high dive. How was this possible?

"Beth, honey? Are you okay?" her mom asked.

"No. I'm not. Stop asking me that. I just got a letter from a dead person." Calmer than she'd been in days, Beth looked straight at her mom. "Please, go away. Let me read this alone."

Without a word, her mom's pale face slunk out the door, easing it closed behind her. Beth felt a pang of regret for having snapped at her, as her mom had been nothing but nice to her over the past few days. She looked back at the letter lying on her bed like it was a snake coiled and ready to bite. Distantly, she noticed that her own hands were shaking too.

She took a deep breath and reached for the letter, then laughed at herself. She was acting as if it really had been sent from beyond the grave. No, it was just another of the endless barrage of cards and correspondence that she and Jessica sent back and forth, this one sent before she died and in transit until today. Tragic timing, but a coincidence nonetheless.

Even so, Beth ripped open the envelope with care, knowing she'd never be getting another such letter in her lifetime. This was the last.

As she pulled out the folded pages of paper, she was surprised at its brevity—usually their letters were long and chatty, full of updates about their lives and loves. This letter was different though, running to just one page of Jess's customary blue-lined binder paper. Even her writing looked heavier, more slanted and hurried. Beth started reading:

My dearest Bethy,

Tomorrow is the big day—the day that I officially become Jewish. I wish I could say I'm more excited, but I'm not. I'm terrified. And I don't want to scare you, I just have this feeling . . . I can't believe I'm saying this, but really, you're the only one I can tell. I should've said something before now, but you're working so hard at school, and I didn't want you to feel guilty about the whole thing.

My friends don't get it, and I think my mom has gone off the deep end. Seriously. She's going crazy over my conversion, saying that my baby can't be Jewish, it's too risky in this day and age, and she doesn't want him belonging to such an outdated conservative faith that didn't even want me in the first place. Basically, after all this time, she's finally caught on to the pressure that Adam and his family—your, our family—have been putting on me, the importance they are putting on my boy child, and now all of a sudden, it's a deal breaker. Or something. I don't even know what is going on with her.

Meanwhile Adam is already planning the bris for after the baby is born—why would you invite all your cousins and elderly relatives to see your son get circumcised? I don't get it. It's all too much for me. I feel like I'm stuck in the middle, like the baby and I are being pulled apart between two worlds that both want us—and don't.

And I'm so sad and alone all the time, Bethy. You're the only person that gets this and soon you'll be grown up and have your own life. Then what? I don't know.

What I do know is that tomorrow, before the mikvah, I'm going to load up on Xanax and sleeping pills. I know I shouldn't, with the baby, but it's just this one time, and it won't be enough to hurt him. Just enough so that I can get through the ceremony itself. I hope. I'm just so scared. Then we'll see, I guess. One day at a time.

I love you so much Bethy. I'm sure I'm overreacting, but I just wanted you to know, no matter what happens tomorrow, that is always true. And hey—you are going to wear your bridesmaid dress to prom, aren't you? And definitely ask that cute guy in English class. Do it. Today. For me.

All my love,

Jess

THE GOD OF VENGEANCE

Bride of Torches

Kenneth Wishnia

This happened in the days of the chieftains, when there was no king over Israel and every man did as he pleased. In retaliation for a surprise attack that left six hundred loyal warriors dead, the army of King Yavin of Kanaan invaded the land of Yisra'el, led by a commander named Sisera. The invaders destroyed the vineyards, lay with the women by force, butchered the children, and hung the babies by their necks. They burned young men alive, and young maidens had no marriage song. Caravan traffic stopped as travelers avoided the war zones. In desperation, the people of the land turned to prophecy and divination.

The Kanaanites blocked the roads and barred any contraband iron goods from coming up from the coast. There were no blacksmiths in the land in those days, so there was no sword or spear made of iron to be found in the land of Yisra'el, and the people had to rely on migrant metalworkers to sharpen their pitchforks, axes, and sickles because the Kanaanite authorities allowed a solitary band of rootless Kenite iron-workers to bring the wonders of Iron Age technology to the farmers and shepherds in the rugged hill country of Lower Galilee.

When Khever the Kenite and his clan of wandering metallurgists reached the village of Beth-Immah, they found the villagers crowding around a wise old woman named Abital who was reading the patterns created by a spoonful of sesame oil shimmering on the surface of the water in a shallow earthenware bowl. The villagers craned their necks, hoping to get a glimpse of the insoluble message.

Abital gazed at the swirling colors and confirmed the worst: "God is angry with us."

The villagers raised their voices in anguish.

"We have turned away from kindness and righteousness, and so God has turned away from us, leaving us to cower in fear and terror before our enemies."

Some wept, tearing at their cloaks, others covered their faces, racked by guilt and shame.

"But—"

The anxious villagers huddled closer. *But what?*

"But . . ." Abital strained to decode the rapidly changing signs. "God will send . . . a *woman* to lead, whose valor will shine like the sun."

A woman?

Who could it be? Devorah of the tribe of Naftali? Ma'akha of the tribe of Issachar?

The clanging of iron jarred them back to the present, as the Kenites announced they had come to trade their goods and labor by banging on cymbals made of a sonorous iron-copper alloy pierced with dozens of silver hoops.

The villagers rummaged about in their kitchens and toolsheds, gathering up armfuls of cracked metal vessels, blunted knives, and cutting tools with dull blades, then scrambled for a place in line so the itinerant metalsmiths could sharpen their farming tools, repair their broken cooking pots, and fix all manner of utensils made of copper, tin, or bronze, all of them pitted and corroded in spots, including a useless hunk of metal that looked like someone had literally tried to beat a rusty sword into a plowshare.

The young Kenite woman tending the fire tied her hair back to keep the tongues of flame from licking her long, wavy locks as her husband's hammer blows sent sparks flying like the sons of He-Who-Burns swarming up from the underworld, for she was the wife of Khever the Kenite, bride of torches. Her mother named her Ya'el because she had long, thin legs and faun-colored hair at birth, and as a youth she ran through the fields like a gazelle. She was more shapely now, and her hair had darkened from constant exposure to the punishing heat of the forges, but it was her voice—breathy and a bit husky from all those years of fanning the flames—that could be relied on to soothe the women and persuade the men to part with their silver for an iron-tipped weapon.

But the residents of this unprotected village were so destitute they had no silver to speak of, bartering for the highly desirable iron tools with baskets of unwinnowed grain and skinny lambs with spotted coats that were considered unworthy of being sacrificed to their god, Yahaweh.

Khever worked the red-hot iron, squinting to avoid the flying sparks and shards of metal. He kept his beard trimmed short because sporting a full beard is pure folly when you make your living working with fire, while Ya'el could only shake her head at the primitive tools they used in these unwalled villages, where the locals had no need of iron bits and horseshoes because they didn't have any horses, no use for spears and arrows because they hunted with slings and stones. They even skinned their animals with knives made of flint. *Flint!*

A little girl with smoky gray eyes and a red ribbon in her coal-black hair to ward off the Evil Eye stared wide-eyed as Ya'el worked the bellows to stoke the flames. When the iron was white-hot, Khever used a metal punch to make a pair of wide, flaring nostrils, and with a few well-placed strokes of the hammer and chisel turned the butt end of an iron pruning hook into the face of a scaly creature with slanted eyes, pointy ears, and flaming red nostrils that hissed and steamed when he plunged it into the water.

When they removed the cold black rod of iron from the water, the girl was still standing there, mesmerized by the transformation she had witnessed.

Ya'el sat back on her heels and wiped the sweat from her forehead with a bit of cloth she used for buffing and polishing.

"What's your name?" she asked the gray-eyed girl.

"Tirzah."

"Watch this, Tirzah," said Ya'el with a furtive wink, as if sharing a trade secret.

She tore off a piece of the cloth, balled it up, and made sure Tirzah was watching as she tilted her head back and stuck it in her mouth, brought a glowing ember to her lips, and set the cloth on fire. Ya'el let the flame dance around inside her mouth for a moment, then closed her lips to extinguish the flame, tilted her head forward, and blew the smoke out through her nose. Tirzah's jaw dropped in amazement. Ya'el spat the charred cloth into her palm, handed it to Tirzah, and warned her not to try this herself.

"I'll show you when you're a little older, the next time we come to your village."

Tirzah nodded gravely, as if already keenly aware that knowledge of many secret rituals awaited her as she got older and the way of women came upon her.

"Where to next?" Ya'el said as the clan of Kenites was packing up their gear for the day.

"North," Khever grunted. "To Khatzor." The capital of King Yavin's realm, where their labors would be more richly rewarded. The men of Khatzor rode iron-wheeled chariots pulled by teams of specially bred Arabian horses with iron bits in their mouths, and there was peace between King Yavin and the clan of Khever the Kenite.

The Kenites were halfway up the rocky trail—the dry, scrubby slopes of Mount Tabor looming over the farmland to the west—when the ground beneath their feet began to tremble. A fierce war cry shattered the stillness of the day, and the rumble of chariots shook the earth as the enemy cavalry overran the village below. Helmeted drivers steered the chariots carrying archers firing iron-tipped arrows at the fleeing villagers, who dropped to the dust as death claimed their souls or screamed in agony as they bled out. Horseback riders slashed at the terrified villagers and menaced them with javelins, herding the survivors together as the army's leader roared in, driving a scythed chariot that cut the victims off at the knees. Ya'el recognized the stubbly beard and piercing gaze of Commander Sisera, his sun-browned cheeks as leathery as an old, cracked wineskin.

At his command, his troops set fire to the village, the dry, worm-eaten roof beams and walls igniting in a flash. A forest of arrows sprouting from the bodies of the dead and dying pointed skyward like smoking fingers as the flames consumed them. Strong winds from the east spread the fires to the storehouses of wool and olive oil, which exploded in flames intense enough to melt clay pots and blacken the mud bricks with a layer of brittle, vitrified earth.

A lone infant sat crying, abandoned amid the smoke and flame, its face and clothing charred by the blast.

Ya'el stirred to help, but Khever held her back with a stern warning: "It's not our fight."

She struggled to break free from his grip while he explained that the clan had survived, even prospered, by keeping out of the dispute between the Kanaanites and the Israelites.

The child was too far away for Ya'el to tell if it was male or female. But she stopped struggling and averted her eyes as the spearmen charged toward the defenseless infant.

The cries of the dying could be heard for miles in the thin mountain air as the nomadic band of Kenites went searching for a new campsite, and Sisera's men sowed the land with a mixture of salt and sulfur to ensure that no food would ever grow in that place again, even unto the tenth generation.

When there was nothing left to slash, burn, or pillage, Sisera and his men withdrew, parading down the trail past Mount Tabor toward the dry riverbed of the Wadi Kishon on the coastal plain, then onward to their stronghold, the city of Kharoseth-ha-goyim, the Foundry-of-the-Nations.

᛫

The Kenites set up camp for the night on a windy ridge overlooking the smoking ruins of the village of Beth-Immah, the women unloading the baggage and the men scrambling about hammering tent pegs into the rocky soil and securing them with threefold cords so they would not be easily broken.

Khever reached out to stroke his wife's long dark hair, but she pulled away and walked to the edge of the camp. She prayed to the God of the Israelites that she would live to see the next cycle of the sun. Since the borders of this disputed territory were continually shifting, they were engaged in a quasi-illicit trade that the Kanaanite overlords often equated with armed resistance and the locals often equated with sorcery, and because it was always a good idea to pay homage to the local gods.

The Kenite tribesmen traced their lineage back to the first metalsmith, Kayin, who was condemned to wander the land bearing the mark of a murderer upon his forehead for an act of violence that shook the foundations of the world and still sent shivers through Ya'el's body after so many centuries. Did her people still bear the guilt of this atrocity—the oldest curse in the world? Had she stoked the fires bearing the mark of Kayin?

The wise women of the tribe said the Kenites were also descended from Yitro the Midianite, father-in-law of Moses the Lawgiver, which made the wandering Israelites her cousins, of a sort. And hadn't the sons of Yisra'el, under their leader Yehoshua, conquered the region with unparalleled ruthlessness, chopping the heads off statues of the Kanaanite gods and setting fire to their sacred posts, burning down the palace, and destroying the city of Hatzor in a firestorm far worse than Kayin's unthinking act of rage thousands of years ago when a jealous farmer killed a herdsman.

And now, it seemed the two groups were caught in an endless cycle of violence.

❦

Ya'el saw the signal fires dancing from hilltop to hilltop, calling for an emergency war council. And when the first rays of the rising sun cleaved the air, bathing the land in the purest light, the sacred fires rose again on the horned altar in the ruined village of Beth-Immah.

Devorah the prophetess, wife of Barak Ben-Avinoam of the tribe of Naftali, took her place among the men of war. A mature woman with strong arms from years of hauling jars of lamp oil from one high place to another across the hill country of Ephrayim, she was a judge now, holding court beneath the palm trees while her husband Barak hauled the jars of oil and kept the fires burning, a dusting of gray in his short, wooly hair.

Devorah summoned her husband before the assembly and said, "Yahaweh, God of Yisra'el, has commanded you to march to Mount Tabor with the men of Naftali and Zevulun to do battle with Sisera's army."

Barak shuffled his feet, aware of the eyes upon him, and said that he wouldn't do it unless his wife agreed to go with him.

Ya'el watched, transfixed, from her clifftop perch behind a break of purple hyssop, as Devorah said, "I will go with you, for there is no greater shame for a warrior than to die by a woman's hand—even more so if we do battle against the enemy's full force of nine hundred iron chariots, a thousand horsemen, and ten thousand spearmen and archers!"

Some of the conscripts went a bit pale as their hearts turned to water, so Devorah summoned a man of God—a hairy man from Gilead with a leather belt around his waist—to curse the enemy before battle.

"You must not fear our enemies! For the Lord your God who led you out of Egypt with a mighty hand is with you!" the man of God cried out, his long gray beard blowing in the wind. "Now, is there anyone here who has built a new house but hasn't dedicated it yet?"

A few dozen hands went up.

The man of God sent them home, lest they die in battle and another man dedicate their house.

"Has anyone planted a vineyard but hasn't harvested the grapes yet?"

Several dozen hands went up, and the man of God sent them home.

"Has anyone paid the bride-price for a wife but hasn't gotten to know her yet?"

A dozen or so hands went up, and the man of God sent them home.

"Right. Any cowards?"

A couple of shaky hands went up, fluttering in the breeze like stalks of barley.

I always catch a few, he thought.

"All right, begone with you," he said, and sent them home as well.

The men of Naftali brought forth a bull and slaughtered it, and splashed its blood on the northeast and southwest corners of the horned altar, so that all four sides of the altar were dripping with bright-red gore. And the man of God raised his hands and *behold*, fire came forth from before Yahaweh and consumed the burnt offering upon the altar! And the people saw, praised God's name, and fell on their faces.

Ya'el couldn't help admiring the Israelites' mastery of such tricky fire-craft, and kept close watch as the skittish warriors oiled their shields— little more than tanned cowhides stretched over flimsy wooden frames and, in some cases, wicker. Maybe they prayed that the grease would deflect the enemies' arrows or keep the animal hides from cracking in the sun, but wood-and-leather shields would be no match for the Kanaanites' heavy iron weaponry, and either way, Ya'el didn't think it wise to depend on a shield that can be set on fire.

Devorah called on a chieftain of Zevulun, a tribe whose people laugh at death. A long-haired Nazirite named Shamgar Ben-Anath, whose name signified he had Kanaanite lineage, came forward and told his people to take heart:

"Shall we bow down and bare our necks like feeble old men? Shall we eat the bread of women? We know these hills better than any invader! But our weapons have grown rusty from lack of use! Arise!" he bellowed, buffeted by the east wind. "Arise—and send word to that butcher Sisera that we will cut off his arm and the arm of his father's house! His armies will flee from us in seven directions! By this time tomorrow, we will place our feet on the neck of King Yavin, lie with his wives, and eat the salt of the palace!"

Ya'el's nose crinkled up, bitterness flooding her mouth as if she had bitten into a rotten vegetable.

An elderly man named Kaleb got so caught up in the martial fervor that he announced, "I will give my eldest daughter 'Akhsa to the man who captures and kills Commander Sisera!"

Ya'el turned away in disgust, seeking the comfort of her tent, when Devorah called upon Ma'akha, the lone female chieftain of the tribe of Issachar, a fierce warrior with flashing eyes and dark brown skin, who raged over the gathering storm:

"May their quivers become empty, may their bows go slack! May Shamash deprive them of sight! Let us fill the mountainside with their corpses and send them down to the belly of She'ol in full battle gear, so they shall never know peace!"

The cry went up: *Khay Yahaweh!* which meant *God lives,* as the sons of Yisra'el tossed their leather helmets in the air. Great was the clamor, the war cries, the rattling of bronze swords and daggers as the tribes of Issachar, Naftali, and Zevulun joined forces. Even the tribe of Benyamin joined the war party, sending a team of seventy handpicked swordsmen, all left-handed.

The women cheered as their cousins and brothers set off with the wind at their backs: the spearmen with their glossy leather shields in front, the archers and warriors trained in special tactics taking up the rear.

By the time the sons of Yisra'el took up positions on the zigzag-incised slopes of Mount Tabor, a thunderstorm was raging westward across the hills.

On the hill overlooking the ruined village, Khever the Kenite had to shout to be heard: "Storm coming! Double the ropes and gather the flocks!"

Ya'el was soaked to the skin by the time she finished securing the ropes. She dashed inside the tent, tossing the mallet and tent pegs aside as she rushed to peel off her clinging wet clothing and wrap herself in a blanket made of nice dry lambswool. She'd have to wait for the storm to pass to dry her clothes over the campfire.

Meanwhile, Sisera's army set forth from the fortress at Kharoseth-ha-goyim and advanced toward the Wadi Kishon, mocking the poorly equipped sons of Yisra'el creeping along the jagged trails on the western face of Mount Tabor. Sisera's archers strutted along the dusty riverbed bearing composite bows and quivers full of iron-tipped arrows that could kill a man at a distance of eight hundred paces and wound a man at more than a thousand. His foot soldiers carried spears with gleaming iron blades and shafts like a weaver's rod, with leather cords wound around them to give the weapons the spin needed to travel farther with more deadly accuracy.

Sisera cursed the sons of Yisra'el, saying, "May the corpses of those who rebel against me cover the land from east to west! May worms feast on their flesh and may their fate be a horror to all who pass by and lay eyes upon them!"

The foot soldiers cheered, his words echoing in their ears as a shadow passed over the land. An ominous dark gray thunderhead loomed over the mountain and unleashed a sudden downpour, the sign for Barak to lead the charge down Mount Tabor, followed by a thousand men.

A great rumbling shook the earth. Lightning bolts crashed about Sisera's army on all sides, striking a dozen upraised spearheads and reducing their handlers to quivering lumps of burning flesh as the Lord's fiery gaze tore up the earth and sky around them.

Heavy waves of rainwater raced down the slopes of Mount Tabor to the hard, dry bed of the Wadi Kishon and rushed toward Sisera's army with the speed of galloping horses, swamping the iron-wheeled chariots and miring them in mud.

Blinded by fury, Sisera ordered his charioteers to punish the river by lashing it with their whips.

The charioteers in their heavy iron armor must have felt as if the very stars in heaven were fighting against them as the lighter, swifter Israelites overran them, hamstringing their horses with short bronze daggers, and raining fire and brimstone on the archers and setting fire to the chariots by lobbing grenades of flaming *naphtha*—black tar from the Dead Sea whose flames cannot be quenched by rainwater.

The Israelite special forces even loosed a mare in heat to confound the Kanaanite stallions, and the left-handed warriors of the tribe of Benyamin cut down legions of swordsmen unused to defending themselves from attack on the right-hand side of their shields.

Charging through the fire and smoke, Barak taunted the enemy commander: "A bit different fighting a *real* army instead of unarmed villagers, isn't it?"

When Sisera saw the day was lost, he alighted from his chariot and fled on foot, heading for the hills, and safety.

The tent roof's goat-hair fibers were still saturated from the heavy rain as the men of the Kenite clan fanned out across the hills, rounding up the livestock scattered by the storm.

Ya'el's clothes were still drying over the campfire, so she was wearing little more than a skimpy linen shift when a badly wounded warrior stumbled into the camp, out of breath, his garments torn, his face streaked with soot and sweat, a hunted look in his eyes as if the gates of She'ol had burst open and the sharp-toothed sons of the storm wind were in hot pursuit, bubbling up through the earth and clawing at his heels.

The men were still rounding up the livestock, so she had to play the role of chieftain and offer this weary stranger hospitality.

"Come in, my lord, come into my tent," she said, bowing low. "You'll be safe here."

Commander Sisera pushed past her and checked the corners of the tent for potential threats. Satisfied, he flopped down on the bedding spread out on the ground.

"Lie down, my lord," she said in her most seductive tones, "and allow your servant to loosen your belt."

Soothed by the sound of her voice, he let her ungird his loins and lay the weapon-laden belt beyond his immediate reach. She removed his muddy sandals and bathed his feet in a basin of water.

"You need to rest, my lord," she said, drying his feet and covering him with a blanket. "You must be exhausted."

She spread some honey on his wounds so they wouldn't fester and prepared a tincture of willow bark to ease his aches.

"Bring me some water for my thirst," he said, a breach of custom that made it clear he regarded his Kenite hosts as inferiors, subject to his dominion.

"As you wish, my lord," Ya'el said, skimming the cream from a pot of fresh goat's milk simmering over the fire.

She cradled his head in one hand and fed him a bowl of warm milk and the choicest curds with the other, wiping the drips off his chin with a cloth.

"Guard the entrance to the tent," he said drowsily, letting his head fall back onto the bedding. "If anyone asks for me, tell them you haven't seen me since daybreak."

"I will do as you say, my lord."

She got up and peered through the tent flaps, but the men hadn't returned yet. It was up to her to take action.

She waited till Sisera drifted off to sleep, then she crept over to him and straddled him like a woman in labor squatting on a birthing stool.

She gently stroked his unshaven chin with the tip of her finger. He wasn't a bad-looking man. His skin was baked from the sun and he was a few pounds heavier than the cut of his clothes suggested, but he must have been quite handsome when he was younger, before twenty years of warfare took their toll.

But any man who so gleefully murders the innocent had forfeited any claim to her sympathies.

He must have been vaguely conscious, because his pulse stirred, his virility began to stiffen, and he started slowly grinding his loins against hers, a low sound emerging from deep within his throat as he purred with pleasure.

Ya'el reached for a tent peg with her left hand and the mallet with her right.

"Anyone would think you're trying to seduce me," Sisera muttered dreamily, reaching for her, caressing the downy skin of her arm with one of his huge, hairy hands.

After a moment's hesitation, she turned his head to the side and gently pressed the tent peg against the skin of his temple.

His eyes grew wide with terror: "Hold—!"

His arm lashed out.

The last thing he saw was the fire in her eyes as she raised the mallet and drove it home, hammering the tent peg through his temple and pinning his head to the ground beneath. And so he died.

"The east wind has broken you, Commander Sisera," she said, spitting twice to cleanse the taste of his name from her lips. "May your name be cursed unto the thousandth generation."

When Khever returned from corralling the runaway goats, Ya'el threw open the tent flaps and stepped out into the flickering light of the campfires. Her dress was soaked with blood, much of it dripping between her legs like a woman who has just given birth. Khever ran up to her, his eyes filled with panic.

"What happened? Are you all right?" He wiped away a bit of blood that had spattered across her forehead. "How did you get this mark?"

There was a great crash of bronze-edged weapons and greased leather as dozens of Israelite warriors burst into the camp. Barak and the tribe of Naftali had been pursuing Sisera from the River Kishon into the hills, following his trail all the way to the Kenite encampment.

"All right, where is he?" Barak demanded.

Ya'el said, "Come, and I will show you the man you seek."

Barak went inside with her and *behold*, Sisera was fallen, dead, with the tent peg piercing his bloody temple.

⅌

And on that day Devorah led the women in a song of victory:

> *Blessed is Ya'el among women*
> *For her strength, for her steady hand*
> *He begged for water, she gave him milk*
> *She struck Sisera with a hammer*
> *Smashed and pierced his temple*
> *Between her legs he kneeled, he fell, he lay.*

They sang of Sisera's mother, Themak, peering anxiously out the palace window, worried, wondering, Why isn't he back yet? Where is the rumbling of his chariot? Her wise ladies said, Surely they must be dividing the spoils. One womb, two wombs for each man, they chortled.

But she did not join in their laughter.

And when Barak sent her son's remains to the palace of King Yavin in Khatzor wrapped in bloody sheets, Sisera's mother cried a hundred times over his body.

> *So may all our enemies be destroyed, O Lord*
> *And may all who love You shine like the rising sun*
> *In all its power and glory*
> *May such fire never die out in Yisra'el!*

The elders complained bitterly that the world had gotten so screwed up that *a woman* could take a man's place on the battlefield, and that they had never seen such an unconscionable rejection of traditional values since the day the children of Yisra'el came up out of the land of Egypt. But Ma'akha, chieftain of the tribe of Issachar, reveled in the unquenchable sisterhood born of the flames.

Ya'el refused to wash the bloodstained bedclothes, insisting that they be burned. And she alone lit the torch that kindled the flames so that the lingering shadow of her encounter with such evil would be purged from her heart. At least she had kept that old man's reckless promise from being fulfilled and spared Kaleb's eldest daughter 'Akhsa from becoming some warrior's prize.

But the Kanaanite gods had clearly grown weak and ineffectual, and couldn't provide for their people anymore. Maybe the time had come to pray to Yahaweh.

And so Devorah sat down with King Yavin and negotiated an end to the wars of conquest, and the land was at peace for forty years.

Or so it is written.

Paying the Ferryman

E.J. Wagner

He tells Judith that he loves her.

They face each other across the butcher-block counter, the one he made fifteen years ago in the first months of their marriage. She slices sweet peppers for their dinner—the peppers are bright green, red, and yellow, and she loves the look of them as she slides them into a big, white bowl.

The window is open, and the May breeze carries the scent of the few blossoms on the recently planted lilacs. The late afternoon sun gilds the two glasses of sherry, which sit side by side on the counter.

He tells her that he loves her and that all through her long and difficult illness he was terrified that she might not recover. He tells her how much he admires her courage and humor, her ability to think quickly in a crisis, the clever little mysteries she writes and sometimes publishes. And how, at the last Shabbat dinner, after she lit and blessed the candles, and he sang the verses of *Eyshet khayil* praising a woman of valor—of strength—he saw her in every word.

She smiles a little as she cuts the peppers.

He tells her that he truly loves her, and has since they met, but that he—and here he smiles sadly—he has fallen deeply, desperately, passionately *in* love with Hadassah Sharon, the Israeli graduate student he is mentoring, and that he simply can't control his feelings because they're overwhelming. It is *bashert*—predestined.

Judith stops smiling.

He sips his sherry.

He tells her that he realizes this is a shock but thinks she must have known that the fire has been leaving their marriage for some time. Although, of course, there is still genuine respect and friendly love between them—and he's sure her grace and wisdom and courage, her *valor*, which he will always deeply admire, will help her understand and feel some empathy for him and Hadassah, since they are both racked—truly—with guilt but are determined to be honest. He explains how very sensitive and intelligent Hadassah is and emotes enthusiastically about his student's brilliant dissertation on death myths, in which she compared the Greek tale of Charon the Ferryman, who guides the dead across the river Styx, demanding payment for the service, with the legendary English black dogs who announce approaching death, and the Hebrew *Malekh ha-moves*—the Angel of Death.

Hadassah, he explains, is an imaginative scholar, witty and insightful, and he hopes that in time, after the divorce (about which he is of course prepared to be most generous), they can all approach each other as friends, in a civilized fashion.

He suggests joint custody might be best. That way, when the children stay with him and Hadassah, Judith will have time for herself—perhaps to take some courses, or travel, or look for a *real* job, and it will give the children time to establish a warm relationship with Hadassah, who is very nurturing, and who absolutely understands that the children's needs are paramount, and, of course, wants to help them adjust to their new situation as painlessly as possible.

Judith stops cutting the peppers.

She still holds the knife.

א

After, her first thought is to call for help—police, emergency services, somebody, anybody—but she remembers her children, both away with her neighbors on a camping trip, thinks of what a life they would have as the orphaned center of murderous scandal, and decides to be resolute. A mother, she tells herself, can do anything for her children. Anything. Especially a woman of valor. *Eyshet khayil!*

She removes the shower curtain from the downstairs bathroom, spreads it next to him, rolls him onto it. She drags him to the bathroom, and then, folding the curtain around him like a sling, pulls him into the tub. It is very difficult, but her recent illness did not affect her strength. She is a big woman, and she is determined.

She walks methodically around the house, collecting what she needs—a box of disposable latex gloves, a roll of large plastic bags, a block of kitchen knives, a book from his shelves. The book is entitled *Field Dressing and Butchering Game*. She carries these into the bathroom and closes the door.

When she emerges a few hours later, she is very pale and carries in her latex-gloved hands two plastic bags, the smaller one the size of a cabbage. She puts these in the wheelbarrow the landscaper has left near the back door, and returns to the bathroom for more. She tries not to dwell on their contents. When the wheelbarrow is full (there are nine parcels in all), she trundles it to the outer edge of the walled garden, near the recently planted lilac bushes. It is almost dark by now, and there are no near neighbors to peer over the fence, so no one sees as she pulls the small young bushes loose, scatters her burdens—all but one—into the vacated trench, adds the used latex gloves, and replaces the plants and soil. She waters deeply, then mulches.

Using a large bottle of bleach, she cleans the kitchen floor and the downstairs bath thoroughly, leaving windows open to allow the antiseptic odor to dissipate. She showers in the upstairs bathroom, washes her hair, dresses in jeans, sweatshirt, and sneakers, puts on an old raincoat of his and pulls a dark blue knit cap over her hair. She rummages through a pile of old letters in her dresser drawer, removes one, and thrusts it into her pocket.

From the garden, she retrieves the unburied plastic bag, and carries it to the garage wearing a fresh pair of latex gloves.

She spreads newspaper on the passenger-side floor of his Corvette and drops the bag and gloves onto it. She slides into the driver's seat, fastens her seatbelt, and backs down the driveway. She drives cautiously.

She pulls up to the dock just in time to see the ferry open the giant jaws of its hold with a groan that makes her think of some great prehistoric beast mournfully protesting extinction.

The boat's name is painted on its side: *The Deep River*. She follows the car ahead of her, careful not to make eye contact with the ferry hand who waves her on. She parks where he indicates, but waits in the car until the few other drivers have left their vehicles and gone above.

She retrieves the letter from her pocket and props it on the dash. She rolls up the newspapers and places them in the plastic bag. Carrying the coat and cap folded over the plastic bag, she locks the car, drops the keys in the coat pocket, and climbs upstairs to the deck. A large purse is slung over her shoulder. There is a chill mist over the water, and most of the passengers are keeping warm inside the cabin.

She leans against the rail, feeling the ferry throb, smelling the salt wind. No one is watching. Spreading the coat open on the deck, she quickly empties the plastic bag—except for the newspapers—onto it, adds the cap, closes the coat over it all, lifts it, and throws it over the rail.

It is dark, and she cannot see it sink—but she hears the splash when it hits the water. The newspapers from the plastic bag and then the empty bag follow with the last pair of latex gloves.

The loudspeaker announces, "The ticket window is now open. Will all passengers please come to the ticket window to buy tickets. The ticket window is now open."

She covers her hair with a scarf from her purse and goes inside. She buys a one-way foot passenger ticket, then takes a seat in the cabin and buries her face in a newspaper she buys at the stand near the ticket booth.

The ferry churns on.

"Will all passengers please come to the ticket booth and purchase tickets. All passengers, please."

The ferry rocks along.

The voice becomes more urgent.

"All passengers, *please*! There is one car without a ticket! Will the driver please come to the ticket window!"

They reach the other side. She gives her ticket to the man at the gate. He doesn't look at her, he is distracted by the increasingly insistent loudspeaker demanding the owner of the ticketless car.

She waits in the darkness of the dock for the return ferry. She wears a lightweight rain slicker from her capacious purse. *The Deep River* won't make the trip—police are searching it, looking for the missing driver. The alternate ferry is called *Great Expectations*, and when it pulls in, she boards it. She buys another foot passenger ticket.

Getting off at her home port, she removes the slicker. It is only a mile to her house—but it is dark, and she is dizzy and sweating. The walk seems to take hours, the heavy purse bumping against her side. By the time she arrives, she is faintly nauseated.

She showers—again using the upstairs bathroom—puts on a dressing gown, and makes a strong cup of tea. At 4:00 a.m. she phones the police and reports her husband missing.

She explains that her husband seemed upset, but wouldn't tell her why, drank a lot of sherry, much more than he was accustomed to, drove off in his green Corvette, and hasn't come home all night. The cop on duty tells her, "Lady, he's probably hoisting a few more. Happens all the time." But he takes the license number—clearly to humor her. Police tend not to search promptly for depressed sherry-drinking husbands.

In the morning, a detective comes to her door. The Corvette was found abandoned on the ferry. There was a note on the dashboard. Does she recognize the handwriting?

"Yes," she says, "yes."

"Darling, I'm so sorry—truly I am," the note says, signed with her husband's name, and looking just a bit more worn than it had seven years before when he had enclosed it with her very belated birthday gift.

The detective speaks quietly, sympathetically. He tells her that she may still hope for some closure. Drowned bodies usually surface. "Not right away, or completely," he says, "but eventually." (He avoids discussing the reasons: predatory fish, decomposition and resultant gases—the poor woman is suffering enough.)

She weeps, finally. Her grief is as sincere as it is overwhelming. The detective makes phone calls on her behalf, and friends arrive—all concerned about her facing such an ordeal after so long an illness.

A few months later she receives a call from the medical examiner. Human remains have been recovered from the water. The fish and boat propellers have done severe damage, and there is only a small portion of a body and part of a stained torn raincoat. But the M.E. is a kind man and spares her the details. He does ask her to view the watch and wedding band found on the "body part." They are neatly sealed in a plastic bag. DNA from her husband's toothbrush is compared with that in the bone and tissue of the recovered part and the match is conclusive.

Several rabbis are consulted but cannot agree on whether a funeral is proper in such a case.

And so there is a memorial service. Hadassah Sharon attends, with the department head, her new mentor. They sit in the back, close together, express their condolences after the service, then slip quietly away before the reception.

Many years pass. The children, who were told only of an accident on the ferry, grow up. They missed their father, but being very young, they were resilient. Not being the center of a murderous scandal, and having a strong mother solely devoted to their care, they grow up well. Their high school grades are excellent; they participate in extracurricular activities, have their teeth straightened, attend good colleges. One becomes a lawyer, the other a certified public accountant. They marry and move away, but they call often, and come home for holidays.

She feels it worked out for the best.

There is, of course, a price to pay.

She is growing old and her joints have begun to ache, and though the winters are much too harsh and the house is much too big, she knows she can never sell it. (For what would happen if the new owners had a dog who liked to dig, or if they put in a swimming pool, or if they just grew tired of the old lilac bushes?)

So she must keep the house, and weed the garden and prune the trees and scrape the icy walks in winter and try not to think of the future.

And sometimes, on a spring afternoon, when she stands at the wooden counter cutting peppers, and the late afternoon sun gilds the single glass of sherry before her, and the May breeze enters through the open window—then it seems to her, that with the fading breath of lilacs, once again he tells her that he loves her.

The Just Men of Bennett Avenue

A.J. Sidransky

85 Bennett Avenue
Washington Heights, New York, NY
Monday, June 17, 2019
6:30 a.m.

A crowd of black-hatted men pushed against the yellow police tape craning to see the body in the alley next to Congregation K'hal Adath Jeshurun. They whispered in hushed, excited tones, their words nearly inaudible to Detectives Tolya Kurchenko and Pete Gonzálvez. Unlucky enough to be reachable at 5:30 a.m.—the duty officer knew where they were, homicide being their business—so here they stood in sweaty gym clothes fresh off the incline bench press, Monday being chest day.

"Have you ever seen anything like that?" Pete said, examining the corpse.

"Seen a lot of dead bodies, but never one quite that color," Tolya replied.

The body, purplish-gray, was the color wheel opposite of the usual greenish-gray typical of the recently deceased. No signs of struggle or contusions, cuts or blood, were evident. The victim's mouth though, was forever locked into an odd, gaping position, like a fish out of water gasping for air. His eyeballs popped out of their sockets. In his right hand, the dead man clutched a bunch of papers so tightly his fingers appeared an even deeper shade of purple than the rest of him.

"Looks like the Chupacabra got him," Pete said, chuckling.

"The what?" replied Tolya.

"A goat-blood-sucking, Caribbean vampire my brothers used to scare me with when I was a kid. I've seen pictures of its victims online. Looks just like this."

Tolya rolled his eyes. He turned to Rabbi Shalom Rothman, standing behind him. "Do you know him?"

Rabbi Rothman sighed. "Yes, sadly, I do."

"Would you like to tell us who he is?" Tolya said, straightening up.

"His name is . . . was . . . Benjamin Andover."

Tolya glanced back at the body. The dead man had a shaggy head of dark, curly hair, face freshly shaven. Dressed in a pair of black linen slacks, a pale turquoise, monogramed shirt, and by the looks of them, bespoke, tasseled loafers, the victim appeared well heeled. "Not one of your congregants."

"No, he's isn't, um, wasn't," replied the rabbi, his voice more nonchalant than Tolya would have expected. "Quite the opposite. Let's go up to my office. I'll fill you in."

❧

TWELVE HOURS EARLIER
85 Bennett Avenue
Washington Heights, New York, NY
Sunday, June 16, 2019
5:30 p.m.

Francisco Abreu stood outside the door of Rabbi's Rothman's office, mop in hand, as he had every day for the past thirty years, save Saturdays which was the Sabbath. He heard shouting coming from the other side of the door and leaned his ear in to listen. So shocked was he by what he heard that he nearly dropped his mop. The sisters at Saint Catherine's would always tell him, don't gossip and don't listen to other people's conversations. It's a sin. Later, he would go to the priest and confess. He would ask for forgiveness.

Francisco jumped away quickly as the doorknob turned. A very tall man in a suit stood in the doorway. He handed a blue folder to Rabbi Rothman.

"Review this," the man said. "As I told you, it's just, well, you know, progress. You can pray anywhere. And let's be honest with each other. I've researched your congregation. It's dwindling, dying, and you know that. You could move into your senior center across the street. Wasn't that your original synagogue anyway?" The man laughed. "Honestly, Rabbi, I intend to take down these buildings. Times have changed. Washington Heights is hot, you're not. I've got the opportunity of a lifetime here."

The man brushed by Francisco as if he weren't there. He bounded down the steps and disappeared. Francisco looked past Rabbi Rothman into the office. The congregation's trustees sat stunned inside. Ten faces looked back at him, their eyes filled with sadness and confusion.

SEVEN HOURS AFTER THE MURDER
New York City Coroner's Office
421 East 26th Street
Kips Bay, New York, NY
Monday, June 17, 2019
1:30 p.m.

Tolya and Pete tried to listen intently as the coroner explained his preliminary findings, but the body of the victim lying on the slab behind the coroner was a bit distracting. The dead man's chest was open, his heart in a white enamel bowl on the table next to them. The coroner emphasized his observations with a laser pointer.

"The victim died of drowning. As you can see, the lungs are bloated, full of fluid."

"Why do they have that odd color?" Tolya asked.

"Because the fluid is blood, not water. One can drown in any liquid."

"You're saying the victim drowned in his own blood?"

"Preliminarily, yes, but not exactly. The volume and viscosity of blood in his body is also severely depleted."

"Why is that?" Pete asked.

"I'm not sure. Never seen anything like it." The coroner moved the laser pointer over the victim's lungs in a circular motion, counterclockwise. "The blood isn't coagulated, but it's much denser than it should be, almost like its water content has been reduced, boiled down. Look at this." He put down the pointer, picked up a scalpel and sliced into a large vein in the stomach cavity. What crumbled out of the vein was more sludge than fluid. It looked like fine, wet sand, dyed a deep reddish-purple.

"Beats me what caused that," said the coroner, shrugging. He picked up the laser pointer again and fidgeted with it. "The toxicology report will be back later this afternoon."

❧

TWELVE HOURS AFTER THE MURDER
Rabbi Rothman's Office
85 Bennett Ave
Washington Heights, New York, NY
Monday, June 17, 2019
4:00 p.m.

Pete texted on WhatsApp as Tolya fidgeted with the folder in his lap, waiting for Rabbi Rothman. "Calm down, brotherman. Probably traffic on the bridge," Pete said, a moment before Shalom entered the room.

"Sorry, gentlemen. I was at a funeral. A longtime member of the congregation died suddenly last night. Francisco found his body this morning. We're required to bury our dead immediately, as I'm sure you know."

"My condolences," said Tolya. "Is this a bad time? We need to discuss something relative to the body we found in the alley this morning."

"No. It's fine."

"We reviewed the security videos from your cameras across the street at the senior center," Tolya said. "Andover's body was dumped in the alley at 4:43 a.m. Francisco found the body at five. The gate appears open on the video. Francisco claims he locked it at ten the night before."

"Francisco has never lied about anything, not in the thirty years he's worked for us."

"Rabbi," said Pete, "the security cam picked up a tall figure in a long, red, hooded cape wearing red spike heels, carrying the body over its shoulder into the alley."

"A woman?"

"Looks that way," said Tolya. "Or a man with a strange fetish for ladies' footwear and dead bodies. What's most interesting is that the victim, your Mr. Andover, was six-foot-six and weighed 238 pounds. Not a small guy. Even for a strong woman, that would be a lot to carry."

"Especially in heels," said Pete.

"Do you think any of your people could have been involved in any way?" Tolya asked.

"Nothing motivates like money," Pete said.

"Detectives, we've known each other for years," replied the rabbi, stifling a chuckle. "I apologize, I don't want to be disrespectful to the dead. You know the congregation. Few of the men are strong enough to lift the Torah during prayers. I doubt any of them could kill a man, especially one Mr. Andover's size. Then this same someone would have had to sling a very large body over their shoulder, don high-heels, and be able to walk in them."

"True enough," Pete said, suppressing a laugh himself.

"Not to pry into police business," Shalom said, "but has the coroner determined a cause of death?"

"Yes," said Tolya. He uncrossed his legs and shifted forward, placing the folder from his lap on Shalom's desk. "It appears Andover drowned. The strange thing is that his lungs were filled with blood, not water. He drowned in his own blood."

"That's odd, and gruesome."

Tolya offered some more bait to Shalom, observing his reaction. "His remaining blood was nearly dehydrated in his veins."

Shalom took a deep breath but remained poker-faced. "How awful." He got up from behind the desk. "Detectives, I want to thank you for keeping me in the loop. It's getting late and we have a trustees' meeting tonight. We need to develop a plan in the event that we do have to move the congregation. Is there anything else?"

"Not right now, but honestly I don't think you'll need to have that meeting," said Tolya. "These are addressed to you."

Tolya handed the contents of the folder to Shalom. It contained copies of the papers Andover gripped in his cold, dead hand when Francisco found him, a signed and notarized deed passing ownership of the land to the congregation. Shalom examined them, speechless. He looked at Pete and Tolya.

"Yes, Shalom, we know what it says," said Tolya. "The question is why."

"And how." added Pete.

TEN HOURS BEFORE THE MURDER
120 Bennett Avenue
Washington Heights, New York, NY
Sunday, June 16, 2019
8:00 p.m.

Francisco placed the CVS shopping bag holding Rav Itzhak's dinner on the lobby floor. He brought the Rav's meals from the community kitchen at the senior center three times a day. Francisco looked forward to seeing the Rav every time he visited. They shared something they never spoke about, loneliness. Francisco had lost everyone in the drug wars of the 1980s. Rav Itzhak had lost everyone too, but in Europe, in the Shoah.

Rav Itzhak was seated at the dining room table surrounded by books. Francisco never liked books. They made his head hurt. But the Rav loved books, and Francisco loved the Rav. So, he loved the Rav's books. "Good evening, Rav Itzhak, here is your dinner," Francisco called out.

"Good evening, Francisco," Rav Itzhak replied. He opened the door to the credenza against the wall to take out dishes. "Will you eat with me this evening?"

Francisco gave him the same answer he did every night. "No, thank you. I've already eaten."

"Will you take something to drink?"

"Yes," said Francisco, "thank you. Some water, please."

"Hmmm, smells delicious, as always," Rav Itzhak said, filling a glass for Francisco.

Francisco slipped into the chair at the end of the table opposite the Rav and sipped at his water. "They had a choice tonight: chicken with the little meatballs or pot roast. I know you like the chicken with the meatballs best, so I brought that."

"How are you feeling today?" Rav Itzhak asked, taking a piece of rye bread, dipping it into the rich chicken gravy.

"Not very good."

"I could tell when you came in. What's bothering you?"

"Something terrible happened." Francisco took another sip. "A man came to see Rabbi Rothman and the trustees. I heard what he said to them through the door of the rabbi's office."

"You were listening?"

Francisco felt bad. Rav Itzhak was like the priest and the sisters at

Saint Catherine's. He was closer to God, and he knew what was right and wrong. "I couldn't help it. He was speaking very loud."

Rav Itzhak put down his fork and knife. "What did he say?"

"He is going to tear down the synagogue and build condominiums."

Rav Itzhak leaned forward. He wiped his mouth with the paper napkin Francisco had folded for him and placed in the bag with his meal. "What is this man's name?"

Francisco took a business card from his pants pocket and handed it to Rav Itzhak. "Here." He watched as Rav Itzhak examined it.

"Where did you get this?"

"Rabbi Rothman's office."

"You know you shouldn't take things from others without asking."

"I know that, Rav, but where will the people pray?"

Rav Itzhak smiled. "Don't worry, Francisco. God provides."

א

THIRTY-SIX HOURS AFTER THE MURDER
Rabbi Shalom Rothman's Office
85 Bennett Avenue
Washington Heights, New York, NY
Tuesday, June 18, 2019
12:30 p.m.

Shalom prayed quietly before opening the Zohar, the "Bible" of Jewish mysticism. While he respected these writings as he did all holy texts, he viewed them with some suspicion and as a source of superstition. Reflecting on what he'd seen in the alley that morning, he recalled an old myth his mother told him about when he was a boy, the legend of the Just Men, the *Lamed-vovniks*.

In the version his mother told him, *Hashem* held the energy of creation in a vessel. The energy was so excited to be part of *Hashem*'s plan that when *Hashem* opened the vessel, thirty-six sparks escaped. Creation was imperfect. To repair the universe, *Hashem* chose thirty-six men to carry the imperfections of the world in their souls. *Lamed-vov* represents thirty-six in Hebrew.

They are pure of heart and faith. They have unshakable belief in the goodness of man and *Hashem*. If one dies, another is chosen. They may be related, say from father to son, or grandson, or nephew, or they may not. When a *Lamed-vovnik* dies, a fine, misty rain falls, the tears of angels.

There are always thirty-six. Never more, never less. The balance of the world depends on them. The thirty-six do not know each other and may not know they are among the chosen. If they do know, they must never divulge it. Their identities remain secret. They have unique powers that they may use only to protect the Jewish community. It's also believed that they will reveal themselves when the Messiah arrives, heralding his coming. Some believe the Messiah will be chosen from among them.

Shalom looked out the window. A fine mist shrouded Broadway. He found the passage he sought, the parsha about creation. He touched the Aramaic dictionary atop his desk to reassure himself that help was there, if needed. And with that he began to read the passage slowly, making sure he understood each word.

⅍

THREE DAYS AFTER THE MURDER
The Captain's Office
34th Precinct,
4295 Broadway, New York, NY
Thursday, June 20, 2019
2:00 p.m.

"Well, what do we know?" the captain asked, leaning back in his chair, his stomach protruding over his belt.

"This is a strange one, Cap," Pete replied.

"My partner here wants to pin this on some mythical Latin American vampire creature or its distant cousin," Tolya said.

"Ah, the Chupacabra," said the captain.

Pete imitated a goat baring his teeth and attacking a neck.

"That's enough, Gonzálvez. This isn't the *X-Files*, and you're not Mulder and Scully. Tell me, Kurchenko, please?"

"The victim is a twenty-nine year-old real estate developer, Benjamin Andover. Single. Lives alone in a two-bedroom penthouse in SoHo. As an associate in the development team that built that building, he was given the penthouse as part of his compensation. There were various articles about him in all the big magazines; *Money, New York, National Real Estate Investor*. He was considered an up-and-comer."

"After he made his windfall on the SoHo building, he developed a small condominium property in Harlem, this time on his own," Pete continued. "He got some bad press with that deal. He convinced an old widow to sell him her bar on Amsterdam Avenue between 143rd Street and 144th Street. Apparently, the deal included the building, but she claimed she didn't understand that. She settled for a cut from the condominium sales proceeds in the end. She died shortly thereafter."

"We considered whether the cases might be related, "said Tolya. "But the old woman had no family. Her estate is managed by a community organization. The estate funds a charter school in Harlem. Everything is completely on the up and up. No one who would be seeking revenge."

"What's your theory of the case?" asked the captain.

"According to the coroner's report, Andover died of drowning . . . technically, anyway. His death was accidental, induced by exposure to insecticide," Tolya said, handing copies of the report's summary to Pete and the captain.

The captain read out loud. "The victim succumbed to overexposure to . . ." he sounded out the next word, "or-gan-o-phos-phates. Can you explain the drowning part, Kurchenko?"

"Organophosphates are used to kill roaches and ants. They break down their respiratory and circulatory systems, and they did the same thing to Andover. The result was that his lungs filled with bodily fluids. He literally drowned in his own blood. There were very heavy concentrations of the chemical in the master bedroom. Apparently, the guy had something of a bug phobia, and according to the super and the porters, he was constantly spraying stuff. The coroner concluded it built up in his system over time, eventually killing him."

"And what about this business with the viscosity of his blood?"

"Inconclusive. They're still working on that. Probably something to do with the collapse of the capillaries and the bleeding into his lungs and cavities."

"Were any empty canisters of this insecticide in the apartment?" the captain asked.

"No," Tolya said. "The building porters collect the garbage from the service vestibules daily. They said that Andover leaves a lot of shit at the service door."

"Sanitation picked up the recyclables that morning before we arrived," added Pete.

"Could any of the synagogue trustees be suspects?"

"I doubt it, Cap," Tolya replied. "They're all over eighty."

"And what about the guy who found the body? Is he a suspect?"

"No."

"Why?"

Tolya glanced over at Pete.

"He's what we now call intellectually challenged," said Pete. "Functions at about the level of a twelve-year-old."

"I see," said the captain. "Any other hard evidence besides the security videos from the synagogue?"

"We found the PIN code for the victim's cell phone with a list of passwords in his desk in his bedroom," said Tolya, "but there's not much there. Some calls between Rabbi Rothman and him. Also, calls made to the group that sold him the leasehold. They claim to know nothing, which I would guess is probably true, judging from the way they reacted when we contacted them and told them Andover was dead. We also have calls to and from his attorney, and what appear to be some friends and pillow pals."

"The attorney had little to say," added Pete. "He wasn't involved in the guy's personal life, at all. He did put us in touch with Andover's parents so that we could notify them of his death."

"And the girlfriends?"

"Mostly pillow pals," said Tolya.

"Any of them fit the description of the woman on the synagogue's security video?"

"Not at all, Cap," replied Pete. "Andover went for short, blond women. He had a lot of overnight guests. The security tapes at his building show them arriving around two in the morning, confirmed by the night concierge. Also, he made a remark to the doorman when he left that he was feeling particularly sexed up, and he was going to Club XXX over on Thompson Street to see what he could find."

"Club XXX?"

"It's an S&M place."

The captain smiled and raised an eyebrow. "Really?"

"He shows up back at his building at 2:13 a.m. It's timestamped on the security cameras," Tolya continued. "He's with a very tall woman. They take the elevator to his floor. They're making out in the elevator. Once they get off, we lose them."

"Can we ID the woman from these videos?"

"No, they're in black and white and they're grainy. Never get a good angle."

"Is there any video of either of them leaving?"

"No."

"Did the neighbors hear anything?"

"We spoke to the residents in the adjacent apartments and those above and below, said Pete. "They didn't hear a thing because the building—which is very new, very high-tech, very high-end—has a 'virtual-silence' system." Pete shook his head. "Rich real estate guys. No end to the bells and whistles."

"How the hell did she get the body out of the building and to the synagogue?"

"We don't know," said Tolya.

"Perhaps she jumped out of the window, flew away?" Pete said, smirking.

"Not helpful, Gonzálvez. Did you find any fingerprints? DNA?"

"There are dozens of fingerprints including his own in the apartment. We don't get a match on any database. There's one specific set on his clothing, however, that aren't his. They match those on the gate to the alley fence at the synagogue. We're assuming they belong to the assailant."

"And DNA?"

Tolya hesitated.

"C'mon, Tol. Tell him," Pete said egging him on, then muttering, "Chu . . . pa . . . ca . . . bra . . ."

Tolya, swiped at Pete's head. "Next time, I won't miss. There's a weird mixture of DNA under his fingernails. The DNA guy said it's contaminated. It's a mix of female human DNA and female mammal-like DNA, but they can't determine what kind of animal. The DNA guy has no explanation. He says sometimes samples can become contaminated, inconclusive."

"There's nothing useful there."

"No, not really. The only evidence we have that's of any real use is the toxicology findings, which you've seen. He bug-sprayed himself to death."

"Maybe he had something kinky going on with one of those girlfriends," the captain said, smirking. "Not something any of them are liable to admit to. Did you try to get DNA from any of these women?"

"No. We'd need a court order for that."

"Let's wait on that till we actually might need it." The captain pressed his index fingers against his lips and thought for a second. "And those papers the victim was clutching?"

"That's the most confounding element of the case," said Tolya. "Those papers are a transfer deed for the land to the congregation as a gift. They're addressed to Rabbi Rothman as trustee of the congregation, signed by Andover."

The captain raised his eyebrow. "Nice gift. Looks pretty suspicious, though."

"We agree," Tolya and Pete said in near unison.

"Notarized?"

"Yes," replied Tolya. "Andover's signature appears to be computerized, which is completely legal, and the notary seal appears legit too."

"We tried to contact the notary," said Pete. "She's an insurance agent with an office on Canal Street around the corner from Andover's apartment. She left for an unexpected monthlong trip to China to visit her ancestral village the morning we found Andover's body. Apparently, her father is very ill. No way to contact her till she gets back."

"Does the rabbi know about the deed yet?"

"Yes, we gave him a copy," said Tolya. "We wanted to see his reaction."

"And?"

"Shock," said Pete.

"There's still the outstanding question of the missing woman," said Tolya. "How did she get out of Andover's building without being seen, and with the body?"

"Keep investigating," said the captain. We have a very tall, very strong, woman in red spike heels to find."

❧

THE NIGHT OF THE MURDER
Rav Itzhak's Apartment
120 Bennett Avenue
Washington Heights, New York, NY
Sunday, June 16, 2019
11:00 p.m.

Rav Itzhak considered what he was about to do.

When he was a small boy in Poland, more than one hundred years earlier, a peasant came to see his father one Friday evening. He apologized

in broken Yiddish for disturbing them on the Sabbath. Itzhak understood most of what they whispered as he hung on his father's pantleg,
searching his pocket for the little candies he knew were hidden there.
When the man leaned in even closer to his father, he mumbled the word
pogrom several times. Itzhak had no idea what that meant. After the
visitor left, Itzhak's father grabbed his hat and headed to the front door
of their small, wooden house.

"Where are you going?" Itzhak called out.

His father looked back at him, eyes filled with dread. "To see your
zeyde."

Itzhak jumped gleefully out of his chair. "Let me go too!" he screamed.

His father knelt in front him. He smiled a smile so loving it filled
Itzhak's heart with joy. "Not this time, *mayn zineleh*. I'm sorry."

The next day, the police chief, Piotr Bogdanski, was found dead
behind the boathouse next to the little river that ran through the town. All
the boys craned their necks to see the body. It was purplish-gray, the dead
man's mouth open in a wide circle like a dead fish, his eyes popping out
of his head. The scene terrified Itzhak. He ran all the way home. When he
arrived, he found his father in the living room, tears running from his eyes.

Itzhak climbed into his father's lap and wrapped his arms around
him. "Are you crying about Piotr Bogdanski?"

His father stroked Itzhak's cheek. "No, my darling son, I am crying
for my father. Itzhak, your *zeyde* has gone to *Hashem*. He died last night."

Itzhak didn't understand what his father told him then, but he understood it now. His father had alerted his grandfather, a Just Man, about a
threat to the community. In the hour of danger, he saved the community.
The price for that act was the Just Man's own death. His father would do
the same some twenty-two years later, passing his heavy burden to Itzhak.
The contact with the profane that was necessary to save the community
would destroy a Just Man's purity of heart and soul.

Rav Itzhak went into the hallway and dug through the bottom of the
coat closet. Way in the back was an old wooden crate. He pulled it out,
his breath catching in his throat. He knew what would happen, but his
resolve only strengthened him. He picked up the old crate with force he
didn't know he had. He carried it into the living room, turned down the
lights, and fetched two elaborate candlesticks from the credenza, placing
candles in each. He lit them and blessed the light over the darkness as his
father taught him on that fateful night in 1941. Then he opened the crate.

Inside were an ancient prayer shawl, which he donned, several old books bound in cracked, black leather, and some small boxes marked with Hebrew letters and symbols. He took one of the books and placed it on the coffee table. Rav Itzhak closed his eyes, mumbled a prayer, then opened the book to a page he marked the night his father passed this cursed treasure to him.

The book was centuries old, the pages so delicate he thought they might crumble at his touch, yet they felt alive, warm and smooth. He squinted in the dim light to find the proper passage, running his finger along the ancient Aramaic words as he read them. There, in the second passage was the name of the being he sought, and in the next the incantation to bring her to this realm.

Rav Itzhak swallowed. He had no choice. If it was his time to leave this world for the next, so be it. The members of the shul had cared for him for years, decades. They had taken him in when he was alone, when his faith was wavering, when he thought he couldn't continue. They brought him joy with every act of devotion they made. *Hashem*'s presence was in everything they did.

He searched for a tiny, red box among the items at the bottom of the crate. It would contain a fine red powder. Remove a pinch and place it in the palm of your hand, the holy book instructed, then blow it toward the flames and mumble the ancient Aramaic incantation, *avra-ca-davra*, "I make, as I say." He completed the task quickly, time being of the essence.

For a long moment nothing happened. Then ever so faintly, a figure appeared in the shadows. Amorphous at first, more a blur than a shape, its edges hardened slowly. As his ancient eyes adjusted, he discerned a woman in a red cape. She was very tall, much taller than him.

Devastatingly beautiful, her skin was the color of alabaster. Her hair, jet black and lustrous, cascaded down her shoulders. Her most alluring and entrancing feature was her eyes. Deep and dark, they sucked him in, like the inkiness of the ocean at night. Rav Itzhak couldn't look directly at them, but neither could he look away. The creature smiled, her ruby-red lips the same color as her cape, full and sensual, so much so that the old man felt ashamed.

"Mmmm," the creature purred. She stretched her arms and shook out her hair. "It's been a long time, Itzhak ben Shimon ben Leib. I've been waiting for you." She took a step out of the shadows and reached out to him. He stepped back, not wanting her touch to pollute him. She laughed, exposing her brilliant, white teeth, the canines just a little too long to appear normal.

Rav Itzhak forced himself to stare into her eyes. "Lilith," he whispered.

Lilith moved back, almost floating, seating herself in an old, velvet club chair, filling it entirely. "Why have you summoned me?" she purred. "As if I don't already know the answer to that question."

"The community is in great peril."

"That's always the answer. How droll." Lilith laughed. "And what's in it for me?"

Rav Itzhak didn't respond. He remembered the words of his father. If he should ever summon her, don't engage in conversation. She's a trickster. She wants something for her services, but she knows she's not entitled. *Hashem* exiled her at the beginning of time. She would serve her penance for eternity.

"You're as quiet as your father, and your grandfather."

"The community is threatened," he repeated.

"You want me to eliminate this threat?"

Rav Itzhak nodded.

Lilith rose from the chair. She tossed her hair back and laughed again. "No."

Rav Itzhak was stunned, confused. He had commanded her. She couldn't refuse.

"You made an error, Itzhak. You left out the last line of the summoning. You brought me to this world, but you didn't specify for how long."

Rav Itzhak's heart pounded. What had he done? He looked down at the ancient book. He reread the passage quickly and with a panic he had never experienced before, not even as he watched his own father die. In his haste, he had left out the end of the incantation. He had loosed Lilith on the world. Quickly, he shouted out the last line of the spell.

Lilith laughed again, this time hysterically. "Too little, too late, as they say."

Rav Itzhak mumbled an incantation, grabbed another pinch of the powder, and blew it at the creature without result.

Lilith became deadly serious. "I will do as you ask," she said. "But this time I will keep my victim's soul. If I have his soul, I can stay in this realm. I can haunt the nights and evenings, the hours before dawn. I've spent too much of eternity a prisoner."

Rav Itzhak thought for a moment, his heart breaking. What else could he do? He had made a serious error, but he would send this demon to destroy Andover anyway. He would do what he must to save the community and try find a solution to the problem of Lilith later. Rav Itzhak handed Lilith Andover's card.

𝔶

Lilith lurked in the shadows waiting for Andover. She was sure he would come. They always did. It was her scent. It worked every time. A few minutes after midnight Andover left his building. She followed him from the shadows as he walked anxiously to his destination, Club XXX, located in an old warehouse on Thompson Street. The entrance was a loading dock. A line of emaciated, sexily dressed, party-wannabees stood in single-file in front. The line wasn't long, but then it was Sunday night.

Lilith waited in the shadows across the street until Andover entered, ushered to the front of the line by a large, burly man seated on a stool in front of the door holding an iPad. The bouncer's beard extended halfway down his chest, its bottom three inches gathered together with a pink scrunchy.

Lilith crossed the street slowly with grace, making sure the bouncer caught her eye. She slid past the line and smiled. He waved her in, mesmerized. Human scent grew stronger as she moved down the dark hallway. The room was cavernous, its interior painted black. Flashing lights played off the walls and the dance floor creating a pulsating effect, which combined with the blasting house music to make the space seem otherworldly. At the back was a long bar painted a high-lacquered ebony with a mirror behind it. She spotted Andover, seated at its middle.

Lilith took a seat farther down. She stared directly at the mirror. "Belvedere, rocks," she said. The bartender nodded and filled a glass with ice and vodka, placing it in front of her. She touched the rim to her lips, watching Andover watch her in the mirror. She turned her head and smiled, revealing her glistening white teeth.

Andover smiled back. She tipped her head ever so slightly. Andover rose from his stool and approached. "May I join you?"

"Of course," she replied, raising her head. His eyes met hers. She held him there for a long second, then knew he was hers.

𝔶

Once in Andover's apartment, Lilith grew excited. Her freedom was near, well, her relative freedom anyway. They'd chatted for a while. Admittedly, he was easier than she'd expected. Men were always like that in the end. They like to impress a woman with their accomplishments. It didn't matter if those accomplishments involved killing a wild boar with a bow and arrow or their latest business triumph, their conceit always came through. She couldn't care less, though she listened attentively to make him believe she was fascinated.

In Andover's case, accomplishment was called "dealmaking." How dull. By the time they had reached their third drink, he leaned in close to describe how he had literally stolen a piece of land from under an old synagogue. Who cared for those ancient Jews anyway, he prattled on, always praying. That land would make him even richer than he was now. What was even more ingenious was the way he had convinced the current owners to sell him the land for a mortgage. He hadn't had to lay out a penny.

As he told his story she could sense his heart rate increasing. She wasn't sure if it was the result of his self-absorbed conceit or her proximity that caused his excitement. She didn't really care, she found him repugnant. Though she had no love lost for the Just Men who had used her for centuries or for their God who had exiled her for eternity, she found this ignorant, self-absorbed thief even more offensive. He clearly lacked the depth and knowledge to understand why these men served their God. "Do you live nearby?" she asked, smiling, her teeth glistening in the semidarkness.

"Yes," he whispered, his hot breath in her ear.

"Let's go," she said, her fingers brushing by his pants zipper.

Andover led her by the hand out of the club into the street and hurriedly to his building. They swept past the doormen and concierge and into the waiting elevator to his apartment. Once inside his bedroom she pressed him against the wall and kissed him hard. Lilith's teeth scraped against Andover's lower lip ever so gently, drawing a drop of blood. She looked deeply into his eyes. Now he was hers. His body became almost jelly-like to her touch. Lilith placed her hands under Andover's arms, her mouth on his. She inhaled, the power of her breath like a windstorm in the desert.

Andover's body began to shake. He tried to pull away but couldn't. He had no strength. Something was happening inside him. It was if his life was being sucked out of him. He felt as if his eyeballs would pop out of his skull. He couldn't breathe. His very blood was boiling. His heart sped up, then stopped.

Lilith released Andover's body. She took in another profound breath, swallowing the life force she had sucked out of him. Andover's soul was hers now. She exhaled a long stream of damp particles. Her mist dissipated around the room as it did on the night the creator sent her to take the first born of Egypt. That mist would kill everything, anything in its path that breathed, moved, crawled.

Lilith rested for a moment. She felt Andover's soul inside her, struggling, frightened. She would absorb it soon enough. The truth was that she so disliked her victim, she wanted to do something to destroy what was left of him. She thought for a moment. She would undo his final deal. That would destroy what was left of his psyche entirely.

An eternity in limbo hadn't cut Lilith off from this world. That was part of her punishment. She could see the world grow and develop, but not participate. Lilith noticed the laptop on Andover's desk. His password bounced around her brain, his soul still not entirely hers. She signed in, searched for the address of the synagogue, and found the file with the title for the leasehold. A quick Google search produced the needed document and in minutes she had a transfer deed. She clicked on electronic signature and then on print.

א

TWO HOURS LATER
105 Bennett Avenue
Washington Heights, New York, NY
Monday, June 17, 2019
4:30 a.m.

Francisco watched from the darkness for the figure of a tall woman in a red cape, just as Rav Itzhak told him to do. He yawned. Rav Itzhak came to his door at midnight. Leaning on his cane, the Rav apologized for waking Francisco, then explained why he needed to speak to him. It was very, very important. The Rav had a job for him.

Francisco was excited, then fearful. What if he couldn't do what the Rav asked?

"Take this," Rav Itzhak said, handing Francisco a small red box filled with powder. "Don't open it now."

Francisco took the box and turned it over in his hand. It felt cold. The top of the box had Hebrew letters on it. Francisco listened as Rav Itzhak continued.

"At four o'clock you will open the gate to the alley of the synagogue from the inside. Then leave the alley by the exit on the 186th Street side. Go to the corner by 105 Bennett and wait in the shadow, not under the streetlight. Watch for a tall woman wearing a red cape and carrying something over her shoulder."

"Yes, Rav."

"She will leave what she is carrying in the alley. When she comes out, she will walk up Bennett Avenue toward my building."

Francisco's fear intensified. What would this woman want with Rav Itzhak?

"When she crosses the street, and she moves quickly so be attentive, you will step out of the shadow. She will not acknowledge you. You will call out to her, 'Lilith.' Say that please."

Francisco hesitated.

"Francisco, this is very important. Perhaps the most important thing you will ever do."

"Lilith," said Francisco, stumbling slightly over the syllables. He repeated the name twice more.

Rav Itzhak put a hand on Francisco's shoulder. "Good, my son, good."

Francisco smiled.

"Then open the little box and blow the powder in the box toward her with a strong breath. Say these words." Rav Itzhak handed a piece of paper to Francisco. "Do you understand?"

"But, Rav Itzhak—"

"No questions. Do you understand?"

Francisco took a deep breath and nodded.

"Good. Do not be frightened. You are doing God's work. When you finish the job, come to my apartment. You will find a wooden crate. Take it to the synagogue. Keep it in your room. In two days give it to Rabbi Rothman."

"But Rav—"

"No, Francisco, no questions." Rav Itzhak put his finger to his lips. He reached out to Francisco and touched his shoulder. "Thank you," he said, then turned and walked away, leaning heavily on his cane.

Now Francisco waited. He sensed the night ending, the first specks of light filtering into the darkness. He spied a figure coming down the hill on Bennett. As the figure drew near, he saw the red cape and something over her shoulder. He would not have thought it was a woman except for the very high-heeled shoes she wore. The caped figure turned into the alley, reappearing a few moments later without anything on her shoulder. She approached Francisco quickly.

"Lilith," he said, stepping out of the shadows.

The figure stopped abruptly and turned, just as Rav Itzhak said she would. She smiled at Francisco, the glistening menace of her teeth evident, even in this darkness. Francisco opened the little box, took a deep breath and blew strongly on the red powder inside. He read the words from the paper Rav Itzhak gave him. The figure in the red cape stiffened suddenly and in just as short a moment dissolved into the air, as if she had never been there to begin with.

❧

FOUR DAYS AFTER THE MURDER
34th Precinct,
4295 Broadway, New York, NY
Friday, June 21, 2019
3:00 p.m.

"Any new developments?" the captain asked, standing in the doorway of the cramped office Tolya and Pete shared.

"Yes," said Tolya. "We just got back from downtown. We know how she got out of the building undetected. There's a glitch in their video security system. They didn't know about it until we found it."

"Imagine," said Pete, "their high-tech, state-of-the-art security system was shutting down on a loop every hour for fifteen minutes. For how long did the security guy say?"

"Two weeks."

"That leaves just one unanswered question," said the captain, leaning against the door frame. "How did the suspect get the body from SoHo to here?"

"Our theory?" replied Tolya. "She had a car, dumped the body in the trunk, drove uptown, parked on Bennett Avenue midblock between 181st and 184th streets by one of the hydrants. No cops out ticketing at that hour. The streets were empty, it was the middle of the night, and it was a Sunday. No one was watching. She dumped the body, doubled back to the car. Drove off."

"But what's her motive?" said the captain.

❦

LATER THAT DAY
Rabbi Rothman's Office
85 Bennett Avenue
Washington Heights, New York, NY
4:00 p.m.

"Hello, Shalom," Tolya said, pushing open the door to Rothman's office.

"What a pleasant surprise," Shalom said, coming around the desk to shake Tolya's hand. "I wasn't expecting you."

"I wanted to clean up some details on Andover. I need you to sign these papers."

Shalom gestured to the chairs in front of his desk. "Have a seat."

"It's your sworn statement. I had it notarized at the precinct, save you the trouble. I figured you wouldn't mind. Just sign the bottom of each page."

"Not at all," said Shalom, signing the first. "So that's it, I guess?"

"For now. We're leaving it open. The missing woman and all." Tolya hesitated for a moment. He looked past Rothman through the window to Broadway, the BX7 rolling by. It was the first clear day since Sunday. "What a weird case."

"What do you mean?"

"The way this guy was found dead in your alley holding the transfer deed for the property. The insecticide overdose, the threat he made to the congregation, the caped mystery woman. I don't know, despite the evidence, I just feel like we're missing something."

Shalom smiled. He leaned back in his chair, hands clasped in his lap. "Sometimes, my friend, something is just what it looks like, an accident."

"Spoken like a true detective, Rabbi," Tolya said, laughing. "I suppose you're right." Tolya hesitated again. "Perhaps we'll know more if we ever find the woman in the red spike heels."

Shalom got up from his desk and went to the bookshelf behind him, scanned the shelves, and reached for a thin volume from the middle shelf. He handed it to Tolya.

"*The Last of the Just*, by André Schwarz-Bart," read Tolya out loud.

"Take your time. Enjoy it." Shalom smiled. "And have an open mind."

Author's Note

The legend of Lilith figures prominently in Jewish folklore, especially among Eastern European Jews. Lilith, Adam's first wife according to the Talmud, angered God by her assertiveness. He banished her spirit as cursed forever. She is believed to lurk in the dark hours, particularly just before dawn, and has been connected to vampire myths. She steals the souls of male infants and toddlers and is warded off by the color red. Superstitions associated with her include placing a red ribbon in the crib of a male baby (my grandmother placed one in mine) and not cutting a boy's hair till after his second birthday to confuse Lilith as to the baby's gender. That's the origin of a custom called *opshern* (a boy's first haircut at age three performed at home by his family) among Orthodox Ashkenazi Jews.

Triangle

Rabbi Ilene Schneider

Murder.

It was my first thought when I heard the name of the new patient.

I am a nurse. Murder isn't part of my vocabulary. Or shouldn't be. Okay, so I favor assisted suicide, which some consider murder. I consider it *rakhmones*, mercy. If I had the energy, I might move to a place where it is legal. But my medications, the same ones that keep my resentments and hatreds under control, sap me not just of the drive needed to enact revenge, but of *oomph* in general.

I long ago discovered the meaning of *bashert*, fate. And now I was experiencing another example of synchronicity.

As is protocol when reporting for work at the ridiculous hour of six thirty in the morning, I met with the nurse going off duty who would update me about the patients. "Whatcha got for me today, shweetie?"

Michelle grimaced. "I'm too tired today to be amused by your Bogie imitation, Rose. And what are you doing here on the day shift? I thought you prefer the overnight one. I missed you last night." We usually work three days on and three days off for twelve hours each shift. I was returning after my time off.

"I have something to do tonight. In fact, I'm taking a vacation day tomorrow."

"Ooh, a hot overnight date?"

"Yeah, right." I wasn't about to let her know what I had planned. She already thinks I'm nuts. So do my therapists. I prefer "eccentric."

"Okay," I continued. "Fill me in on what happened so you can go home and soak in a bubble bath with a trashy novel and a box of chocolates."

"Which I intend to do as soon as I get the kids' lunches packed and them onto the school bus. So, the good news is, no one died. The bad news is, no one got well enough to be transferred to a step-down floor. The worse news is, we have a have a new admission. The worst news is, every bed is filled and Brenda's called out sick. They're still looking for someone to sub for her."

"Worst" was right. Cardiac Critical Care is stressful enough without being short-staffed. It wouldn't be a fun night. And tomorrow would be impossible with my being out too. But there was no way I was going to give up my plans. They were too important to me.

Michelle ran down the important information about the continuing patients and then went into more detail about the new admission. "He's a seventy-eight-year-old retiree, overweight, sedentary, high blood pressure, high cholesterol, Type II diabetes, on meds for all of those, but they barely keep the numbers in check. He was conscious when he arrived and able to give us his medical history. Surprisingly, considering his lifestyle, this was his first heart attack, although he's been having an irregular heartbeat that he didn't bother to tell his doctor about until the chest pains started. Unsurprisingly, he said he really hadn't been paying attention to his diet since his wife died three years ago and he eats out a lot, mostly fast food. One son, who lives in Seattle and is flying in now." Michelle glanced at her watch. "He should be here soon. The patient's name is Max Blanck, no relation to Mel—I asked, and the last name's spelled differently. Jewish, requested a visit by a rabbi. I notified the chaplaincy office."

I had stopped paying attention when I heard the name.

I immediately recognized it.

"Yoo, hoo, Rose." Michelle snapped her fingers in my face. "Wake up. I know you're a night owl, but you haven't even started your shift yet."

"Um, right, sorry. I zoned out for a second."

Michelle looked concerned, but I wasn't going to explain. Not until I could figure out this weird . . . coincidence? I mean, how strange was it for a man with the same name as one of the owners of the Triangle Shirtwaist Company, the site of a fire in 1911 that had been the worst disaster in Manhattan until 9/11, to appear the day before the one hundredth anniversary of The Fire? And for me to be the one to take care of him? *Me*, whose first thought on hearing his name was "murder"? And next thought after that was "murderer"?

Of course, it was absurd even to consider he was the same Max Blanck. If he hadn't already been dead for sixty-nine years, he would now be over a hundred twenty years old. So, he either was a reanimated and surprisingly intact corpse or a young-looking centenarian. I suppose those could be possible, but only if I had entered the Twilight Zone.

I knew all about—well, a lot about—the historic Max Blanck. He and his partner Isaac Harris were found not guilty of manslaughter in the deaths of one hundred forty-six people. Two years later, Blanck was found guilty of again locking the doors during working hours of another factory he owned. He was given the minimum fine of twenty dollars. In 1922, he served time for grand larceny. Eventually, he changed his name to Norman M. Blank and moved to California.

Michelle finished her briefing and went home to make a nutritional lunch for her kids, who would undoubtedly dump it and buy candy bars instead. I did my rounds, changed IVs, checked vital signs, made notes, and finally took a deep breath and went to meet Max Blanck.

"Isaac Harris" is a common enough name that I had met a few, either casually or professionally, through the years but never had a visceral reaction to hearing the name. Never thought "murder," although "murderer" may have crossed my mind.

There's a lot written about the two men together, but I had never found much about Harris without his henchman, maybe because he didn't leave as long a trail of criminal activities as his former partner had.

Why do I know anything about these two men? Even those who have heard of The Fire may not recognize the names. There's a simple explanation. My great-grandmother, for whom I am named, was one of the one hundred forty-six victims. According to family legend, confirmed by newspaper articles I later found in archives, Original Rose, or OR, as I'd taken to calling her, had helped other workers escape until she died of smoke inhalation. I had been raised to venerate her, to emulate her. I felt inadequate to live up to my parents' expectations, so I rebelled at the thought. Chances are, I would have been a "challenging" child, even without OR as an impossible ideal to live up to. But she was a convenient excuse.

"Why," my parents whined to one of my myriad therapists, "would she want to burn down our house?"

"Maybe to recreate her great-grandmother's experience."

My parents found a new therapist.

I can't imagine what my subsequent therapists would have made of the compulsion I felt every year on March 24, the night before the anniversary of The Fire, to light one hundred forty-six *yahrzeit* candles.

So I didn't tell any of them.

There was something about sitting in a darkened room, breathing in the smoke, watching the small flickers of flame that made me feel I was reliving OR's experience. Maybe it was lack of oxygen from all the candles. Maybe it was the adrenaline rush of wondering if I'd burn down my rattrap building. Maybe it was a flashback to my preadolescent act of arson that burned down the family house and sent me into years of residential treatment. Or maybe my great-grandmother was a dybbuk who took over my body every March 25. That's my favorite theory.

After all, there was only one way I could really live up to such an example of heroism and selflessness, and that was to sacrifice myself to save others. Lighting all those candles and breathing in their smoke didn't kill me, but it helped me recreate a bit of OR's death experience. Minus the death. Yeah, that made sense, in a way. I still liked the dybbuk, though.

Max Blanck and Isaac Harris had a lot to answer for in screwing up my life.

But could I murder a man because of his name? I mean, it wasn't as though he was named Adolf Hitler.

I guess in a way, becoming a nurse—helping others while suffering from impossible hours, arrogant doctors who knew very little more than I do, earning a paltry salary compared to the cost of living in Manhattan— was my way of emulating OR.

And now I was contemplating murder. And not for the first time.

Not long before Max Blanck was placed under my care, a phantom of my past was admitted. I won't go through the *gantze megillah*, but the short version is that I was raped when I was fourteen. The new patient had been severely beaten—a cracked skull, multiple contusions and fractures, a ruptured spleen—then put in the trunk of a car that was set on fire. His attackers had tried to kill him because he had sexually molested their ten-year-old sister. It was a miracle he had survived his injuries and burns as long as he did.

I was in an ethical quandary.

Damn it, Jim. I'm a nurse, not a killer.

Yet I really wanted to make the rapist suffer as much as possible. There was little chance he would survive his injuries, and he probably would prefer death to the pain he would be experiencing from his burns. Others in such distress I would have slipped extra morphine so they could die in peace. But I didn't want to help him die. He didn't deserve *rakhmones*.

So I resolved I would only pretend to give him morphine to control his pain.

He died within a few hours. He had received no relief or comfort from me. Even though I hadn't actively murdered him, I had thought about it long enough to know how easy it would be. And I was pleased at how little remorse I felt. In fact, none. I do not believe in any particular god, but I cannot imagine that any deity would find fault with my actions. All these years after I was raped, this revenge was indeed a dish served cold.

And I was the one who took the dish from the refrigerator.

Now, I stared at another inert body, being kept alive only by modern medicine. Was he a relative of the criminal Blanck? I went to the nurses' station and checked Google on my phone, but didn't have the patience to examine the over one million hits on the name. And what difference would it make if he were a descendant?

Still, I knew I would be unable to get any rest until I had found the truth.

The hospital had found a replacement for the ailing—most likely hungover—Brenda. I updated Jeanine on the patients and took a break. I sat on the floor of the coffee room in the lotus position and closed my eyes, so people would think I was meditating. And I was . . . on how to get away with murder.

I began my ruminations by repeating, as though it were a mantra, the vow uttered in grief after Blanck and Harris were acquitted by the brother of a different Rose: "We will get you yet."

The two owners of the Triangle were beyond any retaliation. But what of their families? Thinking about all the young women who did not live to marry or procreate, I wondered why Blanck's and Harris's lines should have continued.

I tried to compute how many more people might now be alive if the one hundred forty-six victims had lived and had children, and they had then had children, who then . . . for one hundred years. I doubt I could have figured it out even with a calculator. Maybe I should just eliminate— murder is such an ugly word—seventy-three people with the surname

Harris and seventy-three with the surname Blanck. But how would I know if they were related to the factory owners? The spelling of Blanck was unusual, but Blank was not. And Harris was *very* common. Should I concentrate on the New York area or, in the case of Blanck, California? Where did Harris wind up? I had no idea. Most of my research had concentrated on the victims and I really had not looked too closely into the perpetrators' later lives. And even if I could find likely direct descendants, what if they turned out to be good people?

Too many questions, no answers. I was frustrated and agitated.

Bad things happened when I am frustrated and agitated.

There was only one solution: forget the questions. Concentrate instead on the logistics of how I could kill one hundred forty-six people and not get caught. I already knew it would be easy to eliminate the first—introduce an air bubble into one of his IV tubes. Simple. Untraceable. No autopsy needed as he was under a doctor's care and the death was not unexpected. Simple.

Maybe there was an easier way.

I was quite good at retaliating without needing a recourse to violence. After all, my sister was in jail for fraud because of me. Yes, my sister was guilty, but I was the one she had embezzled from—or, rather, from the trust fund set up as compensation for the rape and my parents' promise not to go to the press or the authorities—yet I didn't feel the need to kill her. It was sort of similar to the rapist: I'd rather she live in misery and embarrassment than die.

This was becoming an exercise in futility. And it was the antithesis of yoga, making me anxious and jittery. I took a few calming breaths and returned to work.

I was reading Jeanine's notes on her visits and noticed that Blanck had become depressed and weepy and then agitated. It wasn't uncommon following a heart attack, and there was a standing order to sedate him if it occurred. I was about to check on him, thinking it might be a good opportunity to cure his depression and weepiness and agitation permanently, when I heard, "Excuse me, nurse? I'm Richard Blanck. I'm looking for my father, Max Blanck. He was admitted yesterday. I live out west and got the first flight out." He obviously felt guilty he had not come sooner.

I looked up at the middle-aged man, who was kind of cute in a tall, paunchy, balding kind of way. He was casually dressed in rumpled chinos and a polo shirt, as though he had gotten the summons to the hospital while he was heading to a golf course. His looked like he had taken a red-eye flight.

Putting on my professional persona and demeanor, consisting of a quiet voice and sympathetic smile, I turned to him. "Your father is resting comfortably. Come with me. I'll take you to his room. He's asleep now, but I'm sure he'll sense your presence. You can sit with him for a while."

As we entered the room, the son gasped. It was a common reaction to seeing a loved one looking so frail and vulnerable.

"Don't worry," I said soothingly. "The tubes and wires look menacing, but they are mostly monitoring his condition. He's breathing on his own but is receiving extra oxygen. He's being kept hydrated and receives medications through an IV. If you would like, I can find out if his doctor is free to see you, Mr. Blanck."

"Yes, please. I'd appreciate it. And call me Dick. 'Mr. Blanck' is my father." He looked close to tears, but smiled faintly, as though understanding how hackneyed his joke was.

I returned in a few minutes. Dick had pulled up a chair close to his father's bed and was holding his hand. He looked up as I entered and let go of his father's hand. "I hope it's okay. I didn't know if I would disturb any of the tubes, but I've heard touch is good for someone in a coma."

"It's fine. And he's not in a coma, only sedated. Just don't dislodge any of the needles or electrodes. His doctor is being paged." I hesitated for a second, then added, "Tell me about your father. His name sounds familiar."

Dick nodded. "You've probably seen it in the paper lately in connection with the hundredth anniversary of the Triangle Shirtwaist Factory Fire. He shares a name with his distant cousin, who owned the company. Not one of our more distinguished relatives, I'm afraid."

"I've read that some of his descendants think he and his business partner Isaac Harris were dealt a raw hand by history, that they were scapegoats for the deplorable labor standards of the day."

"I don't know," Dick shrugged, "but I do know my father would disagree with the idea that the other Max was a scapegoat. He said his cousin was a nogoodnik. Dad wasn't happy when he learned they shared the same name. But he never talked much about him. Wanna hear something funny? My father is a union organizer, and I'm a labor law attorney. Maybe we're subconsciously making amends for the past."

"Making amends for the past . . ." As I repeated Dick's words, I almost physically felt the anger leaving my body, to be replaced by a sense of relief, of peace, of a purpose other than revenge. Weird. A saying I'd once heard—and rejected as irrelevant—popped into my head: "Living well is the best revenge."

"I'm named for one of the victims," I explained. "She was my great-grandmother and died trying to save her coworkers. Or that's the family history, anyway. She was mentioned in a couple of articles at the time too. But that's because a brother of someone else named Rose accosted the owners after they were acquitted and yelled, 'Murderers! Not guilty? Where is the justice? We will get you yet.' But my great-grandmother didn't have a brother. I think the family liked the story and adopted it as their own."

I hesitated and looked at Max Blanck. Then I turned to Dick. "For much of my life, I've lived by the words 'We will get you yet.' I think I like your words better. After all, there's nothing that can change what happened." I stopped again, then continued, "I finish my shift at seven tonight. Would you like to go out to dinner, then back to my apartment? I always light . . . a yahrzeit candle . . . for my great-grandmother." Telling him I light one hundred forty-six candles would likely convince him I'm as crazy as everyone says. "And, um, a second one for all the other victims. I usually do it alone, but it would be nice to have company." I had already noticed he wasn't wearing a wedding ring. "Also, there's a memorial gathering at the site of the building tomorrow. I'm planning to attend. Would you care to join me?"

Dick looked at his father. "Yes, thank you. I would. It will be a small way of making amends."

Then I recalled an addendum I had read on Facebook to the quote about living well: "Loving well is giving up revenge altogether."

What the hell was wrong with me? I never had those kinds of thoughts. I shook my head to clear it. That night, before leaving work to meet Dick for dinner, I introduced an air bubble into Max Blanck's IV. Damn, it felt good. And was so easy.

I could get used to murder.

AMERICAN SPLENDOR

The Nazi in the Basement

Rita Lakin

What was I thinking?

I nearly passed out behind the wheel on the Bronx-Whitestone Bridge as I headed for my old neighborhood. Whatever had possessed me to come up with that crazy idea?

My close friend Annie had chosen to spend her final days with her family back in New York. So, I'd traveled three thousand miles to attend her memorial on Long Island, recalling loving memories with Annie's children, grandchildren, and even one great-grandchild.

There had been six of us, lifetime girlfriends, all gone now, except for me. Well, that makes me officially the last woman standing; gives me the creeps to even think it.

I was meant to leave on this afternoon's flight back to Los Angeles, then head on home to my small comfort zone of peace in Sherman Oaks.

Instead of flying out, I rented a car at the airport.

When was the last time I'd done that? Forty years ago? Forty years *younger*, that's when. Renting a car at my age? Full of tech-type gadgets I've never seen or used in my life. I was praying that I wouldn't crash. Sweating and nail-biting, I was terrified, recalling a news report about some nutcase hacking into car computers and causing a crash. To expect to survive the lunatic drivers in New York City? I guess I wasn't thinking at all.

I hardly ever drive anymore, even back home. My car, a no-frills 1995 Honda. Nothing electric. No hybrid. No backup camera. No key fob. *Nada.* Nothing but a car that just runs. Maybe I drive to the library, ten blocks away. Or to the nearest Walgreens to pick up new meds. Or to my neighborhood deli for a quick Reuben.

I am, after all, eighty-five years old.

But I needed the rental car. I needed to face my old neighborhood. Like in some Stephen King novel, my old brick building wouldn't let go of me. It has never let go of me. On some level, I always felt that if I went back, I could somehow revisit my demons and erase the pain, once and for all. The building cries out to me. *Come back, I dare you.*

I had tried once before, in the fall of 1977. Not only the Bronx but all of New York City had been in a serious decline, resembling some devastated war zone. Most of the windows in my former building were boarded up, desecrated with spray-painted gang symbols. Rats ruled the putrid garbage cans. I'd assumed I'd never return to this city again.

Right place. Wrong time.

I've told myself over and over again, what happened in the past needs to be left in the past, à la Vegas. Why did I want to do this absurd thing? Because I know it's my last chance. I'll never come back here again.

So, here I am, parked in front of 1070 Elder Avenue in East Bronx, which is adjoined by its Siamese twin building, 1072. Amazed that I didn't drop dead or collide with a truck on the way. Surprised that I even found a parking place on the crowded street. I sit with my head on the steering wheel, trying to remember how to breathe.

I become aware of four young faces leaning in, practically drooling on my windows. Back in the seventies, at the sight of teenagers, I would have expected guns, knives. These are happy, smiling faces grinning at me.

❦

The rent-a-car person had handed me the travel directions, along with the key and car pickup spot info, and advice. "Are you sure you want to go *there*?"

Nosy New Yorkers. They never change. Who asked for her opinion? With teeth gritted, I reply, "Yes, I'm sure. I was born in this city." What I didn't say: it's none of your damn business.

But she wasn't going to let it go. In that annoying nasal accent, she warned me: did I know of the huge changes in the boroughs and that both the Bronx and Brooklyn were jammed with millions of foreigners? From a lot of Third World countries? Snarky grin. "With packs of illegals hiding and praying they won't get forced back."

I tried edging my way out. I know who *she* voted for.

She grabbed my hand. "You won't believe the prices they ask!"

I remember my folks' miniscule apartment had been thirty dollars a month. I was now informed: "Fifteen hundred bucks or more! For those dumps!"

I retrieved my hand and pushed my way out the door, insincerely thanking her for all her unwanted help.

※

The kids look fourteen, fifteen or so. I make assumptions. The tallest—his parents might have been from the Caribbean. The next boy, from China? The third, maybe Mexico? The only girl wears a headscarf, so I am guessing a Muslim. Gone were the triangle-settlers of my growing up years: Jews, Irish, and Italians who ruled this roost for so long. Minorities of that era had white faces.

A whole new world faced me, one I knew nothing about.

The old buildings seem refreshed, and almost new, like they did when I lived there. But I'm still stuck with my bête noire, my enemy.

I look at what these kids are wearing. T-shirts promoting neighborhood businesses like Jo Jo Pizza and ripped-at-the-knees jeans. Not torn Levi's that cost about seventy bucks; these are poor kids who probably wore out those jeans honestly.

I open my door and step out, pulling my cane with me.

They take my measure, up and down, my little diverse audience of four.

"Are you lost, white lady?" asks the tall boy. A question, not asked with malice. Politely.

"I actually live in California."

"Then you are *very* lost," says the Hispanic boy.

All four children laugh.

※

I am now seated on a hard, wooden box dragged over from somewhere for my comfort by Jamarr, whose family, I have learned, came from Jamaica. He joins the others, who are sitting cross-legged on the cement, surrounding me. I am considered a novelty, some kind of white creature that might have come from outer space. We have, by now, introduced ourselves. I let them know my name is Ruth and I grew up in apartment 4J. Eduardo, wearing the pizza tee, is from Puerto Rico, not Mexico. Lee Chang, the smallest of the three boys, has parents who came from Hong

Kong. And our one girl is Barsha. She is not Middle Eastern; her folks come from the Rampur district of Bangladesh.

They have also identified themselves by where they live. Jamarr, 3D. Eduardo, 6B. Both in my six-story building. Lee Chang and Barsha live in 1072.

"Look across the street." I point diagonally over to the corner of Watson Avenue. "Where I used to hang out."

Barsha giggles. "At the Pentecostal church?"

We all stare for a moment at the church now situated there.

I sigh. "In my day it was a wonderful fun store owned by a married couple, Sam and Sadie."

Eduardo says, "A store that sells fun?"

"Much more. You could buy lunch. Snacks. Ice cream. Sodas. Comic books. And the best egg creams in the world."

"What's an egg cream?" asks Lee Chang.

"Move it along, old lady," says Jamarr, cutting Lee Chang off. He's the obvious leader of my little pack. "There ain't no more Sam or Sadie, so why you here?"

Barsha warns, "Now, now, don't hate on an old woman."

Jamarr smirks. "And don't *you* give me shit."

Lee Chang gives him a gentle shove. "Not Gucci, Jamarr. Stick to dumb-talk."

I think I understand. Teen-speak is out. Just be boring with the old broad.

Barsha says quietly, "Sometimes people travel back for good memories." I imagine she is thinking of her early childhood in Bangladesh.

"And sometimes people need to go back for the bad ones," I add, sounding gloomy in spite of myself.

Eduardo is curious. "Why would you do that? I never want to go back to San Juan. Never! Awful things happened to my family there."

"And terrible things happened here too. I was about your age, fourteen, and it was 1944 and we were in the middle of a big war."

Lee Chang raises his hand excitedly, as if he were in his classroom. "I know. World War II, fighting the Axis, made up of Germany, Japan, and Italy. Hitler started that war trying to take over all of Europe."

"Showoff," snarls Jamarr.

"Tell us about when you were there. Were you a soldier?" asks Eduardo, intrigued.

Barsha smiles, "She said she was our age, dummy. And girls weren't soldiers."

"Oh! I forgot." Shy Eduardo is embarrassed.

I don't bother to correct her. There were WACs, women soldiers, Barsha, the Women's Army Corps. WAVES, women's libbers during the war, then sent back to where "they" belonged: barefoot, pregnant, and in the kitchen.

I had intended to come back and deal with those days in private sorrow. These kids don't need to be burdened by my past.

They wriggle around on the cement ground, settling in, making themselves more comfortable. Passing out M&Ms for sustenance. They don't intend to leave this free show.

"A story! Tell us a story," Eduardo cries out.

"Yeah, a *white* story," Jamarr understands sarcasm at his age.

"It's a *war* story." I can give as well as get.

He grins with teeth that haven't met a dentist yet. "That's more like it."

I hadn't expected an audience. Here they sit, waiting eagerly. So, I speak.

"First of all—this is a grown-up saga, not one for kids. Something really bad happened and someone died. There was blame and there was guilt."

"Awesome!" leaps in Jamarr. "Dead people. I dig stories about dead people."

Barsha gives him a gentle push. "Shh."

I am startled by his response. I shouldn't have blurted that out. If they insist on listening, I must find a way to soften it. But part of me thinks, just as I was once in the wrong place at the wrong time, so are they, now. Plus, I think I need to tell someone. I've never told anyone. *Okay, kids, you asked for it.* I start my narrative with mixed feelings.

"It is December 1944. My family consists of Dad, a plumber. Mom is a very reluctant housewife and mother. *I* make the breakfasts and I pack sandwiches for Dad—sardines with onions on a hard roll. *I* have to get myself dressed and rush out to get to school on time. By the way, I have a five-year-old sister, Jodie. Who is just the way all kid sisters are: annoying. She is meant to play quietly until Mom wakes up."

Eduardo can't resist, "I have three annoying sisters."

The others stare fiercely at him. He shuts up.

I have acquired other listeners, including a mother rocking a baby carriage.

"I only learn a little of what's going on in the world when my parents are listening to Edward R. Murrow on the radio, and then they whisper things they don't want me to hear, mixing Yiddish in with their regular English. They are proud immigrants, trying to protect me from bad news, but I am a very curious child. They still think of me as a child, but I'm a teenager now, and I feel I should be treated with more respect. Yeah. That'll be the day."

Eduardo asks, "What's Yiddish?" He backs off when he's glared at again.

"A language many Jewish people know. But the war still seems far away in my small world, and life hasn't yet changed. The bad stuff is months away.

"You need to understand what this neighborhood was like in those days. Italian, Irish, and Jewish families living close. They get along with each other but mostly stick to their own kind. As for the mothers who live in our building, Jewish or not, they are all *yentes*. That's a Jewish word for people who never mind their own business. For example, everybody in the building wants to feed me. Why? Because I'm skinny. Legs like toothpicks. Cheeks caved in. Look at me sideways and I practically disappear. Mom calls it rail-thin, and threatens to send me away to a 'fresh air' summer camp, with the promise I'll come back with an additional ten pounds. The neighbors call me scrawny, unwholesome. Chubby is considered in the pink. Fat is treasured. Mrs. Schwartz would meet me in the elevator. She lives in 5B. 'I have chopped liver I was saving just for you.' She always pinches my cheek. I hate that. I also hate her liver. Always have, always will.

"Or, Mrs. Kelly in 4D calls out from her open door, 'How about some corned beef and cabbage?' Yuck, the stink of cabbage cooking fills the hallway. Or Mrs. Levine, 6B when taking her smelly garbage down to the basement: 'How's about a plate of my delicious brains with *shmaltz*?' No way I am gonna eat anyone's brains. Especially dripping with chicken fat.

"Is it because the entire building knows of my mother's lack of cooking skills? Mom, believer in a 'Handy Cookery' recipe for an Italian-style dinner, would make us overcooked spaghetti with a blob of ketchup plopped on it. Served with white bread and margarine. With a glass of buttermilk.

"I have a secret, a place where I sneak off to and often spend many happy hours. My fourteen-year-old tastebuds are getting sophisticated thanks to the Napolitanos, who live downstairs on the lobby floor in 1A and who feed me on the sly, joining the chorus of those dealing with my so-called weight problem. 'To put some meat on your bones, Ruthie.' I love Lina's cooking—they insist I call them Lina and Salvatore—I am already a fan of rigatoni, cacciatore, and spumoni. My favorite words are *al dente*. And best of all, they have a gorgeous son, Frankie, with black, curly hair, who I have a crush on even though he's seventeen and ignores me. I secretly hope to marry him when I grow up. He has two brothers, Anthony and Johnny, who had enlisted early on. The Napolitanos proudly display the two blue stars hanging in their front window."

The children are puzzled. Lee Chang tosses out the question, "What's that mean, blue stars?"

"Every family who had sons in the army, the navy, or the marines would hang in a small banner with a blue star on a white background their front window."

"Cool," comments Eduardo.

"If the blue star in the window is exchanged for a gold star, it means that a son has died fighting for his country."

Barsha's eyes tear up. The boys frown. This makes them sad.

"My mother wakes up around noon. She's ready to feed me when I return home on my lunch hour, after which she'll go out and visit her sisters or go food shopping or for her weekly trip to the beauty parlor. I never feel ignored because I spend that time with the Napolitanos. Anyway, I always rush home at lunchtime, because I want to get there in time for *Our Gal Sunday*, the radio soap opera."

Eduardo raises his hand; I know what he'll ask.

"No, there was no such thing as TV back then. Radio is king. That's the only part of the day Mom and I share together. I'd eat my peanut butter and jelly—on white bread, of course—and slurp down my Campbell's Chicken Noodle Soup and we'd listen, holding our breaths, to find out whether 'this girl from the small mining town of Silver Creek, Colorado, in the West could find happiness as the wife of wealthy and titled Lord Henry Brinthrope."

"However, that daily hour we spend together doesn't count in my mind. I'm sure they switched babies in the hospital when I was born, I feel I have so little in common with my parents. I would read books, and my mother would say, 'What are you wasting the light for? You think we need to support the electricity company?' And my dad? He would come home from work and say, 'What's to eat?' That was the beginning and end of all conversation. He'd inhale his dinner, then go downstairs to the rented 'clubroom' next door to Sam and Sadie's store, where he met the other husbands who also ate fast in order to smoke and play pinochle all evening."

When I grew up, I realized how little I'd understood my parents. Why their marriage suffered. The rigidity of women's roles. The lack of knowledge about women by those men who married them. My mother had been only sixteen when she married a man eight years older. I finally learned compassion.

Jamarr breaks the agreed-upon silence. "What's this got to do with somebody dying? Jump to the good part."

I am stalling. I will keep stalling. I don't ever want to reach "the good part."

"Well, I have to give you the background. That's what my teacher, Mrs. Brannon used to tell me. She thought I had 'promise,' because I got all A's in spelling and composition. She was impressed with my vocabulary, high for my age. I think I wanted to be a writer someday, and I needed to know these things. And a writer I became. A fiction writer. Because fiction is easy. Truth is hard.

"The war creeps up on us. Changes are happening. Gas is rationed. My dad stops driving his Ford V-8 to work, and uses the subway. We are encouraged to buy war stamps and bonds. Food is scarce and a group of our neighbors take charge of a 'victory garden,' in the empty lot down the street from us. Vegetables are grown and shared. More and more boys go off to fight, and soon windows are filled with blue stars.

"In the steaming, hot summer months with 80 percent humidity, I pretend to eat a typical limp dinner of Mom's tough fried fish and soggy broccoli. I save myself for the really good meal. My mother never questions where I go after dinner. Like father, like daughter, eat and run. Mom has learned to live alone, not counting Jodie.

"I'd rush over to Lina and Salvatore's apartment in time for Lina's fabulous lasagna dinner, and cannoli pastry for dessert. Afterward, I would climb out the window onto the fire escape. The metal slats feel cool against my sweating body. Attempting relief with my useless paper fan, I eagerly listen through the open window for the best part of the evening.

"The three of them would reach for their instruments and play string sonatas. Salvatore on his violin, Lina on her cello, and Frankie playing the viola. The music is heavenly. I've learned nothing in music appreciation in school, but in *this* school I know them all: Bach's Partita Number Two (*Chaconne*), Bartok's Violin Concerto Number Two, Beethoven's Sonata Number Nine—the Kreutzer—Brahms's Number Three in D Minor, Paganini's Caprice Number Twenty-Four. Their music washes over me as if it were a gentle ocean wave."

Momentarily, I am lost in fond memories of those precious evenings. I become aware of street sounds of people strolling by, of others walking their dogs. Chatting friends. The tempting smells of dinner cooking. People walking from the subways, arriving home from work. Lights going on in a few apartments. The air is cooling down.

Barsha's aunt (I guess) comes out of the building to see what has been keeping her niece. But the girl puts her finger up against her lips as if to say, I am listening and I wish to continue to do so. The aunt smiles and returns upstairs. Cars arrive, jockeying for parking spaces. Wait, I want to tell the drivers; soon you'll have my spot.

"My two best friends, Mary and Alice, and I take the subway into the city, feeling the excitement in the air, not recognizing it as fear and anxiety. Manhattan is the Promised Land. Museums, theaters, and dance halls running at full blast. People want to be distracted from the war. Dressed in our party best, we spend Sunday afternoons strolling in Central Park, being whistled at by young sailors, not daring to do more than flirt and giggle. There are temptations, but we are rigidly Good Girls. One Jewish, one Catholic, and one Protestant. Three cowards."

Jamarr is about to ask the obvious, more personal question. I won't allow him. "None of your business," I tell him. Barsha giggles. His pals snicker.

A few more people walk by. Some of them curious, stop and listen for a while, then move on. Others stay, if for no other reason than seeing the young ones enthralled, an unusual happenstance.

We all get comfortable again. The newcomers move in closer. The sun is slowing, doing its daily disappearing act. I wish I had my sweater, but it's in my car.

"Things are getting scarier. In our neighborhood, at our local Ward Theater, we watch the newsreels of the fighting overseas, and war movies depicting how evil the Germans and the Japanese are. We hiss at the villains and applaud how bravely our boys fight.

"We have air raid drills in school and we hide under our desks, but

I can never figure out how that would keep us safe if a bomb fell on us. We have home drills where we have to shut off the lights and pull closed the special blackout curtains so not a drop of light will shine through. We are told that a beam of light could give the enemy planes an advantage. A mistake could kill us.

"One night, when my parents are out, Mom to mah-jongg, Dad to play cards, I am babysitting. My little sister is playing with her little pet turtles on the living room windowsill. The window is open and I am waving to my friend, Alice, who lives in the 1072 building, on the third floor. We have binoculars and we play games with them. Leaning on the windowsill, Alice and I make faces at each other. Sometimes we are naughty and look into other apartments, make notes, and compare them at school the next day. We have favorites. Alice watches the disgusting Mr. O'Connor in 5J, above our apartment. He is a sloppy eater and she mimics him. I watch one of her neighbors, Mrs. LiPuma, who spends endless hours peering at herself in her mirror. I love to imitate her. That's our evening entertainment.

"Jodie is annoying me, pushing her turtles back and forth under my moving arms.

"'Take them someplace else,' I tell her. 'You're in my way, pest!'

"'No, I wanna play here. Hickory and Dickory and Doc likes it here. *You* get away!' She stomps her feet in annoyance.

"Suddenly the air is filled with the horrific sound of sirens. Air raid or drill? No way to know. With a sweep of my arms, I pull the blackout curtains shut, then run to shut off the lights in the room.

"Jodie cries out, 'I'm scared!'

"'Get away from the windows!' I run to her and pull her away. We sit, terrified, on the couch, hugging each until the all-clear siren is heard. I turn the lights back on.

"Jodie screams, a sound that scares me more than the sirens.

"She is at the windowsill, tears rolling down her face. 'Hickory is gone!' Jodie screeches at me. Two of the turtles are in her hands. She tries to stand on her toes to peer out the window. 'He's gone! And it's your fault. You pulled on the curtain and pushed him out. You killed him!'

"'Don't be ridiculous.' I hurry to the window, looking every which way. On the sill, on the floor. Maybe he got tangled in the curtains. No such luck. Hickory is missing in action.

"Mom arrives home. To stop Jodie's tears, she cuts out a star from Jodie's coloring book and colors it yellow. My sister tapes it on the window with her turtle's name crayoned angrily with its fateful message: 'DEAD HICKORY.' Hickory has taken a four-floor plunge and is now a victim of the war. Jodie promises never to forgive me."

"Aww, that's sad," says Barsha.

From Jamarr, the cynic, "It was only a dumb turtle." He turns to me. "This ain't the bad stuff you talkin' about?"

I shake my head. I wish he didn't keep remembering what I wish I could forget. My small group fidgets, but they are still paying attention.

"It's six months later. People seem cheerless, the war news is worse. I hear my dad say something about how the war wasn't supposed to last this long. Rumors that something really terrifying is happening, but this time my parents are whispering behind closed doors. I try to listen in. Are we losing the war? Is that what has my mother in tears? What has this got to do with worrying about my grandmother in Poland?

"Much later, I learn about the horror of killing Jews in concentration camps." Why am I scaring them with this?

Jamall is anxious, but curious. "What did the Jewish people do to deserve this?"

How can I possibly go through the history of those "chosen people," the Jews? I need to get on with my story.

"It's as if winter will never end. None of us want to go to school because the weather is freezing. Children can't play outside, and everyone is restless. The apartment is always chilly. My mom bangs on the icy radiators as her way of complaining to Fritz, our super, who ignores her commands. He always has to be reminded to turn up the heat from the furnaces. He purposely 'forgets' to light the pilot, just to be spiteful. I hate the hissing sound the heater emits when it finally comes on."

It reminds me of snakes. And snakes remind me of Fritz. I hate Fritz.

Sure enough, Jamarr picks up on this. He'll make a great lawyer when he grows up. A prosecutor, definitely not for the defense. "Fritz is your bad guy?" he asks.

"Fritz is a mean guy. He is big and tough-looking and lives down in the basement with two, huge scary German shepherd dogs. As the super, he's in charge of both buildings and he runs them like a prison. He has a way of creeping up on us, and never lets the kids play in the courtyard. He yells a lot. And he always looks like he's going to command those dogs to 'kill!' So we play in the gutter. I spend most of my childhood keeping out of his way."

Time to zigzag away from the subject again.

"I spend as much time as I can in apartment 1A with the Napolitanos. I'm even gaining a little weight, thanks to Lina's mountains of pasta. I can listen to Salvatore for hours playing the violin. Frankie is trying to teach me the harmonica. I have a tin ear. He calls me hopeless. But I practice daily just to have an excuse to sit near him.

"The mailman arrives at the same time every day and it is painful waiting. Mail is so slow in coming these days. Frankie and I wait impatiently. I ignore my family's mailbox. Nobody writes to us. We used to get letters from Poland from my grandmother, whom I'd never met. But those letters stopped coming. I guess it's even harder to get mail from countries at war. My father never likes to talk about his childhood, only that he ran away to America as soon as his older brother, Sam, could put away enough money to send for him.

"Frankie jumps up and down. A letter in their box! The small square official government mail envelope with its red, white, and blue border that tells us it must be from the armed forces. Frankie grabs it and we race back into their apartment.

"Lina leaves her knitting midstitch. Salvatore stops polishing his shoes. We all gather around the kitchen table as Salvatore rips open the envelope to reveal the three-way fold. Both parents caress the letter, and then Salvatore, his hands shaking, gives it to Frankie to read. Lina clutches her husband's hand tightly.

"As usual, many words are blacked out—anything the censors fear might be considered information the enemy could use if the letter were intercepted. We hope that his brothers are still together and in a safe place, if there is such a place anywhere, anymore. The movie newsreels scare us with so many battlegrounds, we don't know what to believe.

"Frankie reads: 'Hi, Mom and Pop and Frankie. We're okay. We can't tell you where we are but . . .' Frankie shrugs; the next words are blacked out. 'Good food is scarce, sure miss Momma's ravioli. Sure wish we could hear some of the old songs we used to sing. We're kinda homesick.'

"Lina picks up a corner of her apron and dries her eyes. Frankie holds up the next part of the letter and shows us where the boys have inked in music notes. 'Poppa, Mama, see here,' says Frankie, 'they're sending us a clue.' All of us lean in to look. The boys have tried to do this before, but the censors caught on. Maybe this time. Salvatore follows the notes with a pencil. He hums the tune. Lina starts to sing. '*Ma nun me lassá, nun darme stu turmiento . . . torna a Surriento: famme campal.*'

"Frankie translates it in English for me. '*But don't leave me, don't give me this torment. Come back to Sorrento, make me live!* They're near Sorrento! They're in Italy!' The family hugs. Italy is not yet considered a bloody battlefield.

"The boys fooled the censors! Then, suddenly, the family is filled with sorrow. A realization their sons might be fighting their kin. Italians killing Italians. For once, I wasn't hungry. My favorite, saltimbocca, sits untouched by any of us."

I rise from my seat with help of my cane, arthritic knees complaining. Then stretch with exaggeration, hoping my young listeners will get the hint. "Time I was leaving, kids. It's starting to get dark and I'm sure dinner is waiting for you."

The teens are about to get up, but Jamarr motions them to stay put. "Haven't you forgotten something?"

Oy, no way out.

I sit back down and sigh. "All right, just a while longer, then I really must leave."

The kids lean forward sensing that the story is building.

"My mom trips and falls one day. She complains bitterly about being helpless. 'Who will do all the work around the apartment?' Her sisters offer to come and stay over. But my father, who isn't too crazy about my aunts, decides *I* can do the chores before and after school for as long as Mom is on crutches. I feel sorry for myself but also guilt-ridden. Selfish teenager, me. Moaning about all the homework I have to do. But the grumbling falls on deaf ears.

"So here I am, sulking and helping with the cooking. Doing the dishes. Sweeping up. Even ironing. But I like ironing. I can daydream while I move the hot iron across our clothes. I have daydreams of being a heroine. I see myself as an army nurse, in the midst of battles, saving boys' lives. In an imagined air raid, I run door to door, gathering the neighbors down in time to reach the shelters. Everyone is grateful, tearfully thanking me for saving their lives. As I iron, I even shed a tear or two."

Barsha can't resist. "I have daydreams too." Then quickly bows her head, sorry to have revealed a secret. I look at Jamarr, whose lips are pursed, egging me on.

Dammit. Why did I let myself get talked into this? They've charmed me, that's why.

I continue. "My mother calls me to the couch where she spends most of the time with her bad leg extended on a pillow. 'Get me my purse, Ruthie.' I do so and she hands me a small, sealed white envelope. 'It's the rent money. You have to take it down to Fritz.'

"Fritz. Even the name makes me tremble. I know the drill. All the tenants have to pay the rent directly to the super, on the first of the month. It has always been my mother's task. And I sure don't want to do her job."

I am terrified of that basement and terrified of Fritz.

I suddenly get the urge to smoke. Even though I gave it up fifty years ago.

Jamarr claps his hands, excited. "That mean old super. Who did he off?"

I need to escape. "I really think I should be getting back to the airport."

There is a quartet of sighs and complaints. They think I'm mean, dangling my story like that, without ending it. They offer me a bribe. A handful of M&Ms. I smile. Who can resist M&Ms?

But I won't talk about the basement. I won't.

"Okay," says Jamarr, arms crossed, belligerently refusing to give up, "So, you didn't want to go in the basement with the envelope."

"No, I didn't." He's forcing my hand, this crafty kid.

"'Do I have to? Can't Dad do it after work?' I beg my mother.

"'*I'm* asking you to help me out. Isn't that enough?'

"I take the envelope. I know better than to argue. I always lose my battles with Mom. 'All right,' I say, not bothering to hide the sulk in my voice. 'I'll do it after school, tomorrow.'

"She turns her hurting body around, to face me more squarely. 'I forgot it was the first, today. You have to do it right now.'

"I look out the window. 'But it's already dark.'

"'It's going to get darker, so go already. And turn down the heat under my soup to simmer.' I stand there waiting for a reprieve, knowing it isn't going to happen. Finally, I slink away. I grab my jacket because it's always cold in the basement. I already feel nauseous. And afraid."

My demons are out. I can't stop now.

My young listeners move closer to one another, believing in safety in numbers. My fear is catching; they're sensing bad stuff is going to happen.

"I open the basement door from the lobby and I am immediately hit with a cold that always makes me cringe. It feels like a refrigerator. It's very dark, day or night. There are no windows. The light bulbs are low wattage, and there is only one dull yellow beam that hardly lights anything. I should have brought a flashlight with me. I pass where the dumbwaiter lands."

"What's a dumbwaiter?" Lee Chang asks.

"A stupid guy who works in a restaurant," Jamarr cackles, enjoying his joke.

I smile and explain. "Our kitchen has a door in the wall that opens to a built-in square elevator. Every kitchen had one. It's where my mother places the day's garbage bags. She presses the buzzer that sends the elevator down the shaft. It's Fritz's job to unload them."

"We don't have that in our apartment." Barsha informs me.

"I suppose they were removed years ago. The smell from all the garbage cans makes my stomach roil. I swear I hear little noises near them. I'm betting there are rats everywhere. I try to walk in the dead center of the room to avoid the cobwebs and anything else lurking in the shadowy corners. The dirt and dust make me sneeze. Pipes up above my head also make odd noises. I think of horror stories I've read. Dead things ending up in a basement. And getting buried there. I move as fast as I can toward the end of this huge space that runs throughout the whole building. That takes me to the door of Fritz's apartment. How can he stomach living down here? But then again, he's a creepy guy living in a creepy place. It fits.

"I am getting close and the barking starts. Those dogs from hell, German—like Fritz—shepherds, with teeth like fangs, report that a stranger is close. Fritz doesn't need a doorbell. He always knows when someone is coming. And I wish I were anywhere but here."

Eduardo jumps up, fearful. "If the dogs had bit you, you could've died from rabies!"

Jamarr pokes him. "Dummy, if that happened would Mrs. Ruth be here?" The kids clutch one another. The tension is getting to them.

"The door is already slightly open. A sliver of light. I bet Fritz never lets anybody in. I bet he never has company. The two dogs' noses poke out. They stare at me with eyes like lasers, drooling, with teeth bared, snarling.

"I'm about to turn and run when I realize Fritz is just standing there, back toward me, ignoring the dogs. He is poised in front of a large, brown chest of drawers, staring at himself in its mirror.

"What I see stuns me. He is wearing a uniform. A uniform I've only seen in movies and newsreels. A Nazi uniform with black belt and high black boots. With the strange armband with double-S design. He plays with the hat, until he is satisfied with its angle on his head.

"He sees me behind him in the mirror and, without turning, says '4J.' That's all he's ever called me. I am only an apartment number to him. I bet he doesn't even know my name. I don't want him to know my name.

"Fritz reaches his hand out though the slit in the door. I shove it at him, the white envelope, now crushed from being in my pocket and sweaty from my nervous, shaking fingers. He takes a receipt book from inside a pocket. He tears off a sheet, marks it with a little stub of pencil, and pushes it at me. I grab it. All the while the dogs hover, waiting for the command to have at me.

"Fritz kicks the door open with one boot. At the same time, he raises his right arm straight up. The dogs bark again. I hear him shout from inside, with passion and pride, '*Heil Hitler!*'

"The apartment is ugly, probably disgusting old furniture that people threw out. On the walls, photos of Adolf Hitler. Swastikas, the symbol of German pride. German flags, guns, and bayonets. Terrifying. I shiver with fright.

"I am ready to run, but Fritz turns to his dogs and with an evil smile on his face, demands they '*Kusse die hubsche kleine Jüdin.*'

"Of course, I don't understand German. I was sure he told them to kill me."

Eduardo gasps. "Did you run for your life?" The children are clutching one another.

I shake my head. "I stood there, paralyzed. I whimpered, 'Mama, Daddy, help,' but I knew there was no help."

"I woulda just died," says Lee Chang, gasping.

Barsa shivers, moaning, asks, "What happened?"

"The dogs, at full attention, stare at me with those beady, red eyes. They look up at Fritz and Fritz nods. I remain frozen, expecting the worst. I read somewhere you see your life flash before you. No, I could only pray I didn't wet myself."

I take a deep breath. "The dogs knock me down and lick my face."

Jamarr, amazed, "What the hell!"

"I know now he told them to *kiss the pretty Jew girl's face.*

"I turn and run, panting, the whole length of the basement until I reach the exit door. Only when I am back in the lobby, do I breathe again."

Mama, why did you make me go down there?

For a few moments, there is silence. Then, all at once the group reacts. The kids call out stuff like, "Wow!" This is from Eduardo. "I would have fainted," from Barsha. Lee Chang, "You had guts, lady."

And Jamarr? Sure enough, he asks what I hoped none of them would ask, "What did your folks say when you told them?"

I practically whisper my answer. "I never told them. Never."

Jamarr shouts, "Never? Why the hell not?"

Lee Chang looks at his watch and jumps up. "I've got to go. Now." He bows to me and smiles. "Thank you, Mrs. Ruth, for your story."

This gives me the excuse to get up once again from my uncomfortable seat. I return the bow and wish him a good evening.

Of course, Eduardo and Barsha jump up as well. "We really must leave too," she says, and Eduardo nods in agreement.

"Hey, don't quit now!" Jamarr yells, but my little tribe has already entered the courtyard of their building.

I smile at Jamarr and shrug. "Dinnertime."

"Now that the fam jumped ship, story's over?" Jamarr tosses the words at me with undisguised annoyance.

"I guess so."

"You never said nothin' to your folks?"

"Never."

"That ain't really the end of the story, is it?"

"Well, you know the end. We won the war."

He begins to walk away, mumbling. "Cheap shot. You made us think Fritz would hurt you or something, maybe sic the dogs on you. Waste my day. Thanks for nothin'."

He doesn't look back, mumbling curse words under his breath.

Sorry, Jamarr, I couldn't face the dénouement. Forgive me.

❦

I sit in my car. Night has fallen. I'm surrounded by blackness, the sky, the streets. It's as if the whole world has closed down. Except for kitchen and dining room window lights from both buildings winking at me.

I can't drive yet, I'm unable to pull myself together.

Jamarr, you expected there was more and you were right. But I couldn't share this with you. I remember it, exactly as it occurred. As if could I ever forget.

Once out of the basement I dragged myself upstairs. Funny, it was the same time of day then as it is here, now. My parents were absorbed by the seven o'clock news on the radio. I tiptoed past them into the cramped bedroom I shared with Jodie. She was already asleep in her twin bed, sleeping in that funny position, surrounded by all her stuffed animals. Were they placed there to keep her safe? Without undressing, I climbed into my twin, heaved the blanket over my head and shivered some more. Never mind about dinner. I didn't think I'd ever want to eat again.

Why didn't I tell my parents? I still don't know. Was I anxious about what they'd say or do to me? I had been so afraid of Fritz. Did I think he would come up and hurt my family? Bring those slobbering dogs? Would he use that gun to go with his uniform? This is something that had never entered my mind until right now. Sixty percent of the building's tenants were Jewish families. Was I afraid he'd blow us all up? God knows, he must have hated all of us. What was he waiting for, working in this despised building? For his *Führer* to win the war?

Why didn't I call the police? Hadn't I read or heard somewhere of a German group of Nazi-followers called the Bund? There were meetings; were they in Madison Square Garden, where prize fighters usually fought? The fascists were allowed to gather in rallies because our country believed in freedom of speech.

There was only one place I could go to where I'd feel safe. Where I could tell what I saw and have people comfort me. I crept out of bed and once again sneaked past my parents, who were still engrossed in the radio.

I started to knock, but their door was open. I hurried inside, but something slowed me down.

It was the silence. No sounds of a family eating dinner. No music. No lights. Except for a small bulb somewhere. Maybe they weren't home? No, they wouldn't leave the front door open.

I followed the light.

To my surprise, they were in the living room, all three of them seated on their couch. I rushed in, words tumbling out; I was unable to slow the flow. "There's a Nazi in the basement!" I shouted. "I saw him with my own eyes! In his Nazi uniform, saluting *Heil Hitler*. He's our enemy, right? What should we do? Call the army? The police? We have to do something. I'm so scared."

Then I realized something was not right. Why were they sitting like that? Close, as if glued together? They looked like statues. Statues that were crying.

Salvatore was holding a letter in his trembling hands. Lina was near to collapse.

Frankie was the only one able to speak. "The War Department wrote. My brothers weren't in Italy anymore . . ."

Lina was keening now. "My boys, my boys . . ."

Frankie choked out the rest of the words. "Tony and Johnny, they're dead. They wouldn't be separated and now they're both dead."

I froze. Oh, how I froze. What could I say or do? I flopped down on a side chair and sobbed.

Salvatore leapt up. It almost seemed funny how the couch pillow billowed out from under where he sat. He came over and shook me. "In the basement?"

I nodded.

I'd never seen him look like this; my mom would have said he looked like death warmed over.

Salvatore raced out of the room and I could hear him in the kitchen. Then there was the rattle of silverware.

The next day, I heard the news in shambling reports. It had blazed all over the neighborhood, like an out-of-control forest fire, that Mr. Salvatore Napolitano, in 1A, crazed with grief, stabbed the superintendent, Fritz Heinrich, with a carving knife. It was gory carnage. The super's two dogs tore at Mr. Napolitano as he sliced the super's body. Twenty times—or fifty times—depending on who was telling the story. Mr. Napolitano was in intensive care in Bronx Hospital. He lived. I didn't know about the dogs.

"Whatever possessed him?" Mrs. O'Reilly, their astonished neighbor next door in 1B was heard to comment. "Such a mild-mannered man."

My fault. All my fault.

The Nazi in the basement is long dead. But not his ghost, who haunts neither this building nor these scars masquerading as memories. I came back but I should have known.

What was I thinking?

I turned the ignition.

Time to go to the airport.

The Hanukkah Killer

Robin Hemley

I was leaving Lady Calvert's house to sell a sack of stolen diamonds when Frank, who was washing his car in the driveway, dropped the hose and said he wanted to have a word with me. If Frank said he wanted a word, you gave him a word. A cross between a mob hit man and a TV detective, even when he smiled, as he did now, it felt the opposite of a smile, a fake, to throw you off. A fact smile. I had learned the phrase "fact smile" the previous year when I'd asked my mother if she'd buy me a hundred-year-old stamp I had seen advertised in a *Fantastic Four* comic book. She'd laughed. "It's an imitation, see? It says right here, 'fact smile.'"

Frank and his wife Joanne, a nurse, were Lady Calvert's upstairs tenants. If we had a family joke, it was that Lady Calvert couldn't have picked better tenants. Frank actually *was* a homicide detective who regularly kicked in doors, creating mayhem in reaction to mayhem, throughout Nassau County. Once he had caught someone trying to break in through a window in the back alley, had put a gun up to the guy's head, and said, "You picked the wrong house, buddy."

Frank led me back into Lady Calvert's house, which was closer to a bungalow than a manor, and told me to sit down at the kitchen table while he went upstairs to get the thing he wanted to show me. While I waited, I took the sack of diamonds from my pocket and loosened the golden threads from at the top of the sack, which had previously held foil-wrapped chocolate *gelt* from last year. The sack bulged with the diamonds, all of them set in rings.

"What you got?" my brother Danny asked, peeking over my shoulder. I pitched the bag and it hit the kitchen door, diamond rings spilling everywhere.

"Nothing," I said as I scrambled out of my seat and started cramming them back into my pocket.

"Wow, are those real?" he asked. "Can I have one?"

"Go away."

"Where did you get them? Give me one."

"Go away. No one likes you."

"No one likes *you*," he said.

"You two should be grateful you have each other," Frank said as he came back into the kitchen. "Always fighting. But someday you're going to remember—"

"Blood is thicker than water," Danny said, like he was reciting a pledge.

"Come here, you two," Frank said without remarking on what we were doing on the floor. We took seats beside him at the dinette table and he withdrew a black-and-white photo from his envelope: a man about Frank's age, with silver sideburns, close-cropped hair. Eyes that, if they were windows to his soul, you would have wanted nailed shut. "This man," he said. "He lives on our block. If you ever see him, you just keep walking. Don't even say hello."

He looked at each of us in turn. Normally, Danny would have asked the obvious question, "What did he do?" But Danny simply pointed at the man, his finger slowly descending as though he wanted to touch the face, but then he withdrew before he was contaminated.

"Don't tell Lady Calvert I showed you this," Frank said, putting the photo back. "She thinks you shouldn't be exposed to some things yet. But I always say–"

"Blood is thicker than water," Danny said.

"No."

"Ha, idiot," I said, and I was going to punch him, but Frank's look told me not to dare.

"The more you know about the world," he said, "the better equipped you are not to grow up to be what my people call a *cazzo* and your people call a *putz*."

"What did he do?" I finally asked.

"You're the putz . . . *cazzo* . . . idiot," Danny chant-whispered to me, loud enough for Frank to hear, but he just raised his eyebrows.

338

"You don't need to know the particulars," Frank said. He kept his finger pointed at us, back and forth like he was going to shoot the first one who said, "Actually, we were planning on inviting him for Hanukkah," which started tonight. That would have earned me a slap for sure, even though Frank had never touched me. But he was capable. At night, he and Joanne raged upstairs. Cries, screams, thuds. It was a regular crime series going on above us, twice a week, at least, but we never said anything because Lady Calvert never said anything. She just turned up the volume on the TV.

Frank whipped the photo and envelope under the table almost as quickly as I had thrown the diamonds when he saw both women entering the kitchen, each with a teacup in hand.

Lady Calvert put on the kettle to boil and retrieved two tea bags to reuse in her tea and Joanne's, something she'd learned to do when she was a young woman in the Depression. She'd never stopped, one of the many things about her that had annoyed my mother, even though Lady Calvert, with or without her title, could afford fresh tea from China now, if she wanted.

"You've got a couple of angels here, Lady Calvert," Joanne said. "Am I right?"

"My poor angels," Lady Calvert said. "At least I know *they'll* never disappoint me." She exchanged a look with Joanne as though they had been discussing a long list of people who had disappointed them, which was probably the case. Lady Calvert was not one to hide her disappointments in front of angels or anyone else. She aired her grievances daily, from the dogs who pooped on her stoop, to cats peeing in her hydrangeas, to kids knocking their Spalding balls into her rose bushes, and at the top of the list, my mother, who Lady Calvert said was shirking her responsibilities by dumping us with her. That my mother was in the hospital was another disappointment, a character defect. If my mother had more brass, she would have been able to get better. "She's got no willpower," Lady Calvert had informed us more than once, a kind of Talmud that might have been called "Commentaries of Lady Calvert" that she recited to us nightly. "She could get better if she just made up her mind." Lady Calvert declared that she had more than enough brass to spare. After all, she had come from nothing but had married royalty and had played the stock market well enough so that she was now a "lady of leisure," who relied on the passive income that her many properties brought her.

About the royalty thing, my mom told a different story. Lady Calvert had met Lord Calvert "of Canadian whiskey fame" at a club where she'd been a showgirl near Niagara Falls. One thing led to another, the big thing being Lord Calvert getting drunk on his namesake, and poof, the next morning, they woke up married. Lord Calvert's family hadn't exactly welcomed my grandmother, and the marriage lasted only a little longer than Lord Calvert's hangover. But my grandmother was allowed to keep her title, and it was the thing that she loved most. Everyone else considered her a *fact smile* Lady, but they went along with it, except for my mom, who refused to call her a lady at all.

I hated that blood saying of Frank's. In my experience, there was nothing thinner than blood. No one in my family was that thick—it was like the opposite of what was true. The Atlantic was thicker than blood. The beach was where we spent all our days, Danny and me, skim boarding, body surfing, building forts, setting off illegal fireworks. The Atlantic was so thick, it helped us forget how thin our blood was.

My mother could be forgiven because she was in the hospital, but my dad's case of thinness was serious. Forget about holidays. He'd thinned us out completely. He'd gone to the west coast where he was following his dreams. *Danny? Barry? Names sound familiar.* So we had to go to Lady Calvert's. Danny had been crying himself to sleep a couple nights a week for the last three months. I pretended not to hear him or care, because that was the family golden rule. Ignore unto others what they would ignore unto you.

But one night in the middle of his crying, I'd interrupted and told him that Mom had called that very day and asked what we wanted for Hanukkah. "I told her you wanted a Hot Wheels Race Set."

"You did?" he said. He hadn't stopped bothering me ever since. Every day, he asked me a thousand times at least whether I thought she'd really get him a Hot Wheels set. I told him I didn't know. I told him not to get his hopes up, but they were up to Everest already.

We weren't a holiday kind of family. My parents forgot all holidays, except for birthdays, when they would go to the grocery store and pick up a cake the same day, sometimes a leftover on sale with some other kid's name on it. In my whole childhood, we had celebrated Hanukkah only once, when we were visiting Lady Calvert. For eight days, she gave us a bag of chocolate *gelt* and a quarter. We lit two dinner candles the first night, then lost track of the days and wound up lighting six candles two nights in a row, eight the day after. When we still lived with our parents, Lady Calvert would send us a rotting crate of Florida oranges around Christmas, regifted from my Aunt Gertie, who lived in Del Rey Beach and sent them up to Lady Calvert every year.

🦌

A week before, while walking by the old boarded-up house on our block, one of the other neighborhood kids, Tony Alfazy, asked if we'd ever wondered what was behind those windows. I was not in favor of wondering what was behind boarded windows. But you couldn't just say that. It would mark you for life, or at least as long as you lived on Kentucky Street. The house, with a large lot, sandy and covered in patches of crab grass, had been abandoned for years and was on the opposite end of the street from Lady Calvert's. In the summers we occasionally played stick ball in the lot when we weren't at the beach. In the winter, we hardly paid attention to the house. This was a time when dares and double dares meant something, and before long we had gone to the back of the house, found the window with the loosest boards, and pried them open. The dull daylight of winter filtered through the house, enough for us to see our breath and the poop and dead birds, some not much more than a pile of feathers, others mummified, one propped on top of the kitchen sink drying rack as though waiting to be put in a cupboard. Animal-like humps of chairs and couches slumped under sheets spotted with mouse or bat droppings.

"I wonder who owns this place," Tony's brother Vince said as we walked up the carpeted stairs to the second floor.

"*Dumkopf*," Tony said. *Dumkopf* was his favorite word, which he'd picked up from Artie Johnson's German soldier on *Rowan and Martin's Laugh-in*. "No one owns it anymore. If they did, they'd be living here."

The second floor was covered in boxes, piled high in the hallway, but only one piece of furniture, just like the vanity in Lady Calvert's bedroom. This one wasn't covered like the other furniture, and it had an oval mirror in a white wooden frame painted with tiny roses. It rested on curving legs and a bench with a red pincushion-like seat and a tear down its middle, stuffing spilling out. My friends started opening boxes, and the house was soon filled with whispered cries as they discovered things that they thought were worth taking. Drawn to the vanity, I opened its tiny drawers—the first two were empty, but the third drawer was full of diamond rings.

"You sure none of this stuff belongs to anyone?" I asked Tony.

"Finders keepers," he said. "You find anything?"

"Nothing," I said. "You?"

"Same, nothing," he said, lifting what looked like a bear suit out of a trunk. We all gathered around it, then tried it on, cracking up as we strutted around the hallway in someone's mink coat.

Over the next few days, we went back and forth to the house and hauled away whatever we could carry that looked like it might have some resale value. No one stopped us, and no one's parents noticed or seemed to care because that was the way people parented on Kentucky Street. The kid leaves after breakfast and returns for dinner. What happens in between is nobody's business.

❧

After Frank's lecture, it wasn't too difficult to shake Danny. I told him go drown in the ocean.

"*You* drown in the ocean, you putz . . . *cazzo* . . . idiot!" he yelled, adding "punk" to his ever-expanding list. Like our mom, upsetting him was the easiest thing in the world. He went off in the direction of the beach as though he was going to follow my command.

I walked up Kentucky, passing the houses of people who knew me or my grandmother, which was most everyone. I wasn't stupid. I wasn't going to try to sell the diamonds to any of them, because word would definitely get back to Lady Calvert. She really *did* think that Danny and I were angels, and that faith in us seemed like the last true belief in our family that could break. But if we were angels, we were pretty poor ones. Our parents seemed to be allergic to angels—our dad had put a whole continent between us, and our mother had to be locked up in the cracker barrel, as Lady Calvert put it.

My plan was to cross Beech Street and head for the bayside of Long Beach, which may as well be another country.

A horn blast announced a fire somewhere in Long Beach. This was the highlight of Lady Calvert's existence. She'd stop whatever she was doing and listen to the blasts. Once she knew where the danger was, she could relax and go about her business again.

Three blasts. That meant West End, Bayside, right where I was headed. I started to run toward the fire and ran smack into another person. I withdrew my hand from my pocket to brace myself, the diamond rings scattering again.

"Watch where you're going, kid," the man I'd bumped into said. I couldn't believe it. The second time within half an hour. I looked up into the face of the guy in the photograph. He was dressed in swimming trunks and flip flops, wearing a Yankees T-shirt, a towel slung over his shoulder. He had a straw fedora with a dolphin on it and carried a straw bag that said "Florida."

"Oh, hello," I said.

Mrs. Hoy, who lived in the house a few doors down from Lady Calvert was peeking through her curtains. She and my grandmother played canasta together every Friday, which was tonight, but it was also the first night of Hanukkah and the beginning of the Sabbath. There was no contest between a holiday and Friday night cards. Canasta would always win. But at least this meant that when I disappeared forever and was chopped up into pieces and thrown into the sea by this guy, they'd have a clue what had happened to me.

"Has anyone seen my grandson today?" my grandmother would ask her canasta ladies. "He didn't come home for dinner."

I was about to die, the first victim of the Hanukkah Killer. I was sure just looking into his eyes would murder me, but he didn't seem to see me at all. "What are those?" he asked, his croaky voice almost a whisper.

"As a matter of fact," Mrs. Hoy would say, "I saw him being dragged down the street by a guy who looked like a murderer. I wasn't sure if I should say anything."

The man turned toward Mrs. Hoy and the curtain fell back into place. He turned back to me and watched me collect the fallen diamonds, picking up a platinum one himself.

"They're rings?" I asked. Everything suddenly felt like it could only be asked, not answered, at least not by me. "I'm selling them for the Salvation Army?"

"They real?"

"It's a charity organization?" I said. "They help people when they're in trouble?"

"The diamonds," he said. "Where'd you get them?"

"I didn't steal them," I said, as though that was what he had asked me. I was a terrible criminal. "Maybe the Salvation Army did, but I didn't."

He looked at me like I was a putz, as Danny called me, and blew on the diamond the way you do when you want to fog something. Then he cradled the ring in his palm and looked at it without expression. "What does the Salvation Army want for these?"

"$9.99?" I suggested.

An upward twitch played around his mouth, but his voice softened and he said, "Okay, then. Let's go back to my place. I was headed to the beach so I'm not carrying my wallet."

I hesitated.

"Or you could give them to me now and I'll pay you next time I see you."

I wasn't going to fall for that, so I followed him to his house, which was at the top of the block closest to Beech Street. His house, like many on Kentucky Street, was made of stucco. Painted white, the first floor was a garage, the second floor the living space with two bedrooms, maybe three.

"Come in," he said, after we had climbed the stairs. He held the screen door open and he wasn't smiling, not even that upward twitch. He was the guy in the photograph, the same one without a doubt that Frank had warned me not even to say hello to. But how bad could he be? He was wearing a straw hat and carried a straw bag. Florida. That was the place full of canasta-playing ladies like Lady Calvert and my Aunt Gertie. I tried to imagine this guy playing canasta. I couldn't do it. Maybe he'd picked the hat and bag off of a dead body.

"I'll wait on the porch," I said.

He tilted his head and looked like he was going through a bunch of options, but I couldn't tell what they were. "Don't go anywhere," he said and closed the door.

When he returned, he counted out a five, four ones, a Kennedy half dollar, a quarter, a dime, a nickel, and nine pennies, one of them a wheat cent from 1939. I handed over the diamonds.

After he counted out the money, I saw just how stupid I'd been to sell him all these diamonds for $9.99. I'd completely forgotten about sales tax. "Okay," he said, which I took to mean *get out of here*. So I did.

I wasn't sure how much tax would be added to the cost of the Hot Wheels Racing Set, but I knew there were three solutions to my problem. I could buy Danny something else, maybe two or three Matchbox cars.

My second option was to go back to Lady Calvert's house and steal a dollar from her purse.

My third option was to pray for a miracle.

When I reached the store, only a few blocks away, a soda fountain that also sold toys and comics and beach supplies, I found one Hot Wheels Racing Set, marked down a dollar to $8.99.

For eight days, a lamp meant to last one day had lit the Temple, and now, for a little over eight dollars, a toy meant to cost almost ten was now within my reach. In response, I made the usual vows to God to be a better kid. I paid for the racing set and had enough left over for a pretzel rod and a comic. Choosing the comic took almost an hour. Tough choices. *Silver Surfer*, *Spider Man*, or *Dr. Strange*? I finally settled on *Silver Surfer* after taking it off the rack and reading the first few pages before being yelled at by Mr. Smorack to stop abusing his merchandise.

By the time I left the store, it was nearly sunset, and I hurried with my loot so I'd be in time to light the first candle—or pretend to light the first candle since I doubted Lady Calvert had bought Hanukkah candles. When I approached the corner of Kentucky Street, there were lights flashing near the house of the guy I wasn't supposed to say hello to. I vaguely thought the flashing lights had to do with me, and wondered if I was in trouble. When I passed the house, I didn't see him but there were a lot of cops on his porch. The front door looked caved in, and that was Frank's specialty, so I figured he was there somewhere too. I crossed the street so no one would notice me and made my way as quick as I could to Lady Calvert's house.

"Don't ever worry your grandmother like that again," Joanne said as Lady Calvert hugged me, and I nearly died from an overdose of her perfume. When Frank returned I thought he was going to scold me like his wife did, or call me a *cazzo,* but he didn't. He just asked me some questions. He asked me if the man had done anything or if he had asked me to do anything.

"Do anything?" I asked.

"You'd know if he'd done something," Joanne said. "Am I right?"

"I guess," I said.

"You're a good boy," Frank said. "A very lucky boy." After Mrs. Hoy saw me walking away with the man in the photo that Frank had shown nearly everyone on the block, she had come running down the street and found Frank in the driveway.

I kept waiting for him to mention the stolen diamonds, for the big revelation that I wasn't an angel at all, but they all looked at me like all they saw were wings. I mouthed the word *cazzo* at Danny but he just stared at me wide-eyed and blinked.

We didn't celebrate the first night of Hanukkah but the second night, we did. To my amazement, Lady Calvert gave us a dollar each and even sang the prayers. My mom called us from the hospital and spoke to me first. She was crying, and I wondered what was wrong with me because I just listened to her cry and couldn't even make my eyes water. I blew on the mouthpiece the way the man had blown on the diamonds and it almost sounded like something real escaping: a sigh, a sob. That was the best I could do and I yelled to Danny to pick up in Lady Calvert's bedroom. Danny thanked her for the Hot Wheels set. "I love it," he said. I was still listening in on the extension.

She started to object but I cut her off. "It's okay, Mom," I said. "I'm not jealous."

"Did I really buy you that?" she asked, and laughed in a way that I remembered and loved, surprised and fleeting, two sharp notes of delight, as though she almost believed it herself.

"You did, Mom," I said. "Do us a favor and just accept it."

Hunter

Jen Conley

The door to the waiting room creaked open.

Lori Kellan heard it from inside her office and breathed a sigh of relief. Her last patient of the day—night, actually, 7:30 p.m.—was ten minutes early, most likely taking a seat in the chair outside her office door. This was good. His name was Hunter and he was a fairly new patient, a bit strange but punctual. Lori liked punctual.

First she had to finish up with Jessica. Jessica, cute and sweet, always dressed in adorable dresses and low-heeled boots, a catch for any decent guy, was anxiety-ridden and nervous because she lived with a shit of a boyfriend. Sure, there were sad stories from her childhood, her parents' contentious divorce and all that went with it, but Lori believed in directing patients like Jessica, those without monstrous childhood trauma, into creating boundaries, taking control, and dropping the victimhood. Lori was trying to gently guide Jessica into making a move—figuratively and literally—but Jessica, twenty-nine, was highly concerned about losing . . . what's-his-name. Lori seemed to always forget the boyfriend's name, even though Jessica talked about him *all the time*. Jessica's sessions had originally been couples' counseling with said shit boyfriend, but he said he was "fed up taking the blame" for their problems, so he stopped coming. He was a clean-cut guy but was indolent and unfaithful, even if he claimed otherwise. During the last of their sessions, while he sat slouched back in the chair, Jessica, sitting on the edge of the sofa, stated that she'd found proof of his unfaithfulness because she saw his text messages. This perturbed him. He said that she had no right to pry. She said that he had no right to cheat. He said the woman in question was just a coworker whom he bantered with, no cheating. Jessica cried and then apologized for snooping.

That was five weeks ago. Lori considered herself an extremely patient therapist but she always struggled with young women who wasted their time with lazy, unfaithful men. Lori had seen enough of fortysomething women, former Jessicas, who, at the dawn of midlife, finally saw the light and kicked their no-good husbands out, only later to complain that they weren't paying child support. The entire scenario was difficult to deal with, especially since Lori had been both a Jessica *and* the forty-year-old who had seen the light.

Jessica's eyes were tearing up now, but she kept talking. "Then I go, 'Josh, this entire thing is making me uncomfortable. Don't you care?' and he says, 'You're making a mountain out of a molehill.' Do you believe it? Classic gaslighting, right?"

"Absolutely," Lori said.

"So then I go . . ."

Lori pushed her glasses up on her nose, handing Jessica a box of tissues but losing all interest in the poor thing. Lori tried to recall what made her stay in her own first marriage for so long. Was it the sex? Sure. She had been young when she met him, twenty-three to his twenty-eight, and he was rugged and handsome and mysterious. She'd been hooked from the moment they first spoke and for the rest of the relationship, she tap-danced to keep him interested. Her mother had called him a "loner" and prophesied that he'd always be a loner, but that didn't deter Lori one bit. Lori had seen her ex-husband as an enigma, a fascinating puzzle she tried to solve for sixteen years until she finally concluded at age thirty-nine that he was simply a fucking sneaky self-centered asshole. She filed for divorce. Moved on.

"Okay, Jessica," Lori announced, turning to her computer. "Why don't we schedule you for next week, same day and time?"

Jessica peered at her cell phone. She was still sniffling. "I can't do that day next week." She had to take her boyfriend somewhere for some reason.

What was his name? Why couldn't Lori remember his name?

They settled on two weeks.

Outside in the tiny waiting room, a small radio played a local soft rock station—Lori's way of drowning out her sessions through the thin walls. Hunter sat quietly staring at his phone, the heavy stink of cigarettes wafting off his puffy coat. Jessica zipped up her jacket and pulled on her oversized, knit mittens. She glanced at Hunter but he didn't look up.

"Okay, Lori," Jessica said. "Thank you. See you in two weeks!"

Jessica was a master of flipping back to Cheerful Woman. It was bizarre.

Aren't we all? Lori thought, standing in the threshold to the hallway, watching Jessica walk away. Other than her next patient, the building was almost empty except for Tom, the custodian, and another counselor, a woman named Judy who used crystals and new-age therapy. Whatever that was. Lori suspected Judy read palms and tarot cards. Her only patients were women. That office was upstairs.

"Hello, Hunter," Lori said.

Hunter finally looked up from his cell phone. "Hey." He was twenty-four, a single guy who'd only had one prior session with Lori. That session had been more of an intake with paperwork and an overview of his goals. He claimed he wanted to be more assertive. "I think that's why I can't get a girlfriend."

Lori had been immediately skeptical when Hunter declared that his problem was a lack of assertiveness. She didn't get the vibe that Hunter was unassertive. She got the vibe that he creeped young women out.

They entered her office and he pulled off his coat, tossed it on the sofa, and plopped in the brown suede chair opposite her. Jessica always sat on the sofa. Her shit boyfriend used to sit in the chair.

Hunter placed his hands on the wide, thick arms of the seat and nodded to Lori. He was dressed in tight jeans and a black hoodie and his hair was a charcoal color—thick, but close to the skull. His features were intense and almost shocking—large blue eyes, heavy dark eyebrows, a large mouth, a five o'clock shadow. Only his nose seemed normal. His hands were enormous, as were his feet, although he probably only stood five-seven. He appeared naturally strong and powerful, as if in a former life he had shoveled coal on the *Titanic*.

"So, I went out on a date," he said. "First real date in four years."

"Good," Lori said. "But what do you mean by 'real date'?" Lori immediately regretted the question. She knew what he meant.

It didn't take long for him to respond. "In the past, the women I've been with have been more . . . opportunistic situations."

A chill ran up Lori's spine.

He looked down. "I mean hook-ups." He paused. "I'm not proud of it."

He means they were prostitutes.

Lori allowed for some silence before asking, "How did the date go?"

"Aren't you curious how I got the date?"

Interesting question, Lori thought.

"My mother set it up. Daughter of one of her coworkers."

"Great way to meet someone."

"She was a bitch."

Lori shifted. She pulled her blue cardigan over her chest. "Why?"

Hunter tapped the arms of the chair. "I bought her dinner and then we went to the bar and I bought her two drinks. Expensive shit too. Ketel One vodka mixed with some pink bullshit. Anyhow, she sees some of her friends across the bar, gets all giddy, and then leaves me to sit by myself. Before I know it, the bitch is walking out the door with them." He glared at Lori. "Nice, huh?"

"That must have hurt."

"It fucking did." He winced. "Sorry for my profanity."

Lori had heard worse. "It's okay. Do your best to curtail it, if you can."

"Sure."

Hunter went on about how his mother kept asking him if he was calling the girl again. He hadn't told her about the ending of the date. "She's a nice woman," Hunter said. "My mother. Always trying to help. I don't want to hurt her."

Lori made another note in her brain.

He talked some more, about his job at a Wawa convenience store working the cash register, his car, which needed new tires that he couldn't afford, about how his mom wanted him to go back to OCC—Ocean County College—but it was just a waste of money. "I don't know what I want to do," he said, shrugging boyishly.

"Perhaps we can focus on that," Lori suggested, hearing the distant sound of the fortune teller upstairs shutting her door, then the clattering of her heels down the wooden stairs. "Sometimes when people find direction in their professional life, then relationships will follow."

Hunter slouched and looked at his big hands. "Yeah . . ."

There was silence as he gazed around her small office. Rick, her husband of three years, painted the walls a peach color and her son, Jake, a senior at Rutgers, put together a long stand where several plants sat in ceramic blue and violet pots. A light-orange and lavender hippyish area rug covered the worn Berber carpet. The idea was to create calm, as if one were inside a seashell.

It appeared by the sneer on Hunter's face that he didn't approve of her decor.

"But you know who I really fucking hate?" he asked abruptly.

Lori glanced at the clock on her desk. She had another twenty minutes with him.

"I hate those fucking Jews. You know what I mean?"

His comment was jarring, but Lori said nothing. She'd heard her patients complain about the local Orthodox and Hasidic community time and time again, although it was never this blunt.

"Those fucking Hasidic, Orthodox . . . whatever. The ones who are taking over? Shit, they come into the store every fucking day with their curls and their wigs and their fifteen fucking kids. Did you know that half of them are on government assistance? I make shit money and I have to pay for *them* to have kids. You know, taxes and all."

Lori scratched her neck. He didn't make enough money to be complaining about taxes.

"Don't they bother you?" he said.

"Do you like your job at Wawa?"

He shrugged again. "Sometimes."

Her cell phone, sitting on her desk, lit up with a text—she should've turned her phone off but she'd forgotten. It was Rick. Probably asking her what type of wine she'd like with dinner. He had told her he was cooking pasta.

Lori folded her hands in her lap. "Did you ever make a list of the things you might be interested in? Career-wise?"

Hunter cracked a smile. "Now you sound like my mother. Are you a mother?"

Lori blinked at him. "I'm definitely old enough to be one."

"You can be a mother at sixteen. Ask the Jews."

She took a heavy breath and leaned forward. "Hunter, one of your goals is to land a girlfriend, correct?"

He cocked his head, his big weird blue eyes bulging. "Yeah."

"Well, I suggest you rethink how you . . ." she paused, trying to find the right words. "How you use this type of language, how you refer to certain groups of people."

Hunter laughed, a loud, garish guffaw. "I think I know where you're going."

She leaned back and slid a finger underneath her glasses and gently rubbed the corner of her right eye. "You seem to have a lot of anger toward one group of people, and that comes through."

"No shit."

"Right. But if you're out with a woman, or if you meet a woman, your tone, which leans toward the angry side, comes across as aggressive. Even if it's not directed at *her*."

He stared at her. Large blue ugly eyes.

"Hunter, women need to feel safe when they're out with a new man, and if you're coming across as aggressive, aggressive toward *anything*, they might feel like you'll be too aggressive to date." She felt relief, as if she'd finished a grueling task.

"Huh," he said. He moved in the chair, placing his big hands on his thighs. "I didn't think of it that way."

"I don't mean to come off as judgmental," she said. "I'm only letting you know how you might be perceived. Perhaps your anger isn't really so much aimed at the Orthodox community as it is aimed more inward, toward yourself. Do you feel that you've achieved everything you imagined yourself achieving?"

He didn't understand.

"When you were a child, did you think you'd be working at Wawa and living with your mom at twenty-four?"

A shadow crossed his face. "You calling me a loser?"

Shit, wrong move. "No, of course not. I am saying you're not really angry at the Jewish people but more frustrated with your direction in life."

He only stared at her.

"I'd like to help you with your direction in life."

Now he smirked. "All right. I see where you're going." He nodded. "So this shit does work?"

Lori laughed, more so out of relief. "It can." She suggested again that he make a list and bring it to the next session.

He smiled even wider. All bright but yellow straight teeth.

"Let's get you set up for next week."

After Lori walked him to the door, through the small waiting room, and waved to him, she returned to her office, taking another deep breath as she sat at her desk, and typed some patient notes into her laptop.

She sent her husband a text and, because it was Friday, she was looking forward to having a nice weekend. She'd been lucky to find Rick, lucky to have remarried, lucky to have a healthy, well-adjusted, good-natured son like Jake. Someone who didn't frighten women.

At a quarter to nine, she shut down the office, turned off the radio in the waiting room, switched off the lights, and locked up. In the hallway, she buttoned up her coat, noticing Tom's broom leaning against the wall, a small pile of dust and dirt clumped in front of it. A lone Christmas ornament, a silver star, hung on one of the office doors she passed—an architect who showed up every few weeks. It was always depressing to see Christmas decorations in January. Lori's mother had loved Christmas, covering the house inside and out with lights and ornaments and candles in the windows, but she'd rip everything down New Year's Day. "I want no reminders of what's gone," she'd say. "I'd rather face the winter with courage, not cowardice. Let's get it over with."

Her mother had died four years earlier, on a cold day in January.

Lori kept walking, clicking her car starter as she reached the glass doors of the building, not that it would warm up her car right away but the lights and the motor would be on, and she felt safer. The parking lot was not well lit. The building was from the 1980s, all forest-green marble, mauve walls, and brass door handles. It hadn't been kept up. Every so often, Rick would drive over and make sure she got out okay. But nothing terrible had ever happened. After all, the building sat on a fairly busy road. It was flanked by a small strip mall and a neighborhood of McMansions, half of which weren't kept up either. There was a small field behind the building, Lori's office looked out on it.

As she walked to her car, something caught her eye on the black-top—a burning cigarette. She stopped and turned around, toward the two-lane road with cars passing by. The parking lot was empty, except for her own car and Tom's old Toyota. But Tom didn't smoke.

Hunter did.

She kept walking to her car, which seemed farther away than necessary. It'd been almost a half hour since Hunter left the office.

But he'd hung around, out here in the cold, smoking, hadn't he?

❦

"He was on his cell phone," she said to herself out loud as she pulled into her townhouse complex. During the entire drive home, she ignored her audiobook, obsessing about the cigarette, but finally arriving at the conclusion that Hunter had been on his phone, or listening to a podcast. Perhaps he lit a cigarette, then rolled down the window and chucked it right before she walked out of the building. Normal.

Inside, her place was warm and smelled of garlic and basil. Rick grew his own herbs in small pots near the back window all year long.

"The house I was telling you about has a four-season room," he said after she had changed into her gray yoga pants and an oversized beige sweater, both a Christmas gift from him. Rick was pushing her to sell their townhouse.

"We could sit in the sun during the winter." Rick poured a glass of sauvignon blanc. He smiled at her. "I read this is one of the better wines from New Zealand. Remember the last one they sent us?" He had recently joined a wine club. "Terrible."

Lori took a sip from her glass. "I needed this."

"Tough bunch today?"

She took a seat at the table. "Just weird."

"Weird is interesting," he said, placing a salad in front of her.

They ate, chattering about politics, him telling her about another Democrat he read about and liked. "Did you hear about her?"

Lori hadn't. She made a mental note to keep abreast of the House of Representatives, especially the Democratic representatives. This way she could enjoy political conversations with Rick.

"I can't believe what's happening to this country," Rick grumbled, shaking his head. "There has to be a change in Washington soon or we're all going to pay."

Lori let him talk more but, like earlier, her mind wasn't on the present conversation. She kept thinking about Hunter and his cigarette. Now she was convinced he hadn't been on his cell phone. That he had been hanging around, waiting for her—her original instinct. She decided to ask Tom if he'd seen anything on Monday.

Later, they sat in the living room, the gas fireplace warming them, Rick watched a documentary about the Roosevelts on Netflix, Lori flipped through her Facebook on her iPad. One of her best friends from college, Janet, had posted a picture of her calico sitting on top of a novel on the coffee table. A glass of red wine nearby. *I have the house to myself and it's a lovely winter night with Rebecca, my book, and my wine. If Rebecca will just let me read!*

Lori commented: *Rebecca! Let Janet read!*

Janet responded: *Miss you, Lori. Let's meet up in the city soon!*

Lori liked the comment and smiled.

Rick caught her. "Anything good?"

"Janet," Lori said. "We're just talking on Facebook."

"Ah," he said, his eyes sailing back to FDR on the television. "I like Janet. Smart woman."

"Yes," said, Lori, wanting to add something else, but too exhausted to think of anything intelligent.

Rick was sixty-one, seven years older than Lori, and retired. He kept himself busy. A stack of library books sat on the floor. His gym sneakers were near the front door. "We should go walking tomorrow," he said. "It's going to be cold but sunny. We'll have to bundle up."

Lori agreed. "Sounds good."

After a while, he paused the television. "Everything okay? You're quiet tonight."

"Long week," she said.

"It's not because I'm bringing up the house, is it?" He meant the house in a retirement village, down by Philadelphia. His daughter lived in Cherry Hill. She had two small boys that he wanted to be near.

Lori placed her iPad to the side and pulled off her glasses. "Jake graduates this spring."

"I'm aware."

"He's going to want to come home for a bit. Find a job. Save some money."

"You sure about that?"

She wasn't sure about it. She hoped it would happen, but Jake was already looking to move out of New Jersey. "California, Mom!" he'd said on the phone to her recently. "You always said you'd love to see the West Coast."

It was one of her personal shames. She'd never been west of the Mississippi.

"Why don't we talk about it in a few months?" she suggested.

Rick shook his head, his voice taking a terse tone. "They already bought two of the units in this complex."

By "they," he meant a family from the Orthodox Jewish community.

"You have to sell *soon*," he warned.

He still said "you" even though after they married, she'd refinanced the townhouse with Rick's cash, and put his name on the deed and the mortgage.

She'd been living in the townhouse since her divorce, when Jake was seven. She'd worked for the state then, a solid government job she'd had since she was twenty-three, but she took classes for years to earn her master's in psychology and, after her mom died, with the money her mother left her, she retired from the state of New Jersey and opened up her own practice. It was only two years old, but she made enough money to help Jake with college. Rick paid for a renovation and update of the townhouse, half the mortgage and most of the bills. He was a retired accountant who still did side work for senior citizens around tax time. When she first met him, she quipped, "A Democrat and an accountant. Isn't that an oxymoron?"

"I don't want to leave my patients," she said, now.

"You can get new patients."

"Do we have to talk about this tonight?"

"Lori, if you don't sell soon, you'll be on the downside of the situation. You won't get your money's worth." He frowned. "We can't be low-balled. We need the money to buy a new place."

"Isn't this a little anti-Semitic?" she said, smirking. Rick prided himself on his support of the LGBTQ community, Planned Parenthood, his love for President Obama, and his ability to give up straws. She was having trouble forsaking straws.

"I don't think I'm being anti-Semitic," he said quickly, glowering at her. "I think I'm being realistic. The bottom line is that you're not going to get the premium amount if you wait much longer. These things happen fast."

Lori had done her best to ignore the situation in Ocean County. Her neighbors, her patients, everyone was talking about the issue which was a version of gentrification—but it was difficult to discuss without sounding anti-Semitic. The Orthodox community was exclusive and they didn't mix with the rest of the population. Their strict religious practices, their clothes, their increasing population, all irritated the people who had lived in Ocean County for decades. The slurs, the nastiness—it was uncomfortable to say the least, and it was tough to let the Hunters of the county rattle on. Lori had Jewish friends, neighbors, and Janet, one of her oldest and best friends in the world, was Jewish. How could she be anti-Semitic? She had no mean opinions about the Orthodox community.

Sure, the traffic was getting more frustrating by the minute, and it was tough to go shopping on Sundays, better to go shopping on Saturdays during the Sabbath, but what could you do? It was part of America. But Rick was speaking the truth—she had to sell soon if she wanted a fair price. Otherwise she'd get lowballed. That's how gentrification worked. Get out early or be left behind.

Back in November, she'd spoken to Janet about the local Orthodox community when they had met in New York for lunch.

"I don't understand the way of life," Lori said bluntly.

Janet picked up her wine. "Every new child is a finger in Hitler's eye."

"Yes, I understand that, but . . ." Lori's voice trailed off.

"Believe me," Janet said, "Just because I'm Jewish, doesn't mean I agree with everything."

Lori played with her salad. "But I don't understand the exclusiveness. Why keep to just one group? Live such strict lives? Why not assimilate? You had children with a Catholic."

Janet laughed. "True. But my children consider themselves Jews."

"My son considers himself an atheist," Lori said.

"Don't they all," Janet said, putting down her wine glass. "But in the eyes of the Hasidic and strict Orthodox, it's not *possible* to assimilate."

"In this day and age, why?"

Janet leaned back in her chair. "History, Lori, history. You know this."

※

"Did you see a guy hanging around last Friday night, smoking outside?" Lori asked Tom Monday evening. She found him in the break room upstairs, eating a sandwich and reading a magazine.

"One of your patients?"

"Yes."

He thought for a long minute. His face was worn and reddish and his fingernails were bitten to the quick, but he had a headful of blondish white hair. She suspected he'd been an alcoholic for years, a drug user, and smoker too, and now he was clean. Sometimes she heard his gravelly voice echoing in the halls, obviously talking to someone on his cell, about keeping to the program, taking it one day at a time, offering to pick them up for a meeting in the morning.

"I'll walk you out tonight when you're done," he offered. "But remember, I'm only here Mondays, Wednesdays, and Fridays." He took a pen and small notepad from his shirt pocket, scribbled down his cell number, tore it off and handed it to her. "Just text me. I'll come down."

Lori took it gratefully. "Thanks. I think it's just Fridays, when he comes."

Tom looked at her. "You gotta go with your gut, Lori. I'm sure you get some real nice people who need help and that's great. But I'm also sure you get the real troubled—people who can't be fixed. Lord knows I've dealt with them. You do what you can to help, but if your safety is in jeopardy, then it's in jeopardy. Some people can't be helped."

It was a concise slap of reality. "It might be my imagination."

He returned to his sandwich and magazine. "All right."

❧

"He's very nice," Marie was saying. Marie was one of Lori's favorite patients. She was about Rick's age and she had three grown daughters, one who worked in the publishing industry in New York City, one who was a stay-at-home mom, and one who taught sixth grade in Old Bridge.

"I'm glad she's found a nice man." Marie was talking about her youngest daughter, the teacher, who was finally dating a good guy.

"That must make you happy."

Marie was sitting on the sofa, her hands in her lap, her round face gentle and kind. "Oh, yes. I'm very happy for her. Especially after she had that trouble with the last one."

The last one had cheated and it had shattered the girl's heart.

Marie gazed through the window, at the open field, but it was almost dark, so nothing could be seen. Lori let the silence fill the air, allowing Marie space to think.

"I had another dream," Marie said.

Lori's heart sank. "You haven't had one in a long time."

"That's true."

Marie had survived years of sexual abuse—rape—from the hands of her father. From the age of ten until she was seventeen. It was a wicked hell. "He taught me how to give a blowjob," Marie had said flippantly in one of their first sessions. But Marie had lucked out and had found a terrific psychiatrist in the 1970s, working through much of the difficult parts of her recovery. Now she came to Lori to "check in." She said she needed someone to bounce stuff off of. "I know some people think therapy is a crutch, but I think it's the crutch I need to stop myself from putting my head in the oven."

Marie was unnervingly blatant about her sexual abuse and its effects.

"How did you feel after the dream?" Lori asked.

"The usual. Sick. Ashamed." Marie had dreams of having sex with her father, sometimes the dreams were about her enjoying it—which she admitted to Lori had been something she felt at times when the abuse was happening. "I was fucked up for little bit there, that's for sure."

The dreams were infrequent but usually occurred when Marie was feeling overwhelmed or stressed. At one point, her husband had joined her in the sessions. He was a darling man, loved her to the moon and back, and did everything to keep her settled. They'd been together since the late '70s and Lori, who didn't always think a woman needed a man, believed that Marie had only been able to survive and prosper in adulthood because her husband loved her so deeply. Not many people had that love, yet Lori thought it was fair. The universe had been kind in this horrific situation.

"Do you think the dreams will ever stop?" Marie asked. "I'm sixty-two. Shouldn't this end by now?"

"It was a terrible thing that happened to you," Lori said, not having an answer for her.

"I've been thinking about retiring," she admitted. She was a kindergarten aide in a small elementary school. "My unit leader—the union—told me to wait until we settled the contract. But that could be another year."

"You don't want to wait that long?"

"My back hurts. My hands ache when I cut construction paper, you know, shapes for the kids. I'm so tired at the end of the day. And we need to sell the house anyhow. It's too much for us these days."

Lori let her think some more.

"I hope I don't have another dream tonight."

❦

Hunter was ten minutes early for his appointment. Marie was long gone, so Lori let him in early.

"I met a girl," he said, the faint trace of cigarettes wafting off his hoodie. He wasn't wearing a coat this time.

"That's good."

He laughed, shifted in his chair, his big hands tapping the arms. "You're not gonna freaking believe this. I know you're not."

"Try me."

"So I'm out back, behind the store, Wawa I mean, and I'm smoking, because the boss makes us go out back and not out front, and all of a sudden this girl comes out of the woods. Like *emerges*, right? They got a bunch of Jew homes behind the store." He stopped himself. "Sorry. There's a neighborhood behind the store where people from the Orthodox community live."

"Much better," Lori said.

"Thanks, Doc." He flashed a quick grin, yellow, straight teeth. "Anyway, so this chick walks out of the woods, they got a path there, and she approaches me. She's wearing a long wig, black, sort of like the woman from the Addams Family wears. You know what I mean?"

Lori grimaced. "Okay."

"Right, and she's got a little makeup on, dressed sort of nice, like you sometimes see some of them. She's pretty, skin that ain't seen the sun like some of these local women who sit on the beach for their entire lives."

Lori listened.

"Then she starts talking to me. I'm like looking behind me, making sure I ain't on some type of YouTube prank thing, but it's all legit." He kept smiling, rubbing his mouth, cocking his head. "She asks me for a smoke. So I look around again, make sure I ain't gonna get beat up, and I hand her one. Even light it for her. Beautiful girl, I'll tell ya."

This is bullshit, Lori thought.

"She starts asking what I do, do I have a car, do I have a girlfriend. She said that to me. And I was like, 'I'm in between women' and she says that she might get engaged soon. I ask, 'This arranged?' She says it sort of is. But we talk and then I get called back into the store. My coworker, Ty, he says, 'You talking to one of them?' and I say, 'Yeah, weird.'"

"When was this?" Lori asked.

"Tuesday. I ain't finished yet."

Lori shifted in her seat.

"She comes back on Thursday. We talk and smoke again. But not for long. Ty called me in again. But you know, she asked me again if I had a car."

Lori didn't believe him. Not one bit.

"How's that for a change of heart, doctor?"

"Interesting."

Hunter scowled at her. "You don't believe me."

Lori stared back at him. "It's a difficult story to believe."

He tapped the arms of the chair. "Because they don't talk to us, right?"

Lori didn't answer. She looked at the clock on her desk. "Do you have your list? Of things you might be interested in as a career?"

He didn't like the question, but he pulled a piece of paper from his hoodie pocket:

Race car driver

Horror novelist

Psychologist

"Very funny," Lori said, handing the list back to Hunter.

"Truthfully," he said, "I'm interested in this psychology thing. I've been here . . . how many times, and I feel like the shit—sorry, stuff—is working. I didn't even drop the f-bomb today. Notice that?"

❧

She sent Tom a text after Hunter left, and he came down, walked her to her car. Luckily there were no cigarettes on the ground. Hunter's car was nowhere in the lot.

But the wind was strong. The cigarette could've blown away.

❧

The following week, Hunter claimed he'd taken the girl to lunch. And then to his

house when his mother was at work.

"Best day of my life. We got a thing going, you know?"

Lori pulled her glasses off and then put them back on. "Hunter."

"What? It's true."

"Did any neighbors see this? Because I'm guessing your mom might not approve."

"I'm twenty-four. She has no say. Besides, she don't care. She'd be happy I've got a girlfriend."

"Do you think it's early to call her a girlfriend?"

"I don't know. We'll see."

The following week, he was still telling this story.

Lori said, "Where do you meet her?"

361

"I told you. Back of the store. She just walks out of the woods and gets in my car."

"What happens on the days you aren't working?"

"Some days I work the later shift. I take her to my house and then drop her off right back at the trail she walked out of and go to work. We got it figured out."

"Do any of your coworkers see this?"

"Don't know. Who cares?"

"The Orthodox community won't approve. She could be severely disciplined."

"She knows. She told me. She said she's thinking about leaving anyway. She'll just miss her brothers and sisters. I could help her leave, you know."

Lori sat back and tried to push the session to something more functional—his future.

It wasn't working.

"She gives an awesome blow job now." He stared at her. "It's sort of fun being the teacher."

A snowstorm was coming. She could see the flakes falling outside the window. "We should cut this short," Lori said. "The roads are going to be dangerous."

"Did I make you uncomfortable?"

"I can handle a lot," she said. "But not bad roads."

He laughed loudly.

❦

Tom walked her to the door. He was leaving too. "It's coming fast," he said, peering through the glass. This time, Hunter's car was in the parking lot, lights on, motor running.

"Something's not right with that kid," Tom said.

"How do you know?"

"Instinct."

She stood with Tom outside under the overhang as he locked the doors. They walked to their vehicles together, Hunter just sitting in his car, smoking. He was parked several spots away, the heavy thumping of music blasting in the silent night. She drove out first, Tom behind her, and then Hunter. Hunter didn't stay behind them for long, making a right when she and Tom went left. The roads were tough and she took it slowly. At a red light she saw she had gotten a text from Tom.

Toss him out. Use the insurance as an excuse.

At home, she saw her son's car out front. She carefully but quickly walked up the short sidewalk and up the steps. Rick had a beef stew cooking and there was bread and merlot.

Her son was at the table, checking out something on his cell phone. He got up immediately and gave her a hug. "Just thought I'd pop in for the weekend," Jake said.

Lori smiled, feeling true happiness. The gas fireplace was on. The snow was falling outside. The house smelled of good things to eat.

But her happiness didn't last long. She was still very much unsettled.

"I'm on season five of *The Sopranos*," Jake announced at dinner. "Never watched it."

"Great show," Rick said. "I still think the worst death was Big Pussy."

"I don't know," Jake countered. "When Ralphie beat that girl to death, that was rough."

Lori ate in silence, still thinking about what Tom said. *Instinct.*

"You ever get one of those patients?" Jake said. "Someone involved in crime? A Tony Soprano?"

She put her fork down and sipped her wine. It was her second glass. "I'm not supposed to discuss my patients."

Jake grinned. "But you *do* discuss them. Right Rick?"

Rick shrugged, digging into his stew. "Not often."

Lori drank more wine. "I have a guy who claims he's having a fling with a woman from the Orthodox community."

"Is he Jewish?"

"No. He works at a Wawa. He says they meet out back, when he's smoking a cigarette, and he takes her to his mom's house, where he lives."

"In the basement?" Jake said. "Those dudes always live in basements."

"He never mentioned a basement," Lori said.

Rick sat back. "You haven't told me about this."

"It's just a bullshit story to avoid talking about his future."

"Is it a bullshit story, Mom?" Jake asked.

She realized she'd said too much. "He's odd. I'm working on helping him get out of the metaphorical 'basement.'"

Rick still didn't like it. "That's really strange."

Lori said, "I think it's a fantasy, a way to deal with his lack of female companionship. I think he's trying to impress me or something along those lines. I haven't figured it out yet."

"Does he tell you details?" Jake asked, his forehead wrinkling up. "Because that's gotta be weird. How do you listen to these nuts all day and night?"

Lori picked up her fork. "I want to help."

There was silence before Jake brought up the house Rick was interested in. "Sounds like you should do it. Start a new practice down there. At least you can get rid of weirdo basement guy."

The following week Lori saw Marie. Marie had decided to put in her paperwork for her retirement. "And the dreams stopped as soon as I did that."

"You took control," Lori said. "The dreams are reminders of when you didn't have control."

"I know that," Marie said. "But I'm not always going to have control over things. I can't have these dreams every time things go out of control. Can't you teach me how to stop the dreams when I'm not in control?"

Lori suggested Marie should parent her child and teenage self. "Tell your younger self this isn't your fault. This is a situation you don't have control of. This was a time when your brain was still developing, therefore your feelings were being manipulated by this man who has terrible inclinations. It isn't your fault."

"Yes, I know." Marie stared through the window. "It is what it is, I guess."

Jessica arrived after Marie. "Josh did it again. He's still talking to that bitch, and he's still denying anything is going on. I said to him, 'It makes me uncomfortable. Is your friendship with her that important that it would override hurting me?'"

"And what did he say?"

"He said that I needed to grow up and trust him. That I can't have control of who he is friends with or not." Jessica played with the bracelet on her wrist. "I mean, that makes sense. I can't be that type of woman. Tell him what to do and who he should see or not. Right?"

Lori felt her breath tighten. Jessica's entire situation was triggering her old self, back when she was married to her self-centered asshole unfaithful ex-husband.

"Jessica," Lori finally said, leaning forward in her chair, deciding to go for the jugular. "Your boyfriend's friendship with this woman is very important to him, so important that he will ignore the fact that he is hurting you. And it doesn't matter that he says he's not having sex with her. That could be true. But what is most important to him is the attention he gets from this woman inflates his ego. This will always happen, whether you like it or not. It will not matter if you get married, buy a house, and have children. You will spend the rest of your life crying and sitting in my office or another office upset about something you will never change. Remember, his ego will always override your feelings. And," Lori added, "usually he will be having sex with a woman he is talking to. Or trying to have sex with her. Your instinct is right. Other women will always be more important than you."

Jessica's mouth fell agape. "You've never been this . . . direct."

"I can give you guidance on how to deal with being second best to his ego, how to deal with his affairs, how to busy yourself with a hobby to distract yourself when he is having sex with someone else, if you want to continue the relationship. Would you like me to give you that guidance?"

"Fuck," Jessica said.

Lori leaned back. She turned to her desk and asked Jessica when she wanted to return.

"I don't know. I'll call you."

In the waiting room, Hunter was there. Jessica slinked out, not saying goodbye or even looking at Hunter. Lori doubted Jessica would call again. But at least Lori had been clear. Sometimes clarity and bluntness was necessary, wasn't it?

"So, I was driving around Jewville," Hunter said.

Lori stared at him. Marie was still on her mind. *It is what it is.* Something in her voice felt off, distant, hopeless. Lori had felt this before with Marie and she'd always come back, safe and sound. They'd even discussed a plan for suicidal thoughts but Marie had always insisted she wasn't suicidal, she was just down, and joking about it made it easier to get through it. But now Lori didn't know. Marie's story seemed to eclipse Jessica and Hunter and everyone else she was dealing with at the moment. Lori knew this was unprofessional and she needed to take everyone's situation seriously but she was struggling. *I'm off my game. Focus.*

"That girl I was telling you about?" Hunter said. "She isn't coming around anymore. I don't know where she went."

"You knew this wasn't a good idea," Lori said, deciding to play along. "She's from a world where your relationship is forbidden. Perhaps she was found out and now she's in trouble."

Hunter nodded. "I'm just hurt, you know? I thought we had something."

Lori still didn't believe most of this story, perhaps a young woman from the Orthodox community had come to the store a few times and spoken to him and now she wasn't coming in anymore—if even that was true. This was all a fantasy, but she had to take his word.

"Does it remind you of your date?" Lori asked. "The girl you took to dinner?"

He nodded heavily. "Yep."

"Hunter, this is dating. Sometimes it's bad."

"I go on Tinder, you know, and I get some girls. They just don't want to stay with me."

This, Lori believed.

"Why don't we discuss your future?" she said. "Why don't you take a break from women?"

"Sure." He was extremely docile the rest of the session. His language was clean, he was agreeable, he even kept his hands in his hoodie.

❧

Friday evening, the wind was blowing wildly and another storm was coming up from the south. Lori sat at her desk for about a half hour, making notes and then reading random news articles on Facebook, prepping herself for dinner that evening. Rick was going to want to discuss politics, as he usually did. He'd also been pushing her again to put the townhouse up for sale. "Another unit was sold. That's five total. It's time put an exit plan into fruition."

Five? She thought now. Wasn't it three? Did he tell her the other two had been sold?

She picked up her phone to send Tom a text message, but then remembered that he'd texted her earlier, saying he had an emergency with a friend but he'd be around at nine to lock up the building. *Just wait for me.*

At nine, Tom sent another text. *Be there at 9:30.* She didn't want to wait that long and closed up the office and waiting room, locked the door and walked to the foyer. She pressed her car starter and then walked out to the parking lot. The wind was loud and strong.

There was no cigarette, no car. He was definitely gone. She sent Tom a quick text saying that there was no need to come back.

All right, he wrote back, adding, *Stay safe.*

❧

At 3:46 a.m., Lori got out of bed and went into the kitchen. She'd been up for a half hour, listening to Rick's breathing. Jessica had sent a message through the secure patient portal at 2:43 a.m., saying she was discontinuing therapy for good. *Thank you for your services, Lori.*

She was relieved Jessica had quit, as awful as that was. Her mind kept going back to Marie, though, and she was worrying again. All through Rick's dinner, and his discussion about the newest nonsense out of Washington, Lori had agreed, had added some points of her own, but her mind was somewhere else. The wind had died down, but now it was snowing, falling quickly, heavily. She stood in the dark at the counter, then walked to the window by Rick's herbs. She squeezed a basil leaf with her fingers and then brought the sweet smell to her nose. "I can have a garden too, if we move," Rick had said.

She wanted to call Marie, but it would be highly inappropriate in the middle of the night.

Why was she even up? Marie had been depressed before and she'd made it through. Lori decided she would call Marie in the morning, just to check in.

This decision made it easier for Lori to return to bed. But sleep didn't come for another hour.

❧

In the morning, while Rick and Lori sat at the kitchen table, Rick reading the newspaper and Lori finishing her phone call with Marie—she was fine, feeling good—a text came through Lori's cell. It was her son, Jake.

Tell me this isn't your patient who lives in his mom's basement.

He'd attached a local news story.

Hunter Carlson, twenty-four, was in custody for the murder of an eighteen-year-old woman. The news report said the victim was from the Orthodox Jewish community.

Lori gasped and dropped her phone.

❧

Later, Hunter would tell the police she was his girlfriend, that they were secretly seeing each other, although there was no evidence from Wawa's store cameras this was true. There was indeed a trail in the woods that some people from the Orthodox and Hasidic neighborhood would walk through to get to the store, but nobody had ever seen the two of them talking, never mind a female getting into his car.

But somehow she *had* gotten in his car. Whether it was by force or not, she had been in his car. Her body had been located fifteen miles away in the Pine Barrens of Manchester Township. An older man and his dog found her in the woods, just off a narrow trail.

Hunter claimed they had a fight, that she'd decided not to leave "the Jews."

Commentators on Facebook left prayers and sad emojis but tucked in between were nasty words and unsettling jokes:

One down and five-point-something million to go.

Glossary

blekh – tin, metal sheet

[*der*] *eyver iz nit in der keyver* – one's penile member isn't in the grave (it rhymes in Yiddish)

farkakteh – shitty, crappy

farmisht – mixed up, confused

ganef – thief

gantze megillah – a long-winded story, the whole song-and-dance; lit. the entire scroll, one of the five biblical *megilloth* (Song of Songs, Ruth, Lamentations, Ecclesiastes, Esther)

gelt – money, gold

Gey kakn oyfn yam – Go take a shit on the ocean

goyish/e/er – non-Jewish, Christian

Hashem – the name; used in place of the (forbidden) name of God.

idi na khui – Russian/Ukrainian, usually translated as "go fuck yourself" but literally means "go to the dick." A popular slogan among Ukrainians during the Russian invasion of 2022.

keynehore – no evil eye (from Yiddish/Hebrew *keyn ayin ha-ra*)

kharoset – sweet mixture of nuts, apples, wine, etc. used at the Passover Seder

mayn zineleh – my dear son (diminutive of *zin*)

mikvah – ritual bath

mishegas – craziness, nonsense, BS

peyes – sidelocks (from Hebrew *payot*)

sheyner punim – pretty face

shikseh – a Christian woman

shivah – one week of mourning

shtik drek – piece of shit

tateleh – father dear (diminutive of *tateh*)

tfiln – phylacteries (also written *tefillin*)

yente – gossip, blabbermouth

zaftig – often used to mean chubby (a presumed negative), it literally means *juicy* (clearly positive). So there.

zeyde – grandfather

Contributors

Gabriela Alemán, based in Quito, Ecuador, has played professional basketball in Switzerland and Paraguay and has worked as a translator, radio scriptwriter, and film studies professor. Her literary honors include a Guggenheim Fellowship in 2006 and being a member of Bogotá 39, a 2007 selection of the most important up-and-coming writers in Latin America of the post-Boom generation. *Poso Wells*, chosen as an Indie Next Pick in August 2018, is her first full-length work to appear in English.

Twice an Edgar Allan Poe Award winner and the record holder in the Ellery Queen Mystery Magazine Reader's Award competition, **Doug Allyn** is one of the best short story writers of his generation—and possibly of all time. He is also a novelist with a number of critically acclaimed books in print. The author of a dozen novels and more than 130 short stories, Doug Allyn has been published internationally in English, German, French, and Japanese. More than two dozen of his tales have been optioned for development as feature films and television. Mr. Allyn studied creative writing and criminal psychology at the University of Michigan while moonlighting as a guitarist in the rock group Devil's Triangle and reviewing books for the *Flint Journal*. His background includes Chinese language studies at Indiana University and extended duty USAF Intelligence in Southeast Asia during the Vietnam War.

Jill D. Block is a writer and an attorney, not always in that order. Her stories have appeared in *Ellery Queen's Mystery Magazine*, *Mystery Tribune*,

Title, and several anthologies. Jill's first novel, *The Truth About Parallel Lines*, was published in 2018. Jill grew up celebrating both Christmas and Hanukah, and she has never kept kosher for Passover but once fasted for most of Yom Kippur. Although she did not have one of her own, she has been to more bar and bat mitzvahs than she can count.

Lawrence Block has been writing crime, mystery, and suspense fiction for more than half a century. He has published in excess of one hundred books and no end of short stories. He apprenticed under various pseudonyms in the late 1950s; the first time his name appeared in print was for his short story "You Can't Lose," in *Manhunt* (Feb. 1958), and the first book published under his own name was *Mona* (1961), reprinted by Hard Case Crime under the author's original title, *Grifter's Game* (2005). Block is best known for his series characters, including cop-turned-PI Matthew Scudder, gentleman burglar Bernie Rhodenbarr, globe-trotting insomniac Evan Tanner, and introspective assassin Keller. Block is a Grand Master of Mystery Writers of America, and a past president of Mystery Writers of America and the Private Eye Writers of America. He has won the Edgar and Shamus awards four times each, and the Japanese Maltese Falcon award twice, as well as the Nero Wolfe and Philip Marlowe awards, a Lifetime Achievement Award from the Private Eye Writers of America, and the Diamond Dagger for Life Achievement from the Crime Writers Association (UK). He's also been honored with the Gumshoe Lifetime Achievement Award from *Mystery Ink* magazine and the Edward D. Hoch Memorial Golden Derringer for Lifetime Achievement in the short story. In France, he has been proclaimed a Grand Maître du Roman Noir and has twice been awarded the Société 813 trophy. He has been a guest of honor at Bouchercon and at book fairs and mystery festivals in France, Germany, Australia, Italy, New Zealand, Spain, and Taiwan. As if that were not enough, he was also presented with the key to the city of Muncie, Indiana. (But as soon as he left, they changed the locks.) https://lawrenceblock.com.

Craig Faustus Buck has won numerous awards for his neo-noir novel, *Go Down Hard*, and his short stories. Many of these stories are available free at http://craigfaustusbuck.com. He is also a screenwriter, having written and produced network series, pilots, movies, and miniseries for more years than he cares to admit. Some ancient highlights include the seminal miniseries *V: The Final Battle*, the Oscar-nominated short film *Overnight Sensation*, and the famous episode where the Incredible Hulk dropped acid. Finally, he is a pitmaster extraordinaire.

Jen Conley is the author of the Anthony Award–winning YA novel *Seven Ways to Get Rid of Harry* and the Anthony-nominated short story collection, *Cannibals: Stories from the Edge of the Pine Barrens*. She lives in Brick, New Jersey.

Dawna Maria Bivins-Smith, or simply "Maria," writes fiction under **D.M. Evans**. Maria is a native of Flushing, New York. She is a clinical psychologist, consultant, and founder of Wellsmith Life, an online wellness home. Her latest nonfiction work is *Control Your Crazy: Work the Good. Tame the Bad and Ugly*. *Return to Murder*, her crime fiction novel, is in the works. She and her husband live in the Atlanta metro area.

Robin Hemley is the author of fourteen books of fiction and nonfiction, and has won fellowships from the Guggenheim Foundation, the Rockefeller Foundation, three Pushcart Prizes in both fiction and nonfiction, the Nelson Algren Award for Fiction from the *Chicago Tribune*, and many others. His book *Borderline Citizen: Dispatches from the Outskirts of Nationhood* was published in 2020, and his novel *Oblivion: An After Autobiography* followed in 2022. He is director of the George Polk School of Communications at LIU-Brooklyn and director of the MFA in Writing and Parsons Family Chair in Creative Writing. His website is https://robinhemley.com.

Ellen Kirschman is an award-winning public safety psychologist and author of *I Love a Cop: What Police Families Need to Know*; *I Love a Firefighter: What the Family Needs to Know*; lead author of *Counseling Cops: What Clinicians Need to Know*; and three mysteries, *Burying Ben*, *The Right Wrong Thing*, and *The Fifth Reflection*, all told from the perspective of police psychologist Dr. Dot Meyerhoff. She blogs with *Psychology Today* and is a member of Sisters in Crime, Mystery Writers of America, and the Public Safety Writers Association. She publishes an occasional newsletter. Sign up on her website at https://ellenkirschman.com.

Sara Kitai (translator of "Mosquitoes over Bamako" by Yigal Zur) was born in New York and has been a translator for several decades. Her other translated works include *Lineup* and *Asylum City* by Liad Shoham and *Death Comes in Yellow* by Felicja Karay.

Rita Lakin spent twenty-five years in television in LA as a writer of series, movies, miniseries, finally becoming producer/showrunner on her own shows. *The Only Woman in the Room: Episodes in My Life and Career as a Television Writer* is her memoir of those years. She is also known for writing nine comedy mystery novels featuring Gladdy Gold and her zany geriatric partners in crime-solving, starting with *Getting Old Is Murder*. The sixth novel in the series, the IMBA bestselling *Getting Old Is a Disaster*, won the Left Coast Crime Lefty Award for Best Humorous Mystery in 2009. She has just competed numbers eight and nine. Other novels include *The Four Coins of the Kaballah* and *A Summer Without Boys*. Her many other awards and nominations include Writers Guild of America, Mystery Writers of America, Edgar, and the Avery Hopwood award from the University of Michigan. And most important, she is part of the prestigious WGA Television Academy Archives collection. She has written articles and short stories for anthologies such as *Bronx Noir*. She taught screenwriting at UCLA, the University of Wisconsin, and Dominican University of California. She has also written two plays.

Joy Mahabir is the author of *Miraculous Weapons: Revolutionary Ideology in Caribbean Culture* (2003) and the novel *Jouvert* (2006). She is coeditor of *Critical Perspectives on Indo-Caribbean Women's Literature* (2012) and has published essays on literature, music, and jewelry. She is a professor at Suffolk County Community College, New York.

Jeff Markowitz is the author of five mysteries, including the award-winning dark comedy *Death and White Diamonds*. His latest book, *Hit or Miss*, was released in December 2020. Part detective story, part historical fiction, part coming-of-age story, *Hit or Miss* was an Amazon Hot New Release in political fiction. Jeff spent more than forty years creating community-based programs and services for children and adults with autism, before retiring in 2018 to devote more time to writing. He is past president of the New York chapter of Mystery Writers of America.

Chantelle Aimée Osman is the editor of Agora, an imprint of Polis Books, which focuses on crime fiction with unique social and cultural themes. Books she has edited have been nominated for multiple Edgar, Anthony, Lefty, Macavity, and Strand Critics awards. The former editor in chief of *RT Book Reviews* magazine and a freelance editor for over ten years, she is also an instructor at the Virginia G. Piper Center for Creative Writing, Authors at Large and LitReactor. Chantelle is the author of the nonfiction series on writing The Quick and Dirty Guides To . . . and has also published numerous works of short fiction, in addition to serving as editor for several anthologies. She was named a *Publishers Weekly* Rising Star honoree in 2020, and a guest of honor at Left Coast Crime in 2016. Find her online at https://chantelleaimee.com and on Twitter @SuspenseSiren.

As the daughter of a religious studies professor and a *New York Times*–bestselling mystery author, **Zoe Quinton** has stories in her blood. She earned a master's degree from the London School of Economics, then in 2007 began working as her mother's business manager and head publicist. After a decade in the publishing industry, Zoe established her own freelance editing and publishing consultancy business in 2017. Since then, she has edited both aspiring and many-times-published authors as well as helping others find agents or navigate the ups and downs of self-publishing. When she's not reading for work or pleasure—which is rare—you can find her working out, drinking good coffee or wine, gardening, and spending time with her partner, their two small people, and a very loud Siamese-tortoiseshell cat in their lovely home in Santa Cruz, California.

Eileen Rendahl is a national-bestselling and award-winning author of mystery, paranormal, and romance novels and teaches creative writing at Southern New Hampshire University. Eileen was born in Dayton, Ohio. She moved when she was four and only remembers that she was born across the street from Baskin-Robbins. Eileen remembers anything that has to do with ice cream. Or chocolate. Or champagne. She has had many jobs and written under many names and lived in many cities and feels unbelievably lucky to be where she is now and to be doing what she's doing. https://www.eileenrendahl.com

Rabbi Ilene Schneider, one of the first female rabbis in the US, has decided what she wants to be when she grows up: a writer. Despite spending her retirement (from earning a regular paycheck) birding, gardening, streaming movies, binge-watching TV series, traveling (prepandemic), and oversharing on Facebook, she is the author of the award-winning Rabbi Aviva Cohen Mysteries: *Chanukah Guilt*, *Unleavened Dead*, and *Yom Killer*. The fourth is *Killah Megillah*. She is the writer of award-winning short stories and the nonfiction *Talking Dirty—in Yiddish?*. She created an ongoing website of questions and answers about Hanukkah (https://whyninecandles.com) and edited *Recipes by the Book: Oak Tree Authors Cook*. Contact and follow her at https://rabbiauthor.com.

Terry Shames writes the Samuel Craddock series, set in small-town Texas. Nominated for numerous awards, her books won the Macavity Award for Best First Novel and an *RT Reviews* award for Best Contemporary Mystery. MysteryPeople has twice named Terry one of the top five Texas mystery authors of the year. Her latest short story is "Double Exposure" in *Bullets and Other Hurting Things: A Tribute to Bill Crider* (Down and Out Books, 2021). Terry lives in Northern California and is a member of Sisters in Crime and Mystery Writers of America. For more, go to https://www.terryshames.com.

A.J. Sidransky's published novels include *Forgiving Maximo Rothman*, *Forgiving Stephen Redmond*, *Forgiving Mariela Camacho*, and *The Interpreter*. He is currently working on *The Intern*, the next installment in the Interpreter Series, and *The King of Arroyo Hondo*, a novella set in the Dominican Republic. His published short stories include "La Libreta," (The Notebook) in sx salon: a small axe literary platform, "Mother Knows Best," in *Noir Nation 5*, "The Glint of Metal" in the *Crime Café Short Story Anthology*, and "El Ladron" (The Thief) in *A Rock and a Hard Place* magazine. He lives in New York City.

Lizzie Skurnick is the author of *That Should Be a Word* and *Shelf Discovery*, as well as many books in the YA *Alias* series, and the editor of the anthology *Pretty Bitches*. She lives in Jersey City with her son, Javier.

Crime-historian/storyteller **E.J. Wagner** has written and lectured widely on the folklore and history of forensic science. Her book *The Science of*

Sherlock Holmes was awarded an Edgar Award, and her work has appeared in *Ellery Queen, Smithsonian, Lancet,* and the *New York Times.* She was founder and moderator of the Forensic Forum at Stony Brook University. She researches her material by hanging out in such places as the Armed Forces Museum of Pathology in Maryland, the Suffolk County Office of the Medical Examiner, and the crime laboratory of London's Metropolitan Police (Scotland Yard). Website: http://ejwagnercrimehistorian.com. Blog: https://ejdissectingroom.wordpress.com.

Kenneth Wishnia's novels include *23 Shades of Black,* an Edgar Allan Poe Award and Anthony Award finalist; *Soft Money,* a *Library Journal* Best Mystery of the Year; *Red House,* a *Washington Post* "Rave" Book of the Year; and *The Fifth Servant,* an Indie Notable selection, a *Jewish Press* Best Mystery of the Year, winner of a Premio Letterario ADEI-WIZO, and a finalist for the Sue Feder Memorial Historical Mystery Award. His short stories have appeared in *Ellery Queen, Alfred Hitchcock, Queens Noir, Long Island Noir, Send My Love and a Molotov Cocktail!, Denim, Diamonds and Death,* and elsewhere. He edited the Anthony Award–nominated anthology *Jewish Noir* for PM Press. He teaches writing, literature, and other deviant forms of thought at Suffolk Community College on Long Island. https://kennethwishnia.com.

Steven Wishnia is author of the novel *When the Drumming Stops* (Manic D Press), in which four aging rockers face the Great Recession; *A-String to Your Heart,* an anthology of writings on music; the short-story collection *Exit 25 Utopia*; and *The Cannabis Companion,* which has been translated into six languages. A veteran journalist specializing in labor and housing issues, he wrote the last article ever published in the *Village Voice.* Bassist in the 1980s punk band the False Prophets, he now plays klezmer in Kvetch, spoken-word rock in Blowdryer Punk Soul, and in the multimedia shows of artist Mac McGill. (His memoir essay "Wie Bist Die Gewesen Vor Punk-Rock?" was published in *Jews: A People's History of the Lower East Side.*) He received the title of Zeyde in 2019 and is now pitching a children's book manuscript, *The Baby Ate Brooklyn!* He lives in New York, the proud city of bodega cats and real bagels.

Xu Xi 許素細 is the author of fourteen books of fiction and nonfiction, including five novels, a memoir and eight collections of stories and essays.

Titles include the novel *That Man in Our Lives, Insignificance: Hong Kong Stories*, and most recently *This Fish is Fowl: Essays of Being*. She is cofounder of Authors at Large and recently established the Mongrel Writers Residence. An Indonesian-Chinese-American diehard transnational, she previously inhabited the flight path connecting New York, Hong Kong, and the South Island of New Zealand. And her family really did reside, for many years, in the building where Bruce Lee died. These days, she splits her life, unevenly, between the state of New York and the rest of the world. Follow her @xuxiwriter on FB, Twitter, Instagram, LinkedIn.

Elizabeth Zelvin is the author of the Mendoza Family Saga, Jewish historical fiction that includes the current story, as well as the Bruce Kohler Mysteries, featuring a recovering alcoholic who, like Liz, is a life-long New Yorker and a wiseass with heart. Liz's short stories have been nominated three times each for the Derringer and Agatha awards and have appeared in *Ellery Queen's Mystery Magazine, Alfred Hitchcock's Mystery Magazine*, and *Black Cat Mystery Magazine*. Her editorial credits include two anthologies: *Me Too Short Stories* and *Where Crime Never Sleeps: Murder New York Style 4*. Liz is also a psychotherapist, an award-winning poet, and a singer-songwriter with an album called *Outrageous Older Woman*.

Yigal Zur is a noted Israeli writer and tour guide. He served in the military, spending time on the front lines in the Golan Heights during the 1973 Yom Kippur War. Toward the end of the war and the imminent conclusion of his military service, he began to repeat to himself like a mantra: "When it's all over, I'm going to India." For seven years he traveled the world with only a knapsack on his back and irrepressible curiosity, his eyes gaping in wonder. His thriller series features the Israeli former security services operative turned private investigator Dotan Naor. Two novels in the series, *Death in Shangri-La* and *Passport to Death*, have been translated into English. Zur has written novels, a movie script, and guides to India and China. In 2020 he published an Israeli noir, *Southern District*, the first in the Nimer Bekerman series. Born to a Bedouin Muslim father and Jewish mother from Russian origin, he currently lives in Jaffa, Israel. https://yigal-zur.com.

ABOUT PM PRESS

PM Press is an independent, radical publisher of books and
media to educate, entertain, and inspire. Founded in 2007
by a small group of people with decades of publishing,
media, and organizing experience, PM Press amplifies the
voices of radical authors, artists, and activists. Our aim is to

deliver bold political ideas and vital stories to all walks of life and arm the dreamers
to demand the impossible. We have sold millions of copies of our books, most
often one at a time, face to face. We're old enough to know what we're doing and
young enough to know what's at stake. Join us to create a better world.

PM Press
PO Box 23912
Oakland, CA 94623
www.pmpress.org

PM Press in Europe
europe@pmpress.org
www.pmpress.org.uk

FRIENDS OF PM PRESS

These are indisputably momentous times—the financial system is melting down globally and the Empire is stumbling. Now more than ever there is a vital need for radical ideas.

In the many years since its founding—and on a mere shoestring—PM Press has risen to the formidable challenge of publishing and distributing knowledge and entertainment for the struggles ahead. With hundreds of releases to date, we have published an impressive and stimulating array of literature, art, music, politics, and culture. Using every available medium, we've succeeded in connecting those hungry for ideas and information to those putting them into practice.

Friends of PM allows you to directly help impact, amplify, and revitalize the discourse and actions of radical writers, filmmakers, and artists. It provides us with a stable foundation from which we can build upon our early successes and provides a much-needed subsidy for the materials that can't necessarily pay their own way. You can help make that happen—and receive every new title automatically delivered to your door once a month—by joining as a Friend of PM Press. And, we'll throw in a free T-shirt when you sign up.

Here are your options:

- **$30 a month** Get all books and pamphlets plus 50% discount on all webstore purchases

- **$40 a month** Get all PM Press releases (including CDs and DVDs) plus 50% discount on all webstore purchases

- **$100 a month** Superstar—Everything plus PM merchandise, free downloads, and 50% discount on all webstore purchases

For those who can't afford $30 or more a month, we have **Sustainer Rates** at $15, $10, and $5. Sustainers get a free PM Press T-shirt and a 50% discount on all purchases from our website.

Your Visa or Mastercard will be billed once a month, until you tell us to stop. Or until our efforts succeed in bringing the revolution around. Or the financial meltdown of Capital makes plastic redundant. Whichever comes first.

Jewish Noir

Edited by Kenneth Wishnia

ISBN: 978-1-62963-111-0
$17.95   432 pages

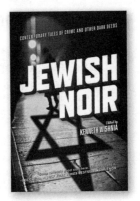

Jewish Noir is a unique collection of new stories by Jewish and non-Jewish literary and genre writers, including numerous award-winning authors such as Marge Piercy, Harlan Ellison, S.J. Rozan, Nancy Richler, Moe Prager, Wendy Hornsby, Charles Ardai, and Kenneth Wishnia. The stories explore such issues as the Holocaust and its long-term effects on subsequent generations, anti-Semitism in the mid– and late-twentieth-century United States, and the dark side of the Diaspora (the decline of revolutionary fervor, the passing of generations, the Golden Ghetto, etc.). The stories in this collection also include many "teachable moments" about the history of prejudice, and the contradictions of ethnic identity and assimilation into American society.

Stories include:
- "A Simkhe" (A Celebration), first published in Yiddish in the *Forverts* in 1912 by one of the great unsung writers of that era, Yente Serdatsky. This story depicts the disillusionment that sets in among a group of Russian Jewish immigrant radicals after several years in the United States. This is the story's first appearance in English.
- "Trajectories," Marge Piercy's story of the divergent paths taken by two young men from the slums of Cleveland and Detroit in a rapidly changing post-World War II society.
- "Some You Lose," Nancy Richler's empathetic exploration of the emotional and psychological challenges of trying to sum up a man's life in a eulogy.
- "Her Daughter's Bat Mitzvah," Rabbi Adam Fisher's darkly comic profanity-filled monologue in the tradition of Sholem Aleichem, the writer best known as the source material for *Fiddler on the Roof* (minus the profanity, that is).
- "Flowers of Shanghai," S.J. Rozan's compelling tale of hope and despair set in the European refugee community of Japanese-occupied Shanghai during World War II.
- "Yahrzeit Candle," Stephen Jay Schwartz's take on the subtle horrors of the inevitable passing of time.

"Stirring. Evocative. Penetrating."
—Elie Wiesel (on Stephen Jay Schwartz's "Yahrzeit Candle")

"Wishnia presents the world of Ashkenazi Jewry with a keen eye for detail. Wishnia never judges his characters, but creates three-dimensional people who live in a very dangerous world."
—The Jewish Press on "The Fifth Servant"

23 Shades of Black

Kenneth Wishnia
with an introduction by
Barbara D'Amato

ISBN: 978-1-60486-587-5
$17.95   300 pages

23 Shades of Black is socially conscious crime fiction. It
takes place in New York City in the early 1980s, i.e., the
Reagan years, and was written partly in response to
the reactionary discourse of the time, when the current
thirty-year assault on the rights of working people began in earnest, and the divide
between rich and poor deepened with the blessing of the political and corporate
elites. But it is not a political tract, it's a kick-ass novel that was nominated for the
Edgar and the Anthony Awards, and made *Booklist*'s Best First Mysteries of the
Year.

The heroine, Filomena Buscarsela, is an immigrant who experienced tremendous
poverty and injustice in her native Ecuador, and who grew up determined to devote
her life to helping others. She tells us that she really should have been a priest,
but since that avenue was closed to her, she chose to become a cop instead. The
problem is that as one of the first *latinas* on the NYPD, she is not just a woman in a
man's world, she is a woman of color in a white man's world. And it's hell. Filomena
is mistreated and betrayed by her fellow officers, which leads her to pursue a case
independently in the hopes of being promoted to detective for the Rape Crisis Unit.

Along the way, she is required to enforce unjust drug laws that she disagrees
with, and to betray her own community (which ostracizes her as a result) in an
undercover operation to round up illegal immigrants. Several scenes are set in the
East Village art and punk rock scene of the time, and the murder case eventually
turns into an investigation of corporate environmental crime from a working class
perspective that is all-too-rare in the genre.

And yet this thing is damn funny, too.

"Packed with enough mayhem and atmosphere for two novels."
—*Booklist*

"From page-turning thriller to mystery story to social investigation, 23 Shades of Black
*works on all levels. It's clear from the start that Wishnia is charting a unique path in
crime fiction. Sign me up for the full ride!"*
—Michael Connelly, author of *Lost Light*

Send My Love and a Molotov Cocktail: Stories of Crime, Love and Rebellion

Edited by Gary Phillips
and Andrea Gibbons

ISBN: 978-1-60486-096-2
$19.95   368 pages

An incendiary mixture of genres and voices, this collection of short stories compiles a unique set of work that revolves around riots, revolts, and revolution. From the turbulent days of unionism in the streets of New York City during the Great Depression to a group of old women who meet at their local café to plan a radical act that will change the world forever, these original and once out-of-print stories capture the various ways people rise up to challenge the status quo and change up the relationships of power. Ideal for any fan of noir, science fiction, and revolution and mayhem, this collection includes works from Sara Paretsky, Paco Ignacio Taibo II, Cory Doctorow, Kenneth Wishnia, and Summer Brenner.

Full list of contributors:

Summer Brenner
Rick Dakan
Barry Graham
Penny Mickelbury
Gary Phillips
Luis Rodriguez
Benjamin Whitmer
Michael Moorcock
Larry Fondation

Cory Doctorow
Andrea Gibbons
John A. Imani
Sara Paretsky
Kim Stanley Robinson
Paco Ignacio Taibo II
Kenneth Wishnia
Michael Skeet
Tim Wohlforth

The Colonel Pyat Quartet

Michael Moorcock
with introductions by Alan Wall

Byzantium Endures
ISBN: 978-1-60486-491-5
$22.00   400 pages

The Laughter of Carthage
ISBN: 978-1-60486-492-2
$22.00   448 pages

Jerusalem Commands
ISBN: 978-1-60486-493-9
$22.00   448 pages

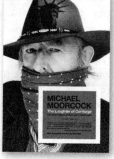

The Vengeance of Rome
ISBN: 978-1-60486-494-6
$23.00   500 pages

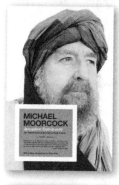

Moorcock's Pyat Quartet has been described as an authentic masterpiece of the 20th and 21st centuries. It's the story of Maxim Arturovitch Pyatnitski, a cocaine addict, sexual adventurer, and obsessive anti-Semite whose epic journey from Leningrad to London connects him with scoundrels and heroes from Trotsky to Makhno, and whose career echoes that of the 20th century's descent into Fascism and total war.

It is Michael Moorcock's extraordinary achievement to convert the life of Maxim Pyatnitski into epic and often hilariously comic adventure. Sustained by his dreams and profligate inventions, his determination to turn his back on the realities of his own origins, Pyat runs from crisis to crisis, every ruse a further link in a vast chain of deceit, suppression, betrayal. Yet, in his deranged self-deception, his monumentally distorted vision, this thoroughly unreliable narrator becomes a lens for focusing, through the dimensions of wild farce and chilling terror, on an uneasy brand of truth.

Everyone Has Their Reasons

Joseph Matthews

ISBN: 978-1-62963-094-6
$24.95   528 pages

On November 7, 1938, a small, slight seventeen-year-old Polish-German Jew named Herschel Grynszpan entered the German embassy in Paris and shot dead a consular official. Three days later, in supposed response, Jews across Germany were beaten, imprisoned, and killed, their homes, shops, and synagogues smashed and burned—Kristallnacht, the Night of Broken Glass.

Based on the historical record and told through his "letters" from German prisons, the novel begins in 1936, when fifteen-year-old Herschel flees Germany. Penniless and alone, he makes it to Paris where he lives hand-to-mouth, his shadow existence mixing him with the starving and the wealthy, with hustlers, radicals, and seamy sides of Paris nightlife.

In 1938, the French state rejects refugee status for Herschel and orders him out of the country. With nowhere to go, and now sought by the police, he slips underground in immigrant east Paris.

Soon after, the Nazis round up all Polish Jews in Germany—including Herschel's family—and dump them on the Poland border. Herschel's response is to shoot the German official, then wait calmly for the French police.

June 1940, Herschel is still in prison awaiting trial when the Nazi army nears Paris. He is evacuated south to another jail but escapes into the countryside amid the chaos of millions of French fleeing the invasion. After an incredible month alone on the road, Herschel seeks protection at a prison in the far south of France. Two weeks later the French state hands him to the Gestapo.

The Nazis plan a big show trial, inviting the world press to Berlin for the spectacle, to demonstrate through Herschel that Jews had provoked the war. Except that Herschel throws a last-minute wrench in the plans, bringing the Nazi propaganda machine to a grinding halt. Hitler himself postpones the trial and orders that no decision be made about Herschel's fate until the Führer personally gives an order—one way or another.

"A tragic, gripping Orwellian tale of an orphan turned assassin in pre-World War II Paris. Based on the true story of the Jewish teen Hitler blamed for Kristallnacht, it's a wild ride through the underside of Europe as the storm clouds of the Holocaust gather. Not to be missed!"
—Terry Bisson, Hugo and Nebula award-winning author of *Fire on the Mountain*

The Cost of Lunch, Etc.

Marge Piercy

ISBN: 978-1-62963-125-7 (paperback)
       978-1-60486-496-0 (hardcover)
$15.95/$21.95   192 pages

Marge Piercy's debut collection of short stories, *The Cost of Lunch, Etc.*, brings us glimpses into the lives of everyday women moving through and making sense of their daily internal and external worlds. Keeping to the engaging, accessible language of Piercy's novels, the collection spans decades of her writing along with a range of locations, ages, and emotional states of her protagonists. From the first-person account of hoarding ("Saving Mother from Herself") to a girl's narrative of sexual and spiritual discovery ("Going over Jordan") to a recount of a past love affair ("The Easy Arrangement") each story is a tangible, vivid snapshot in a varied and subtly curated gallery of work. Whether grappling with death, familial relationships, friendship, sex, illness, or religion, Piercy's writing is as passionate, lucid, insightful, and thoughtfully alive as ever.

"The author displays an old-fashioned narrative drive and a set of well-realized characters permitted to lead their own believably odd lives."
—Thomas Mallon, *Newsday*

"This reviewer knows no other writer with Piercy's gifts for tracing the emotional route that two people take to a double bed, and the mental games and gambits each transacts there."
—Ron Grossman, *Chicago Tribune*

"Marge Piercy is not just an author, she's a cultural touchstone. Few writers in modern memory have sustained her passion, and skill, for creating stories of consequence."
—*Boston Globe*

"What Piercy has that Danielle Steel, for example, does not is an ability to capture life's complex texture, to chart shifting relationships and evolving consciousness within the context of political and economic realities she delineates with mordant matter-of-factness. Working within the venerable tradition of socially conscious fiction, she brings to it a feminist understanding of the impact such things as class and money have on personal interactions without ever losing sight of the crucial role played by individuals' responses to those things."
—Wendy Smith, *Chicago Sun-Times*